Praise for Chloe Neill's
Chicagoland Vampires Novels

Drink Deep

"Three cheers for the Chicagoland Vampires series and Neill's latest addition! . . . Neill manages to keep the action going and the tension tight as Merit struggles to fulfill her obligations and make sense of the ever-changing world around her." —*RT Book Reviews*

"Chloe Neill knows how to write a well-rounded book full of emotional depth that will easily suck the reader into Merit's world . . . a completely unpredictable read that left me more than satisfied." —A Book Obsession

"Chloe Neill is a master at storytelling. . . . Ms. Neill has proven that the Chicagoland Vampires are worth the wait." —Night Owl Reviews

"Neill has another powerhouse entry to this series with *Drink Deep*, and her legions of fans are sure to be delighted." —SFRevu

Hard Bitten

"Delivers enough action, plot twists, and fights to satisfy the most jaded urban fantasy reader." —Monsters and Critics

"A fast and exciting read." —Fresh Fiction

"A descriptive, imaginative, and striking world . . . rich with real-world problems as well as otherworldly creatures . . . roughly fantastic from beginning to end, with one of the best endings in urban fantasy history." —*Romantic Times*

Twice Bitten

"The pages turn fast enough to satisfy vampire and romance fans alike." —*Booklist*

"Neill continues to hit the sweet spot with her blend of high-stakes drama, romantic entanglements, and a touch of humor . . . certain to whet readers' appetites for more in this entertaining series!" —*Romantic Times* (4½ stars)

Friday Night Bites

"Wonderfully entertaining, and impossible to set down." —Darque Reviews

"First-rate fun!" —*Romantic Times*

continued . .

A CHICAGOLAND VAMPIRES NOVEL

HOUSE
RULES

CHLOE NEILL

NEW AMERICAN LIBRARY

New American Library
Published by New American Library,
a division of Penguin Group (USA) Inc.,
375 Hudson Street, New York, New York 10014, USA
Penguin Group (Canada), 90 Eglinton Avenue East, Suite 700, Toronto,
Ontario M4P 2Y3, Canada (a division of Pearson Penguin Canada Inc.)
Penguin Books Ltd., 80 Strand, London WC2R 0RL, England
Penguin Ireland, 25 St. Stephen's Green, Dublin 2,
Ireland (a division of Penguin Books Ltd.)
Penguin Group (Australia), 250 Camberwell Road, Camberwell,
Victoria 3124, Australia (a division of Pearson Australia Group Pty. Ltd.)
Penguin Books India Pvt. Ltd., 11 Community Centre,
Panchsheel Park, New Delhi - 110 017, India
Penguin Group (NZ), 67 Apollo Drive, Rosedale, Auckland 0632,
New Zealand (a division of Pearson New Zealand Ltd.)
Penguin Books (South Africa) (Pty.) Ltd., 24 Sturdee Avenue,
Rosebank, Johannesburg 2196, South Africa

Penguin Books Ltd., Registered Offices:
80 Strand, London WC2R 0RL, England

First published by New American Library,
a division of Penguin Group (USA) Inc.

First Printing, February 2013
1 3 5 7 9 10 8 6 4 2

Copyright © Chloe Neill, 2013

◼ REGISTERED TRADEMARK—MARCA REGISTRADA

LIBRARY OF CONGRESS CATALOGING-IN-PUBLICATION DATA

Neill, Chloe.
House rules: a Chicagoland vampires novel/Chloe Neill.
pages cm. — (Chicagoland vampires)
ISBN 978-0-451-23710-1 (pbk.)
1. Merit (Fictitious character: Neill)—Fiction. 2. Vampires—Fiction.
3. Chicago (Ill.)—Fiction. 4. Paranormal romance stories. I. Title.
PS3614.E4432H68 2013
813'.6—dc23   2012040751

Set in Caslon 540

Printed in the United States of America

PUBLISHER'S NOTE

This is a work of fiction. Names, characters, places, and incidents either are the product of the author's imagination or are used fictitiously, and any resemblance to actual persons, living or dead, business establishments, events, or locales is entirely coincidental.

The publisher does not have any control over and does not assume any responsibility for author or third-party Web sites or their content.

To Jeremy, Baxter, and Scout, with love and squares,
and to Krista, for her incredible patience, hard work, and amazing memory.

Death waits for no vampire.
—*Ethan Sullivan*

I like bacon.
—*Merit*

HOUSE
RULES

✠

◆◆◆

CHAPTER ONE

BOXER REBELLION

Mid-December
Chicago, Illinois

It was like a scene from a divorce: belongings divided into piles; books labeled with one owner's name or the other; and everyone emotionally exhausted.

But in this case, there was no breakup. Not of the human variety, anyway. This was more of a secession. A declaration of independence.

It was a rebellion, and the golden-haired vampire next to me was leading the charge. Ethan Sullivan, the unofficial co-Master of Chicago's Cadogan House, and my boyfriend.

That was still a strange thing to say.

Ethan, looking exceptionally handsome in black pants, a button-down, and a black tie, examined a slim, leather-bound book.

"This one belongs to the GP," he said, glancing at the spine. "*The Metamorphosis of Man*," he read. "*From Opposable Thumbs to Descending Fangs.*"

"That's an awful title," I said.

"It's their awful title now." Ethan's words were humorous, but the tone in his voice wasn't. The entire House was nervous, the building fogged with magical tension as we waited for the final countdown: Seventy-two hours remained until our official split from the Greenwich Presidium, the European council that ruled American vampire Houses, and the pendulum swung over our heads like Damocles' sword. The GP's members were traveling to Chicago for the sole purpose of formally expelling the House—of breaking up with us in public.

Our preparations had been largely uneventful. We'd been separating and packing up the GP's goods and readying our finances, which seemed to be in order. The GP had been unusually quiet since we'd announced our intention to leave, communicating with the House only about the details of the ceremony and their travel arrangements to Chicago.

Ethan found that silence very suspicious. He'd gone so far as to appoint a "transition team" comprised of vampires and other supernaturals from whom he'd sought advice about the split.

Ethan leaned back and glanced at the bookshelves that lined a long wall in his large office. "This is going to take a while."

"Yes," I agreed, "but our other option is letting Darius do it himself. And I don't think we want that."

Darius West was head of the GP. He was very proper, very British, and very much not a fan of our House.

"We don't want that," Ethan agreed. He handed his book to me, our fingers grazing as he passed it over.

My blood warmed instantly, my cheeks flushing at the intensity of his emerald gaze. Ethan and I had been officially a couple for only a few weeks, and the honeymoon period wasn't over. I may have been fierce with a katana—the samurai sword that vampires, including myself, carried for protection—but my heart still fluttered when he looked at me.

But we had many books to get through, so I pulled away and placed this one into the old-fashioned, brass-hinged steamer trunk on the floor.

"Work now, play later," I reminded him.

"I find mixing business with pleasure makes both more interesting."

"I find I'd rather spend my off-hours not packing away dusty books."

"Being a vampire isn't always about getting what you want, Sentinel. Although I'll concede I can imagine more enjoyable ways of spending our time." Sentinel was my title, a kind of House protector. Ethan used it when he was aggravated with me, or when he was trying to make a point.

"Then you probably shouldn't have irritated the GP so much they kicked you out."

He gave me a flat look. "They didn't kick us out."

"I know. We voted to break up with them before they could break up with us."

This time his flat look was accompanied by an arched eyebrow, Ethan's signature move. He wore the expression—much like everything else—very well.

"Are you purposely riling me up?" he asked.

"I am. Is it working?"

He growled, but there was a smile on his face as he did it.

I turned back to the books. "Can't we just randomly grab half the books and throw them into the trunk? Will Darius really know the difference?"

"He might not, but I would. And so would the librarian." He looked at me askance. "I'm surprised at you, Sentinel. You're usually the bookish type."

I had a master's degree and then some, so I agreed I was the bookish type, and I was proud of it. But his statement wasn't exactly a ringing endorsement. I narrowed my eyes. "I'm not sure you mean that as a compliment."

"I'm not sure, either," he said with a wink, and handed me another book. "But your point is well taken." As I added the book to the trunk, Ethan stepped back and scanned the shelves.

I did, too, looking for anything obviously out of place. The *Presidium Guide to Alienating the American Houses* or the like. But before I found anything remotely appropriate, Ethan sidled next to me, a hand propped on the shelf.

"Come here often?" he said.

"Excuse me?"

"I see you're here in this"—he gestured at the shelves—"library all alone. You must be a student here?" He traced a fingertip down the hollow of my throat, lifting goose bumps on my arms.

Since my mind hardly worked when he did things like that, it took a moment for his words to register. Was he initiating a bout of role-playing . . . about a library?

"Ethan Sullivan," I marveled. "You have a library fantasy."

He smiled slyly. "I have a doctoral-student-turned-vampire fantasy."

Before I could respond, he whipped a hand around my waist and yanked my body toward him like a pirate on a romance novel cover. I nearly laughed at the move, until I met his gaze. His eyes smoldered, deep green warring with silver.

Ethan leaned down, his lips at my ear. "You aren't laughing now."

"No," I hoarsely said. "I definitely am not."

"*Ahem*," said a loud voice in the doorway.

We looked over. Luc, former captain of Cadogan's guards, now tied for the position of House Second, stood in the doorway. As House Sentinel, I was an unofficial member of the guards, which made Luc my pseudoboss.

"Sentinel," he said, "the guests are going to be here in an hour, and we're nearly done setting up outside. Since this is your party, perhaps you'd like to join us at some point?"

He was right about the party; I was the House's social chair, an appointment Ethan had given me as both a punishment and an incentive to get to know my fellow Cadogan vampires. But he was wrong that I'd been avoiding my party-prep duties. I'd cleared my being here with the boss, or at least the one currently wearing a suit.

I slid Ethan a suspicious glance, but kept our conversation private, activating the telepathic link between us. *I thought you told Luc you needed my help getting this done before the party?*

He shrugged lightly. *I thought we'd finish this particular job with plenty of time to spare.*

We might have, if his flirtations hadn't kept slowing us down. But what was done was done. I had arrangements to make, and he had guests to greet.

"Apologies, Luc," I said. "Miscommunication on my end." I'd let myself be distracted, after all. I could take responsibility.

Suddenly nervous, I straightened the hem of the fitted leather jacket I'd paired with slim jeans and a flowy tank, a look I managed because the weather had been unseasonably warm the last few weeks. "I truly hope this was a good idea."

Ethan grabbed his tailored suit jacket from his desk chair while I walked to the doorway.

"Inviting every Rogue vampire in Chicago into our backyard?" Ethan asked. "However could that go wrong?"

Most of the country's vampires lived in twelve Houses scattered from coast to coast: Navarre, McDonald, Cabot, Cadogan, Taylor, Lincoln, Washington, Heart, Lassiter, Grey, Murphy, and Sheridan. Three of those—Navarre, Cadogan, and Grey—were located in Chicago.

All twelve Houses fell under the authority of the Greenwich Presidium—at least until seventy-two hours from now, when that number would drop to eleven. Now that we were defecting, we were joining the Rogue vampires who didn't live in Houses. They managed on their own or banded together into unofficial tribes. Either way, they didn't believe the GP had the right to rule them from across the pond.

Rogues were, in their way, America's vampiric colonies.

Pretty soon we'd be Rogues as well, which made it perfectly reasonable that I'd arranged a meet-and-greet for Rogues and Cadogan vamps on the expansive grounds that surrounded Cadogan House.

Yes, we were *finally* having a mixer.

The party would provide an opportunity to ease Cadogan vampires' concerns about the Rogues—who they were and what we were about to become—and let the Rogues get to know us, too.

Luc offered a sarcastic laugh. "It's Cadogan House, and Merit is our social chair. I'm thinking this is a recipe for disaster." Luc, much like Ethan, enjoyed riling me up.

"Har, har," I flatly said, waiting while Ethan slipped into his suit jacket. "If it is, serves Ethan right for making me social chair."

"You did attack him for changing you into a vampire," Luc pointed out.

"Only because he didn't do it very well."

"I reject the notion I am capable of doing anything 'not well,'" Ethan offered.

"So modest, our Liege," Luc said.

Luc called Ethan "Liege" even though Ethan wasn't techni-
cally Master of the House anymore. That honor fell to Malik, the
vampire who'd taken over during Ethan's brief demise. Now that
Ethan was back, even though we hadn't made any official changes,
everybody acted like the old guard was in charge again—Ethan as
Master, Malik as Second, Luc as Guard Captain. It was simply easier than treating twice as many vampires as senior staff members,
or figuring out what to call them. Ethan certainly didn't object to
playing Master, and the others didn't seem to mind giving up their
promotions.

"In any event," Luc said, "sorry to interrupt."

"No, you weren't," I challenged.

"No, I wasn't." He patted my back collegially. "It's entertaining to see you flustered. So very human. Reminders like that keep
a girl grounded."

"She's plenty grounded," Ethan said, joining us in the doorway.
"And not just because I knock her off her feet every time we train."

"Only in your dreams, Sullivan." Ethan had undertaken to
help me with my training as Sentinel. With four hundred years of
experience under his belt, he usually bested me. *But not always*, I
thought with a grin. I'd surprised him a time or two, and those vic-
tories were particularly sweet.

"My dreams are much more interesting than that, Sentinel."

Luc swept an arm toward the hallway. "Your guests are arriving
soon, and I am plenty disturbed and have no desire to learn more
about those dreams, so let's be on our way, shall we?"

Ethan made a sarcastic noise. "Lucas, I rue the day I promoted you."

"Probably so, boss. Probably so. You do wonders for his sense of
humor," Luc said to me.

"Funny, I wasn't aware he had one."

"And now it's two against one," Ethan said. "God willing, our guests are more generous."

Luc chuckled. "As much barbecue as we're piling up outside, they should be."

It didn't surprise either of them that I hoofed it down the hallway at the mention of barbecue. But this time, I wasn't just hurrying because of the smoked meats.

It was the supplier I was looking for.

The House's main hallway led through the first floor to the cafeteria and the door to the backyard.

We stepped outside. The lawn—an expanse of grass that had long since yellowed—swarmed with Cadogan vampires adjusting decor and arranging chairs and tables, all of them sending excited magic into the air. The Black Keys' "Howlin' for You" echoed through outdoor speakers, the result of a special permit we'd managed to acquire from the city and the playlist Lindsey, my closest friend in the House, and I had put together for the party. Social chair duties, I figured.

Luc trotted into the yard, waving his arms at a reporter attempting to climb the fence around the House for a shot of the party. Paparazzi loved vampires and parties. The two together, I imagined, were irresistible.

But before Luc reached him, the reporter squeaked and disappeared back behind the hedge.

He'd undoubtedly been found by our hired security, Chicago's mercenary fairies. They detested humans, and wouldn't take kindly to the reporter's attempt to breach the shield around the House.

That mild drama addressed, preparations for the *invited* guests were well under way. I felt a jolt of guilt about having been distracted by Ethan. On the other hand, we'd been through plenty as a couple, and we took our moments together when we could find them.

Normally, stepping outside in Chicago in winter was a chilling venture, which made the lawn a questionable location for a social event. But we were taking full advantage of the unusually warm weather, and stand-up heaters handled any residual chill in the air. Giant white balloons floated lazily in the mild breeze, and a white, open-sided tent offered tables and a small parquet dance floor, its roof a dome of stretched fabric and arched iron, like something you might have seen in Beaux Arts Paris. There were hundreds of unaffiliated vampires in this city, and we aimed to impress them, at least with our stylishness and good taste.

And, of course, there was the food. You couldn't have much of a party without it, and it certainly wouldn't have been gracious to invite the Rogues into our domain and refuse to feed them. Vampires craved blood and needed it for nutritional purposes, but that didn't diminish our desire for human food. If anything, our faster metabolisms made the hunger worse.

I had planned appropriately, ensuring our tables were filled with roasted meats of the most popular barnyard persuasions— pork, beef, and chicken—and all the appropriate sides. Chicago had once thrived as a cattle town, and that legacy lived on today. It wasn't difficult to find the choicest or homeliest cuts of meat, depending on your preference.

It especially wasn't difficult when you knew where to look. In this case, I looked to a slender woman in jeans and an apron, an aluminum tray of steaming food in her hands, who was walking toward the tables.

She was Mallory Carmichael, a recently confirmed sorceress

and my (maybe) best friend. Our relationship had been strained by her recent efforts to unleash an ancient evil, which nearly destroyed Chicago in the process. Go figure.

Her hair was a newly vibrant shade of blue—or shades of it, actually. She'd dyed her hair in an ombré style; it darkened from pale blue at the roots to indigo at the ends. Tonight it was pulled into a messy bun because she was working as an official employee of the Little Red Catering Company.

Since loosing a fallen angel on the world, she'd been hired by the North American Central Pack of shape-shifters as a girl Friday in their Ukrainian Village bar and diner, Little Red. They were usually a self-contained bunch, but they were concerned enough by Mallory's behavior that they made an exception. She was now getting the *Karate Kid* treatment—doing manual labor while she learned to control herself and tolerate the magic that bubbled beneath her skin.

The Pack also realized that with a sorceress attempting to redeem herself, they had enough staff to increase their income. Little Red already produced top-notch Eastern European food, so they'd ventured into the catering business, prepping full-on meals for Chicago's supernatural denizens. Only supernaturals for now, because humans weren't yet sure that victuals prepared by shape-shifters were safe to eat.

Mallory put her trays on the table, where they were immediately arranged by the Cadogan House chef, Margot, a vampire with a signature bob of sable hair.

"Mallory looks good," Ethan said, still beside me.

I nodded, feeling as relieved as he sounded. Fortunately, Mallory was recovering from the addiction to black magic that had led her astray. But the wounds were still fresh, and vampires had long memories. We were in the process of rebuilding our relationship, and this wasn't the kind of betrayal that was solved by a pint of ice cream or a cathartic cry. I would need time before I could trust her again, and I had the sense she needed time to trust herself, as well.

I didn't see her nearly as much as I used to, so it was reassuring to see her here, now, helping others instead of creating magical mayhem. That's precisely why I'd asked Margot to hire Little Red for the catering. Supporting the bar meant supporting the shifters' new business venture and Mallory's recovery efforts. It seemed like a good idea all around.

"She does look good," I agreed. "I'm going to go say hello."

"Do that," he said, a hand at my back. "I'm going around to the front to greet the guests as they arrive."

"And formally invite them to the House so they don't break any points of vampiric etiquette?" Vampires did love their rules.

"Just so," he said with a smile. "And perhaps we'll finish our library discussion later?"

I barely contained the blush that brightened my cheeks. "We'll see," I said coquettishly, but the knowing look in Ethan's eyes told me he didn't buy the bashfulness.

My evening plans addressed, I caught up with Mallory as she began to walk away from the table, probably to grab another tray of meats.

"Hi," I said, suddenly self-conscious, our interactions still a little awkward.

"Hey," she said.

"I like your hair." That was the absolute truth, but it was less the hair than what the hair symbolized that thrilled me. Mallory's hair had been blue as long as I'd known her . . . except for her period as the Wicked Witch of the Midwest. It seemed to me to be a good sign.

She smiled and touched the top of her bun. "Thanks. It took forever, and I lost four towels in the process, but I think it turned out."

"It definitely turned out. The ombré works for you."

"I need to get some more stuff from the truck," she said, gesturing toward the front of the House. I nodded and walked beside her.

"You ready for this shindig?" she asked.

"As ready as we can be. We're trying to mix two groups of people who've basically sworn to have nothing to do with each other. You do the math."

"That good, eh?"

"I'm expecting some tension," I said honestly. Many of the Rogues had purposely avoided the House system, and now we were inviting them here to socialize.

A shifter carrying four stacked aluminum trays that smelled of porky goodness walked past us, and I couldn't help but stare as all that meat disappeared from sight. "I need to find him later," I absently said. "How's work?"

"Shiftery," she said, pointing to a white delivery truck that was parked at the open gate in the Cadogan fence. "I feel a lot better, but I've developed a new problem."

"What's that?" I asked, fearing a new magical addiction or another demigod with an attitude.

The answer came quickly, and it was decidedly shorter than a demigod.

"Mishka!"

Mallory frowned as a barrel-chested woman with bleached hair stepped out of the truck and headed our way. She was a shifter named Berna, and she tended bar and worked the kitchens at Little Red. She also supervised Mallory, apparently to Mallory's chagrin.

"She calls you Mishka?" I wondered.

"Among other things. And she's driving me crazy." Mallory picked up more aluminum trays, then turned to Berna with an obviously forced smile. "Yes, Berna?"

As soon as Berna reached us, she poked me in the arm. She was always concerned I wasn't eating enough—which was never the case; it was just my vampire metabolism—so the poke was actually an affectionate hello.

"Hi, Berna. The food looks good."

"You eat enough?" she asked in her heavy Eastern European accent.

"Always," I assured her.

"You eat more," she said, then poked Mallory. "You back to work."

"I was just saying hello to Merit."

Berna made a sarcastic noise and pinched my arm. Hard. "Still too thin," she pronounced, then walked away, yelling at another shifter who was heading toward the back of the house carrying plastic bags of yeast rolls.

"I should get back to work," Mallory said. "She has a very specific plan about how this gig should operate."

"I take it you two aren't getting along?"

"She's driving me up the freaking wall."

"Berna's intense," I said, rubbing the sore spot on my arm. "Motherly, in her way, but intense."

"That's precisely the problem. It's been a long time since I've been mothered, and twenty-eight is too late to start."

Mallory's parents had been killed in a car accident years ago, and she didn't have any living relatives.

"I can see how that would be awkward."

"It is. But she means well, so I'm going to shake it off later with a hot bath and stack of gossip magazines."

I wondered whether she'd also shake it off by talking to Catcher Bell, her boyfriend—or at least, he'd been her boyfriend before her unfortunate magical incidents. I wasn't entirely sure where they stood, but since she didn't bring it up, I didn't either. Not that the curiosity wasn't killing me.

"Do the bath and magazines help?" I asked.

"Less than they should. But when you aren't supposed to use your magic, you do what you can. It's like the world's worst diet."

"Mishka!"

"I'm coming!" Mallory yelled, then smiled apologetically. "It's good seeing you, Merit."

"You, too."

She looked up at me a little shyly. "Hey, maybe we could do something sometime? If you're up to it?"

It killed me a little that I hesitated before responding. But I still needed time. "Um, yeah. Okay." I nodded. "Give me a call."

She smiled a little brighter, then jogged back to the truck to arrange food at Berna's command.

Say what you would about Mallory, but the girl was trying to claw her way back into her life. I had to respect that, and I truly hoped she could make it stick.

CHAPTER TWO

PAS DE DEUX

An hour later, the yard was full of vampires of the Rogue and Cadogan persuasions. They seemed to be mixing relatively well—which was the entire point of a mixer, really. If the fashion was any indication, the crew here today was much more eccentric than the Rogues who'd previously visited the House. A few were outfitted in the black military-style duds we'd seen before. But the others wouldn't have passed a military inspection. They wore heavy biker leathers and tie-dyed shirts, classic Goth ensembles and cocktail dresses.

Some of them had been snubbed or excluded by the House system, and some of them had purposely chosen the Rogue life. None of them seemed the worse for it.

Ethan worked the crowd like a master diplomat, moving from cluster to cluster of vampires, shaking hands and listening attentively while they chatted.

Luc stepped beside me. "Not bad for a last-minute party."

"It was only a last-minute party because we've been focusing on the transition," I pointed out.

Ethan appeared at my side and gestured across the lawn to a broad-shouldered man who chatted with Kelley, who'd served as the captain of Cadogan's guards when Luc was promoted. I guess now she was a cocaptain, since Luc had essentially reassumed the position. Seriously, our leadership structure was a mess.

"Noah's just arrived," Ethan said. "Let's say hello."

I hadn't seen Noah since he'd offered me a spot in the Red Guard, a clandestine organization of vampires whose mission was to keep an eye on the Greenwich Presidium and the Houses' Masters to ensure vampires were treated fairly.

I'd accepted Noah's offer, and Jonah, the captain of the Grey House guards, had been appointed as my partner.

Ethan didn't know about the RG or Jonah, or that Noah was affiliated with the organization. Seeing Noah again made my stomach clutch with nerves. I wasn't much of a poker player, but I was going to have to bluff my way to nonchalance on this one.

I followed Ethan across wet grass and toward Noah. He stood in a clutch of black-clad vampires who looked like the type of Rogues I was familiar with. Noah looked up as we moved closer, giving both of us slight nods of recognition.

"Ethan, Merit," Noah said, then looked at his crew. "I'll find you later," he told them, and they disappeared into the crowd.

"Everything okay?" I wondered.

"Personal matters," he said without elaborating, then smiled. "You two look happy and healthy. I was glad to hear you successfully managed Mallory and the Tate twins."

Seth Tate, the former mayor of Chicago, was also an angel who'd been magically linked to his demonic twin brother, Dominic. He'd slain Dominic and left Chicago to seek redemption for the crimes they'd committed while sharing a psyche. We hadn't heard from Seth since.

"So were we," Ethan said, "although it was touch-and-go for a while."

"Well, you put an end to the crisis, and that means something." He took in the sweeping height of Cadogan House, our home in Hyde Park. The mansion was three stories tall, made of pale stone and iron ornamentation. It was built around Chicago's Gilded Age, when cattle and manufacturing made the wealthiest citizens flush and they built stately homes to prove it. Some of those homes were gone, and some had been split into apartments. A few still existed as single-family homes . . . but only one was home to a pride of vampires.

"Are you ready to say good-bye to the GP?" Noah asked, dropping his gaze to us again.

"Only time will tell what it's like on the other side," Ethan said. "Although given the venom the GP's been spewing in our direction lately, I don't anticipate a significant change. If they're going to hate us, they might as well do it without our tithe. You and yours have managed well enough."

"With care and technique," Noah said. "We keep our ears to the ground and our bodies out of the GP's line of sight."

"Is it that bad?" I wondered aloud. Ethan had told me the GP took an all-or-nothing approach to its membership—the vampires within its purview were members, or they were enemies. But I'd never seen the GP take aim against a Rogue vampire. They seemed more interested in harassing the Houses and punishing those within the system who didn't adhere to their standards of behavior.

"Most of our drama lately has been internal," Noah said. "Issues among Rogues, not Housed vampires. But there was a time when the GP kept the lines between the Houses and the Rogues clearly marked and enforced those lines at sword point."

"So many things in the world to worry about," I mused, "and they decide to create animosity for no particular reason."

"Oh, there's a reason," Ethan said. "If they convince the Houses that those outside the Houses are bad, the GP is good by default. They offer constructive criticism and protection from all that's bad."

"So the GP is a protection racket," I said.

"A year ago," Ethan said, "I'd have said that proposition is ridiculous. Now I fear it's not far off the mark. But they aren't here, and we haven't been Decertified yet. So for now, let us eat, drink, and be merry."

"For tomorrow we . . . ?" Noah asked.

Ethan smiled slyly. "We'll see." He glanced across the crowd at someone I couldn't see, and nodded before looking back at us. "If you'll excuse me, I'm being paged from afar. Be nice to our new allies, Sentinel."

"Har, har," I muttered, enjoying the view as he walked away.

"You seem smitten," Noah said.

My cheeks warmed. "I am, as it turns out. Although God knows how that happened."

"He's not the type I would have imagined you with."

"Me, either, and not just because he's fanged." I'd initially planned to avoid dating vampires; that plan hadn't succeeded. "But whatever the reason, we work. We complement each other. I can't explain it, as much as I like to try."

"Connections like that are a rare and fortunate thing," Noah said, with enough bleakness in his voice that I thought he had experience with that rarity.

"Jonah indicates your relationship with Ethan won't affect your RG involvement?" He asked the question casually, although it seemed unlikely he'd have asked at all if he'd actually believed Jonah's answer.

Margot walked toward us with a tray of delicate crystal glasses shimmering with golden champagne.

"Drink?" she asked.

Nodding, I pulled one from the tray and took a hearty sip. Noah did the same.

"I made a commitment," I promised when she was out of ear-shot again. "And I intend to keep it."

"See that you do," Noah said. His tone was just mild enough that I wasn't sure whether he was confirming my allegiance—or questioning it.

When dinner was served, I joined Lindsey at a table beneath the tent.

She was blond and fit, and incredibly bright. She also had a great sense of fashion, a piercing sense of humor, and a strong streak of loyalty, which had nearly tanked her burgeoning relationship with Luc. She'd been afraid a relationship would ruin their friendship, but they seemed to be doing okay.

Across from us at the table were two Rogue vampires.

Alan, who wore a button-down plaid shirt, looked as happily average as they came. He explained that he worked in insurance; I didn't entirely understand his job, but it seemed to involve a lot of math and, fortunately, allowed him to work at night.

Beth, who dressed with Gothic flare, was a tattoo artist with a shop in Wrigleyville and a part-time burlesque dancer. She had dark, wavy hair and a curvy figure with a nipped-in waist, and she snorted a little bit when she laughed, which she did a lot.

Alan and Beth had recently met on an Internet dating site for Chicago vamps, and my mixer was their very first outing together. I took an obscene amount of pride in that, even though their finding each other had nothing to do with me.

Alan put down the bottle of root beer he'd been drinking. "You know, the GP may call you Rogues, but there's still a big difference between you and us."

"How do you mean?" Lindsey asked.

"You're Housed," Alan said. "Even if you aren't in the GP, you're still part of a unit. You've agreed to live and work together, to hang out together. It's basically a vampire fraternity, right?"

I actually hadn't agreed to live and work in Cadogan House— I'd been attacked by a Rogue vampire and left for dead. Ethan had made me a vampire to save my life. Membership in Cadogan House had been the side benefit. Or cost, depending on your perspective.

"Alan," Beth scolded, but he shrugged off the concern.

"I'm not trying to be rude," he said. "I'm just being honest. That's the perception of a lot of Rogues—that you think you're in a club and that makes you better than everyone else."

That thought hadn't even occurred to me, and I doubted it had occurred to Lindsey, either. We weren't the elitist type. If anything, Cadogan was the least elitist House in Chicago. Navarre, in my humble opinion, was snootier, and the vampires of Grey House, which was all about athletics, had a built-in tendency to hang together.

On the other hand, he was right that we were part of a club. There were three hundred vampires associated with Cadogan House. Nearly one hundred of us lived together in Cadogan House in our dormlike rooms, ate together, worked out together, and sometimes worked together. We had positions and titles, rulebooks, and T-shirts and medals that proclaimed our membership to the world.

"We kind of are a fraternity," I said. "That makes us loyal to each other, and willing to work for the House's good. But I don't know anyone in the House who thinks we're better than anyone."

"Well, I think you seem cool," Beth said.

"She is cool," Lindsey said. "For a nerd."

Beth and Alan also seemed cool, and they certainly didn't seem miserable just because they lived outside the Houses.

Beth smiled. "And it's not that we think anything's wrong with living in a House. We just don't do it."

The clink of metal against glass brought our attention to Ethan, who stood nearby, a champagne flute in one hand and a fork in the other.

"If I could have your attention," he said, placing the fork on a nearby table while the crowd quieted. "I'd like to take this opportunity to welcome the unaffiliated vampires of this city to Cadogan House. I hope you've felt our door was open to you, and I certainly hope that you'll feel that way after our status changes. It is true that we're a House. But we are now, have always been, and will continue to be a collective of vampires. We have chosen to come together just as you have chosen to stand as proud individual vampires, and we respect your decisions to do so. We are searching for a new way to live and thrive as vampires." He smiled rakishly. "We may come to you for advice."

There were a few appreciative chuckles in the crowd, and a few suspicious grunts. It was becoming clear that the city's Rogues weren't just going to welcome us with open arms; we'd have to prove our worth to them just as we had to the GP. Maybe, unlike the GP, the Rogues would actually listen.

Ethan looked down at the ground for a moment, his forehead wrinkling in the center. That was a sign he was worried, and when he looked up across the crowd again, the concern in his eyes was clear.

"These are strange times," he said. "We have been tested, as this city has been tested. Recent events have been difficult for vampires and Chicago, and they may become more so. Other supernaturals' announcements of their existence, while taking some of the spotlight off vampires, have made humans increasingly nervous about our presence. Tate's antics did nothing to improve the humans' esteem; nor has the new mayor offered any help."

There was no disagreement with that point. Diane Kowalcyzk, Chicago's new mayor, wasn't bright, and she seemed to be overtly prejudiced against supernaturals. She'd even made friends with McKetrick, first name unknown, a former military type with a raging hatred of vampires.

"At the risk of speaking ill of our soon-to-be former leaders, it probably won't surprise you to learn that the Greenwich Presidium has turned a blind eye to those developments, and has refused to accept the changing world. We don't think that's fair, and we think it's time for a change. This week we take our stand. We cannot predict the future," Ethan said. "We do our best, and we hope—with love and luck and friendship—that we survive these turbulent times."

He held up his champagne glass. "May the winds blow fair through your journeys, wherever they may lead. Cheers."

"Cheers," responded the crowd, and everyone took a sip.

Without missing a beat, Ethan walked to Noah's table and shook his hand. The chatter returned to normal levels, vampires digging back into their proteins while two of the most important vampires in the city made nice in front of their minions.

I had to give it to Ethan: He was right that times were precarious, but he'd managed to convince a chunk of the city's unaffiliated Rogues to venture into our domain, break bread with us, and toast our collective futures. Fanged or not, the man had a way with words.

Fortunately for me, his skills weren't limited to his vocabulary.

As if sensing the somewhat lurid direction of my thoughts, Ethan turned toward me and smiled, my toes curling just from the heat of a look.

His conversation with Noah done, he walked toward me, every female eye—and some of the men's eyes, too—on him as he moved, the embodiment of masculinity. A vampire in his prime.

He stopped behind my chair and held out a hand. The entire table went silent.

"Dance with me," he said.

My cheeks warmed. "There's no music."

Before he had time to respond, the quartet in the corner—a group of Cadogan and Rogue vampires with musical talents—began to play a jazzy tune.

I gave him a sardonic look. "Did you just telepathically direct them to start playing that?"

"What's the point of being telepathic if you can't use the connection for a wee bit of wickedness, Sentinel?"

I heard the yearning sigh of a female vampire to my right, and caught the dreamy-eyed gaze of a male vampire to my left. Ethan was an equal-opportunity crush.

He wiggled his fingers. "Merit?"

With the audience's eyes on me, it would have been difficult to say no to Ethan even if I hadn't had feelings for him. That I did made it virtually impossible.

"Of course," I said, putting my hand in his and letting him lead me to the makeshift dance floor.

Oh, my God, could he move.

Ethan whipped a hand around my waist like he'd trained with the cast of a televised dance competition. With moves that were a mix of swing and tango, he led me around the floor like a dance master, all the while keeping those ridiculously green eyes focused on me. Fortunately, I'd been a ballerina in my former (human) life, so I managed to keep up with him. I even tried to put on a good show—or at least as good a show as pants and a fitted leather jacket would allow—to the surprise of Rogue and Cadogan vampires.

The song ended, and Ethan dropped me into a dip, his smile mischievous and his eyes twinkling. The rest of the world came rushing back in a roar of sound as the vampires on the margins of the dance floor burst into applause.

Ethan brought me back to my feet, my ponytail bobbing over a shoulder. "And that, Sentinel, is how you impress a crowd."

My cheeks warmed as I waved a little at said crowd, acknowledging their applause.

But when I caught sight of Noah surrounded by the same black-clad vampires he'd been speaking to earlier, I realized my fun would be short-lived. There was no mistaking the distress in Noah's expression, or the fact that his companions kept sneaking anxious looks in our direction.

Delicately, I put a hand on Ethan's arm and leaned toward him, my lips just brushing his ear. It was a move the crowd would mistake for a show of affection, which was a perfect bit of sleight of hand.

"Something's up," I whispered. "Noah's surrounded by Rogues, and they look worried. They're at your eight o'clock."

In the guise of pressing a light kiss to my cheek, Ethan glanced over his shoulder. "So I see," he said, turning back to me again. "Can you get the gist of it?"

As predators, vampires had uniquely strong senses—hearing, sight, smell. But there were too many vampires in the crowd, and too much magical energy, for me to tell what trouble was brewing.

"I cannot," I said. "Perhaps an invitation to your office?"

"That seems wise," he agreed. He took my hand and, with smiles and waves to the crowd, stepped out of the spotlight.

"Keep the guests busy," he whispered to Luc, who nodded obediently and stepped into the middle of the dance floor.

"It's a party!" Luc said, clapping his hands together as a jaunty David Bowie tune filled the air. "Let's all dance."

With Luc's encouragement, vampires spilled onto the dance floor.

We slipped through the tent to reach Noah and the worried Rogues. Fear marked their expressions, and they radiated tense magic that made my skin feel tight from the contact.

"Is everything all right?" Ethan asked.

Noah glanced among his Rogues, meeting the gaze of a female vampire with cropped hair and small silver spikes above both eyebrows. Her look was edgy, but her tearstained eyes belied her appearance. She nodded at Noah, giving him approval for something. Rogue democracy at work.

Noah paused, as if weighing a decision. "Perhaps we could speak privately?" he asked. "We have a concern, and we'd appreciate your thoughts."

"Of course," Ethan said, gesturing toward the door. "Let's go to my office. We can speak there." He glanced across the group of Noah's friends. "You're all welcome to join us."

But they edged away like feral kittens nervous about being led indoors.

"I'll be back," Noah said to the rest of the Rogues, then supportively squeezed the hand of the spiked girl. Both of them followed us into the House.

We walked silently down the hallway, and Ethan closed the office door when we were all inside. Noah immediately headed toward the conversation area and took a seat in one of the leather club chairs there; the female vampire followed him. I took a seat on the opposite couch, and Ethan did the same.

"What's on your mind?" Ethan asked when all were settled.

"Two of my vampires have disappeared, and we're afraid they might be in trouble."

Ethan's eyes widened. "I'm sorry to hear that. Start at the beginning, if you would."

Noah nodded. "Last night we had a gathering—a meeting—that we hold monthly for Rogues in the city. Nothing formal, nothing official, just a chance for us to get together and chat. Some Rogues aren't interested in attending; some are. On average, we get thirty to forty vampires. Most of them are regulars, including a couple of kids named Oliver and Eve. They came up from Kansas City when the GP consolidated the Rogues down there into Murphy House. Living in a House wasn't their bag, so they moved up here. But they didn't show up at the meeting."

"Is that so unusual?" Ethan asked.

"Unusual enough," Noah said. "I can't recall a meeting they've missed since they came to Chicago."

"They broke pattern," Ethan said, and Noah nodded.

"Precisely. And that's gotten a few of our Rogues worried."

"Understandable," Ethan said.

"I'm going to be honest with you—I'm not convinced there's anything to this. Oliver and Eve are generally quiet kids, and I don't tend to ask a lot of personal questions. It's not impossible they had business to take care of that they simply didn't want to tell us about. Kansas City vampires tend to be reserved like that."

"If they didn't attend the meeting, when were they last seen?" Ethan asked.

Noah's expression darkened. "A place we all have to go sooner or later."

That cryptic response sent my imagination on a tear. To what places did vampires have to go? Fang orthodontists? Plasma centers? Vampiric couturieres?

"A vampire registration center?" Ethan flatly guessed.

Chicago's politicos had decided, in a fit of ethnocentrism, that forcing vampires to register with the city would somehow make Chicago safer. The conclusion might have been correct, but for the wrong reason. Registration scared and angered vampires, precisely the emotions humans wanted to avoid. There were a handful of registration offices across town, their existence funded by the fees vampires paid to register.

Noah nodded. "Exactly. Two nights ago, Eve took a picture on her phone when she and Oliver were in the registration line. She sent the pic to a few of her friends, including Rose." He gestured at the vampire beside him.

"Given what you've told us about them so far, and their reason for moving to Chicago, I'm surprised they decided to register at all," Ethan said.

Noah nodded. "So was I. Most of us haven't registered. Many Rogues feel that if registration of vampires is the first step, internment is the second. They don't even align themselves with Houses of their own kind; they certainly aren't going to set themselves up for de facto incarceration by humans."

I could understand his concerns, even if I couldn't evade them. My father was a real estate mogul, and my picture had been in the paper. I was too well known to avoid registration even if I'd wanted to, which was why my laminated registration card was safe and snug in my wallet, even as much as it offended me.

"If they were last seen two nights ago," Ethan said, "what's made you nervous tonight?"

"Rose got a call from Oliver's phone earlier this evening. She didn't actually talk to Oliver; no one was speaking on the other end. But she thinks she heard something in the background."

I glanced at her. "What did you hear?"

Her voice was soft. "I don't know. I thought he'd called me accidentally—like a misdial. Nobody was speaking, but I thought I heard something loud, and then voices, but they were muffled. I'm not really sure. . . ."

She glanced at Noah, and seemed hesitant about offering more, so I gently nudged.

"Anything else?" I asked.

"I thought I heard . . . maybe a scuffle? Or a fight? Like furniture moving or people falling down? That kind of fleshy sound?"

Ethan nodded, then returned his gaze to Noah. "Have you advised the police Oliver and Eve may be missing?"

Noah shook his head. "I haven't, and I don't plan to. We aren't fans of the city's police establishment. Their history with vampires leaves something to be desired."

Noah linked his hands together, elbows on his knees, and leaned forward. "Look, maybe this is something; maybe it's not. Oliver and Eve have left a vampire community before. This could be the same situation. And we aren't crazy about involving others. Bringing you into this is . . . challenging for us. But it's unusual enough that we think it's worth checking into. I apologize for the timing; we certainly hadn't planned to bring trouble to your door tonight."

Ethan shook his head, dismissing the worry. "You're troubled, and we're colleagues. We're happy to listen."

Nicely subtle bit of politicking there, I thought.

Noah nodded. "At the risk of ungraciously putting you on the spot, perhaps you could make some inquiries? You have certain connections. Your grandfather, for one," he said to me. "Chuck Merit's a good man. I'd appreciate any help he could offer."

I nodded in agreement. My grandfather was unquestionably a good man. One of the best, in my opinion. He'd been the city's supernatural Ombudsman, at least until Mayor Kowalcyzk did away with the position. But my grandfather wasn't dissuaded from his mission; he set up shop in his own house.

They both went quiet for a moment. Ethan, I suspected, was considering whether we had the resources to take on someone else's problem, especially when it wasn't entirely clear there was a problem at all.

"I know you have a lot on your plate right now," Noah added. "But you're the House that listens."

Ethan looked at me. *Are you willing to discuss this with your grandfather?* he silently asked. *As Noah notes, I do have a bit on my plate.*

Of course, I said. *And besides—if we don't help, who will?* The new mayor wouldn't much care, and the other Houses avoided politics and controversy at all cost.

There was a flash of pride in Ethan's eyes. He was glad that I hadn't shrunk back from the problem, that I was willing to face it head-on. I was glad of the same from him—that he wasn't letting appearances and political considerations sway him from a course we needed to chart. Of course, now that we were leaving the GP, those considerations were even more flexible.

"We're on board," Ethan said. "Perhaps we could review the photograph Eve took outside the registration center?"

"I'll do you one better," Noah said. "I'll escort you to the spot."

Ethan advised Malik and Luc of our plans and ensured the party was well tended. Rose went back to her group of Rogue friends, and we met Noah in the House's foyer. We were all dressed severely in black, and we looked displaced among the House's holiday decorations.

"Do you need a ride?" Ethan said, but Noah shook his head.

"I have things to take care of when we're done. I'll meet you there?"

Ethan nodded; Noah had already given us the address of the registration center, a spot in Chicago's Little Italy neighborhood near the University of Illinois at Chicago. "We'll be right behind you."

Ethan, being a senior House staff member, had a coveted parking spot in the House's basement. He wouldn't have to dig his car out of a Chicago snowstorm, have someone hold a spot on the street as he neared the House, or attempt to parallel-park between gigantic cars and a mountain of snow that cemented into a secondary curb.

We took the main staircase to the basement, and he keyed his way into the garage. I stopped short in the doorway.

In Ethan's parking spot, which an Aston Martin had temporarily filled, sat a shiny two-door coupe with a deep red finish and grinning grille.

"What is that?" I asked.

Ethan *beeped* the security system and walked to the driver's side. "This, Merit, is a Bentley Continental GT."

"It looks brand-new."

"It is."

I glanced around the parking area; his Aston Martin was nowhere to be found. "Did something happen to the Aston Martin?"

"No," he said, frowning. He opened the door. "The Aston just didn't do it for me."

Ethan had lost his former car, a sleek Mercedes convertible, in an unfortunate run-in with the Tate twins before their separation. Tate had thrown the car off the road—with us inside—and the Mercedes hadn't survived the fall.

I understood well the bond between car and driver. I was still driving the boxy orange Volvo I'd had for years. It wasn't much, but it was paid for, and it got me where I needed to go.

Still. He'd had an Aston Martin. A brand-new, right-off-the-lot Aston Martin delivered to him by a very pleased salesman.

"All due respect, a brand-new Aston Martin 'didn't do it' for you? That's James Bond's car."

"I'm no James Bond," he cannily said. "I loved the Mercedes. It fit me perfectly. The Aston just . . . *didn't.*"

"So you traded up?" I asked, walking toward the car and opening the door. "Do you treat your relationships in the same way?"

"Yes," Ethan gravely said. "And I spent four hundred years shopping before I met you."

It was comments like that that kept me around, even when Ethan was being otherwise insufferable. He popped them into conversation just often enough to make my heart melt.

"Then by all means," I said, "let's see what she can do."

＊ ≡◆≡ ＊

CHAPTER THREE

FOUNDING FATHERS

We drove to Little Italy, which was southwest of downtown Chicago.

In all fairness, the Bentley handled like a dream, which I suppose was the point of spending so much money on the car. Along with impressing your friends and intimidating your enemies.

The street Noah had identified was quiet, a weekday neighborhood of small businesses—banks, tailors, Realtors' offices. Most of the buildings were stand-alone and three or four stories tall, their windows bearing signs promising future condos and apartments.

As we neared the street number Noah had given us, Ethan pulled the Bentley into a parking slot in front of a sushi restaurant that now stood vacant. A dry cleaner was next door, and in the next building was the insult to our existence, the vampire registration office. Tonight was a weekend, and the building was dark. But come Monday at dusk, a line of vampires would appear outside the door awaiting the opportunity to give away their blessed anonymity to the bureaucracy of the city of Chicago.

Ethan and I got out of the car and strapped on our katanas. Chicago cops would probably lose it if they realized we were carrying dozens of inches of honed and tempered steel, but I wasn't going to let that stop me. There was no telling what kind of drama we might find, and I wanted to be prepared.

I jumped as a nearby car door slammed shut. Noah, who'd parked on the street a few cars back, walked toward us.

"You all right?" Ethan asked, glancing back at me.

"Fine," I said with a nod. "The sound startled me."

Ethan squeezed my hand supportively. "So Oliver and Eve came here to register," he said, glancing around. "Why this particular center?"

"They lived not far from here," Noah said. "So probably proximity."

"Sentinel? Thoughts?"

"They probably wouldn't have been alone," I suggested. "There would have been other vampires here, or the employees operating the registration center. Maybe they saw something, or could tell us if Oliver and Eve actually made it through the registration process? That might help us nail down the time line."

"That's something to check," Noah agreed.

"There's also no blood," I said. My vampiric instincts would have been triggered if there'd been a quantity of blood around. I hoped that meant Oliver and Eve hadn't succumbed to any harm.

"I'm not suggesting anything untoward has occurred," Ethan said, "but if it did, could they have been targeted because they were registering?"

"Maybe," Noah said. "But registration is supposed to soothe humans. Why punish vampires for doing what you've asked them to do?"

"Perhaps it wasn't humans who did the punishing," Ethan said.

"Other Rogues might have been less than thrilled they'd decided to register. They might have seen it as a betrayal."

I thought Ethan had a point, but Noah wasn't thrilled at Ethan's implication. His look was arch. "You're suggesting we've created our own problems?"

But Ethan wasn't intimidated. "I'm asking. Is it possible?"

"I'd like to think not. But I don't control them."

So two vampires were missing, vamps we knew had visited a registration center. There weren't any obvious signs of violence or anything else that linked them to the site, or that suggested where they might have gone—or been taken—afterward.

Hands on my hips, teeth worrying my bottom lip, I glanced around the neighborhood. It was either very late or very, very early, depending on your perspective—and the area was quiet. Across the street from the registration center was another set of buildings: a pizzeria, closed for the night, and a boarded former apartment building surrounded by chain-link fence. But in between them, something interesting—a tidy, narrow, three-story condominium . . . with a suited doorman.

I glanced back at Noah. "Do you have the picture of Oliver and Eve?"

"On my phone, yeah."

I gestured toward the doorman. "He's on the night shift. Maybe we'll get lucky and he was on the night shift two nights ago, too."

A corner of Ethan's mouth curled. "Well done, Sentinel," he said, then gestured across the street. "Ladies first."

I waited until a very odiferous garbage truck rumbled past, then jogged across the street, Ethan and Noah behind me.

The doorman, the brass buttons of his burgundy coat gleaming, looked up nervously as we moved toward him, his eyes widening, his heartbeat speeding. If he'd had magic, I'd no doubt have felt the bitter pulse of his fear yards away.

As if protecting his castle from marauders, he stepped in front of the door. "Can I help you?"

"Noah," I said, extending my hand until he placed his phone in my palm. I checked the screen, saw the gentle smiling faces of two blond vampires—one male, one female.

I held it toward the doorman. "Our friends have disappeared, and we're trying to find them. We think they might have been across the street two nights ago. Do they look familiar to you?"

Without bothering to check the screen, the doorman crossed his arms over his barrel chest and narrowed his gaze at me.

"Not even a little peek?"

He blinked slowly.

"Perhaps this will jog your memory," Ethan said, extending a folded twenty-dollar bill between his fingers.

The doorman took it and slipped it into his coat pocket, then crossed his arms again. I guess Jackson wasn't his favorite president.

"How about President Grant?" Ethan asked, offering a fifty in the same way.

The doorman cast a suspicious gaze at it. "I prefer Benjamin Franklin's commonsense advice and down-home humor. But President Grant has his finer qualities." He took the bill and tucked it into his pocket. "What can I do for you this evening?"

I bit back a smile. "These two," I reminded him, wiggling the phone. "Have you seen them?"

This time his gaze slid to the screen. "I saw them," he said with a nod. "They went to the registration office."

"How do you remember them?" I wondered.

"They took photographs of themselves in line, like they were heading into a concert instead of registering with the city." He shrugged. "I don't know. I guess that seemed unusual to me."

It seemed unusual to me, too, but I didn't have a strong enough sense of Oliver and Eve to know whether it was unusual for them.

"What happened after that?" I asked.

He shrugged and looked straight ahead again.

"Really," I flatly said.

He cast me a sideways glance. "Inflation, don't you know."

Irritation building, I put a hand on my sword and stepped forward.

Sentinel, Ethan silently cautioned, but it was time to walk the walk.

"This sword isn't for show," I said. "It's honed steel, and it's very sharp, and I'm very good at using it."

"She is," Noah and Ethan simultaneously agreed.

"We aren't asking you for much—only information, for which we have handsomely paid." I tapped the top of the sword's pommel. "I can't imagine your residents would be thrilled to learn that you irritated people carrying weapons instead of simply telling them what they wanted to know and allowing them to be on their way."

He scowled.

"Commonsense advice," I reminded him with a saccharine smile.

The doorman scowled again, his upper lip curled, but relented. "They went in, came out again."

"And got in their cars and drove away?" I wondered.

"Actually, no," he said. He pointed across the street. "Car pulled up in the alley."

The dry cleaner sat on one side of the registration office, the alley on the other.

"A car?" Noah asked. "What kind of car?"

He shrugged. "Didn't see it. Just the headlights—they were shining out of the alley. The vampires walked over there like they were checking it out, maybe talking to the driver. Then headlights dim like the car's backing out of the alley."

"Did you see them leave again?" I asked.

The doorman shrugged. "Don't know, don't care. Maybe they were meeting up with friends? This is America. I don't keep track." Thinking he'd been insulted, he turned his gaze blankly back to the street again. We'd lost his interest.

"Thanks," I told the doorman. "We appreciate it."

He didn't look much impressed by the thanks, but he nodded anyway. "You're blocking the door."

Ethan touched my arm. "Let's check out the alley," he said, and with the doorman scowling at our backs, we crossed the street once again.

I tried to imagine I was a cop—walking a beat like my grandfather had—except with added vampire sensibilities.

I walked to the edge of the alley, then closed my eyes and breathed in the night air, let the sounds around me unfurl. Unknown droplets fell ahead of us in the alley, which smelled of dampness and garbage, rusty metal and dirt. Luckily I got no obvious sense of violence—no scents of blood or gunpowder.

When I was sure the coast was clear, I stepped into the darkness. It wasn't the first alley I'd seen; in Chicago, they mostly looked the same: puddles of dirty water on the ground, brick walls, a Dumpster, and an emergency exit or two.

I looked for any clue that would have explained why Oliver and Eve walked into this alley.

After a moment of scanning the ground, a glint caught my eye, and I crouched down. There were chunks of glass on the ground. Not shards, but square pieces. It was safety glass, the kind used in car windows.

"What did you find?" Ethan asked, stepping behind me.

"There's glass here. Could be from the vehicle the doorman sort of saw."

"Very long odds of that," Ethan remarked. "If the glass was broken, surely the vampires out front would have heard it and investigated."

"Probably," I agreed, standing up again and dusting my hands on my pants.

The shrill ringing of a cell phone filled the alley. Instinctively I checked my phone, but it was dark and silent.

"Is that yours?" Ethan asked, and I shook my head and scanned the alley, realizing the sound was coming from a few feet away, near a red metal Dumpster.

I walked closer, the sound growing louder, and kicked aside a few windblown bits of trash. A vibrantly pink phone lay on the concrete, flashing as someone tried to reach the phone's owner.

No—not just someone. The screen flashed with a phone number and name; the caller was Rose, Noah's Rogue friend. I had a sinking suspicion I knew whose phone this was, and my stomach flipped uncomfortably.

"Noah," I called out, and felt him move behind me, his nervous energy tickling the air.

"That's Eve's phone," he solemnly pronounced. "I'd know it anywhere. It's old and does pretty much nothing but take calls, but she refuses to upgrade. Rose is probably trying to reach her—to check on her again. She's worried. She keeps calling. I've told her to stop, but . . ."

I understood that fear, and sympathized. But I didn't think finding Eve's phone in an alley signaled very good news.

"Perhaps Eve just dropped it here?" Ethan wondered. "Oliver did call Rose earlier. There's a chance this is all a misunderstanding."

Ethan's tone was optimistic, probably intended to keep Noah calm. And he was right: We really had no idea how or why the phone had ended up here, although it did confirm that Eve had been in the alley. But it also made her and Oliver's disappearances look less and less like they might be voluntary.

"It seems unlikely she'd have just left it," Noah said. He rubbed a hand over his face, seeming suddenly exhausted.

The ringing stopped, leaving the alley silent . . . and a little grim.

"Do you have a handkerchief?" Ethan asked. "We'll want to get it to the Ombud's office—they have connections—but we don't want to disturb any evidence."

He was right. There could be fingerprints or biological material on the phone, evidence that could help us figure out exactly what had gone on.

"Bandanna," Noah said, pulling one printed in pixilated camouflage from his pocket and handing it over.

Gingerly I picked up the phone with the cloth. While I was gathering evidence, I walked back to the pile of glass and snagged a square. I folded the packet carefully, then looked at Noah.

"I'll give this to Jeff Christopher, and we'll have him check Eve's call log. Maybe there's a clue about where she might be."

Jeff was one of my grandfather's pseudo-employees, an adorable and quirky computer genius. He was also a shape-shifter and member of the North American Central Pack. Along with Catcher, a rogue sorcerer, my grandfather's admin, Marjorie, and a "secret"

Housed vamp I hadn't heard about in a while, they kept an eye on supernatural comings and goings and helped us manage whatever crises popped up. Since their office had been closed by the mayor, they'd all been working together at my grandfather's house.

A black cat hopped down from the neighboring yard's retaining wall, gazed at us warily, and trotted to the Dumpster, presumably to look for a snack. Oblivious to the danger, birds began to chirp nearby, a cheery song that announced the impending break of morning.

I glanced up at the sky. The eastern horizon was just beginning to pale. Sunrise was on its way, which meant we were running out of time. Vampires and sunlight didn't mix, not without fatal consequences.

Ethan checked his watch. "We've not quite an hour before dawn. We should get back to the House."

"The world continues to turn," Noah said.

"So it does," Ethan agreed. "And hopefully for Oliver and Eve, as well." We walked back toward the alley entrance, the birds singing behind us.

"We'll find them," Ethan said.

Noah nodded, but didn't seem convinced. "I hope so. They're good kids."

"We don't doubt it," Ethan said. They shook hands, and Noah walked back to his car. We followed and climbed silently into the Bentley.

"Do you really think we're going to find them?" I asked, leaving unspoken the fear that we'd find them, but too late.

"I don't know," Ethan said. "But we will do our damnedest to try."

Of course we would. But would our damnedest be enough?

I had evidence that might help lead us to Oliver and Eve, but I was about to be forced offline. The sun was our ultimate weakness, an allergy that rendered us permanently nocturnal. This being winter in the Midwest, we were out of the investigation game for the next nine hours.

On the other hand, the members of the Ombud's office—the Ombuddies, as I preferred to call them—who usually adopted supernaturals' overnight hours, were at least capable of venturing about in daylight. So I used the fancy electronics in Ethan's car to dial Jeff's number, hoping he'd be sympathetic to our predicament.

"Yo," Jeff answered, his voice ringing through the Bentley's impeccable stereo system.

"Hey, it's Merit."

"Merit. Have you finally decided to ditch the zero and get with the hero?"

Ethan cleared his throat—loudly—while I bit back a smile. I didn't see anything wrong with reminding Ethan that I had other options. Even if they were slightly goofy options I'd never actually take advantage of.

"Jeff, you're on speakerphone in Ethan's car. He's driving."

There was an awkward pause.

"And by 'zero,'" Jeff quickly corrected, "I meant, you know, you should . . . um . . . start liking the White Sox. Go, Sox," he weakly added, as I was a notorious Cubs fan with an unwavering love of all things Cubbie.

"Hello, Jeffrey," Ethan dryly said.

Jeff laughed nervously. "Oh, hi, Ethan. Hey, look, it's Catcher. Catcher, why don't you join us?"

"Vampires?" Catcher asked, his voice a bit farther away in the room.

"Ethan and Merit," Jeff confirmed.

Catcher made a sarcastic sound, but whether a snort or grunt was impossible to tell through the phone.

"Trouble?" I wondered.

"I've got a River nymph panicking about a zoning change on Goose Island and another who's panicked some Oak Street shop won't hold a pair of designer heels until she has time to pick them up. Because that's the kind of work our office does. We are personal assistants for the supernaturals of Chicago."

Catcher's tone was dry, and I sympathized. The River nymphs were petite, busty, and fashionable ladies who controlled the ebb and flow of the Chicago River. They tended toward the dramatic, and they liked expressing that drama in public screaming matches and other shenanigans. Catcher might not have liked listening to their quarrels, petty or not, but he was performing a service by keeping them out of the paper, even if it made him grouchier toward the rest of us. And his baseline level of grouchy was already pretty high.

"I'm sorry about the theatrics," I said. "And not to add to your plate, but we have a problem. Two of Noah's Rogues—Oliver and Eve—are missing."

"We've just left the last location where we can place them," Ethan put in. "Near the registration center in Little Italy."

"Find anything?" Catcher asked.

"What looks like safety glass and Eve's cell phone," I said. "We talked to the doorman across the street, and he saw Oliver and Eve go into the reg center, then come out again and approach a car in the alley. No info about the car's make or model; he only saw the headlights. Oliver and Eve didn't come out again. The glass and cell phone were all we found."

"I'm not sure that bodes well," Catcher said.

"I'm not sure, either," I agreed. "But at least they're clues. The sun, of course, is rising, and we're on our way back to the House. Is there any way you can get your CPD contacts to look at it during business hours? We're afraid to wait until tonight."

"Chuck might have to call in a favor, but we'll get it done. Maybe leave the goods with the fairies?"

I glanced at Ethan, checking for approval, and he nodded. "We'll arrange it," he said.

"Noted. Do we know anything else about these kids?"

"They were generally quiet, hailed from Kansas City," Ethan said. "They seem to have strong connections among Rogues and are well liked."

"No enemies?" Catcher wondered. "Even though they decided to register?"

"We wondered the same thing," Ethan said. "But if there's trouble in that corner, we don't know about it."

"Well, I'm sorry to hear they're missing. I didn't know them, but if they were friends of Noah's, I'm sure they were good people."

Were, he'd said, as if their fate was a foregone conclusion. But I refused to give up.

"We'll call you as soon as the sun goes down," I said. "If you learn anything that explains where they might be, you win the bonus prize for the evening."

"What's the bonus prize?"

And that was the problem with spur-of-the-moment offers. "Um, I'll order pizza for the office?"

"Make it double meat and you've got a deal," Catcher said.

"Done," I said.

The perky sound of a country song—the lyrics about partying hard after a long day of work on the graveyard shift—suddenly filled the car, emanating from the speakerphone.

Catcher muttered a curse and the sound went silent. But the silence didn't eliminate the questions.

"Was that—was that your ringtone?" I asked, simultaneously comforted and amused by the weird contradiction that was Catcher Bell. He was built, gruff, and an expatriate of the Order, the sorcerers' governing body, which had kicked him out. He was also a protector of Mallory—at least until her magical misanthropy—a lover of Lifetime movies, and, so it seemed, a lover of country music.

I had no objections to country music. It just wasn't the type of thing Catcher would ever admit to. Except that it was on his ringtone, for God's sake, and I had two independent witnesses.

Some nights there was justice in the world, even if it was meted out only in a dribble of *Billboard* country/pop crossover.

"Enjoy the country music, do you?" I wondered.

"Don't push your luck," Catcher grumbled. "This is the South Branch nymph calling, and I need to go deal with her. We'll talk to you tonight."

The line went dead before we could respond—or I could harass Catcher any more about his ringtone.

"You're going to use that against him, aren't you?" Ethan asked.

"As much as possible," I agreed.

The Ombud arrangements made, I texted Jonah—my RG partner—to let him know Noah had pulled us into the investigation. Jonah was also Noah's friend and RG colleague, so there seemed little doubt Noah had already told him about the missing vampires. But he needed to know we'd undertaken the assignment, so to speak.

ADVISE IF NEED ASSIST, he messaged back.

I promised I would, but that wasn't the end of the conversation.

ALSO RG INITIATION IMMINENT. DETAILS TBA.

I stared at the message for a moment, my heart thudding with my sudden nerves. I'd known the RG ceremony was coming, but I hadn't known precisely when. It wasn't so much the initiation that made me nervous as the commitment to the RG. My relationship with Ethan was just getting off the ground, and the House was in a precarious situation. I believed in the RG's mission—keeping an eye on the GP and the Houses—now more than ever. But that didn't make me feel any more comforted about making my ties official and unbreakable.

"Trouble?" Ethan asked, sparing me a glance.

"Nothing I can't handle," I said, tucking the phone away again. I hoped it was true.

One crisis at a time, I told myself.

I told myself that a lot. Unfortunately, our world rarely worked that way.

Cadogan House had three aboveground floors, all equally posh and full of expensive furniture and lush decor. Ethan's apartments—we shared them, but they bore his stamp—were on the third floor.

We met Malik on the stairs, also on his way to bed, and exchanged updates about our evenings. We filled him in on our visit to the alley; he reported on the party.

"Two thumbs up for the catering," he said, "and everyone seemed friendly enough. But your absence was noted. The mood deflated a bit when you left."

"I was afraid of that," Ethan said. "Two families throw a party and the heads of the families disappear? It doesn't read positively."

"The Rogues are aware of Oliver and Eve's possible disappearance. Some are concerned for their friends and are glad we're on board. Others are concerned Rogues will be dragged into Cadogan politics."

Ethan lifted his gaze to the ceiling, as if exhausted by the premise. "We engage in politics because it is required of us. If vampires would simply act appropriately, there'd be no need of it." He glanced at me. "We should have that embroidered on a T-shirt."

"It's not exactly catchy, but I could make that happen."

"I'm sure you could. In any event, Malik, thank you for handling it."

"Of course, Liege."

Ethan winced at the title. "Please stop calling me that. You're still officially the Master."

"Oh, I know," Malik said. "But much like Merit, I find it amusing to irritate you."

As Malik walked down the hallway and around the corner, Ethan turned his pointed gaze on me.

I shrugged innocently. "I can't help it if I'm a trendsetter."

Ethan humphed but took my hand, and we continued to the third floor and down the hallway, saying good night to the vampires we passed.

Luc was returning to Lindsey's room, which was only a few doors down from Ethan's. Given the look of adoration on his face as she opened the door for him—even though her hair was tucked into a messy bun and her face was covered with a layer of green goo—I'd say things were working out just fine between them.

"Avocado mask," she explained, before I could ask exactly what the green goo was. "It's *great* for the skin."

"You were making guacamole and you had extra, didn't you?"

"My girlfriend, the salad," Luc said. "Yummy."

"Keep it to yourselves," Ethan good-naturedly said, putting a hand at my back and steering me gently down the hallway. "And you don't give me that look," he said with a chuckle. "They're your friends."

"They're your guards."

"I didn't hire them for their senses of humor. That's why you're better positioned as Sentinel. Guards are expected to be obedient."

That was quite an opening. "And Sentinels aren't?" I asked with a smile. "Because if you're willing to concede that I don't fall beneath the umbrella of your authority, I can work with that."

He tucked his hand into mine. "Don't push your luck."

This hadn't been the most pleasant of evenings; thank God for the little things that reminded us we were home.

I used my key, now sharing the ring with keys to my Volvo and my grandfather's house, to unlock the door. Ethan obviously had a key of his own, but he allowed me the ceremony.

His posture changed the moment he walked into his apartment. His shoulders relaxed, as if he'd dropped the mantle of power and authority that usually weighed him down.

His apartment consisted of three rooms—a sitting room, a bedroom, and a bathroom. Like the rest of the House, all three were decorated with a kind of European-chic flair: tall ceilings, crown molding, and expensive paintings.

The sitting room was bathed in the warm glow of lamps and candles that had already been prepared for our arrival. Circles of light contrasted with the deep shadows that covered the corners of the room. The furniture was oversized and built of dark wood. I could easily imagine Marie Antoinette returning to a similar room at the end of a night of French carousing.

A portion of the sitting room had been dedicated to mementos of Ethan's centuries as a vampire. A table held runes and weapons, and a tall glass case held an egg made of gold, enamel, and precious stones. The egg was wrapped in a ruby-eyed dragon, and it was displayed under glass and a beam of light that made its gems sparkle magically.

The egg had been a gift to Peter Cadogan, the House's eponymous Master, from a member of the Russian aristocracy, who also happened to be a fairy. I wasn't sure of the reason for the gift, other than a vague "favor" done by Peter, but the egg's beauty was undeniable.

Since I lived in the apartment, too, Margot had left a snack with the drink that was waiting for Ethan on a tray on a side table. I got a chocolate truffle; he got a bottle of seltzer water. Finding a bedtime snack at the end of the night did not suck.

Still, the most remarkable things about our evenings weren't those little luxuries. It was the simple fact that we were here together. I'd challenged Ethan after I'd learned he made me a vampire; our relationship had a tense, stop-and-start history, and his brief period of mortality hadn't helped. I was still in awe that we'd come together in a relationship that seemed to be working. He was stubborn and political and an utter control freak, and there were certainly times when his bossiness chafed. But he loved his vampires, and he undoubtedly loved me, and I tried to be thankful for all the little moments we had together, even those as simple as our bedtime rituals—of the teeth-brushing, pajama-donning, prepping-for-the-day-ahead variety.

He disappeared into his closet, which was as large as my former dorm-sized bedroom and furnished as well as the rest of the apartment.

I kicked off my boots and threw my jacket on the bed—it was also nice to have someone who cleaned up after me every night—and flopped down onto my back. The linens were lush and fluffy, and I sank into the middle of the bed and closed my eyes.

"So, your first outing as social chair wasn't entirely successful," Ethan called out.

"I can't keep an eye on every Rogue vampire."

"True. You can barely keep an eye on yourself."

I rolled my eyes, but got up and walked toward the closet, which I could have counted as another room. The floor was covered in thick carpet, and the walls were shelved in cherrywood. Clothes were divided into sections—jackets, pants, shoes, ties, and coats, and long, flat drawers for folded items. Ethan had graciously offered room in each of those sections to me, although my simple wardrobe didn't take up much space.

The middle of the closet held a storage unit that looked like an expensive piece of European furniture, and a leather bench for changing clothes or putting on shoes. Mirrors filled empty bays, and track lighting illuminated the whole room like a perfectly prepped *Vogue* set.

Ethan wore a suit nearly every night, and the closet was filled with well-fitting black jackets and pants. But even the value of the fabric and tailoring was second to the artifact that hung in an alcove on the opposite end of the closet: In an ornate gilded frame was a moody painting by Van Gogh. It was a landscape at dusk, a golden field of wheat topped by a dark indigo sky, Van Gogh's telltale swirls of clouds hovering above it.

I leaned against the doorway and crossed my arms as I admired it. It was a simple painting, and a small one, only a few inches across. But there was depth in the scene that appealed to me... not unlike the vampire disrobing a few feet away from it.

Ethan wore only boxer briefs, his long and lean body exposed to my salacious glance. It was easy to appreciate him in a purely aesthetic way—his body was like a perfectly honed sculpture: curves and flat planes of muscle, golden skin that should have given way to vampiric paleness some time ago. And on the back of one calf, a mysterious tattoo he wouldn't explain, even to me.

Thank God he had no idea how much control was required of me just to be near him. Although given the knowing glance he offered when our eyes met, maybe he did.

I closed my eyes to reset the visual. As intriguing as he was, we had more pressing issues.

"Oliver and Eve," I said. "What do you think?"

"There are too many possibilities for us to even theorize at this point. This could be a simple miscommunication. Or perhaps Oliver and Eve were reacting to a slight and chose not to contact Noah and the others for a time."

"Maybe Oliver and Eve fought with others about the fact that they decided to register. That couldn't have thrilled everyone."

"And Eve's phone in the alley?" Ethan asked.

"Maybe she threw it in anger? Like an 'I'm furious they're furious at me for no reason'"—I mimicked hurling something at him—"kind of reaction."

Ethan flipped off the closet light and walked toward me, an eyebrow arched. "I certainly hope that's not your best pitch. Because it was pathetic."

I smiled at his attempt at humor, at ending our night on something other than a note of fear and despair. The sun was rising and there was nothing we could do for Oliver and Eve while it was up. But we could be ourselves, and for those few moments of peace and solitude in the home we'd made together, we could find joy.

"You wouldn't know a good pitch from a hole in the ground. And my athletic prowess is unsurpassed," I asserted.

Ethan stopped, that eyebrow still irritatingly cocked, and put a hand against the doorjamb, leaning over me.

"Your athletic prowess?"

"Just so," I said, using one of his favorite phrases. "I have all the right moves."

With a look hot enough to melt me into a puddle of girl, he caught my hand, then whipped my body against his.

"Okay, you have all the right moves," I said, my lids dropping as the sun began to rise . . . and as he moved his hands to the small of my back and pressed me tighter into his body.

"You gave in so quickly, Sentinel," he murmured. He maneuvered me backward toward the bed, which left little doubt about the reason for those moves. He was a predator in full alpha mode . . . and he was ready for action.

With his hands at my hips, his mouth found mine. His kiss was intense, nearly brutal in its force. It was a show of arousal and an expression of something. His feelings for me, certainly. His frustrations at the world, possibly.

The back of my legs hit the edge of the bed. Unbalanced, I tottered, but he kept me upright. "I have the advantage."

"I'm not fighting back."

"In that case," he said, slipping an arm behind my knees and tossing me onto the bed, "there's no reason to play coy."

Ethan covered my body with his. My heartbeat quickened, as did the pulse of blood through my veins. It was as if my heart knew his scent, his body, and his magic, and anticipated his bite. As if our vampiric natures had connected on a biological level separate from our hearts and minds, like our predatory souls had found kindred spirits.

I leaned up into the kiss, taking full advantage of the things he offered—things that I'd missed and only truly come to appreciate while he'd been gone, taken by a stake through the heart.

Dawn drew closer, bringing with it the hazy exhaustion that struck all vampires. We fought back sleep with the press of skin and the rhythm of our bodies, and as the sun breached the horizon with a crown of orange and gold, we pushed each other under, and slept together until the sun fell again.

CHAPTER FOUR

+━━◄◆►━━+

VISITING HOURS

I woke in Ethan's arms, my consciousness triggered by the *whirring* retraction of the automatic shutters that covered his windows.

"Good evening," he said, pressing a kiss to my bare shoulder.

I humphed and pressed my face back into the pillows. The room was chilly, and I was entangled with a handsome and powerful man. I really had no incentive to get out of bed ... except for my solemn duty to the House and my friendship with Noah. Vampires were missing, and I had work to do. First item on the list? Calling Catcher for an update.

Begrudgingly, I sat up and pulled my hair out of my face, twisting it loosely behind my head. It wouldn't stay there for long, but at least I could make it out of bed without blinding myself in the nest of it.

Ethan sat up beside me, his back against the headboard as he scanned his phone for news and updates.

"Anything new?" I asked.

"The fairies have confirmed Catcher retrieved the packages

we left with them. And more updates from the transition team," he said. "I've invited them to the House, you know. I thought it would be advantageous to have them here in person. And, frankly, they provide a bit of insulation against any shenanigans Darius attempts to pull."

I nodded. "The dailies said people would be visiting, but there weren't many details yet. I don't think the travel arrangements had been finalized." "Dailies" were the reports of House happenings Luc prepared for the Cadogan guards. Vampiric travel arrangements were often complicated by our sunlight restrictions.

"Who got the official transition team invites?" I asked.

"Paige, who has maneuvered her way into the librarian's heart."

"As I predicted." Cadogan House had a gorgeous library and a knowledgeable, if crabby, librarian. Paige was a redheaded sorceress who'd gotten mixed up in Mallory's midwestern rampage, and she'd spent time at Cadogan House after Dominic Tate torched her house to punish her. She'd recently found a place of her own—a third-floor walkup also in Hyde Park—but she'd remained a frequent visitor to the House . . . and the librarian. Both lovers of books and knowledge, they'd made a quick love connection.

"Mm-hmm," Ethan noncommittally mumbled. "They're perusing the library for precedents regarding the Decertification."

"Precedents?" I wondered.

"It might not surprise you to learn the members of the GP are sticklers for rules." His voice was dry as toast; the fact was completely unsurprising.

"And there are lots of rules," he said. "The Decertification of Houses doesn't happen often—only twice since the GP was formally established. The problem is, when the GP disbands a House, it doesn't usually wave a polite good-bye and go on about its business. So they're checking the other Decerts to determine if the GP pulled any shenanigans they might try to repeat here. Our financial adviser's also on the team, and a security auditor, Michael Donovan. We've asked him to provide an unbiased perspective on our security protocols. Luc and I have been communicating with him for the last couple of weeks, but it seemed appropriate to bring him in for the final battle, as it were."

Luc hadn't mentioned Michael Donovan to me, which made me wonder whether he was irritated that Ethan had hired an auditor to look over his shoulder. But Ethan was the boss. Unofficially, anyway. "Sounds like a good plan."

But Ethan went suddenly—and unusually—quiet.

I cocked an eyebrow at him. "What?"

"Lacey will be one of the visitors."

Lacey Sheridan was the Master of San Diego's Sheridan House. She was tall and blond, with enviably long legs and a history with Ethan. She'd visited once since I'd been a member of the House, and she made it quite clear to me then that she wanted to rekindle their relationship. Ethan might have moved on, much to her chagrin, but she wasn't ready to give up on him.

Part of that bond, undoubtedly, had been formed when Ethan made Lacey a vampire and helped train her to lead her own House. She was the only one of Ethan's vampiric "children" to have her own House. With only twelve Houses in the United States, that made her a very valuable ally.

On the other hand, he also knew that Lacey had been a thorn in our side before, which made me wonder about his real motivations. How was she so vital?

"She and Darius have a unique friendship," Ethan said, as if guessing my concern.

"Romantic?" I wondered.

"No. More an affinity. A kinship. They are two of a kind."

Darius was fastidious and proper, and the Cadogan vampires called Lacey the Ice Queen. She was as carefully styled and modulated as Ethan—without the endearing personality. A friendship between her and Darius actually made a warped kind of sense.

"Darius is a member of the old guard," he said. "We challenge the authority of the GP and, by virtue, his authority. By becoming Rogues, we become that which they despise: outcasts and traitors. I'm hoping that Lacey's presence—an ally of his own, in a sense—will mitigate his more dictatorial sensibilities."

Ethan ran his hands through his hair, then crossed them behind his head and leaned back against the headboard again. He looked concerned, and was obviously unaware of how the move tightened the muscles in his torso and made him look even more like a distracted cologne model from a *GQ* spread.

I couldn't fault his logic. It was entirely reasonable that he'd ask Lacey to visit. I wasn't crazy about the idea—mostly because I wasn't crazy about her—but I was also a grown-up.

"Okay," I said.

He looked at me with suspicion in his eyes. "Okay?"

"Okay," I repeated with a smile. "I appreciate your honesty. I don't trust her any farther than I can throw her, but I'll deal."

"Why don't you trust her?" I saw the pain in his eyes; he was afraid I thought he'd be unfaithful. But it wasn't him I worried about.

"She's still in love with you."

"She is not in love with me," he countered, but there was a hint of pink in his cheeks.

"I assure you she is, and she's all but willing to take me out to get to you."

He looked mildly amused . . . and flattered in an ego-driven, masculine kind of way. "And you know this because?"

"She stares at you, she hangs on every word . . . and she told me."

He looked surprised. "She told you?"

"She told me." Maybe not in so many words, but she'd gotten the point across.

"Merit, Lacey has lived in Sheridan House for years. She is the only Master in a city with hundreds of vampires, and—I say this without personal interest—she's a perfectly attractive woman. I assure you—if she wanted a suitor, she could find one."

Not when she's holding out for you, I silently thought, but kept that to myself. If he was truly that naive about her feelings, I figured that benefited me. It would be harder for her to woo him away if he had no romantic thoughts of her.

"Okay, then."

Ethan looked at me. He watched me, really checking my mood and whether that "okay" meant okay in the male sense ("okay") or the female sense ("possibly okay; it depends on what you say next").

"You mean that," he said.

"I do. I trust you. I'm not entirely sure I trust her, but I trust you." I put my hand on his. "And more important, I know you're worried about the House—and about Darius and the GP. Do what you need to do. I'll live."

Without warning, he pounced, wrapping my body in his, his warmth penetrating through to my core. As a vampire, I was often cold; Ethan Sullivan was by far the best blanket a girl could ask for.

"What time do they arrive?" I murmured.

"Hours yet." He nipped at my neck and pulled me closer, a suggestion of exactly how we might spend those hours.

Unfortunately, that wasn't in the cards for me tonight. "You've got work to do, and I need to get moving. We've got missing vampires and an Ombudsman who's probably already left half a dozen messages on my phone."

"That should fill out your schedule for the night," he said.

Still beneath him, I stretched out and snagged my cell phone from my nightstand. No calls or messages, which was unusual, but we were only a few minutes past dusk. Perhaps Catcher hadn't seen the point in sending a message I wouldn't have been able to read for hours anyway. "Barring a zombie attack, yes."

"More likely a human attack than a zombie attack," Ethan said.

"Potato, *potato*. Either way, the attacks would be mindless, and they'd be out for blood. Hey," I said, poking his chest. "What do zombies chant at a riot?"

"*Grrarphsnarg?*" he asked, in a surprisingly well-done bit of mindless zombie imitating.

"No, but that was really good. Disconcertingly good."

"I was deceased for a time."

"True. But anyway, the rioters get all riled up, and they chant: 'What do we want? Brains! When do we want them? Brains!'" I fell into a wave of appropriately boisterous laughter; Ethan seemed less impressed.

"I truly hope the stipend we pay you doesn't get spent on the development of jokes like that."

"It gets spent on smoked meats to supplement this House's paltry smoked-meats selection."

"There's probably a twelve-step program for meat addiction, and I imagine the program starts by admitting you have a problem."

"Loving smoked meats isn't a problem. It's a birthright. Especially for the fanged. All right," I said, slapping Ethan on the butt. "Off. I need to get dressed, as do you."

But he didn't shift the weight of his body; instead, he cupped my face in his hand. "Be careful out there."

"Yes, Liege," I dutifully said.

Ethan turned to his side, and I climbed off the bed and headed toward the shower. But I paused in the doorway just long enough to wink. "And do try to keep your hands to yourself."

His smile widened. "Michael Donovan is an attractive man, Sentinel. But I'll do my best."

Ethan Sullivan, registered smart-ass.

I quickly cleaned, loofa-ed, and shampooed, spending less time in Ethan's roaring shower than I would have liked. When I was just clean enough, I toweled through my hair, pulled it into a high ponytail—my signature move—and brushed out my bangs.

Ethan dipped into the shower as I walked back into the bedroom to dress. My clothes were easy to assemble—leather pants, shirt, leather jacket, and boots. An ensemble that would protect me against the chill in the air and serve me well in a fight . . . in case that became necessary.

I already wore the gold medal around my neck that identified my name and position and marked me as a member of Cadogan House. I tucked a sleek dagger—a gift from Ethan that bore a coin in the hilt similar to my House medal—into my boot, and grabbed my scabbarded katana from the table near the door. I hadn't pulled it last night, but I was planning on visiting the Ombuddies tonight, including Catcher. He'd given me the katana and trained me in how to use it, and there was no way I'd carry it near him without ensuring it was clean.

With a *whip* of sound, I unsheathed it, the light pouring down its honed steel. It looked pristine, but out of caution I pulled a sheet of rice paper from a drawer in the table—the sword-cleaning drawer, as I'd named it—and wiped down the blade. Better safe than sorry, especially when a gruff sorcerer might demand an inspection. It wouldn't be the first time.

"You're going to see Catcher, I presume?"

I looked up. Ethan stood in the doorway in unbuttoned slacks, scrubbing a towel through his hair.

It was not an unpleasant sight.

"Yes," I said, forcing myself to meet his eyes. "I'm going to call him as soon as I grab some blood and breakfast."

"And Jeff?"

There was a funny little twinge in Ethan's voice. Surely not jealousy, as he'd sworn he was so sure of our relationship that he wasn't capable of it. Jeff did, admittedly, have a pretty obvious crush on me. But since he was in some kind of on-again/off-again relationship with a shifter named Fallon—the only sister of the head of the North American Central Pack—I didn't think Ethan had much to worry about. Even if I weren't in love with him, and even if I did have a thing for Jeff, I was not about to cross a shifter, much less one in line for the Pack throne. I hoped to squeeze at least a few years out of my immortality, thank you very much.

"Yes, and Jeff. I enjoy seeing him, and he enjoys seeing Fallon," I reminded Ethan.

"Fair enough. Keep your wits about you, Sentinel."

"I will. And I'll be back in time to say hello to our guests." I might have wanted to refuse Lacey's entrance into the House, but Ethan wanted her here, so I could take one for the team.

"I wouldn't have it any other way," he said with a wink.

But before I could make my brilliant exit, there was a knock at the door.

"Likely Helen," Ethan said, "with information about ceremony planning."

He was partially right. Helen, who was basically the House's den mother, stood in the hallway when I opened the door, but she didn't look pleased about it. She stepped inside, her gaze searching for Ethan, with a cloud of floral perfume and nervous magic about her.

Ethan stepped into the room, hair still damp, but now dressed. "What is it?" he asked, concern in his expression. He must have picked up the same magical notes.

"They're here. Early."

Ethan's expression went stone cold. "They" could only have been the GP, and their arrival a day early couldn't have signaled anything good.

"Sentinel," he said, grabbing his suit coat and heading for the door.

I pushed my sword into its scabbard and tied the belt around my waist. "Right behind you," I said, and followed him down to the House's first floor.

In addition to Malik and Luc, seven men and women stood in the foyer in an inverted V, with Darius West, head of the Greenwich Presidium, directly in the middle. These were the members of the GP, some of the most powerful vampires in the world.

Darius—tall, with a shaved head and an aristocratic manner—had the personality of an egotistical hall monitor.

The other GP members, four men and two women, didn't look familiar. I knew their names, and that they'd wreaked havoc in our House from an ocean away. But I could identify only one of them—Harold Monmouth, a class act who'd once helped Celina Desaulniers, the former Master of Navarre House, dispatch a woman who'd stood in her way. Celina had tried to kill me on several occasions, and when she threw the stake that killed Ethan, I returned the favor. Morgan Greer, whom I'd dated for approximately five minutes, took over as Master of the House after her bad behavior.

There was a gap in the V between the last two individuals on the left-hand side. That was the spot, I guessed, that had once been held by Celina. But she was gone, and that was no doubt another reason why the GP didn't care much for me.

Ethan smiled thinly at Darius. "You're early."

"But not unwelcome, I presume," Darius said. Ironically, the statement was incredibly presumptuous.

Before Ethan could get himself into any more trouble, Helen stepped beside us.

"I've spoken with the manager at the Dandridge," she said. "Your rooms have been prepared and are ready at your convenience."

The Dandridge Hotel was one of the most exclusive luxury hotels in Chicago, small but chic, and apparently the only place good enough for the GP to stay this time around.

Darius nodded. "We'll settle in and be in touch about the ceremony."

"As you say," Ethan said.

Like a flock of birds, the vampires turned in unison, then filed back through the gate to waiting limousines.

For a moment we all stood there.

Ethan muttered a curse, but when he turned back to us, he slipped his hands into his pockets, his body tight with the swagger and confidence of a Master vampire. He might not have been official Master of Cadogan House, but he was a Master vampire all the same.

It was comforting to see him confident, even if he was bluffing.

"They will think of us what they think of us," he said. "That doesn't matter. What matters is what we are together, and that is stronger than we could ever be as GP automatons and subjects of a would-be king."

He looked at Malik. "Assemble the House tonight. We'll wait until an hour before dawn."

"To assure Darius is tucked in at the Dandridge and can't spy on us?" Luc asked.

"Precisely," Ethan said. "I'll speak to the Decert at the ceremony, so whatever the night brings, plan to be back at the House by then." He nodded at Luc. "Call Paige and the librarian. He's up to something, and I want to know what it is. *Now*."

"Liege," Luc acknowledged.

"Go on about your business," Ethan said. "I'll see you all soon enough."

I wouldn't be a vampire if Ethan hadn't changed me, and I wouldn't survive without regular doses of blood. Even though the process had become a fairly routine endeavor, I still needed it. So I dropped by the House cafeteria and plumbed for snacks. A bag of blood from our retail supplier, Blood4You, was a necessity, as was a mini chocolate candy bar that I stashed in my jacket pocket for later. For now, I grabbed a bagel with a smear of peanut butter and took a bite as I nuked the blood and poured it into a travel mug, just another Chicagoan on her way to the office.

There was something about the first bite of food in the morning—maybe the relative absence during sleep, maybe the reawakening of the taste buds—that made my simple breakfast seem nearly majestic.

I am only barely exaggerating. The depth of my relationship with food is no doubt thrilling to some and strange to others. It probably has something to do with the fact that I grew up feeling removed from the rest of my very wealthy, very fancy family. I'd entertain myself with my other great love—books—during a hot Chicago afternoon, usually with something to nibble on. I was especially fond of foods that could be dipped—tortilla chips, celery sticks, apple wedges, chocolate drops. Eating them was an activity in itself, a repetitive movement that was almost Zen-like.

Fortunately, I was athletic enough then that my weight stayed manageable. I'd danced ballet for many years, and had the toes to prove it. Also fortunately, my speedy vampiric metabolism now meant I could eat all night with no ill repercussions. Not that I had time for that kind of grazing. Not when vampires were possibly being abducted and our House was facing an uncertain future. And not when Lacey Sheridan was on her way.

Yes, I believed in me and Ethan, but I was still a girl. The last thing I needed was for her to find me wrist-deep in a bucket of Frank's Finest fried chicken.

Although that did sound delicious. I made a mental note to grab a celebratory Cluckin' Bucket after we found Oliver and Eve safe and sound. I really hoped we'd do that.

When I emerged into the main hallway with breakfast in hand, the House's tension was palpable. We were forty-eight hours away from the severing of our GP ties, and they'd already made an appearance. The hum of nervous magic was becoming a torrent of full-on worry. I could feel it in the prickly air, the haze of anticipation that flowed through the House. The vampires of Cadogan House might trust both their Masters—Ethan and Malik—but they were entering unknown political territory.

I held the bagel with my teeth and fished the keys to my ancient Volvo from my pocket. Unlike last night, it was bone-chilling cold outside, the kind of cold only a hot bath or a roaring fire could cure.

Tonight the lawn was bereft of fragrant food trucks and revelry, but the nearly identical mercenary fairies still stood watch in front of the House. When I walked through the gate, their expressions were typically stoic, but they both nodded in acknowledgment. That was a recent development—and a hard-won victory. Fairies bore no strong love of vampires, but we'd had interactions recently with Claudia, the fairy queen, that seemed to have bridged the gap between us.

Windshield wipers flapping against the glass, I drove south to my grandfather's modest house. Traffic wasn't bad, but the drive still took a few minutes. I used the opportunity to check in with Jonah.

It took four rings for him to answer the phone, but his handsome, auburn-haired visage eventually popped up on the screen.

"Busy?" I wondered.

"Unfortunately, yes. Your House drama has spread. We've got already aggressive vampires mouthing off about the GP and talking about seceding."

"Already aggressive?" I asked.

"Jocks," Jonah said with a smile. "They spent their human lives lifting weights and destroying linemen. The adrenaline doesn't fade."

"Why do they want to secede?"

"They want to drink."

Vampires or not, that was actually surprising. Most American Houses had sworn off drinking from humans or vampires. Their only source of blood was Blood4You, and they drank only from the bag or cup. Banning drinking from another person was supposed to help vampires assimilate; it kept their less endearing behaviors hidden from human view. Cadogan was one of the few Houses that still allowed drinking, and we took crap around the country—and from the GP—for doing it.

I was still a relative novice when it came to drinking, but I was experienced enough to know that nothing made me feel more like a vampire—and less human—than drinking from Ethan, or letting him drink from me.

"You should join us," I said. "It's hard to be the only target in this game of GP dodgeball."

"You couldn't pay me to be in your position."

"We manage," I dryly said.

"For now. But you should know we're hearing things about the GP and the Decert that aren't exactly promising."

"Such as?"

"Such as the GP wants to cause you as much trouble as possible."

That revelation made my stomach flip uncomfortably, even if it wasn't entirely surprising. Ethan and the others had centuries of experience with the GP, and had previously trusted that it operated with the Houses' best interest in mind.

I'd been a vampire for just a few months, but I knew it operated with only one thing in mind—its own interest. It seemed to me keeping power in the GP's hands was its number one priority.

"Unfortunately, that squares with the fact that they're here a day early."

Jonah whistled. "That's not promising."

"I know."

"I hate to say Cadogan House is screwed. . . ."

"Then don't say it. It would be considerably more helpful if you could give me any details about what you think they're going to pull so I can adequately prepare my House."

"Reason and logic will only get you so far. All I know is, the GP's contract with Cadogan House is key."

I wasn't sure which contract he meant, but I'd figure it out. "Your information comes from other RG members?"

"From our communications network," he said, "which I can't loop you into until you're official. Which you will be tomorrow night."

The night of the GP ceremony. The timing for the RG ceremony could hardly be worse, although I appreciated the irony. I would be joining the RG—and thereby promising to watch over the GP—even as we left the GP because of its tyranny.

"Where and when?" I asked.

"I'll let you know. I've got to make sure I can get out of here, too. I'll try to message you later tonight."

"Okay. FYI, I'm heading to my grandfather's. We picked up glass and Eve's cell phone last night at the reg center they visited, and I asked them to take a look."

"Does your grandfather have that kind of facility?"

"Not unless he's remodeled the rumpus room," I said. "But he's got friends in high places, and it's the only lead we've got so far."

"Good thinking. I hope the investigation gets some momentum."

"You and me both. The night is young. I'm hoping against hope Oliver and Eve will call Noah and tell him they had to make an emergency trip to KC or something."

"It would be a happier ending," Jonah agreed. "Good luck with it."

"Thanks. I'll let you know if there are any developments."

"Do that. And in the meantime, I'll do my part to keep Grey House on Darius's good side."

I made a sarcastic sound. "Since the well-being of your House is clearly at the top of my list, that comforts me."

"That's my girl," he said, and ended the call.

I wasn't, but he hung up before I could argue. Probably better for both of us.

My grandfather's house was small and quaint—white clapboards, metal storm door, stubby concrete porch. As I drove up, the lights were on and half a dozen cars were parked in the driveway and on the street. Most of them were tiny roadsters, which meant only one thing.

River nymphs.

I guessed Catcher hadn't managed to resolve the shoe crisis.

When I reached the front door, I could hear music and the squealing of voices. I didn't bother knocking, but walked inside.

I could not have been more surprised.

The front door opened directly into my grandfather's living room, and it was full of people, among them my grandfather and half a dozen nymphs in their typically short, cleavage-baring dresses.

They knelt in a semicircle around what looked like a new television, and squealed while Jeff Christopher stood in the middle with a video game controller in his hand.

But that wasn't even the strangest part.

Jeff Christopher, geek extraordinaire, was in *costume*.

He wore a pale green tunic, over which he'd slung a forest green cape trimmed in brown, and knee-high leather boots. The tunic's hood was up, just perched at the crown of Jeff's head, but his shoulder-length brown hair shone at the edge of it.

Jeff was tall and lanky, and the costume fit him surprisingly well. But for his lack of longbow and horse, he might have stepped out of a medieval forest.

By the look of the screen, his costume was modeled after a character in the game, who was currently flailing at green, goblin-like creatures with a golden sword. The excitement in the room built as Jeff's character, a ranger of some kind, pummeled the creatures with his steel, until—with a final killing blow—he finished off the last goblin.

The room erupted into a flurry of hoots and applause. The nymphs jumped to their feet and surrounded their victor in a cloud of wavy hair, rayon, and fruity perfume.

I pressed my back against the door to avoid the crush. I'd been snagged by River nymphs before, and I wasn't much interested in another round.

"Merit!" my grandfather exclaimed, finally realizing I'd stepped into the room. In his typical button-down plaid and grandfatherly slacks, he walked over and enveloped me in a hug.

"What's all this?" I asked.

"Diplomacy in action," he quietly said. "The nymphs were giving Catcher fits, and Jeff thought they might be calmed by a show of virtual strength."

It wasn't the type of show that would have occurred to me, but it was clearly working for the ladies. After a moment, Jeff pulled himself away from the cluster of girls; his expression turned serious when he saw me.

He clapped his hands together. "Ladies, thank you so much for squeezing me into your schedule. I need to get some work done, but do you think you could find me some cheat codes for the next level? That would be awesome."

To a one, they squealed and clapped their hands together at the assignment, then jiggled out the front door until the screen slammed shut behind them.

The sudden silence was deafening, at least until the game console reminded us Roland of Westmere was ready for his next quest.

"The nymphs like video games?" I wondered. "They don't really seem the gaming type."

"Not the games themselves," Jeff said, pulling back his hood, his hair damp beneath. Digital adventure or not, he'd definitely gotten a workout. "They like watching shifters win games. They think it's manly."

I frowned in sympathy, then moved closer to wipe a crimson stain from his cheek. "Well, Mr. Manly Man, you have a drugstore's worth of lipstick on your face."

Jeff sighed and scrubbed the mark. "That's not gonna work. I'm supposed to meet Fallon later."

"I don't think she'd be thrilled about their interest in you. Or the evidence."

"She'd go ballistic," he said. "She's got history there, I guess, with cheating."

"Ah," I said. I didn't know enough about her to say more than that.

"The good news is, we've discovered they're easily distracted. Catcher couldn't calm them down, so they went nuclear about a minor issue—*again*—and drove over here. We discovered a few minutes of gaming calms them down and gets them talking rationally again."

"They have to band together to solve problems," my grandfather said. "And this is much less messy than paintball."

"Whatever works," I said with a smile, then gestured at Jeff's getup. "And what's this you're wearing?"

"The ensemble of Roland of Westmere. He's a character from 'Jakob's Quest'—that's the game I was playing."

"I can't imagine being so involved in a video game that I'd want to wear a costume. I mean, what's the appeal?"

"What *isn't* the appeal? I get to have someone else's drama for a little while instead of my own."

Okay, that I could understand. My Sentinel leathers were a kind of costume for me—an ensemble that let me feel a little more kick-ass and bluff a little more easily. Not that the role didn't come with its own drama.

"Fair enough," I told Jeff.

He gestured toward the back of the House. "I'm going to change real quick and then I'll come fill you in. Catcher's in the back if you want to talk to him."

"Do you need a drink, baby girl?" my grandfather asked.

"No, I'm good. But thank you. I'll go find Catcher."

I walked down the hallway to the former storage room my grandfather had turned into an office for his volunteer crew. Catcher sat at a homely-looking desk. No costume for him, fortunately. He wore a flat expression, jeans, and a T-shirt that pictured a velociraptor, teeth bared, riding a giant kitten and wearing his own T-shirt that read, KTHXBAI.

"FYI," I said, stepping into the room, "I think the Internet threw up on your T-shirt."

Catcher rolled his eyes. "Is it just me, or is there always vampire drama to attend to?"

"Unfortunately, there is, and I'm attending to it. Although I could say the same thing about sorceress drama. And speaking of, how's yours?"

I meant Mallory, of course, because I wanted—from at least one of them—an update about their relationship.

Uncharacteristically, Catcher blushed. I took that as a good sign.

"We're talking," he said.

"That sounds promising. Especially since you're living in her house."

Before the onset of her magical addiction, Mallory and Catcher shared her brownstone in Wicker Park. When Mallory decamped to live with the shifters, Catcher stayed put.

His blush deepened, and I gave myself five more points. Advantage: Merit.

"Our relationship is a movie of the week," he admitted.

Jeff, having quickly changed, walked into the room wearing a pale-blue button-down shirt with the sleeves rolled up, and khakis. The combo was his unofficial uniform. He sat down at his desk and began tapping on his keyboard, which was actually a conglomeration of keyboards he'd turned into one Frankensteinian monstrosity.

"I checked Eve's calls," he said. "She'd cleared out her call list within the last day or two, so there are only a couple of phone calls on it: to Rose, to the registration center."

"Crap," I said. "I was hoping for more of a lead there. She probably called the registration center to see if they were open."

"That's what I was thinking."

"What about biological material on the phone? Fingerprints, anything like that? Or the glass?"

"We've asked Detective Jacobs to take a look," Catcher said. Detective Jacobs was a solid cop and a friend of my grandfather's. Unlike some of the other CPD members, he didn't assume we were troublemakers just because we were vampires.

"Good," I said.

Jeff swiveled in his chair to face me, fingers intertwined over his abdomen. "It is good. The problem is, the CPD is already backlogged. Even pulling in a favor, it could be a few days before we find anything out."

I sat down and blew out a breath, deflated. I'd been hoping for something more from those two little bits of evidence. They were the only leads we had, and they were looking like pretty crappy leads.

"I'm out of ideas," I said.

"It's possible there's nothing to this," Catcher said. "Maybe they aren't missing. Maybe this is just about two vampires who decided to make their own decision, go their own way. They are Rogues, after all."

"Yeah, but even Rogues follow patterns. And from what Noah was saying, it was out of character for these two to completely up and disappear."

"Merit?"

We all looked up. My grandfather stood in the doorway. "There are some folks here I think you'll want to see."

His expression was neutral, and I found my hopes lifting. Was it Oliver and Eve? Had they dropped by to tell us they were fine, and this had all been a big misunderstanding?

I followed him into the hallway, Catcher and Jeff at my heels, and then back into the living room.

In front of the door, tucked into jackets against the cold, stood Noah, Rose, and a third vampire I didn't know. Rose's eyes were red and swollen. The new girl, who had tan skin and sleek, jet-black hair, had an arm around Rose.

Their expressions didn't bode well; nor did the melancholic magic that accompanied them into the house.

"We're sorry to barge in," Noah said.

"Not at all," my grandfather said. "Please come in. I can take your jackets, if you like."

"No, we're okay," Noah said, as they stepped inside.

My grandfather smiled gently and gestured toward the sofa. "Have a seat."

Noah nodded, and the trio moved silently to the couch.

"You know Rose," Noah said when they were seated. "This is Elena."

"Catcher and Jeff Christopher," I said, motioning to the pair, who stood behind me. "And my grandfather Chuck Merit. What's happened?" I asked Noah.

"We found them," Noah said.

As Rose broke into a sob, Noah pulled his cell phone from his pocket, pushed a button or two, and handed it to me.

+—◆—≡◆≡—◆—+

CHAPTER FIVE

VAMPIRES, INTERRUPTED

I'd braced myself for the worst, and that was hardly preparation enough. The picture was grainy and the colors were mottled, but there was no denying the subject matter.

Oliver and Eve were dead.

There were few guaranteed ways to kill a vampire—aspen stake, sunlight, total dismemberment, decapitation. The latter two options were why vampires carried swords into battle. Our blades were a sure weapon to fell an immortal foe.

Whoever had done this deed, whatever dark-hearted monster, had chosen decapitation.

They lay side by side on a wood floor in a pool of blood. They were holding hands, their fingers intertwined in a final act of love—a denial of death. Their arms were covered in tattoos that seemed to flow together, as if they'd been inked arm over arm by the same artist.

They both had blond hair, but it was matted with blood. Their throats had been cut completely, their heads severed but resting only centimeters away from their bodies, a mockery of their immortality. They might have survived other wounds that would kill most humans; vampires healed quickly, and gashes might have eventually closed. But decapitation was, quite clearly, a mortal wound. A cruel cut.

There were no other signs of trauma. They might have been sleeping . . . other than the obvious insult.

I'd seen death before, and I'd taken life myself—always in the heat of battle, and always to protect someone or something that I'd loved. That was different. Unless Noah had information about Oliver and Eve we just didn't understand, this was cold-blooded, and shocking in its brutality.

My stomach swooned. My skin felt clammy, and a cold trickle of sweat slipped down my back. My head spun. I was swamped by the sudden memories of the loss I'd suffered a few months ago, before Ethan had been brought back to me. . . .

Shakily, I handed the phone to my grandfather, then looked at Noah, Rose, and Elena. "I'm so sorry for your loss."

Noah nodded. "We aren't troublemakers. I don't know who could have done this."

"A monster," my grandfather said frankly, handing the phone to Catcher and Jeff, then looking at Noah, Rose, and Elena in turn. "I'm sorry for your loss, as well. I know that's little consolation, but I'm sorry for it."

I wondered how many times he'd spoken those words in his decades-long career as a cop.

"You took the picture?" Catcher asked.

Noah nodded again. "A friend of ours is a professional photographer. He loves to take shots of urban decay: building husks, graffiti, rusting steel, things like that. There's an old document warehouse not far from his studio. It was built in the nineteen forties, and he didn't think it would last much longer. He wanted to take a look before it was torn down or fell down, so he was walking through it with a colleague."

Noah cleared his throat, as if the explanation was getting more difficult. "They were walking around one of the upper floors, and they smelled blood, but they couldn't figure out where it was coming from. No visible source anywhere. James—that's the vampire—eventually found a latch. There was a secret room, a vault of some kind at the back of the room. They opened the door . . . and found Oliver and Eve."

Rose sobbed. My grandfather offered a box of tissues housed in a cozy knitted by my grandmother. Elena pulled a few out and handed them to Rose, who pressed them to her face but only cried harder.

"We took a look—just to confirm it was them—then came here. I left others to retrieve their remains. In case there's other evidence there, we wanted someone to know."

I looked at my grandfather, silently seeking his advice. A murder would fall under the purview of the CPD, but it wasn't as if the city's sentiment toward vampires was friendly right now. We were, after all, animals that required licensing.

"I can make a discreet phone call to the CPD," my grandfather said. "In the meantime," he told Catcher, "you might take a look at the scene for any other evidence." He glanced at Noah. "If that's all right with you?"

Noah nodded.

"Merit and I will go," Catcher said.

Noah was a big and buff man, but I caught a glint of relief in his eyes. He didn't want to return to the crime scene, and I didn't blame him. "Yeah," he said. "That's probably best."

"I hate to ask this," Catcher said, "but is there any chance James or his friend is involved?"

Noah shook his head. "I know you have to ask, and no. I've thought about it, and I truly believe he had nothing to do with it. Oliver and Eve were good kids. Ditto James. He prefers cameras to weapons, and he volunteers at a halfway house for guys with addiction problems. The service-oriented type."

Catcher nodded. "Then we'll start with the building. Jeff, while we're gone, check the property records for anything interesting. The owner, the history, anything that might tell us why the building was picked."

"Will do," Jeff said. He stood and waved gallantly down the hallway. "If any of you would like to join me in my office, you're welcome to. You could lend your expertise."

Noah rose and followed Jeff down the hall, leaving Elena and Rose on the couch, curled together in their grief.

My grandfather looked around the room. "Why don't I make some coffee, or perhaps tea?" He smiled gently at Rose and Elena. "Would either of you young ladies like that?"

"Tea would be great," Elena said gratefully, and my grandfather nodded and disappeared into the kitchen.

"We'll be back," I assured Elena. "Noah knows how to reach us if necessary."

"Find something," she said, and I truly hoped we would.

Catcher volunteered to drive to the address Noah had given us, which was also in Little Italy. Unfortunately, it made a grim kind of sense that the killer would do the killing not far from the registration center where Oliver and Eve were taken.

On the way, I took a moment to update the House. I called Ethan, but didn't get an answer, and opted not to leave a grim voice mail. This was news I'd deliver in person.

"Two dead vampires," Catcher said when I tucked the phone away again. "And by all accounts, decent, innocent vampires."

Two vampires who'd lain down together, hands intertwined, and wouldn't awaken again. I wasn't sure why I kept coming back to that detail. Perhaps it was the former grad student in me. I'd studied medieval literature, and there was something about the image that evoked Romeo and Juliet.

Had that been the killer's purpose? Not just to kill vampires— or to kill these two vampires—but to paint an image of sweet and sad and bitter death?

There was something terrifyingly foreign about the idea. I understood killing in the heat of battle. I could understand killing for anger or revenge; the motivation was clear. But killing for poignancy? Killing to shock or offend? That was something much stranger, and I couldn't quite wrap my mind around it.

"The killer was setting a scene," I said. "Arranging them just so. They couldn't have held hands through . . . what happened to them."

"And he knew how to take out a vampire. He knew decapitation would do it, or he got really lucky on the first try."

I nodded. "Staking would have been easier. Aspen is so fast—a second and they'd have been gone. But if they'd been staked, ash would be the only thing left."

"Sunlight also would have been faster," Catcher said. "If he'd wanted them really, truly gone, there are lots of ways to hide that evidence, and we'd never have found them. So that's the first question—what's he trying to tell us? And second, why these vampires in particular? Why Oliver and Eve? Did he mean to kill them . . . ?"

"Or did he just mean to kill?" I wondered.

Not exactly the most comforting thought.

The rain fell in a whispery mist, adding another layer of bleakness to the evening. We parked the car on an empty side street and stared up at our destination—a white brick warehouse with WILKINS painted across the side in peeling blue paint. The windows were mostly boarded now, and the site was wrapped in torn plastic fencing to keep out visitors. Unfortunately, the warehouse's condition was similar to that of the other nearby buildings. They were old or dilapidated, in serious need of paint and rehab.

Catcher lifted the collar of his jacket and buttoned it up against the irritatingly constant rain and chill in the air. "Into the deep?" he asked.

I nodded and prepared to take the lead when a figure emerged through the darkness on the other end of the block. I put a hand on the pommel of my sword.

"Merit," Catcher whispered, a warning.

"He's a vampire," I quietly said when the familiar magic reached me. "No hostility that I can sense."

He was tall and angularly thin, with long arms and legs tucked into an old-fashioned black suit complete with vest beneath his trim jacket. His dark hair was short, a striking contrast to his muttonchop sideburns.

The light of a passing car reflected in his eyes, which were completely silver.

Vampires' eyes silvered when they were in the throes of strong emotions. Unfortunately, I couldn't tell which emotion he was feeling; his magic, although nervous, was otherwise neutral. Was he so adept at hiding his feelings, or was his reaction merely biological?

"You're Merit?" he asked.

I nodded, but kept a hand on my sword, a warning that I was

prepared for action, and funny business wouldn't be tolerated. (Although in stressful times like this, I rarely said no to a good bit of sarcasm.)

Catcher watched him warily. "I'm Catcher, and you have us at a disadvantage."

"Horace Wilson," the vampire said, extending a hand. "Corporal, if you prefer it, although Horace is fine, too."

"You serve?" Catcher asked.

"Served," he said, emphasizing the past tense. "Eleventh Maine Volunteer Infantry."

That would have made him a soldier in the Civil War, and at least a century and a half old.

"We're sorry to hear of your losses," Catcher said.

"Appreciated, although I didn't know them myself. I'm just here to help. Rogues have a public service corps—purely volunteer, but we take care of things that need to be done. Some of them grimmer than others."

Horace glanced around the neighborhood, which seemed quiet and asleep, but we were odd-looking enough that we'd attract attention eventually.

"Let's get inside," he said. "We've taken care of the kids."

"Kids?" I asked.

"Oliver and Eve. They were relatively young. Kids to me and most in my circle." He waved us toward a bit of fence that was rumpled, then lifted it so we could sneak beneath. When we were inside the barrier, we followed Horace toward the building and a set of double entrance doors.

He looked over at me. "You're a kid yourself."

"Vampire since April," I said.

"Good transition?"

"It's had its moments," I said.

The doors, heavy and industrial, hung poorly on their hinges. Horace pushed them open with two hands, sparks flying up from the grate of steel against the concrete pad below. When he'd made a gap large enough to squeeze through, he switched on a flashlight.

We followed him into the building and directly into a stairwell. We climbed up to the third floor and emerged into a gigantic empty space, presumably where the documents had once been stored.

It might have previously been a warehouse, but its storage days had long since passed. No furniture, no shelves, no operating lights. Graffiti marked the exposed brick walls, and water dripped from ceiling tiles into puddles on the scarred wooden floors.

Horace shined a flashlight across the huge room to other side, where the door to the hidden room that James had found stood open.

"That's it," he said, then offered the flashlight to me. "I've been in once, and that was plenty for me. I'll wait out here."

I took it and nodded. Catcher beside me, the circle of light bobbing in front of us, we walked across the room, footsteps echoing across the worn wooden floors.

We reached the secret door, a tidy slab of faux brick that, when closed, would have slotted neatly into the rest of the wall. But for the blood, James never would have found it.

The door rotated on a single point that balanced its weight. A brick to the right of the door stuck out a bit farther than the others. That, I assumed, was the hidden latch that opened the door.

"It's an interesting contraption," Catcher said.

"For someone wanting to hide something, sure."

The scent of blood spilled from the vault, and I was glad I'd had blood before I left the House. Intellectually, I had no interest

in the spilled blood of two murdered Rogues. But my baser predatory instincts didn't much care for ethics, and the blood's origin
didn't diminish its desirability. I was a vampire, and blood was
blood.

We stepped inside.

Oliver and Eve—as Horace had promised—were gone. But the
evidence of their brutal murders remained. Their deaths had been
marked by the pool of dark blood on the floor, still damp in the
night's humidity.

A wave of scent washed over me, and I closed my eyes for a
moment against the instinctive attraction.

"Keep it together," Catcher whispered, moving ahead of me
toward the puddles.

"In the process," I assured him. When I was positive I was in
control, I opened my eyes again, then ran the beam back and forth
across the room in the event any clues might be found there. The
room was big enough on its own, probably thirty by thirty feet
square.

There were no windows, no shelves, no goods a warehouse
would actually store. As in the rest of the space, the walls were
made of exposed brick. Other than the size, and the hidden door,
there was nothing here that differentiated it from the rest of the
warehouse.

"Maybe they used this for secure storage?" Catcher asked.

"Maybe," I said. "Customers pay a little more, and their goods
get locked into the hidden room."

"If this place was built in the forties," Catcher said, "that means
wartime. We aren't far from where the Manhattan Project operated. There could have been sensitive scientific information here,
which would explain the security measures."

I nodded, walking back and forth, moving the flashlight a few inches with each sweep, like a TV crime scene unit. And just like in a forensic television show, I didn't hit pay dirt until the end, when a bit of something on the floor caught my eye.

"Catcher," I called, freezing the beam on the spot. There in the dust and grime was a small sliver of wood.

Now that I knew what I was looking for, I scanned the area . . . and found more of them. Two, then a dozen, then a hundred scattered in a triangle about ten feet across at its base.

"What did you find?" Catcher asked.

I picked one up—no larger than a toothpick, but much more jagged—and extended it in the palm of my hand. "Wood slivers. And I'll bet they're aspen."

"McKetrick?" Catcher asked.

"It could be shrapnel from one of his aspen bullets," I reluctantly agreed. McKetrick had invented a gun that shot bullets of aspen intended to quickly dispense of vampires by turning them to ash. He'd tried to shoot me with it. Fortunately, the gun had backfired. He'd caught the worst of the resulting explosion of metal and wood shrapnel, and I hadn't seen him in person since. I also hadn't assumed we'd seen the last of McKetrick, but nor was I thrilled about the possibility he was making a move again. Unfortunately, this evidence pointed that way.

Catcher knelt on the ground and picked up another sliver. "Oliver and Eve were decapitated. If he had a gun, why didn't he use it to kill them? Was he trying to scare them first?"

"I don't know. Maybe it was his first stage of attack, his warning weapon. Maybe that's what got them into the room. If he did this . . ." I murmured, my anger beginning to rise at the possibility McKetrick was involved and that he'd taken the lives of two innocent vampires.

"We don't know McKetrick killed them," Catcher said. "Maybe

he used the weapon; then someone else finished the job. There's no direct evidence he's involved."

But I had a hunch. "This is *exactly* the kind of thing McKetrick would do. Taking out vampires attempting to register? Proving that we're damned even if we try to abide by human rules?"

"You're absolutely right," Catcher said. "But that's not good enough."

And I knew he was right, but that didn't make me feel any better.

We thanked Horace for his help and drove back to my grand-father's house. Noah, Rose, and Elena were gone. They'd helped Jeff garner what information he could before taking Rose, who was overwhelmed with grief, home again.

Jeff was at the computer when we walked inside. I offered up the wood sliver.

He knew of McKetrick's penchant for aspen, and he whistled at the sight. "Is that what I think it is?"

"That's what I need you to find out. Can you get it tested?"

"I'm on it."

Catcher sat down at his desk and kicked up his feet, then rubbed his hands over his face. Since his day had started with an evidentiary pickup hours and hours ago, he was probably ex-hausted.

"The property?" he asked. Catcher was evidently too tired to spare a verb.

"As you saw," Jeff said, "the building is a former warehouse. But I haven't been able to find anything about who actually owns it."

I leaned against the opposite desk. "Any other ideas?"

"Not until the labs come back," Catcher said. "That'll take a little while, but we'll let you know."

I nodded and stood up. "In that case, I'll leave you to it. I need to update Ethan and Luc. Can you dig into Oliver's and Eve's backgrounds a little more? Maybe this isn't a random attack. Maybe they've been somewhere or done something that really pissed someone off and completely explains this."

I knew that was unlikely, but I needed to believe there was some reason, some logic to what I'd seen.

Jeff nodded. "Safe driving. And let us know if you find anything interesting."

I was hoping to find anything at all.

I drove back with the car's window cracked. I needed the bracing chill to wipe clean the scents of blood and dilapidation.

I parked the car and jogged into the House, then headed immediately to Ethan's office. The door was open, and he stood in front of the conference table, perusing documents piled there.

He looked up when I entered, a line of worry between his eyes as he looked me over. "Merit?"

I walked inside. "Oliver and Eve are dead."

He closed his eyes for a moment. "How?"

I moved closer to him so I could lower my voice. There was no need to publicize the gory details.

"Decapitation," I said. "They were in a warehouse in Little Italy, in a secure room tucked into the back of one of the storage floors. Their bodies had been arranged, but there was no other notable evidence except wood slivers on the floor. Lots of them, just like the kind produced by McKetrick's gun."

Ethan's eyes narrowed dangerously. "There's evidence he's involved?"

"Only circumstantially. There's nothing but the wood at the moment. Jeff and Catcher are sending a sliver to Detective Jacobs;

the phone and glass we found in the alley are already there. Unfortunately, that's all the information we've got. The property records were a dead end."

He walked closer and put a hand on my cheek. "And how are you?"

"Disturbed," I admitted. "Noah and the others are clearly grieving, and we've got nothing but potential lab results. Although Jeff's going to look into Oliver's and Eve's backgrounds, see if anything pops there."

He rubbed his thumb along my jawline, and pressed a kiss to my forehead. "It's a good thought, Sentinel."

"Any word from Darius?" I wondered.

"No," Ethan said. "But I expect I'll hear something soon enough. Darius rarely acts without an ulterior motive."

"Has Paige ferreted out anything about what that ulterior motive might be?"

"Not yet. The other Decertification records weren't helpful. They were many years ago, and the disputes involved alchemical equations and the treatment of tenants. The lessons aren't entirely applicable in the modern age."

"Huh." I remembered Jonah's comment about the contract being the key, and feigned a bright idea. "You know, since vampires are, as you said, sticklers for rules, maybe there's something in the rules themselves. I assume the House has some kind of contract with the GP about sharing investment funds and stuff; is there anything in there about the transition?"

Ethan's brows lifted in surprise. "That's not a bad idea, Sentinel. I'll suggest it to Paige." It wasn't a positive development, but at least it was movement. I'd take progress any day.

There was a knock at the door. A dark-haired man stood in the doorway. His jaw was square, his cheekbones honed. His face was angular, but not unattractive, mostly because of his eyes. They were big, dark, and hazel, with lashes long enough to tangle at the corners. He wore black trousers and a white button-down. On his right hand he wore a gold signet ring. He was handsome, but in an almost severe way. Like he might have been a Spartan in a past life.

"Am I interrupting?" he asked.

"You're just in time," Ethan said, walking forward with a hand extended. "It's nice to see you."

They shook hands at the elbow, one of those masculine rituals that suggested they were, as Ethan had said, already acquainted.

"Good to see you, too, Ethan." The stranger slid a glance my way. "And this is her, I presume?"

Ethan smiled slyly and extended an arm toward me. "This is her. Merit, this is Michael Donovan, our security auditor."

"Merit," I offered, extending a hand. Michael's grip was strong, confident. His magic was subtle, checking me out and testing my measure. He wasn't the first vampire to try such things on me—Celina was famous for doing it—but since Ethan trusted him, I let him get away with it.

"Michael Donovan," he said. "You stand Sentinel?"

"All night long."

He smiled, a dimple alighting at one corner of his mouth. "She's clever, Ethan."

"Yes, she is," I agreed, glancing between the two of them. "And how do you know each other?"

"We met a few years ago," Ethan said. "Michael was acquainted with Celina."

I glanced at him cautiously, and held back the snark that would have normally followed a comment like that. God knew I wasn't a fan of Celina's, but there were plenty of vampires—including the members of the GP—who thought differently.

"Oh?" I simply asked. "Were you a member of Navarre House?"

"I was not," Michael said, leaning toward me, eyes twinkling. "Nor was I an admirer of Ms. Desaulniers's."

"Then you're on the side of right and justice, and I won't hold it against you."

He held out a hand collegially. "I think that's entirely fair."

We shook on it, and I found myself liking Ethan's new security guru.

There was another knock at Ethan's door; his room had apparently become the House's Union Station.

Malik stood in the doorway. "I'm sorry, but could I interrupt you for a moment? Our banker has a time-sensitive question."

"Of course. Excuse me." Ethan smiled politely, then followed Malik out of the room, leaving Michael and me alone.

Their obvious friendship aside, I was curious why Ethan felt the need to hire an outside security expert, given that he had a full guard in the House and mercenary fairies outside it.

"What exactly do security auditors do?" I wondered.

I didn't mean for my voice to carry a tone, but I could hear the suspicion just as clearly as Michael Donovan undoubtedly could.

I blamed my father for that one. He was a managerial whiz, but through the course of his business dealings, I'd seen come and go dozens of outside "consultants" whose only value, as far as I was aware, was validating whatever my father told them. They were highly paid yes-men who brought nothing to the table except a willingness to praise my father and snipe at others who posed a threat to their careers.

"We do not facilitate synergistic synergy," Michael said.

"I'm sorry?"

"Synergistic synergy. It's one of those bullshit business phrases that make you pretty confident I'm going to steal money from your House."

I could feel the blush from my toes, mortified that he'd called me out.

He crossed his arms and smiled a little. "I appreciate your obvious skepticism. It's easy to call yourself an auditor. It's harder to provide a meaningful service for your clients.

"In brief, my job is to ensure the House is stronger after the split than it was before. Among other things, I've been reviewing the House's crisis preparedness and its physical and technical security. I'm trying to identify chinks in the House's armor and fill them, at least in the limited time we've had since the House voted to leave."

"And have you found them yet?"

He nodded. "Not many—Luc knows what he's doing—but there are things we can improve. Your infosec protocols—information security—aren't as strong as I like, and we've been updating them. Your House evac plan is top-notch, but I'd prefer if your alternate housing options were stronger." He leaned in a bit. "And frankly, I'm not a fan of the House's choice of outside guards, but Ethan won't hear a thing about it."

"The fairies can be fickle," I agreed.

"Indeed they can. But ultimately, this all comes down to the GP. I'm also no fan of Darius West's, but the man's got balls of steel and the vampiric prowess to back it up."

"Unfortunately, I'd agree." The members of the GP were reputably the strongest of the strong, with physical and psychic skills—like the ability to glamour humans—that gave them a leg up on other vampires. That was precisely why they'd been chosen to lead us, although it seemed clear that strength did not equal leadership ability.

"I don't know about you," Michael said, "but I'm also trying to speed up Ethan's reinvestment as Master of the House. Malik and I both believe it would help solidify the House's position. Ethan disagrees."

That was new information, but I certainly didn't mind that Michael was sharing it with me. "Why does he disagree?"

"I suspect he wants his reinvestment to be a more enjoyable occasion. A celebration, not undertaken in fear of the GP."

That made some sense.

"My turn with the questions," Michael said. His posture changed; he crossed his arms and dropped his chin, eyes narrowing as he looked at me skeptically. He was in security mode now.

"You were a graduate student?"

"I was. University of Chicago. English lit."

"And twenty-seven at the time of your turning."

"Nearly twenty-eight."

"You were part of this year's class?" Michael asked.

"I was. Commended in April as Sentinel."

"Did Ethan have to woo you?"

"Excuse me?" Was he asking about our relationship?

"Into the House, I mean. It can't be a coincidence that you're Joshua Merit's daughter. I assume that's why Ethan sought you out? Not that you don't have your own achievements, I'm sure."

My beginnings as a vampire weren't common knowledge—the fact that Ethan had made me a vampire to save my life after a vicious attack. Unfortunately, it wasn't unusual for someone to accuse me of having gotten my golden ticket to vampirism and immortality by using my father's connections.

"Ethan didn't recruit me because of my father." Quite the contrary: Ethan hadn't recruited me at all, although it would have been wrong to say my father hadn't been involved.

Michael looked at me for a moment, his expression perfectly neutral.

"Very well," he finally said.

"Was that a test?" I wondered. "To see how I'd react?"

"In part. And partly simple curiosity. Ethan often stands alone. To hear that he'd chosen someone to share his life with was a surprise."

Ethan walked back into the room.

"Is everything okay?" I asked.

"Fine," Ethan said, but he stopped and looked between us. He must have caught the hint of tension in the air. "Is everything okay here?"

"Everything's great," Michael said. "We're just testing each other's defenses."

So we were, I thought.

"It's in your natures," Ethan said, then put a hand on my arm. "We've got work to do, Sentinel, if you'd like to head to the Ops Room and update Luc on the Rogues."

I could tell when I was being dismissed. I gave him a mild salute. "Of course, Liege."

Ethan rolled his eyes.

"Merit," Michael said. "A pleasure to meet you. I'm sure we'll see each other again."

If he was here to guide Cadogan House through the final stages of the transition, there seemed little doubt of that.

On the way to the stairs, I found a message from Mallory on my phone, asking if I wanted to grab pizza.

I missed her, truly. Lindsey was a great girl, and I was glad I had friends in the House to commiserate with. But Mallory and I had history, and the comfortableness that had come from a long friendship.

I was suddenly struck with melancholy, missing my former life, when my only worry would have been whether I was ready for the next day's classes at U of C. I'd worried about due dates and dissertation chapters and grading papers, about whether my car would last through another Chicago winter (it had) and the Cubs would win another pennant (they hadn't).

These nights, I worried about murder, the safety of my House, and whether my best friend could keep her hands out of the black magic cookie jar.

But with those supernatural hassles came Ethan and the thrill of knowing I was truly helping the vampires of my House.

Tonight, that House came first.

CAN'T TONIGHt, I texted back. MIDINVESTIGATION. RAIN CHECK?

OF COURSE, she said.

I put the phone in my pocket. Someday, hopefully, Mallory and I could get back on track.

CHAPTER SIX

LADIES AND GENTLEMEN, THE REPLACEMENTS!

The Ops Room was the headquarters of Cadogan's guard crew, the place where we strategized about supernatural problems and looked for solutions. It was also the hub of House security, where guards at closed-circuit televisions and computer monitors kept an eye on the House and its grounds and any activities that might pose a threat.

The room was high tech, outfitted with computer stations, a large conference table, and state-of-the-art technology. It was also right down the hall from the House's training room and arsenal, giving us access to practice space and weaponry if the need arose.

I wasn't exactly a guard, but I generally played one when things went bad. And they'd been going bad with some frequency lately.

There were three veteran guards on staff—Juliet, Lindsey, and Kelley, Luc's temporary replacement. There were also a handful of temp guards, hired by Luc to fill the guard corps' vacancies.

Tonight, the Ops Room was quiet. Kelley was gone, probably

on patrol, and Juliet, lithe and redheaded, sat at the bank of monitors that displayed the House's security feeds.

Lindsey sat at the table in front of a tablet, a cup of yogurt and a plastic spoon in hand. Luc sat at the end of the table, reading a newspaper, ankles crossed on the tabletop. It was like walking into their breakfast nook.

"We need to give you two a couple name," I said, taking a seat on the opposite side of the table. "Lucsey, perhaps?"

Luc didn't bat an eyelash; he simply turned a page of the newspaper. "Call us what you want, Sentinel. We already have a name for you."

That was alarming. Not that there was a way to avoid it, but I wasn't sure I wanted them discussing my relationship around the Ops Room table. "No, you don't."

"Yes, we do." Lindsey stirred her spoon noisily around the walls of the yogurt cup to get the remaining drops. "You're Methan."

"We're what?"

"Methan. Merit and Ethan. Methan."

"Nobody calls us that."

Every vampire in the room turned back to look at me, sardonic expressions on their faces. They nodded simultaneously, and I sank back into my chair a little bit.

"Yes, we do," Luc said, speaking for them. "I mean, we try not to talk about you constantly. We all have more important things to do than dissect your relationship—"

Lindsey held up her spoon. "I don't."

"Okay, everyone except Lindsey has more important things to do, and I'm not going to take that personally. Anyway, since we skipped over it before, good evening, Sentinel."

I humphed. "Good evening. The security auditor's here. Ethan's talking to him. He said you'd already spoken with him?"

"We talked," Luc confirmed. "Frankly, I think his suggestions are unnecessary—not dangerous, but even more conservative than best practices would be—but if they make the big man feel better, so be it."

"I met him earlier tonight," Lindsey said, tossing her yogurt cup and spoon into a wastebasket across the room. Her aim was perfect, and the shot echoed into the trash. "He's hot," she said, wiping off her hands. "Tall, dark, and a little bit dirty."

"I'm right here," Luc said.

"Yes, you are, even as I admit a man wholly unconnected with you is hot."

Luc grumbled, but let her get away with that. "Sentinel, what's new in your neck of the woods?"

"Not much," I said, then told them about Oliver and Eve, the mourning Rogues, and what we'd found in the warehouse.

As I talked, Lindsey got up and pulled over our favorite standby—a giant whiteboard on which we could track our leads and thoughts—and began filling in what we knew.

"The wood slivers, if they're aspen, will lead back to McKetrick," I concluded.

Lindsey stilled and looked at Luc, and there was nothing pleasant in the exchange.

"What?" I asked.

"We have something you need to see." He tapped a bit on a screen built into the tabletop until an image appeared on the projection screen on the wall beside us.

He'd selected an Internet video of a news broadcast from earlier in the day.

On-screen, Diane Kowalcyzk, Chicago's mayor, appeared behind a podium. Beside her stood McKetrick. We'd seen him in this position before, sucking up to Kowalcyzk and standing nearby like a malicious human Sentinel.

He wore a suit, a change from his usual brand of military fatigues. The scars he'd received from his encounter with his aspen gun were unavoidable. His face was cratered, crossed with scored and bubbled skin from neck to hairline. One of his eyes was milky white; the other eye was clear and alert, and there was no denying the obvious malice in his stare.

Luc adjusted the tablet. "Let me get the audio up."

The volume slowly increased, marked by the growing green bar across the bottom of the screen and the rising volume of Kowalcyzk's beauty pageant voice. She was a handsome woman, tidy and attractive, but her anti-sup politics were hateful.

"This city was founded by humans," she said. "We live here; we work here; we pay taxes."

"We live here, work here, and pay taxes," Luc muttered. "And we've been here doing those things longer than she or any other human being in the city has been alive."

"Chicagoans deserve a city that is free from supernatural drama. Violence. Rabble-rousing. But Chicagoans don't cower away from our problems," she said, her accent suddenly thick and Midwesterny.

"We face them head-on. Once upon a time, the former mayor thought it was important to have an office where 'supernaturals,' as they're known, could call the city with their problems. It was called the Ombudsman's office, and I'm proud to say I closed it. We didn't need it then, and we don't need it now. What we do need—what the city of Chicago needs—is an office for humans with supernatural problems."

"Oh, God," I said, anticipating what was coming next.

"That's why today I'm pleased to announce the creation of the Office of Human Liaisons, or OHL. I'm also pleased to announce that I've asked John Q. McKetrick to lead that office and serve as the head liaison."

Oh, this was very, very bad. She'd hired as her new "liaison" a man whose goal was to rid the city of vampires by any means necessary. She'd given him a title, an office, a staff, and total legitimacy. Which meant that if he was behind Eve's and Oliver's killings, he was now politically untouchable.

My grandfather was going to lose it.

"Not all supernaturals are criminals; we know that. But this man wears the scars of his interactions with the undesirable element, and I believe he has much to teach us about those with whom we share our city."

Unmitigated fury flashed through me. McKetrick bore his scars because he was a killer with a vendetta against vampires. He'd done those injuries to himself—quite literally. I'd been the intended victim of his misanthropy.

McKetrick smiled at the mayor and replaced her at the podium. "The city is not what it seems. We live in a world of light and sun. But at night a darker element emerges. For now, we are still in control of this city, but if we are not vigilant, if we do not stand tall and strong, we will become the minority in our own town."

I gaped at the prejudice McKetrick had apparently been hired by the mayor to spew on supernaturals. Was this what public discourse was coming to?

"This administration aims to shine the light on Chicago. That's my job: to protect humans from supernaturals' whims and to ensure this city continues to be, not the Second City, but the best city in the world."

There was a smattering of polite, probably scripted applause until Luc turned off the video.

"That guy," Lindsey said, "is a douche. Asterisk, I hate him. Footnote, he can suck it."

"We got it, hon," Luc said, not unkindly. "Although I don't disagree with the sentiment. And, man, I do not want to tell Ethan."

"As if he needs anything else to worry about right now," I said, my heart aching for him. "Now he has a fearmonger with a title. We'd better hope McKetrick didn't kill Oliver and Eve, because if he did, the mayor just appointed a killer to her cabinet."

Whether she did or didn't, the wood slivers still implicated him and had to be investigated.

"Once I've talked to Ethan, I'll advise the other guard captains," Luc said. He swore out a curse. "And John Q. McKetrick? As in 'John Q. Public'? How does she not know that's not his real name? It's obviously fake."

"Because she's ignorant," I said. "She'd have to be in order to believe giving this guy power was a good idea."

My phone buzzed with a message, and I plucked it up. It was from Jeff. DET. JACOBS SAYS NO PRINTS OR OTHER MATERIALS ON EVE'S PHONE, it said. BUT WOOD WAS ASPEN.

That was all the information I needed. I stood up and headed for the door.

"And where are you going?" Luc asked.

I glanced back at him, fire in my eyes. "Two vampires are dead, and the crime has McKetrick's stamp on it. Since I now know how to find Mr. McKetrick, whatever his first name, I think it's time we had a little chat."

It was late, nearly midnight, and most city offices would be empty. But McKetrick had been assigned to the supernatural beat, and since most sups were nocturnal, I figured the odds were in my favor that he'd still be around.

Besides, I suspected the man of murder; I wasn't going to visit him at home or at the "facility" we'd once heard he operated. The city's administration might not have been huge fans of vampires, but an office visit seemed much safer than the alternative.

I found his number on the Web, then picked a quiet spot on the first floor and dialed him up.

"John McKetrick."

"It's Merit. I hear you've been promoted."

There was a pause, although I'd have sworn I heard the quickened beating of his heart. "So I have," he finally said. "What can I do for you, Merit?"

"I thought we might meet. Maybe you could give me a tour of your office?" *And*, I silently thought, *explain to me exactly why you decided killing innocent vampires was justifiable?*

He hesitated for a moment, perhaps considering the outcome of our last encounter—when he'd walked away with scars. But he must have decided the risk was worth it.

"What a good idea," he said, and his tone sounded like it. That wasn't exactly comforting, but I didn't think he'd hurt me in his office, not this soon into his job. He didn't have the political capital yet to kill a vampire in the Daley Center.

Or so I hoped.

"I can be there in half an hour," I guessed.

"I'll let security know you're on your way. And, Merit? I look forward to seeing you."

The man made my skin crawl. And even though I didn't think he'd commit vampiricide in his office, I texted Jonah to let him know where I was headed, and then Jeff. Just in case.

I paused for a second, glancing at Ethan's office. Luc knew where I was going, so I didn't have to tell Ethan about my plan. Which was good, because I didn't think he'd approve of a late-night trip to visit our primary political enemy on his home turf.

This was one of those situations in which it was better to forge ahead and seek forgiveness later than get permission in the first place.

Sometimes being an underling meant managing up.

I drove downtown and found a parking spot on a side street. The Loop was dark and quiet, most of the neighborhood's business traffic having gone home for the night—probably on the El back to the suburbs—hours ago. Anticipating guards and metal detectors, I left my sword and dagger in the car.

Outside the building I looked up, and my nerves kicked into overdrive. The Daley Center was an intimidating building—a huge Federal-style structure marked by columns that ran halfway up the building like a stone crown.

"Come here often?"

My heart skipped a beat at the break in the silence, until I looked beside me at the man who'd made it. It was Jeff, hands in his pockets and a rather large grin on his face.

"What are you doing here?"

He shrugged. "I decided you needed backup."

Jeff was a shape-shifter and undoubtedly strong; I'd seen him fight, although I'd never actually seen him shift. Not that I was hoping for a zoological throwdown between Jeff and McKetrick inside the Daley Center.

We walked around the building to the plaza alongside it, where an enormous sculpture by Picasso stared out into the night. The steel glowed rust-red in the spotlights, and arced into the sky like a robotic insect. Behind it stood three huge flagpoles that had already been stripped of their canvas for the evening.

As we walked across the plaza, I felt suddenly small: a single impotent vampire in the midst of a human empire that wasn't much concerned about my survival.

"You're okay?" Jeff asked.

I nodded. "I'm fine. Just nervous."

"I can go up with you, if you want."

I shook my head. "It's better if you stay here. I don't want him to feel like he's been cornered, and I don't want to put you in his line of fire. I'll be fine. It's just the anticipation. I'm sure my gumption will kick in once I get to his office." It had better, because McKetrick had things to answer for, and this wasn't the time to be a shrinking violet.

Nerves on edge, we walked into the marbled main lobby, past the various homages to Richard Daley and toward the security desk. A man and woman with tidy hair and wearing security ensembles looked up.

"I'm Merit," I said. "I'm here to see John McKetrick in the Office of Human Liaisons?"

If my name rang a bell, they didn't seem to care. The man read off a floor number, then directed me to metal detectors, X-ray machines, and security gates. Good thing I hadn't brought my weapons.

Jeff and I walked toward them, and he squeezed my hand. "You can do it."

I nodded. "If I'm not back in an hour, call someone."

He chuckled and pulled off a surprisingly cocky expression. "Mer, if you aren't back in half an hour, I'm coming to get you myself."

"They have guns," I reminded him, but he just smiled.

"I'm a shifter."

My backup plan in place, I blew out a breath and walked toward the gauntlet.

McKetrick's office was on the fourth floor, tucked between a mayoral staff office and a traffic courtroom.

The door to his office bore his name and position in gold foil letters. I wanted to key the glass and scrape them off, but I managed to hold myself back.

I was secondarily glad my fear was giving way to anger. Anger was so much easier to bear.

Inside, I found an empty reception desk and an open door. I walked to the doorway and found McKetrick standing in front of a window, looking out over the dark plaza with a mug in hand.

He looked back at me and smiled thinly, the scars on his face even more jarring in person than they had been on television. His skin looked uncomfortably tight in places and paper-thin in others. There seemed little doubt they caused him pain.

"Merit. So nice of you to come by and wish me well."

I glanced mildly around the office. "So this is where Mayor Kowalcyzk is keeping you: in your own little office behind a mask of legitimacy."

"I have my bona fides," he said. "Unlike some."

"I'm a duly registered vampire," I assured him. "I can show you my card if you don't believe me."

Smiling, he walked back to his desk and took a seat, clearly enjoying the repartee.

"You know what your problem is, Merit? You think you're better than the rest of us. I know what vampires think—that you're an evolutionary advancement, a genetic mutation. But being a vampire doesn't make you special. It makes you a pest." He linked his hands together on his desktop and leaned forward. "And I'm here to protect the city from your particular specimen of vermin."

"You're a new brand of racist."

"I'm a man with a staff, an office, and mayoral privilege. She believes me, you know."

"She believed Tate, too. And you saw how well that worked out. The entire city saw his bat wings."

He shook his head. "And to think—I thought you'd actually show me some respect now that my views have been validated."

I didn't think the mayor's stupidity equated to a validation of his beliefs, but it was hardly worth the argument.

"Does that validation mean that you're allowed to take vampires out?"

McKetrick looked amused. "You mean our little incident on the Midway?" He meant the last time we'd met, when he'd pointed his aspen gun at me. "That's in the past, Merit."

"I mean the two vampires you killed. Good Samaritans who were murdered for no reason."

"I didn't kill any vampires." He smiled wolfishly. "Not recently, anyway."

His tone was casual, and that pissed me off. My anger rose and blossomed, heating my blood instantaneously and silvering my eyes.

His eyes widened with fear, which I enjoyed more than I should have.

"Two vampires are dead, and your aspen gun was used to subdue them."

He looked surprised at the accusation, his expression either really well faked or inexplicably honest. But how could he have been surprised?

"That's impossible," he said, gaze flattening again. He might not be thrilled at a pissed vampire in his office, but he was warrior enough to keep himself under control.

"I saw the wood slivers, and we've had them tested. They were aspen."

I watched him for a moment, opening my senses to his reactions to my accusations. If I listened hard enough, I could hear the thud of his heart and the rhythmic pulse of blood in his veins. Both seemed fast, but not alarmingly so. He may not have been utterly calm, but he wasn't a frightened predator, either.

"Quit using your magic on me."

I doubted he knew whether I actually had magic, but it was my turn to bluff. "I don't know what you're talking about."

"As if I'd trust anything you say. Look at my face, Merit. Look what you did to me."

There was zealotry in his eyes; he'd managed to convince himself that I was the cause of his injuries, even though the precise opposite was true. I guess deciding I'd been at fault was easier than admitting he'd done it to himself.

"Your gun exploded," I reminded him. "A gun you decided to use on me, even though I didn't have a weapon."

"Lies," he simply said.

This was getting us nowhere, so I went back to details. "Tell me why you picked Oliver and Eve. They were trying to register— doing exactly what the city wanted them to do. Why did you kill them?"

"I don't know who you're talking about." McKetrick smiled a little. "But regardless, if you want to accuse me of something, you'll have to do it officially."

"McKetrick, you can sit and smile in this office all you want, wearing a suit and pretending to be bestest friends with the mayor. But you're a killer, and we all know it."

He smiled again, and this time the expression was one of pure malice—hateful enough that it made me nervous.

"And you need to remember who's in charge here." He poked a finger at his chest. "Me, not you or your band of heathen vampires. Not anymore. My name is on the door, Merit. The mayor has given me the authority to help the humans of this city against the infestation of those like you."

A security guard appeared at the door, ready to throw me out. I guess my silvered eyes had scared McKetrick plenty. So he didn't just hate vampires; he was afraid of us?

I wasn't going to fight a security guard who was just doing his job, even if it was for a lame-ass like McKetrick. "This isn't over," I promised him.

"Oh, I know it isn't," McKetrick called out, as I was escorted to the door. "That's what makes this so fun."

Lindsey was right. That man truly did suck.

Wisely, Jeff let me stew a few minutes before asking questions about my visit, not that there was a lot to tell. He'd found a parking space not far from mine, so he let me stay quiet until we reached the cars again.

"I'm not sure he did it," I finally said. "I'm not sure he's innocent, either, but I think if he knew who Oliver and Eve were, he would have gloated. At the very least, he would have hinted about it."

Jeff leaned against the Volvo. "And he didn't gloat?"

"Not really. He gloated about his position, but the aspen gun thing—he seemed completely surprised by that."

"Maybe somebody stole a weapon from him," Jeff said. "He's got a facility, right? And henchmen?"

"Yeah," I said. We weren't sure where the facility was, only that he had one. We'd seen his henchmen in action plenty of times.

They preferred the black fatigues he'd worn before he'd taken office.

How had those become the good ol' days?

I looked at Jeff. "Is that our theory? Someone stole an aspen gun from McKetrick's facility and decided to take out two vampires?"

Jeff crossed his arms. "It's not a bad theory. Maybe one of McKetrick's flunkies found out he was going to take the city job, figured his boss was a sellout, and took action on his own."

I nodded. "That's a possibility. But it doesn't get us any closer to finding the killers. He'd never give up a colleague, even if they did steal a weapon. That would be like choosing vampires over humans."

"The ultimate betrayal," Jeff said, and I nodded.

"I should get back to the House. Thanks for meeting me out here." Before he could object, I wrapped him in a hug. Jeff was thin and tall—taller than me—but surprisingly solid beneath that lanky frame.

"Uh, you're welcome," he said, awkwardly patting my back before I released him again. His cheeks were crimson. "I've got a girlfriend."

"Of course," I gravely said. "Anyway, thank you."

"Later," he said, and climbed into his car for the drive back to my grandfather's house. I was headed in the same general direction, and there seemed little doubt we'd both find drama when we reached our destinations.

I didn't, however, expect to find the House completely silent.

The foyer was empty, as was Ethan's office.

I heard a sudden crack of sound in the foyer, followed by the sound of feminine cursing. Fearing the worst—riot, attack, supernatural temper tantrum—I hurried back to the spot.

I found Helen there, kneeling in the foyer, picking up a spoiled bouquet of flowers from the floor. A large, clear vase—apparently plastic, since it hadn't shattered—lay beside her. She wore a well-tailored tweed skirt and jacket and sensible heels, and she knelt like Coco Chanel might have—with feminine care and careful style.

"I'll help," I said, bending down to help gather up the stems. They were white roses just past full bloom, their flowers limp and beginning to brown, the stems emitting the faint aroma of decay.

"Thank you," she said, gathering an armful of flowers and rising to her feet again. "I was just replacing the arrangement on the foyer table. I caught a thorn and it startled me. Such a small thing," she added, "but there you go."

Not so small that it hadn't drawn blood; the pungent aroma of the drops she'd spilled was a low note beneath her perfume and the smell of the flowers.

"No problem." I put the vase on the table again, picked up the remaining bunch of roses, and followed her into the kitchen, where we dumped the mess into one of Margot's large trash cans. "Where is everyone?"

"They're in the training room. Ethan has decided to put our new security consultant to the test."

I was running down the stairs almost instantaneously.

CHAPTER SEVEN

THE CASE OF VAMPIRE VS. VAMPIRE

There were two parts to the training room at Cadogan House, which sat next door to the Ops Room: the tatami-covered floor where the participants fought, and the balcony that ringed it, a place for spectators to watch the proceedings below.

The fighters hadn't yet stepped into the ring, so I found a seat on the balcony beside Lindsey, Luc, and half the Ops Room temps.

"How did your meeting go?" Luc asked.

"McKetrick didn't try to kill me, but I'm not sure he's involved in the killings, either. He didn't much care they were dead, but he did seem surprised about the aspen gun."

Luc looked surprised. "He claims someone stole it from him?"

"He didn't say, but I'm wondering."

The balcony erupted into applause, and we peered over the railing as Ethan walked inside, wearing black martial arts pants and a top belted at the waist. He was shoeless, and his hair was pulled tight at the nape of his neck, all but a lock of golden blond that fell across his face.

A burst of pride filled my chest. The man was walking power and confidence, and he was all mine.

"Seriously," Lindsey whispered, "well done."

"I know, right?"

Ethan walked onto the mat and bounced on his toes, stretching his arms above him as he not-so-subtly scanned the balcony for me. He met my eyes, and I offered a supportive wink.

Go get him, tiger, I silently told him.

Shouldn't you be working? he asked.

Yes, I said frankly. *But the world outside these walls is depressing, and I need the distraction. You may begin impressing me now.*

He smiled wickedly, his expression public, but the reasons—and the conversation between us—for our ears only.

Michael stepped into the room to the good-natured clapping of the vampires in the balcony. He'd opted for white martial arts gear, the same styling as Ethan's. But the color contrast was notable. They were both tall and fit, but their coloring and mannerisms were noticeably different. Michael had dark hair and a casual, athletic bounce to his step. Ethan, golden haired and green eyed, made clear that every move was precise and calculated.

Michael pressed his hands together and bent forward at the edge of the mat, bowing toward Ethan. Ethan did the same, his expression unreadable, and they met in the middle.

The battle started almost instantaneously.

Michael jumped into a high spinning kick that sent Ethan to the floor, and he rolled away before Michael could attempt contact again.

"Not bad," Ethan said.

"I'm only worth your House's money if I can teach you a trick or two," Michael said, executing a side kick that Ethan neatly blocked, then moving forward with a jab-slash-punch combination. Ethan dodged him, flipping backward out of the way—and at least ten feet into the air—before Michael could hit him again.

"Clearly four hundred years of practice has its benefits," Michael said, grunting as he used his right forearm to block a crescent kick that Ethan landed perfectly, the sound of bone on bone ringing across the room.

We winced sympathetically. That couldn't have felt good for either of them.

They kept at it, the advantage switching back and forth as they worked through what seemed like every weapon in their arsenals: strikes, punches, kicks, and flips.

Michael was good. His form was strong and he made quick decisions, although his responses weren't as creative as Ethan's. Maybe Ethan was helped by the years of practice, of experiencing the "special" relationship with gravity that helped vampires stay airborne.

But what Michael lacked in creativity, he made up for in pure strength. He was brawnier than Ethan, lean, but broader in the shoulders compared to Ethan's lithe frame.

They separated and paused for a moment, both breathing heavily, each watching the other carefully. Assessing and calculating their skills.

After a moment, Michael broke the silence. "If you want to improve, you've got to be willing to get dirty."

"That's what she said," Luc whispered beside us, Lindsey coughing to hide an obvious snort.

"Dirty?" Ethan asked. Hands on his hips, a single eyebrow arched in aristocratic doubt, he gazed back at Michael.

"Dirty," Michael repeated. "You fight like a prince. Honorably. And that's all well and good in the sparring room, but if you're fighting for real, there's a good chance they don't give a rat's ass if you're following vampiric etiquette. They won't be checking the *Canon* later. You have to be willing to fight back the way they're fighting you. Otherwise you risk losing a fight—being killed or injured—or not disabling a foe when you have a chance. And that puts the burden on someone else."

For a moment, the training room was silent as we all watched Ethan, waiting for his reaction to the advice. Ethan wasn't frequently corrected, especially when it came to fighting. But he held out a hand toward Michael.

"I appreciate your candor. As often as we train in the traditional methods, it's easy to forget the purpose of the learning—protecting ourselves and those we love."

"Precisely," Michael said, nodding as they shook hands.

They separated just as Malik walked through the door and headed for Ethan, not bothering to wait for an invite.

"Good lord," Lindsey muttered. "And just when I was enjoying myself. What is it now? Robots? Monsters? Is McKetrick outside with a torch, ready to light the House on fire?"

"Possibly worse," Luc said, checking his phone, then raising his gaze to me. "Kelley just messaged me. Lacey Sheridan is nearly here."

The vampires in the balcony around me went silent, all eyes on me as if waiting for my reaction, their questions obvious: *Will she throw a tantrum? Scream and cry? Pout and storm out of the room?*

My cheeks burned at the apparently universal belief that I was an insecure basket case. "I already knew she was coming."

"Thank sweet Christ," Luc said with much drama and obvious relief. "I did not want to drop that bomb right now."

I gave him a flat look. "I'm not that bad."

"Yes, you are," said most of the vampires in my vicinity.

I managed not to give them all an obscene gesture, but followed suit when Luc stood up. "Let's go downstairs and make nice." He pointed a finger at me. "And no staking the guests."

Unfortunately for Luc, it wasn't the guest I was thinking about staking.

We walked upstairs again and waited for a few moments while Lacey completed her journey and Ethan changed into business attire again. The senior staff milled about in the foyer, although Michael was nowhere to be found. Ethan had probably stashed him in an office or the library to keep things moving forward.

I'd been prepared. I knew she was coming, and I knew she'd look like a supermodel ready for a strategy session—blond hair and makeup perfect, her lean frame draped in an expensive suit that hugged her body like it had been made especially for her. And it probably had.

But this . . . this I had not been expecting.

"What is she wearing?" Lindsey asked. "Why isn't she in a suit? She's always in a suit."

"Jeans," I quietly said. "She's wearing jeans."

More specifically, jeans, knee-high riding boots, and a very chic caramel-colored sweater. She had dressed down—casually even—despite being Master of a House, returning to serve Ethan, her own Master, as he managed the transition of his House.

Certainly she wasn't the first vampire to wear jeans. Most Cadogan House vamps did when we weren't on duty, and even Ethan had made the transition. But Lacey Sheridan wasn't any vampire.

The clothes weren't the only change. Her hair was short like it had been before, but she'd angled her blond bob into a cut that fell to points at her jawbone. The look was modern and daring, and it accentuated her blue eyes and perfect cheekbones.

"She's . . . changed," Lindsey whispered. "She looks good, but it's weird to see her dressed so normally."

"Weird," I said, "and probably completely intentional."

"A makeover to bring her a little more in line with Ethan's current tastes?" Lindsey whispered, glancing at me. "The probability is high."

Lacey picked that moment to look through the crowd and meet my eyes, and there was an unmistakable dare in her gaze. I assumed she knew Ethan and I were in a relationship, although it appeared she didn't much care. She meant to have him, and she wasn't going to let me stand in her way.

I sighed.

"That was a pretty sad sigh," Juliet said.

"I really, really hate drama," I said. "And I'll bet you twenty dollars she's bringing a load of drama with her."

"Not in those jeans," Lindsey said. "She's not getting anything else in that two-hundred-dollar skintight denim."

I elbowed her, which made me feel a little better.

Ethan gestured toward me, beckoning me forward.

"Rock her socks off," Lindsey whispered.

I made a vague sound of agreement and moved forward. When I reached them, Ethan put a hand on my back. "Lacey, you remember Merit."

"The Sentinel," she said. "Of course. Nice to see you again, Merit."

Ethan had a habit of calling me "Sentinel" when he was in work mode. I guess Lacey had picked up the same habit. It made sense, since she seemed to view me more as an employee than a colleague. But I could take the high road.

"You, too," I said. "I appreciate your coming out to help Ethan."

Her expression momentarily faltered. My comment had been

polite, but it had also been a subtle reminder of my position in the House—at Ethan's side.

Ethan smiled and looked at Lacey. "Do you need time to freshen up? I know it was a long night's travel."

"Maybe for just a few minutes. Perhaps I could take my bags upstairs and get settled, and then join you in your office?"

"Please," he said.

Helen appeared at Ethan's side, taking one of Lacey's suitcases and holding out a hand toward the stairs.

"You're in the guest suite," she said.

Helen escorted Lacey up the stairs, and the rest of the vampires—except the guards—dispersed.

"A moment, Ethan?" Luc asked.

"My office," he said, and we funneled inside, as if we were simply going about our evening . . . and the head of a vampire House thousands of miles away hadn't just shown up dressed like me.

It was undoubtedly going to be one of those nights.

Since we'd been on the first floor to greet Lacey, Ethan's office became an assemblage of senior staff. We gathered in a huddle, waiting for someone to break the bad news to Ethan. I was happy to let Luc take that one.

He got immediately to the meat of it. "The mayor has appointed McKetrick the city's new Ombudsman. He's got a different title, of course, but the job seems the same."

Ethan's eyes went wide. "She did what?"

"He's got an office and a staff," Luc said. "Which makes him, if not untouchable, a lot harder to touch."

Ethan looked skyward. "God save me from ignorant humans." He looked at me. "Do we have anything linking him to the vampires' deaths?"

"Jeff has confirmed the wood in the warehouse was aspen. But that's not enough to link him to Oliver and Eve. Not really. He also has flatly denied he's involved."

Ethan stilled. "And you know this because . . . ?"

"Because Jeff and I paid a visit to his office, which we believed was the safest possible location to confront him about his involvement."

Ethan made a vague sound that suggested we weren't finished discussing this particular topic, but he wouldn't push it in front of present company.

Also, interesting how I was learning to interpret male clicks and grunts.

"Have you heard anything from Paige?" Malik asked.

"He's about to."

All heads turned to the doorway. Paige—a lithe redhead with brilliantly green eyes—stood there, the librarian beside her, a file box in his hands. Neither looked happy.

"You were right," she said, joining us as the librarian dropped the file box on Ethan's conference table. "The contract is the key. The GP doesn't care if they lose you as a House; they care if they lose you as a set of assets."

I said a silent thank-you that Jonah had shared that tidbit and we'd been able to lead Paige to the right spot.

"And they don't use traditional mechanisms," the librarian said. "They look through the House's contracts with the GP for loopholes, and they exercise them."

"What loopholes?" Ethan asked. "Peter negotiated the House's contracts himself. There were no loopholes. I've read them."

"Not in the main contracts," the librarian said, pulling from the file box a red leather folio and extending it toward Ethan. "But there are other documents."

Frowning, Ethan took the folio and carried it to the conference table, where he placed it atop the other stacks of materials and untied the silk ribbon that bound it shut. Malik at his side, they perused the documents.

Luc and I exchanged a worried glance.

"What's in there?" I quietly asked Paige.

"The aforementioned loopholes," she said. "Extra 'parts' of the contract that were supposedly signed by Peter Cadogan."

Ethan turned back to us. His face was expressionless, but it was easy to see he was concerned. "The documents are signed. The terms are unconscionable and lopsided, but there is little doubt the signature is Peter's."

"What do they say?" I asked.

"In essence," Paige said, "that the bulk of any material gain obtained by the House since its creation belongs to the GP. That the House leave the GP with what the House brought to the GP—virtually nothing."

The room dropped into stunned silence. We'd believed the House had generally been in good financial shape because Ethan and Malik had made solid investments since the House's founding. We also lived in some luxury: The House was in immaculate condition; our rooms were simple but well furnished; food was always available; and our stipends were more than sufficient for personal necessities.

But it sounded like the GP was arguing that nearly all our funds belonged to them.

Ethan cursed. "We'll have to pay them off. And even if we negotiate down the figure, the check will be substantial. It will clear out a significant portion of our saved funds. We won't be bankrupt," he said. "But if the worst-case scenario holds, we could lose the nest egg that we've built."

"How does it serve their long-term purposes to put vampires on the street?" Paige asked. "That would only create public panic."

"Because it would strongly discourage any other House from attempting to leave," I predicted, and Ethan nodded his agreement.

"They're using you as an example," Paige said.

Ethan rubbed his temples. "That's likely correct. But for now, it's irrelevant. We focus on what we presently know, and whether we can negotiate a different result. It's quite possible the GP will be satisfied with hobbling us a bit, rather than destroying us altogether."

Given what I knew of the GP, I wasn't sure I'd put "destroying us" past them. For an organization created to help vampires survive human hatred, they weren't doing much to keep the Houses whole and healthy.

"I'll turn in the Bentley," Ethan absently added. "It was an extravagance, and certainly something I can do without." He looked at me. "I may need to borrow your car until we can replace it with something more . . . suitable."

"How 'bout a Schwinn with a saddle pack?" Luc asked.

"Denied," Ethan said.

"Hey," Luc said with a chuckle that was still tinged with insecurity. "We can do this. We've been through hard times before. The Great Depression? The 'seventy-three oil crisis? Capone's reign of terror?"

Ethan nodded. "We will survive and be stronger as a result. We merely have to get through this bit first." He picked up the folio again and passed it to Malik. "Have these materials messengered to the lawyers. I want them reviewing the documents first thing in the morning."

Malik nodded. "Liege."

"Is there any chance they can fix this?" Luc quietly asked.

"Not without a court battle, and the last thing we need is protracted litigation on a contract issue American courts don't have the precedent to deal with."

In the silence that followed that statement, he looked up at us and smiled mirthlessly. "Sorry. I've already talked to the lawyers tonight. It means there's no other law on the issue, so the courts would have to interpret a contract between vampires that was written centuries ago. The effort would be expensive, and the results unpredictable."

Ethan looked at Malik, and they shared a long, silent look. Perhaps they were communicating telepathically.

Malik nodded, and headed for the door, folio in hand. Whatever they'd discussed was a done deal.

Ethan looked at his watch. "I'm speaking to the House in an hour. We'll address it then. You're dismissed," he said, and the vampires filed out.

Cashing in my "girlfriend's prerogative" chip, I stayed behind, waiting until we were alone again before looking at him.

"You're all right?"

He ran his hands through his hair, which fell in a halo of golden blond around his face. "I will manage. We all will." He crooked a finger at me. "Come here, Sentinel."

I walked into his arms, and he embraced me with relief, as if the act of touching me removed the weight from his shoulders. That might have been the most flattering compliment I'd ever received from him, nonverbal as it was.

We stood there in his office for a long moment, until a loud grumble echoed across the room.

I stood back and grinned at him. "That was your stomach growling, wasn't it?"

He put a hand against his abdomen. "I have Merititis. Gnawing hunger," he clarified, which made me roll my eyes. "We've a bit of time before I speak to the House. Perhaps a bite to eat?"

"Are you asking me out on a date?"

He glanced around the shambles of his office—normally pristine, now covered in boxes, binders, and stacks of paper. "In these humble surroundings, yes."

"For you, I can manage 'humble.'"

"You actually meant 'for food,' of course, but I'll take what I can get." This time, his back was turned when I rolled my eyes.

CHAPTER EIGHT

EGGSACTLY

As usual, Margot outdid herself. Ethan had asked for comfort food, and Margot decided on a full diner-style breakfast: eggs, toast, potatoes, and sausage. Wearing her chef's whites, she rolled in a cart, silver domes covering the food and a glass pitcher of orange juice on the side.

"That smells delicious," Ethan said, clearing space at the conference table for Margot to place the trays.

"We aim to please here at Cadogan House," she said with a smile, winking at me as she uncovered the plates and lit a silver candle in the middle of the table. "Ambience."

"Appreciated," Ethan said.

Margot made a small bow, then rolled the cart back out again and closed the door behind her.

Grandiosely, Ethan pulled out a chair for me and gestured toward it. "Madam."

"Thank you, sir," I meekly said, taking a seat.

Ethan took the seat at the head of the table, perpendicular to mine, and poured juice into our glasses. "A toast," he said, holding up his glass. "To Cadogan House. May she stand strong, financially and otherwise."

We clinked our glasses together and I took a sip. The juice was delicious, with the fresh bite and lingering umami of freshly squeezed oranges.

"So Michael knew Celina," I said, digging into scrambled eggs.

"He did. Not all Masters are fortunate enough to have relationships like I did with Peter. Some are more like the relationship I had with Balthasar," he ominously said.

Ethan met Peter Cadogan, the House's namesake, after Ethan had traveled Europe with his sire, a vampire named Balthasar who'd rescued him from a battlefield. Ethan had once said he'd considered himself a monster after he'd become a vampire; I'd wondered if he'd thought the same of Balthasar.

"Fortunate that you met Peter," I said.

Ethan nodded. "I was. He was a good man, and I'm better for knowing him. Many of us mourned his passing."

"I don't think I've ever asked. How did Peter die?"

He genteelly pressed the napkin to his mouth. "Extract of aspen."

My eyes widened. An aspen stake through the heart was one of the very particular ways to kill a vampire. But extract of aspen? That was a new one.

"I didn't even know there was such a thing."

"It's usually goes by more poetic names. Sometimes bloodbane or bloodberry, because the particular variety of extract turns crimson as it's prepared. It had a role in alchemy and earlier sciences. Its secondary effect on vampires was a later discovery."

"What does it do?"

"It's a slow, death-dealing poison," he said. He shoveled a mound of eggs onto his fork.

"When was the last time you ate?" I wondered.

"Yes," was all he said, loath to admit to his girlfriend how poorly he'd been taking care of himself.

I took a bit of eggs that seemed positively dainty by comparison. "The complete reorganization of a political system can be difficult for the schedule."

Ethan snorted through his eggs, then coughed his way through a laugh. "Well said, Sentinel. Well said."

"So, back to Peter. He was poisoned. By whom? And why?"

"His beloved's parents, unfortunately."

My eyes widened. I loved a good story—I'd been a literature student, after all—and this one sounded like a doozy. I plucked up a sausage roll and bobbed it at him like a magic wand. "Elaborate."

"Peter was a vampire. He fell in love with a woman who was not."

"Human?"

"Fairy," he said, and I winced, recognizing the drama.

"Yikes."

"Indeed. Cadogan House was situated in Wales at the time, but we'd traveled to Russia. Her name was Anastasia. She was the daughter of fairies of some repute—politicos with connections to Claudia, who was still in Ireland at that time—and who'd gained a title in the Russian aristocracy. Keeping face was very important to them, and they were staunch believers that fairies shouldn't mix with humans or anyone else.

"But Peter was in love," he said, a smile crossing his face. His eyes went slightly vacant, as if he were recalling. "You'd have liked him. He was a man's man. Brawny. Like me, a soldier before he became a vampire. He had a warrior's mentality, and that didn't stop simply because he joined the night brigade, so to speak. He was Welsh, didn't really believe in vowels to speak of. He had a ruddy complexion—more like an Irishman than a Welshman, although he wouldn't even hear of the possibility that there was Irish blood in his veins."

He looked at me again, his gaze sharpening and the corners of his mouth dropping again. "It was a great love," he said. "A big love, and very emotional. Equal parts love and hatred, I think, although neither Peter nor Anastasia would have admitted that. Unfortunately, her parents hated Peter, hated that Anastasia was 'lowering' herself by being with a nonfairy, and a vampire to boot. He was a Master vampire, but he was neither fairy enough nor wealthy enough for their preference."

"So what happened?"

"She wouldn't end the relationship, so her father decided to end it for them. Anastasia had a retainer—a weasel named Evgeni. He was a sneak, a liar, and a murderer. And, unbeknownst to Peter, he was doing her parents' bidding."

"He poisoned Peter," I said, understanding dawning.

Ethan nodded. "Slowly, and over time. Long enough and little enough that the poison accumulated in his heart. By that point, it was equivalent to a staking, although unfortunately a slower process. As it turned out, Evgeni's motivations weren't solely about his hatred of Peter and his sycophancy to Anastasia's father. He was infatuated with her."

My eyes widened. "That's a nasty love triangle."

"Indeed. One evening, after he dosed Peter with what he imagined was the fatal bit of extract, he confronted Anastasia. Whatever the faults of her people, she was very much in love with Peter, and had no interest in Evgeni, who was, frankly, an asshole."

"He sounds like it."

"But he didn't take her rejection seriously; he'd convinced himself Peter had glamoured her, that she wanted Evgeni and Peter was in the way. So when she said no . . ."

"He pushed?"

"And then some. He assaulted her," Ethan said flatly. "Peter heard her scream. By then he was so weak. We thought he'd been cursed by a witch." He laughed mirthlessly. "How silly that seems now."

"Actually, it doesn't. Consider what Mallory did. Also consider the fact that you're here right now because of her magic . . . and you're eating your toast with a fork. Why are you doing that?"

He shrugged. "It's how it's done."

"That's very much *not* how it's done, and I'm pretty sure I've seen you eat toast before."

Ethan was trying to lighten the mood, I realized. Doing something unbelievably pretentious—even for Ethan—and trying to make me laugh. But this story was too sordidly, horribly interesting for me to be distracted by vampiric foibles.

"Anyway," I said, "Peter heard her scream?"

"He ran to her. I rushed into the room just in time to see him pull Evgeni away. Anastasia was petite—a wisp of a thing—but she fought him like a hardened soldier. She just wasn't big enough. . . ." Ethan trailed off, shuddering at the memory. "Weak as he was, Peter was still a vampire. He threw Evgeni across the room, and then he collapsed. Her parents rushed in and thanked Peter for saving their daughter's virtue—Evgeni was a fairy, but his caste was too low for them. A few seconds later, it was over. Peter was gone."

"He turned to ash?"

"Before our eyes. Extract works more slowly than staking. And the worst of it was, there was nothing that could be done in the interim."

"He knew he was dying?" I quietly asked.

Ethan nodded. "And we knew it wasn't a curse. Evgeni forcibly confessed to it, and to Anastasia's parents' role. But Peter's act of saving her seemed enough to sway them. The floor was stone—big chunks of stone with jagged edges. I kneeled there beside him as he passed. My knees ached from it—from kneeling on that cold stone." He looked up at me. "Isn't it odd that I remember such an insignificant thing from so long ago?"

"Memory is a powerful thing," I said. "The pain probably set the memory, sealed it. I bet you remember the smell of the room, too."

Ethan closed his eyes. "Amber," he said. "Anastasia's home always smelled warm and rich. Heady summer roses. Roasted meats. Ale. But mostly amber." He opened them again. "I haven't told that story in a long time. I'm glad I'm telling it to you. It's important that someone know the history, especially since it's being rewritten as we speak."

I reached out and put a hand over his. "I'm really sorry for your loss. Peter sounds like a good friend."

Ethan nodded. "The curse of being immortal, Merit, is watching the passage of those you love—even those who aren't supposed to leave."

We sat quietly for a moment. "What happened to Evgeni?"

His eyes flattened. "He was dispatched."

My blood chilled a bit. "You killed him?"

"I avenged Peter's death and Anastasia's attack. Her father was too cowardly to do it."

That was an effective reminder that Ethan had lived most of his life in another time, a time during which life and death were bargained differently. I wouldn't call him cold, but he had the capacity for detached violence if he believed it was necessary and honorable. Violence he didn't shun, and for which he wouldn't apologize.

"What about Anastasia?"

"I don't know. I lost track of her after Peter passed. As far as I'm aware, her parents went back to insulating her from the world, at least the vampire portion of it."

"They must have been relieved," I said. "I mean, horrifically so, but still."

"They were thrilled, at least as much as fairies will ever show. Two problems addressed at once. The vampire wooing their daughter was dead, as was the fairy who'd attacked her." He crumpled his napkin on the table and crossed his legs. "You've met Claudia," he said. "I take it you're familiar with the fairies' conception of value?"

"They like money and treasure," I said. "They're less big on emotions, including love, at least that they'll admit." Claudia had had an affair with Dominic Tate, Seth Tate's evil twin, and although she'd clearly been infatuated with him, she denied love was anything fairies deigned to involve themselves in.

Ethan nodded. "All true."

"The dragon's egg," I said, suddenly realizing. "Luc said a Russian duchess gave Peter the egg. That they'd 'bonded.' Anastasia's mother was the duchess?"

Ethan smirked. "She was, although I believe his summary changes a bit in each retelling."

"Like a game of 'telephone'?"

He looked at me quizzically. "What's the game 'telephone'?"

"It's a party game," I said. "You sit in a circle, and one person whispers something to the person beside her, and she whispers it to the person beside her, and so on and so on, until the last one tries to guess what the person at the beginning said. The answers are always different after having been passed around."

"Ah," he said. "Then yes. It's very much like that, although Luc's got the gist of it. The egg was a thank-you to Peter from the duchess and her husband for what he did for Anastasia—if a posthumous thank-you. And it was a priceless thank-you, as far as the fairies were concerned."

Priceless not only because of its intrinsic value or its value to the fairies, but because they'd actually *thanked* the vampires, when clearly there was no love lost between them.

"Score one for supernatural relations," I said.

There was a knock at the door, which opened. Helen stepped inside. "The vampires are assembled."

"Thank you, Helen. We'll be with you in a moment."

Helen nodded and exited again, closing the door behind her.

By the time I looked back at Ethan, he was well into Master vampire mode: his expression blank, his shoulders back, his chin authoritatively set. He adjusted the cuffs of his shirt before glancing at me.

"I think you'll enjoy this particular performance, Sentinel," he said.

I wasn't sure exactly what he had in mind, but I wasn't about to doubt him.

And, of course, I took a moment before heading inside to share the evening's most important news in a quick text to Mallory: ETHAN EATS TOAST WITH A FORK.

It took a moment before she responded. DARTH SULLIVAN = PRE-TENTIOUS HOTTIE, she responded.

I really didn't have a reason to disagree with that. But I loved that we were talking again.

The House's ballroom was on the second floor, right beside the House library. It was a beautiful space, with wood floors, high ceilings, and majestic chandeliers that cast golden light around the room, although the nervous magic felt electric enough to illuminate the space on its own.

Michael Donovan stood with Lacey in the back of the room. They chatted together quietly and familiarly, probably having known each other during Lacey's time at Cadogan House. They both glanced at me as I followed Ethan inside. Michael's glance was pleasant; Lacey's was suspicious.

I smiled pleasantly back at both of them—I was a grown-up, after all—as Ethan made his way to the raised dais at the front of the room. Hands in his pockets, he waited until the vampires quieted.

"Good evening," he said. "Thank God it's been quiet here tonight."

The crowd offered a good-natured chuckle. We all knew when to laugh at the boss's jokes. But the tone changed quickly.

"I'm going to dispense with the pleasantries," he said, "and get to the point. Tomorrow, in a ceremony here at midnight, we will exit the GP. The ceremony is not long, but I expect Darius will have no shortage of wisdom to pass along. When the ceremony is complete, our House will no longer be affiliated with the Greenwich Presidium. Nor will we be members of the North American Vampire Registry."

Ethan reached up and touched the gold medal around his neck. "Tomorrow," he said, "we will return our medals to the GP."

There was a cacophony of noise, of fearful shouts and angered outbursts. No one wanted to give up their medals, including myself. The golden disks were our dog tags, our identification, our badges of honor. They marked us as vampires, as Cadogan vampires, as Novitiates of a proud and noble House. They also marked us as members of the NAVR, which was precisely Ethan's point.

"Novitiates!" Ethan yelled out, and the crowd quieted. "We have no choice; nor would I give us any. It is the right and honorable thing to return the badge of the GP's authority over us. But I will be the first." He reached up and unclasped the medal from his neck. He held it in his fist for a moment before dropping it into a box on the dais beside him.

"If we are to do it," he said, "let us do it in solidarity."

Luc was next, then Malik. Then Kelley and Juliet and Helen. One by one, every vampire assembled in the ballroom walked to the podium, pulled the medal from his or her neck, and dropped it into the box at Ethan's feet.

I did the same, sharing a glance with him before I returned to my spot. He nodded, and I slipped back into the crowd.

"We also anticipate the GP will use its contracts with the House to contend it is the rightful owner of some of our assets. Part of that anticipated claim we must honorably accept; another part we will dispute. Regardless, to address our alleged debt, tomorrow we will give a substantial sum to the GP."

He paused while the vampires whispered nervously.

"This House has existed for centuries, and it will continue to do so. But we must tighten our belts. We will live, for the time being, more as humans, and less as vampires with decades upon decades of compound interest. Our assets will be consolidated. Some antiques will be sold. My vehicle, which was admittedly ostentatious, will be returned to the dealership."

There were masculine moans of disappointment from the crowd.

Ethan smiled with understanding and raised a hand to quiet the crowd. "This exercise will prove two things to us. First, that the GP is exactly what we believed it to be: selfish, motivated by fear, and unconcerned about the needs of individual vampires. Second, that we are strong. That we appreciate fine things, but we do not need them to survive. For we are Cadogan vampires."

There were appreciative hoots in the crowd.

"We are, of course, on our way to becoming Rogue vampires, at least of a sort. You may know two of our Rogue brothers and sisters were recently killed. Oliver and Eve were, by all accounts, lovely and caring individuals. Let us take a moment of silence in their memory. And let us hope that we soon can lead the murderer to justice."

The room went silent, even the magic calming as we offered our thoughts to Oliver and Eve.

"There is one more matter to attend to," Ethan said. "Our arguments with respect to the disputed contract provisions may not be strong. But we believe there is one act that will help simplify and solidify our position."

The lights suddenly went out, causing a moment of panic among the vampires, at least until they realized a golden glow emanated from the front of the room.

I moved quietly through the crowd to get a better look.

"Malik," Ethan said. "Come forward, please."

Malik stepped onto the dais holding a small white taper candle. The room was utterly silent but for the soft pops of the flickering flame as we all waited to find out what the hell was going on.

Ethan looked at him. "You're sure?"

"I am."

"You have the paperwork?"

"I do," Malik said, placing the candle on a holder in the dais. He took a folded piece of paper from his lapel pocket, then held a stick of red wax over his candle's flame. Droplets of wax began to bead as the wax melted.

Candlelight casting shadows across his face, Malik looked across at Ethan. "Upon this night, I set my seal upon this page and I relinquish the House to you, my Liege, its only and rightful Master."

We roared into applause and joyous shouts.

Ethan was taking his place again as Master of Cadogan House.

Malik moved the stick of red wax, and it dripped—thick and scarlet and fragrant—onto the paper in his hand. He put down the stick and pulled a handled brass seal from his pocket, pressing it into the wax and making official the act we'd been anticipating for so long.

The deed done, Ethan sighed with what sounded like relief. But even as he did it, his shoulders straightened, as if he'd donned again the mantle of House power and was ready to wield it. This time, my goose bumps were for a completely different reason.

He looked over the ballroom of vampires. *His* vampires. His eyes blazed as they made contact with mine.

"I am alive," he said. "I am alive and well and in good health. The House has been relinquished to me, and I have undertaken its leadership once again. I presume none of you object?"

Once again, the ballroom exploded with applause. The world might end tomorrow, but for tonight, our Master was back, and he was most definitely in charge.

Ethan stayed behind to answer questions from the vampires. Because dawn was rising, I headed upstairs to get ready for bed, and found a message on my phone. It was from Jonah.

"The lighthouse," he said. "Tomorrow night. Nine p.m. Look for the rocks. We'll be there." That was it.

The lighthouse stood in Chicago's main harbor, and provided light for ships seeking safety from Lake Michigan's breaking waves and rocky coastline. The lighthouse helped them find safe passage; now, ironically, it would be a place of reckoning for me.

I sat down on the bed and turned the phone over and over in my hand. As my initiation moved closer, I became even more swamped with guilt, and even less sure I was doing the right thing for the right reasons.

Times were so perilous. We were facing a fundamental change to our identities as vampires, and in the midst of the chaos, I was scampering away to join a rebel organization. And not just that, but an organization I couldn't tell Ethan—or anyone else—about. That didn't exactly make me feel honorable, or honest.

On the other hand, there seemed to be little dispute the RG was going to help the House. I wasn't even a member yet, and they'd already informed us of the GP's asset grab.

The RG was the kind of help we needed.

Stop whining, I warned myself, and sent a response to Jonah.

I'LL BE THERE. AND THANKS FOR THE CONTRACT TIP. YOU MAY HAVE SAVED OUR ASSES.

I put the phone away as the apartment door opened.

I'd made the decision to join the RG a long time ago. But for now, Ethan was home, so I rose to join him. The night would be over soon enough, and the fear would wait for later.

CHAPTER NINE

THE ICY PRECIPICE

Hours later, night fell again as it had so many times before. The sun dropped beneath the horizon, the shutters opened, and vampires awoke.

Tonight we would leave the Greenwich Presidium and strike out on our own.

But as relieved as we were to have the House under the control of a single Master once again, the drone of anxious magic made me feel as if I were standing beneath power lines.

I felt Ethan stir behind me. He was awake, and undoubtedly could feel the magic, as well.

"The House is nervous," I said.

"Hmm. It's a big night."

I struggled for the right words—something that would acknowledge the giant step we were taking but express confidence that he could lead us through it.

Maybe it wasn't what he could say, but what he could do. . . . I sat up and swung my legs over the bed, then glanced back at him, his hair a golden mess around his face. "Let's go for a run."

"A run?"

"For exercise. Around the neighborhood. It will help you burn off some magic."

He arched an eyebrow. "As I'm not currently being chased, I see no need to run."

"No, you have no desire to run. That's different. It'll give you a chance to alleviate some stress."

"Is this about Lacey?"

"It's about the House being on the precipice of something monumental, and your needing to lead them through it. And if they think you're nervous, they'll freak out."

His gaze narrowed. "Are you attempting to manage me, Sentinel?"

I put my hands on my hips and gave him back the same authoritative look he was giving me. "Yes. I am, and according to the House rules, I have that right. Get dressed."

He grumbled, but scooted out of bed, confirming that I was, in fact, the power behind the throne.

It was winter and cold, so I opted for layers. Capri-length leggings. A sports bra, tank, T-shirt, and slim jacket. My shoes were well worn, and it was probably time to find a new pair, but they still had enough bounce to keep me moving.

Ethan wore track pants and layered long-sleeved shirts, and on his wrist was a huge watch.

No, not just a watch: a GPS watch—the kind serious runners use to keep track of their pacing and mileage.

My gaze narrowed. "I thought you hated running. I thought you only ran when chased?"

He smiled slyly. "You once told me you preferred unprocessed foods."

"Touché," I said. "Exactly how badly are you planning to outpace me here?"

"Time will tell."

"Har, har," I mocked, but I was getting nervous.

We walked downstairs in silence, both of us warily eyeing the other, the competition-fueled adrenaline already calming us down. And a calmer Master, I figured, meant a calmer House.

He pressed a button on his watch to start the timer, and then he was gone—already down the steps and running through the gate to the quiet streets of Hyde Park.

"Crap," I muttered, pushing off and bounding down to the sidewalk. Ethan stood one hundred feet away at the corner, one hand on the fence, the other on his hip. It didn't take more than a few seconds to reach him, and he grinned at me as I jogged closer.

"What took you so long?" he asked.

"I gave you a head start. As I've said before, and undoubtedly will again, age before beauty."

Ethan made a decidedly sarcastic sound and pushed off the gate, then lined up beside me on the sidewalk. "Nine miles," he said, then identified the landmarks that would mark our loop around the neighborhood and back to the House again. The trip would be long for humans, but a bit of light exercise for vampires.

"I can only assume you're telling me where to go because you know I'll be out front?"

"Or because I'll completely lap you," he said.

"Does your ego know no bounds?"

Ethan Sullivan, Master of Cadogan House, smiled wickedly and slapped my ass. "Not when it's well deserved. I'm ready when you are, Sentinel."

I didn't give him the opportunity for a faster push-off. "Go!" I yelled, but I was already past him and sprinting feet away toward our first landmark—the church four blocks down the street. Vampires were predators, and we were naturally faster than humans.

But like humans—or cheetahs or lions or any large predators—the superspeed could last only so long.

Ethan let me take the lead, and I took full advantage, pushing myself at a sprinter's pace to get as large a lead as I could. I was lighter, but he was taller and had longer legs. He'd also been running for *centuries*. There seemed little possibility I could outpace him to the end of the race, so I did what I could for now.

It wasn't enough.

He caught up two blocks later, and I risked a glance behind me at the sound of his footfalls. His arms and legs were swinging, every muscle honed and triggered, his form impeccable. If only Olympic races were run at night.

He caught up to me, his breathing barely increased, and jogged beside me. "I believe you cheated, Sentinel."

"Sentinel's prerogative. I'm sure there's a rule in the *Canon* about it."

He made a sound of doubt. "Grateful Condescension requires total obsequiousness to the Master of the House."

"You've been a Master for a matter of mere hours and you're already a cruel despot."

"Hardly, although you are a Sentinel in need of an attitude adjustment."

I opened my mouth, and would have given back the same snark he was giving me, but some silent alarm went off in a marginal part of my psyche.

I slowed to a jog, then a stop, hands on my hips, my breathing still elevated, as I looked around.

Ethan realized something was wrong, stopped. He'd moved a few steps ahead; ever cautious, he walked back to where I stood.

"What is it?"

I scanned the neighborhood, opening all my senses to figure

out what had tripped my trigger. Other than the rasp of our breathing, there were no other unusual sounds. A car door opening up the block. A mewling cat in an alley. The rumble of traffic on nearby avenues. I saw nothing unusual, and even the smells were typical—the cold, smoky scents of a night in the city.

"I don't know. I just had a feeling. Internal alarm bells."

I'd probably have made a sarcastic comment if Ethan had said the same thing to me, but there was no humor in his eyes. I took it as a grave compliment that he trusted I'd sensed something, even if I wasn't sure what it was.

"Instinct is important," he said. "Occasionally the senses detect things the rational mind can't yet analyze."

I reached out and squeezed his hand, moving my body closer to his and pushing him a little farther away from the street and a little closer to the retaining wall that bounded this part of the sidewalk.

Being the good Sentinel, and an Ethan Sullivan trainee, I began to plan. We weren't far from the House, and we could easily run back if necessary, but that would leave both of us more exposed than I liked. A phone call to Luc, asking him to pick us up, would be safer, but I didn't want to give myself over to an agoraphobic fear without some kind of evidence.

"Merit?" Ethan asked.

"I hate to pull rank," I told him, "but I'm playing Sentinel, and I'm getting you back to the House in one piece. And without argument. Stay at my side."

"Yes, ma'am," he said, and I was pretty sure he meant it lasciviously.

"Keep jogging to the end of the block. Human pace. And no showy stuff."

He grunted with disdain at the idea of dialing back his effort, but complied. We made a slow and silent jog toward the end of the block . . . and that was when I heard it.

The slow scratch of tires on gravel.

Hear it? I asked Ethan, activating our silent link. *Car behind us, seven o'clock?*

American, by the sound of it. Strong engine.

Of course that would be your contribution, I kidded to ease the tension. *Slow down just a smidge.*

We slapped back a gear, moving with less speed, our feet barely lifting off the ground. A slow jog for humans, barely a shuffle for healthy vampires.

And still, the vehicle crept forward. I hadn't yet seen it, but I could hear it behind us. Moving as we moved, tracking our speed. But was this friend or foe?

Was this someone who watched us, wanted to speak with us . . . or wanted to end us?

On three, stay where you are. I'm going to make a move.

You'll be careful?

Liege, I parroted back, using one of his favorite phrases, *I'm immortal.*

One, I silently said. I squeezed his hand for luck. *Get a look at the license plate if you can.*

Ethan nodded. *Two*, he silently said.

Three, we said together, and I bolted.

I darted to the street. The car, half a block back, caught me in its headlights and came to a squealing stop. I couldn't see the car for the lights, but it was high enough that I could tell it wasn't a sedan or convertible, more like a truck or SUV.

For a moment, we faced each other.

The vehicle revved its engine, and I stared it down with feigned bravado—because my heart was beating like a timpani drum.

We could stand here all night, but I wasn't going to learn anything about this threat—if it was a threat—unless I made a move.

One hand on my hip, I crooked a finger at the car, daring the driver to move forward.

The driver took the dare.

With the squeal of rubber on the road, the driver mashed the accelerator and pushed forward. I squeezed my fingers into fists, even as my heart thudded beneath my chest, willing myself to stay where I was until the vehicle was closer, until I had a chance to catch sight of the driver. But it was dark, the windows were tinted, and the glare was too much to see through.

With only nanoseconds and a few millimeters to spare, I half turned and flipped backward, barely moving out of the way in time. I'd have sworn I felt the slickness of the vehicle's clear coat beneath my toes as we passed each other.

I hit the ground in a crouch and turned back to stare after the car.

It was a black SUV. No plates. We'd seen similar vehicles before; McKetrick's thugs had driven them when he'd confronted us in the past.

I nearly jumped when Ethan put a hand on my arm. "You're all right?" He scanned my eyes.

"I'm fine. It wasn't even close," I lied. "But I couldn't see the driver. Did you see anything?"

"Nothing at all."

"Weird. Why get this close without taking action?"

"Maybe they're watching us," Ethan said darkly, which was somehow even more disturbing.

"For what purpose?"

"I'm not sure," he said, obvious concern in his voice. "Let's get back to the House."

I wasn't about to argue with that.

When we walked into the foyer, Malik stood beside the door, awaiting our return. Ethan must have signaled him telepathically.

"You're all right?" he asked, his gaze shifting between us; he must have sensed the spill of magic.

"We were followed by a black SUV. No clue who it was or what he or she was after. The vehicle drove off when Merit confronted them."

Malik looked at me. "Merit confronted them?"

"I approached; they left."

"Any word yet from the GP?" Ethan asked.

Malik shook his head. "They've been completely incommunicado. I presume they'll be here when it's time for the ceremony, but they haven't reached out."

"Is it just me, or is that completely unlike them?" I asked, glancing between them. "Why bother to get here early if they aren't going to use the time to harass us?"

Ethan nodded. "Unfortunately, I tend to agree. And a bit of last-minute drama isn't out of the question." He glanced at Malik. "I'm going to head up and take a shower. Please tell Luc about the SUV, and let's warn the House in the event they're still out there."

Not exactly the most comforting of thoughts.

I was also grungy from the run, so I grabbed a shower as soon as Ethan was finished and climbed into my leathers, as I had no idea what the night might bring.

I pulled my hair into a ponytail and touched the hollow of my neck where my Cadogan medal formerly would have rested.

I'd given back the medal I'd been wearing during last night's ceremony. But that was only one of the two I owned. The first I'd been given had been stolen, and I'd eventually gotten it back. Last night's medal had been the replacement; the original sat in a small box in the bottom of my nightstand in Ethan's room. Because I hadn't been wearing it last night, I hadn't had an opportunity to give it back.

But now that I remembered, I still didn't offer it up. I wasn't going to wear it; that seemed dishonest, especially when all my fellow vampires had given up their own. But this medal had been stolen and returned by Seth Tate, and I had no idea what magic he'd done while he'd had it. Maybe nothing; maybe wicked acts.

The medal would stay in its box, at least until I was sure one way or the other.

By the time I was ready to go, Ethan was dressed as well, in a perfectly fitted suit. Every molecule of clothing on his body was bespoke and perfect, from the slacks that ran the length of his long legs to the suit jacket that fit his shoulders as if it had been hand-sewn for him by an elderly European gentleman with small needles and thick chalk.

Come to think of it, I bet that was exactly how it had been made.

Whatever its origins, he looked sharp. He looked in charge, and every bit the Master of the House.

"Do you need anything for the GP ceremony?"

"No," he said. "One night without drama would be appreciated, but that seems unlikely in the near term."

I hardened my heart against the half lie I was about to tell—or at least the substantial omission. "Since we've got a bit of time before the ceremony, and unless you need me here, I'd like to check in about the murders. I might visit my grandfather, see if they've learned anything. It bothers me that we still don't have a lead, especially when we gave our word to Noah. Plus, I'm stressed about the murders and the GP"—*and the other thing I'm not supposed to be telling you about*, I silently thought—"and my grandfather usually offers me Oreos. I like a good Oreo now and again."

"Is there anything you won't do for food?"

I struck a pose with a hand on one cocked hip, and grinned at him with lowered lids. "It depends on the food."

His gaze was appreciative. "I'm not sure if we're discussing food or innuendo. Either way, this may be the best conversation we've ever had."

I walked over and pressed my lips to his, lingering a moment longer than I might have, basking in the moment.

The moment before everything changed.

Before I swore allegiance to the Red Guard.

Before he pulled the House's allegiance to the Greenwich Presidium.

Ethan tilted his head at me. "You're all right?"

"Nervous," I said honestly. "Big night."

He made a vague sound of agreement. "One of the biggest. And we'll see what comes of it."

Before the night was through, I was sure we would.

I had some time before the ceremony, and I did intend to make good on my promise to visit my grandfather. Or at least check in with him before my visit to the lighthouse.

Thinking blood and food were in order before I headed downstairs, I walked down the hallway to the kitchen to grab a snack.

There were bagels on the counter, but Margot had skipped the cream cheese, probably as a cost-cutting measure.

I'd just tucked one into a napkin and pulled a bottle of

Blood4You from the fridge when Lacey stepped into the kitchen. Once again, she wore skinny jeans, and she'd paired them with a trendy striped top and boots.

With no acknowledgment of me other than the mild glance she offered in my direction, she walked to the fridge and grabbed a bottle of very expensive water. Only the best for the best, I supposed.

She shut the door, then leaned back against it. "I've heard you two are seeing each other."

No need to ask whom she meant. I glanced back at her. "We are."

"You aren't good for him."

I'd been heading for the door—hoping to avoid any drama and hit the road—when I stopped short. "Excuse me?"

"You aren't what he needs."

Anger bit me with a sharp ferocity. "And what is that, exactly?"

"Not just a tool. Not just a fist. The House is precarious; although I've got my own House now, don't doubt my love for Cadogan. This place is in my blood. It's where I was made, and I'll be damned if I'll let you run it—and him—into the ground. You're the reason this House is leaving the GP. If it falters, that's on you."

I managed to form words, which was more than I would have thought possible given my anger. "My relationship—his relationship—is really none of your business."

"It is my business," she countered. "This House is my business, and the Master who made me is my business."

Master or not, she was pissing me off. "Your business is in San Diego. You left this House and Ethan when you went there. I don't appreciate your poaching on what is, quite clearly, my territory."

Before she could answer, two other Cadogan vampires—Christine and Michelle—both in workout clothes, walked into the kitchen. They waved at me and said polite hellos to Lacey—

Grateful Condescension, I supposed—before grabbing sports drinks from the fridge and bananas from a bowl on the counter.

They said nothing more to either of us, but their heads were bowed together as they left; they were undoubtedly chatting about the kitchen encounter between Ethan's lover and his lover-in-waiting. I didn't even try to catch their whispers; I wasn't sure I wanted to know what they were saying . . . mostly for fear that they were right.

She moved a step closer. "Suppose you're correct. Suppose it isn't my business whom he dates. Suppose it's yours. Then maybe you should think long and hard about the kind of vampire he deserves. Are you that girl? Or does he deserve someone better? Someone loyal and true?"

"Someone blond?" I dryly asked. "Someone exactly like you, perhaps?"

My phone rang. Fearing another crisis, I whipped it from the pocket of my jacket. It was Jonah, probably calling to ensure I'd show up at the initiation. I turned off the phone and put it away again, but not before Lacey watched me with obvious curiosity.

"Are we keeping you from something?"

"I'm trying to solve a double murder," I reminded her. "Just checking in."

She smiled a little. "I have plenty of decades under my belt, Merit. Decades of having worked with him, watched him, known him. You think, what, eight months of being fanged is going to tell you what you need to know about a Master vampire? About what an immortal needs?" She arched her eyebrow in a perfect imitation of Ethan. "You're a child to him. A momentary interest."

If Lacey was working to make me even more insecure—to plant the seeds of doubt—she was doing a damned good job of it.

"Leave me alone," I said, my anger growing.

"No problem." She walked to the kitchen door. "Just remember, I don't trust you, and I'm keeping an eye out."

"What a witch," I muttered when she was gone, but I stood there in the kitchen for a moment, my hands shaking with vaulted anger. Was she right? Was I nothing more than a liability to Ethan?

No, I thought. He loved me, and he knew better than anyone what was or wasn't right for him and the House. He was a grown-up, by God. It wasn't like I'd somehow teased him into a relationship.

I snapped off the bottle cap and chugged the bottle of blood as I stood there, until the gremlin inside me quieted down again.

I presumed her plan was to make me crazy. To make me uncertain about our relationship until I drove Ethan crazy from neediness . . . or ended the relationship to "save" him.

Lacey had once called me a "common soldier," but she'd confused soldiering and martyrdom. My job was to stand strong for my House and my Master, not give myself away like a wilting violet because I was afraid I'd ruin him.

I wouldn't ruin him. Just as I'd told him before when he needed to be reminded, we were stronger together than we were apart. Two souls different from the rest who'd found solace in each other.

She couldn't take that away from us.

At least, I hoped she couldn't.

My mood soured and my nerves even more jangled, I walked downstairs to the Ops Room. Everyone but Juliet was in the room; it was her night for patrol, I guessed. Luc, now officially entrenched as Guard Captain again, sat at the head of the table, just as he usually did.

Lindsey's gaze found me when I walked into the room, and the question in her eyes was easy to read: *What's Merit's emotional state now that Lacey has spent an evening in the House?*

Since she was highly empathic, I didn't feel a need to inform her.

"Sentinel," Luc greeted me. "Glad to see you're here without your panties in an obvious twist."

"They're getting there," I said ominously. "Any word from the Ombud's office?"

"Not a lick. We thought we'd wait for you and give Jeff a call."

I sat down at the conference table. "Thanks. Let's do it."

Luc nodded and leaned over the table to the conference phone, where he hit the second speed-dial option.

"Who's number one?" I wondered.

"Saul's Pizza," Lindsey said. "You've ruined us for all other deep-dish."

Damn straight, I thought. Saul's was my favorite deep-dish joint in Chicago, a little hole-in-the-wall in Wicker Park, near Mallory's brownstone. I'd introduced it to the House.

"This is Jeff," Jeff answered appropriately.

I linked my fingers together as Lindsey moved the whiteboard closer. "Hey, Jeff. It's Merit in the Ops Room, on speakerphone as per usual."

"I've got an update. Which do you want first? Good news or bad news?"

"Bad news."

"The glass from the alley is a dead end. It's safety glass from the side window of a passenger vehicle. Could have been dozens of models, so it doesn't really tell us anything."

Bummer, but not entirely surprising. Lindsey erased GLASS from the whiteboard, and I suddenly felt I was playing a game show in which the prizes were disappearing with each wrong answer.

"What else did you find?" I asked.

"We checked out Oliver's and Eve's backgrounds. Nothing pops there. No arguments with neighbors, no personal feuds, no money problems. If the killer picked them for a reason, it's not obvious to us. But I'll send you the documents in case you want to review them."

Luc leaned forward. "That would be great, Jeff. Thanks. We've got a security consult in for the transition. Maybe we'll have him take a look."

"They're on their way. And now for the good news," Jeff said. "I was checking out satellite images of the registration center. Turns out there's a bank across the street. And banks have lots of security."

I crossed my fingers. "Tell me there's video, Jeff."

"There's video," he confirmed. "But not much of it. I'll send it to you."

By the time Luc had dabbled with his touch screen, it was already registering receipt of a new file. He hit the "play" button.

The video was grainy and dark, and it stuttered along more like time-lapse photography than film, but the setting was right. The shot was focused on the spot directly in front of the bank's ATM machine, but it caught the edge of the registration center across the street and the alley next to it.

"What's the timing?" Luc asked.

"This starts eight minutes before Oliver and Eve show up. Now, ignore the guy at the ATM, and watch the alley."

The guy at the ATM was broad shouldered and dark skinned, and he wore green scrubs as he cheerfully pulled cash from the ATM. He was easy on the eyes, but Jeff was right; the action was behind him.

Traffic rolled past the registration center across the street.

Some of the cars pulled to the curb, where vampires spilled out to get into the line gathered outside the door.

"There they are," Luc said, pointing as Oliver and Eve hopped out of a car not far from the ATM and walked across the street, hand in hand. The car took off again.

My heart clutched. I wanted to urge them back into the car, and felt utterly powerless watching them walk into danger . . . and that much more determined to find their killer.

Oliver and Eve joined the line with the rest of the vampires. The focus at that distance was pretty awful, the queue looking more like a snake of pixels than a distinguishable line of vampires.

"Keep an eye on the next car up," Jeff said.

"Watching," Luc absently said, eyes glued to the screen. And he wasn't the only one. Every vampire in the Ops Room stared at the screen as a large, dark SUV drove past the registration center.

No—not drove. It *cruised* past the registration center, barely moving, as if scoping out the center and the line in front.

"That could be the same vehicle that followed us this evening."

"You were followed?" Jeff asked.

I nodded. "Yeah. Ethan and I went for a run. A black SUV followed us, then drove away in a hurry when we moved closer."

The SUV in the video moved out of view before backing up into the alley, its headlights shining out from the darkness just as the doorman had explained.

"And we have a car in the alley," I quietly said.

We squinted at the screen, watching as the headlights flashed a couple of times and figures—pixilated blobs—moved toward the car.

I knew instinctively who the blobs were: Oliver and Eve, heading for the alley and the SUV that had parked there. The video was silent; maybe they'd heard something in the alley we couldn't pick up.

But before we could see what happened next, a large gray armored car crept into the frame, parking directly in front of the bank and blocking the view of everything else.

I began shooing the screen. "Get out of the way! Get out of the way!"

The video stopped.

"The armored car sits there for forty-five minutes," Jeff said. "By the time it leaves . . ."

"Everything's over," I finished.

"Exactly."

The Ops Room was quiet for a moment. "Whoever was in the SUV lured them into the alley," Luc concluded.

"That's exactly what happened," Jeff said. "Marjorie talked to one of the staff members in the registration office. Gal named Shirley Jackson—she's worked for the city for two decades—who got transferred to the office when it opened. Turns out, her desk is next to the front window. She remembered hearing some kind of engine noise from the alley, like a car had trouble starting. She saw a couple—a 'nice-looking couple'—walk past the window. She didn't remember seeing them again, but said she didn't think anything of it."

"Nor would she have," Luc said. "You hear engine trouble, but someone goes to help and the sound disappears? You figure some Samaritans offered their assistance, and the problem was fixed."

"Yeah," I said. "But unfortunately wrong this time. Oliver and Eve were lured into the alley. The SUV faked some kind of car trouble, and Oliver and Eve went to help. And they were killed because of it."

I shuddered, wondering if that's what had been in store for me and Ethan on our run.

"And that's why Jeff found nothing in their backgrounds," Luc said. "The killer probably wasn't targeting Oliver and Eve specifically. He was targeting people outside the registration center. He was cruising for prey."

"For vampires," I clarified. "He was outside a registration center, so he was targeting vampires."

"And the car you saw tonight?" Luc asked.

"Maybe cruising the House, looking for vampires?" I suggested. "Ethan and I happened to be the ones on the street. Maybe he was hoping for a more subtle approach, which is why he drove off when we got closer."

Luc shrugged. "Hard to say."

"Thank you for the update, Jeff," I said.

"Sure thing. We'll keep looking on our end. I'm going to dig through the video a bit, see if that SUV makes another appearance."

"Good plan," Luc said. "We'll be in touch."

He clicked off the speakerphone and the video, and I looked back at the whiteboard. While the video had rolled, Lindsey had filled out the whiteboard with key bits of data. OLIVER AND EVE. ROGUES. TAKEN AT REGISTRATION CENTER BY SUV. KILLED IN WAREHOUSE.

A time line of murder, of sociopathic violence. But what did it mean?

I cast a glance at the clock on the wall. The hours were ticking down, and it was time to hit the road for the lighthouse. I steeled myself for my next omission of the evening, which was extra tricky, since there was a vampire with strong psychic abilities, Lindsey, in the room.

I rose and stuffed my hands into my pockets. "I think I'm going to go for a drive. I need some fresh air."

Luc nodded. "It's good for you. It'll help you process this, maybe make a connection."

I nodded, casting a slight glance at Lindsey to see if she'd caught a whiff of anything unusual. But if she had, I couldn't see it in her face.

"You'll be back for the ceremony, I presume?" Luc asked, tone dripping with sarcasm.

"I wouldn't miss it for the world." Much like taxes, if not death, it was unavoidable.

CHAPTER TEN

GOLD MEMBER, RED GUARD

I slipped out of the gate and jogged to my car, and before anyone was the wiser, I was zooming away into the night, ready to reaffirm my commitment to the RG.

The drive wasn't comfortable. My stomach was still raw with nerves, and I was discomfited by the fear that I was betraying Ethan all over again.

But how could acting in the House's best interest be a betrayal?

Per Jonah's instructions, I drove toward Lake Michigan, then headed north to the marina at the edge of the harbor.

It was December, and the marina had long since closed for the season. A security booth marked the entrance, and a black-and-yellow-striped bar kept cars from driving in.

Not entirely sure how to proceed, I drove up to the security gate and cranked down the window. The woman who sat inside looked me over, then pressed a button to lift the gate.

A friend of Jonah's, perhaps? Or the Red Guard's?

I got out of the car and zipped up my jacket, then glanced

around. The small parking lot was virtually empty except for a few cars scattered here and there.

The lake was dark and quiet, filled with ice even in the unseasonably warm temperatures.

A line of concrete and rocks led away from the pier and into the water, forming a harbor for boats and leading to the harbor lighthouse, which flashed its warning across the water.

I took a long, hard look at the boulders and concrete blocks that made up the harbor wall. They were large, icy, and, by the looks of them, treacherous. Then again, they'd been placed in the harbor to provide protection for boats, not to provide a winter path for vampires.

"This had better be worth it," I muttered. Arms extended, I began to pick my way across the rocks.

I'd danced ballet for many years, and that certainly helped me keep my balance. But the leather soles of my boots weren't made for slick rocks, and I was only ten feet into the journey when I lost traction. I went down on my knees, which sent a shock of pain right up my spine.

"Mother lover," I muttered, wincing there on my knees for a moment, waiting for the pain to subside. When it felt slightly less like someone had taken a mallet to my kneecaps, I rose and continued the journey.

After a few minutes of half walking, half crawling, I reached the ladder that led up to the concrete platform surrounding the lighthouse.

"You made it."

The words, quietly spoken, seemed tremendously loud in the silence of the lake. I glanced up.

Jonah stood at the top of the ladder, hands tucked into the pockets of a black, calf-length wool coat. He wore jeans and boots beneath it, and his auburn hair swirled around his face in the wind. His cheeks, honed like sculpted marble, were pink from the cold.

"Merit." He gestured me up, and I climbed the ladder—which was cold, rusting, and rickety—hand over hand until I reached the platform at the top. Jonah helped me scoot onto the platform.

"Nice location," I said, stuffing my hands into my pockets against the chill. It was colder on the water, with no protection from the wind or elements.

He smiled at me, Buddha-like in his calm. "The RG path isn't easy, and that lesson shouldn't be forgotten."

"My knees will remember," I assured him.

We looked at each other for a moment, magic and memory sparking between us.

Jonah and I had complementary magic—magic that operated on a similar frequency. A supernatural kinship, of a sort. He'd also once confessed that he'd had feelings for me, but had gracefully withdrawn when I'd told him of my feelings for Ethan.

Now we were partners, and we were about to make that official. Ironically, only hours before Cadogan's political breakup with the GP.

"Let's go inside," he said.

"Inside?" I hadn't imagined I'd be out here on the lighthouse platform, much less actually going inside it. It excited the nerd in me.

"Membership has its privileges," Jonah said, as I followed him around the platform to a red wooden door on the other side. He flipped aside a brass plate that looked like a doorbell, revealing a small scanner. He pressed his thumb to it, and the door unlocked with an audible thump.

"Fancy," I said.

"Only the best at RG headquarters."

"This is RG headquarters?"

"It is," he said, closing the door behind me as I took a look around. The building consisted of two small rooms that flanked the central lighthouse like bookends . . . or something decidedly more genital. The floors were tile, and all the walls were marked by windows with views of the water or the city. The decor was sparse and probably last updated in the 1970s. A spiral staircase split the middle of the room in half and led, I presumed, up to the actual light.

"Well, such as it is," he said.

"So this is what the inside of a lighthouse looks like."

"At least in 1979, when this place was last staffed," Jonah said.

"That explains the faux wood and brass."

"Yeah," he agreed. "It's not like we've filled it up with equipment, so I guess it's more of a safe house than a headquarters. But it serves its purpose. Excuse me a minute." He walked to the spiral staircase, put a hand on the rail, and called up the stairs, "We're here! Come on down."

With a cacophony of shoes on metal treads, eight men and women came down the stairs, most wearing some version of Midnight High School gear. MHS was the unofficial (and secret) calling card of RG members.

Jonah joined me again, and the group assembled in front of us. A few of them looked familiar; I'd probably seen their faces in crowds at events the RG had seeded with members.

One of them looked more specifically familiar. Horace, the Civil War veteran from the warehouse, stood beside a shorter, curly-haired girl with dark skin and smiling eyes. He still wore antique-looking clothes; she favored Converses and jeans, which made me like her immediately. Their hands were intertwined, their feet just touching as they stood beside each other.

They gave off a good vibe, and they weren't the only ones. All eight of the members stood together in pairs, presumably by partners. Another of the couples held hands, and from the closeness of their bodies, it was clear they weren't just being friendly.

Jonah had once confessed he'd had feelings for me. Seeing these vampires together, I wasn't sure which had come first—whether RG members had sought out their partners because of their skills and the romance had followed, or romantically intertwined couples simply made good RG spies. Whatever the reason, there seemed to be more than just business between the partners. And here Jonah and I were, the only noncouple in the group of obvious couples.

Awkwardness growing, I gnawed my lip.

"Everybody," Jonah said, "this is Merit. You've got a big evening yet," he said to me, "so we'll save the formal introductions for another time. Suffice it to say, these are Chicago's Red Guards."

I waved a little weakly as my heart thudded uncomfortably. Jonah had bowed out when he'd learned I was in love with Ethan . . . or had he? Was he holding onto hope that we'd somehow end up together? Because as far as I was concerned, and much like Lacey and Ethan, that just wasn't in the cards.

That would be such an uncomfortable discussion, but there was no way around it. There was no way to avoid the issue, not if I was going to fully commit. To put it frankly: I could commit to the RG. I could commit to Jonah as my RG partner. But I'd already committed my heart to Ethan, and I wanted to make that crystal clear.

I turned to him. "Could I speak to you for a moment? In private?"

Jonah smiled a little, as if he'd been anticipating the request. "Of course."

He shifted his gaze to the vampires behind us. "All right, show's over."

There were good-natured grumbles, but every vampire made a polite good-bye to me and Jonah before they headed up the spiral staircase or out the door.

He waited until we were alone before looking at me again. "I'm not propositioning you."

I felt simultaneous embarrassment and relief, and my cheeks flamed hot enough to light up the room.

"I know. I mean, I didn't think you were. I just . . ." I cleared my throat, the sound just as awkward as the moment. "I just want you to know where I am."

"I know where you are," he said. "It's not unheard-of for RG partners to become romantically involved. We call it the *Moonlighting* effect."

I arched a very Ethan-esque eyebrow. "From the TV show?"

"Yeah. For the years of their membership, they work together, often undercover. You don't sign up to be someone's partner if you don't have a rapport." He pointed at me, then himself. "We have a rapport. But it doesn't have to be romantic."

"You're sure?"

"Yes, Merit," he said with a smile. "It's not all about you."

I rolled my eyes, glad we were back to sarcasm. Sarcasm was definitely within my comfort zone.

"So we're good?" he asked.

"We're good."

Jonah nodded. "Then let's get this ceremony started."

"You don't want to invite the rest of them back in?"

He shook his head. "We're partners. This part's just for us."

Jonah picked up a wooden box from a table beneath one of the windows. The wood was deep and red, and from the faint tingling

in my hands, I guessed it held steel. It was an aftereffect of the
tempering of my own sword: My blade had been tempered with
my blood, and as a result I had a sensitivity to metal.

Jonah lifted the lid. Inside, nestled on a piece of crimson vel-
vet, was a striking dagger. Made from a single piece of gleaming
steel, the blade was twisted from its base to tip, creating three hundred and sixty degrees of deadly.

"That's beautiful," I said.

"Hold that thought," he said with a small smile. He held the
blade up, letting the light slink down the steel like a trailing ribbon.

"We walk a knife's edge between worlds—vampires and
Houses—and rarely feel fully a part of either. We see things most
vampires prefer to ignore, but that knowledge gives us power. It is a
curse and our greatest weapon. It can be cruel, and it can set us free.

"As a member of the Red Guard, you stand for honor, not pride.
You stand for vampires, not associations. You stand for those who
cannot speak for themselves, and for honoring what we are."

Jonah touched the point of the blade, pricking his finger. A
droplet of blood appeared there, sending a sweet, metallic scent
into the air.

"You stand for me," he said. "And I stand for you."

He swept the droplet across the curve of the blade, which
shimmered from the magic of spilled vampire blood, just like my
sword had done.

"Your turn," he said.

Cringing in anticipation of the pain, I pricked my finger, as
well, then touched my fingertip to the blade. The dagger, already
marked with Jonah's blood and magic, glowed faintly red.

"May this blade never spill your blood or mine again," he said.
"And may the steel always remind us of the strength of friendship,
of honor, and of loyalty to our comrades."

He looked at me. "Do you swear your loyalty to vampires, irrespective of House, irrespective of allies, irrespective of affiliation? Do you swear to be a guardian of order, fairness, and moderation, and to rise up against any authority that threatens those who cannot defend themselves?"

I swallowed hard, knowing that this was the moment. This was my final chance to say no to the Red Guard . . . or to commit myself to two decades of service.

The calling was honorable, and my choice was clear.

"I swear," I said, knowing that I had made the right choice.

He reached out and kissed me on the cheek, a peck that was unquestionably collegial, but still carried the magical spark. "In that case, we're partners, and you're stuck with me, kid."

I smiled at him. "I'll do my best. Not that I could do much worse than the GP right now."

"Truth," he said.

He put the box and the knife back on the table, then pulled open a drawer and reached inside. "There's one more thing," he said, handing me a small silver coin.

It was about the size of a quarter, and it was engraved with the image of a man on a horse and the caption SAINT GEORGE.

"Saint George?" I asked.

"The patron saint of warriors," Jonah said. "We've adopted him for the RG, too. It's a token, a reminder that you aren't alone, and there are more of us out here willing to help."

"Thank you," I said, and tucked the medal into my pocket.

"You know, your life is about to get a lot more complicated."

"Oh, good," I said lightly. "I was getting bored with the status quo."

"Yeah, it seemed that way. I'm actually rescuing you from tedium and despair."

"I haven't seen tedium since I became a vampire."

"Well, it's certainly not going to start now." He put a hand on my arm. "I know it feels overwhelming, but you can do this."

I nodded, and let him have confidence for both of us.

"Let's get you back to the House. Ethan would throw a fit if you were late for the ceremony."

"Lake Michigan isn't large enough to hold the fit he would throw."

"We're done," he called out, and there were hoots of pleasure from the vampires who'd gone upstairs.

We walked back outside, and he closed the door and tugged the doorknob to ensure it was locked. I looked out across the harbor and the twinkling lights of Streeterville.

"Jonah, of all the places in this city, all the spots you could have put a safe house, why here?"

"Listen," he said quietly.

We stood in a narrow outcropping of concrete and rock two hundred feet into Lake Michigan; the world was quiet here, even the lap of waves all but silenced by the water's freezing. There were no distractions. Nothing but quiet and stillness and winter's chill.

"Ah," I said. "The seclusion."

Jonah nodded and smiled a little, as if I'd correctly answered. "It's the nature of our positions that sometimes we're forced to be too involved in the world. This is our little respite. If you need solace or shelter, or you can't find me, come here. You can find help. Oh, and there's one more thing: I've got something for you in my car."

I was curious what that might be, but the walk back took all my concentration. Carefully, we retraversed the stones back to his car, where he dug into his backseat, finally pulling out a glossy paper bag, which he handed to me.

"What's this?"

"Swag," he said.

Eyebrow raised suspiciously, I peeked inside the bag. Inside were Midnight High School T-shirts in two colors, a hoodie, and a windbreaker featuring the MHS mascot, a spider.

I closed the bag and looked at him. I did have one problem in regard to swag.

"What?" he asked.

I figured I might as well be honest with him; he was my partner, after all. "I'm living with Ethan."

Jonah opened his mouth and closed it again. "Ah. I see."

"Yeah. So I have to be careful. Really careful."

"The Lake Michigan–sized fit and all. Yeah. That's part of the RG cost. The benefit, of course, is that the world is a better, safer place."

"Of course."

"While we're here, any developments regarding Oliver and Eve?"

"There are, as it turns out," I said, and quickly filled him in.

"What's your next step?" he asked.

"Honestly, I'm not really sure. I think we're at a dead end unless Jeff comes up with something else."

He nodded and climbed into his car. "He'll come up with something. Keep me posted."

I gave him a little wave as he drove away, then climbed into my car and let it warm up for a moment before pulling out of the parking lot and back into my life.

By the time I arrived at the House, we were minutes away from the GP ceremony. Bag in hand, I climbed out of the car, but then stopped to think.

Taking a bag of RG swag into the House might not be the best idea; the House was chaotic enough without adding more drama. I unlocked the trunk of my car and stuffed the bag into it, somewhere between the padded gloves I'd used twice for a kickboxing class, the blanket I kept for winter emergencies, and the emergency road kit that hadn't been opened in all the years I'd had the car.

A car squealed to a stop in front of me, parking parallel.

I put a hand on my sword, but it was Lacey who got out of the car. Still tall, still blond, still effortlessly attractive. She slammed her door shut, and then began walking toward my Volvo.

And she looked very, very happy.

"Well, well, well," she said as she approached. "I guess we all have our secrets, don't we?"

My heart fell into my stomach. *Oh, God,* was the only coherent thought I could manage. What had she seen?

"Our secrets?" I asked, slamming the trunk shut before she came around the car.

She walked around and leaned against the car, a hip against the metal, then crossed her arms and leaned forward just a smidge.

"I know where you were," she said. "I know where you were, who you were with, and what you were doing."

I felt sick with panic. She'd seen me and Jonah, and she knew about the RG. But there was no turning back. I could only hope against hope that she didn't yet know why I'd been there.

Keep bluffing. "I don't know what you're talking about."

"You know damn well. I saw you in the parking lot. I saw you with *him*."

My anger sprouted quickly. "Did you *follow* me?"

"I'm keeping an eye out for my Master and his House."

"Your Master does just fine on his own, and his House is in good hands."

"That's not how it looked to me. And I can't decide which betrayal I find more disturbing—that you're betraying him for Jonah, or that you're doing it tonight, one of the most important of his very long life."

I swallowed down a burst of guilt and fear that she was correct. But I bluffed just as I'd been taught to do.

"I'm betraying no one," I said. "You have no idea what you're talking about."

"Really?" she said with a cunning smile. "Great. Then let's go talk to him about it right now and clear the air, right before the GP ceremony. You truly have excellent timing."

"Maybe you could mind your own business."

"Maybe you could stop screwing around with things you don't understand." Her voice was suddenly fierce, suddenly ferocious, and I stared back at her. I knew she had feelings for Ethan, but even if she was jealous, this seemed like a lot of emotion to be mere jealousy.

"I understand everything, and very well, thank you. He took a stake for me. I mourned for him."

She barked out a laugh. "Ha! You mourned for him? You, who'd known him for a matter of months before he died? You think you have any idea what grief is like?" She pointed at me. "You failed to protect him. You were his Sentinel, and you failed, and he died. It's only by a freak magical accident that he's alive again, no thanks to you."

"Is that what you think happened? You think I was standing around, shooting the shit with the mayor, and I let Ethan get staked?"

"You were there," she said. "That's all I know."

God, she sounded just like Seth Tate, blaming me for what had gone on in that room, even though I'd been an innocent bystander.

Was this grief? The pent-up emotions she'd had to face when

Ethan had died? Anger that he hadn't come crawling to her when he'd been resurrected? Whatever the cause, it was deeply felt, and strong enough to drive her to spy on me.

"He took a stake for me," I said. "Celina threw a stake at me, and he stepped in front of it. He saved me from that. How dare you minimize what he did."

She pointed at me, her eyes hot with anger. "You are a damned liar."

"I am not a liar."

She must have caught the truth in my face, because her expression fell, and for a moment she looked like a sad human being, a girl who'd been dumped. She looked vulnerable and a little pathetic, and my heart ached for her. Not a lot, but still.

She'd had feelings for Ethan, and had assumed facts about their relationship and what she meant to him—and more important, what I meant to him. And if I was right, I'd proven her seriously wrong. Lacey didn't seem like the type who liked being wrong.

She sniffed delicately, and then, like she'd flipped a switch— and as if she hadn't lost her composure in front of me—she was back to cool, calm, and collected again.

Well, I could play calm and collected, too. If she really thought she had something, she'd take it to Ethan right now, the GP be damned. But she didn't know what she'd seen, not exactly. She knew only that I'd met Jonah in a parking lot. She didn't know that I'd met him because of the RG and because I'd just been initiated as a member.

"You'll tell him," she said.

"There's nothing to tell."

"You'll tell him, or I will." She took a step closer. "How dare you preach to me about the sacrifices he's willing to make for you when you won't give him the truth."

Unfortunately, she had a point there, one that made my stomach curl.

"Tell him," she reiterated, her lips curving into a slow and eerie smile. "Tell him, or give me the satisfaction of proving what I've known all along. Just how common you really, truly are," she whispered, her words falling like poison. "You have twenty-four hours."

And then she turned and walked away, her heels clicking as she strode down the sidewalk again and toward the House.

I stood there, my stomach in knots, trying to think what to do.

Regardless, I was pretty sure I was screwed.

Heart thudding, I walked back into the House, cold sweat blooming on my skin. The House was aflutter, and so was I. I needed time to compose myself, so I ran up the stairs to my second-floor room, the one I wasn't sharing with Ethan, unlocked the door, and locked myself in again.

I ripped off my jacket, dumped it on the floor, and headed for the bathroom, where I splashed cold water on my face until my bangs dripped with it, hands gripping the edges of the sink.

Lacey knew.

Maybe not everything, but enough, and there was no way she wasn't going to use this against me. She loved Ethan, hated me, and thought I wasn't good enough for him. (Despite, ironically, my graduate degrees, fighting skills, rich parents, and obviously rich sense of humor.)

I looked at myself in the mirror, bangs wet and matted, skin paler than usual, House medal absent. We were all remaking ourselves, from members of an international vampire collective to something different. I was part of that process, having gotten my fangs as a member of Cadogan, and now making the switch with the rest of them. But what, exactly, was I becoming?

I grabbed a towel and pressed it to my face, reluctant to go downstairs and join the *other* drama that was preparing to take over the House.

Nights like this made me wish I had an "undo" button, that I could simply rewind my actions or mistakes—or notice nosy vampires trailing me across town—and start fresh.

But that was impossible. What was done was done, and I was going to have to deal with it and the consequences like an adult. Instead of the twenty-seven-year-old cloistered graduate student I wished I were again.

I fixed my ponytail and applied some lip gloss, then brushed out my bangs until they shone. When I looked respectable again, and I'd locked my fear away, I walked downstairs to the first floor.

CHAPTER ELEVEN

IMMORTALLY IRREVOCABLE

E than, Luc, and Malik were already downstairs, dressed to the nines in classic black suits. Ethan nodded when he caught sight of me.

I stepped into the foyer just as Darius and the rest of the GP walked into the House, once again in their birdlike V formation. Like members of a dance team, they each had a position to fill, although their routine was much more conniving.

As I slipped into the crowd of Cadogan vampires who'd also assembled to greet them, Lacey stepped up to say hello. That's when the pleasantries began. Ethan had been right; however much I may have hated her, Darius definitely liked Lacey Sheridan.

"Lacey," Darius said, his voice saccharine sweet. He held out his hands and took hers, and they exchanged back-and-forth-and-back European-style cheek kisses.

"Sire," she said deferentially.

"You're looking well," he said, taking in her perfect black suit.

"As are you." Her gaze traveled down the line of vampires who'd accompanied him, and she made eye contact with each.

I told you they had a bond, Ethan silently said.

So you did, I said. *And clearly they do.*

Lacey pressed her hands together, then lifted them to her forehead, an obvious show of Grateful Condescension. Or brown-nosing.

"Sires, I am honored by your presence."

"I doubt that sentiment is universal," Darius said, looking back at Ethan, and an awkward silence fell.

"Darius," Ethan said, and the word fell heavy like a gauntlet, or a challenge. Darius was still Ethan's sire, his king, his commander, at least for a few more minutes, and calling him by his first name wasn't exactly respectful.

Darius's eyes narrowed. He'd taken the slap, and he didn't like it. But then a smile blossomed, and that was even scarier.

"Ethan. Apparently we've chosen to act like peasants before the deed is done," he said, the insult clear. "But no matter. Soon these issues will be resolved. Shall we get to it?"

"By all means," Ethan said, extending a hand toward the back of the House.

I guessed he hadn't forgotten all of his manners.

It was late and cold, but we were most definitely awake, Cadogan House's vampires silent as we gathered together around the brick fire pit on the back lawn.

We'd been joined by about half of the Cadogan vampires who didn't live in the House but wanted to show their support, our size swollen in solidarity against our future enemy. I recognized friends and colleagues in the crowd, but I found I couldn't approach them. I felt like a betrayer, a violator of Ethan's trust and the House's. Separate from everyone else who wasn't currently being black-mailed.

Across from us stood the vampires of the Greenwich Presidium. Numerically, we outnumbered them, but we radiated nervous energy, as if they held the power to destroy us with a flick of their hands.

They were all dressed professionally. Every one of them wore a suit of some sort, and to a one, their hands were clasped together in front of them, an angry jury ready to pronounce its verdict upon us.

Except that we'd already entered a plea in the metaphorical court. And tonight we were making it official.

"Who stands for this House today?" Darius asked.

"I do," Ethan said, stepping forward.

The members of the GP exchanged looks of obvious surprise.

"You are not the Master of this House," said a petite woman, gazing at him above the top of her glasses.

"I am the Master of this House by concession of its former Master and my formal reinvestment." Ethan held out his hand, and Malik handed him the papers they'd signed and sealed last night.

Ethan held up the sheaf, showing it to the GP, but unwilling to hand over the documents. Not that I blamed him. They might have gone directly into the fire.

"We were not invited to the ceremony," Darius mused.

"It wasn't a ceremony for you," Ethan said. "It was for this House."

Darius looked singularly unimpressed. "So you stand Master now?"

"I do."

Darius smiled falsely. "I don't see any particular need to draw this out. Ethan Sullivan, as you are apparently Master of Cadogan House, you and yours have voted to remove yourselves from the Greenwich Presidium. Do you agree?"

"I agree."

"From this night forward, you and your vampires shall be unaf-filiated, and your House, the House of Peter Cadogan, shall be De-certified. You shall not be entitled to the rights or privileges afforded to members of the Greenwich Presidium. Do you agree?"

"I agree."

"You reject the authority of the Greenwich Presidium over you and your vampires, and you submit to the authority of humans and hereby do join the world in which they live?"

It was becoming apparent the GP hadn't updated their script in a while. But that didn't stop Ethan.

"I agree," he said.

"Before you take an irrevocable step, we offer you one last chance," Darius said. "Agree to follow the appropriate dictates and we will allow you to remain within the GP on a . . . *trial* . . . basis."

Ethan smiled thinly and crossed his arms. "I can easily guess what those dictates are. In the course of preparing for our depar-ture, you realized the economic significance this House provided to the GP. And you've decided that our leaving the GP doesn't have quite the favorable ring that it once had. Here's the thing—we don't need you or your organization. We can and will survive on our own."

"What you don't appreciate," Darius said, "are the benefits you received from your membership. That you weren't fully aware of them doesn't mean they didn't exist. Do you honestly think Peter Cadogan would be happy to learn what's happened to his House? That the members of his House have elected to leave the GP—the institution that protected them for so long?"

Silence descended, but magic rose.

Ethan dropped his chin, gazing back at Darius beneath a hooded brow. "Peter Cadogan believed in his vampires. They were his first priority, and they were and remain mine. I'm not sure you've ever understood that, Darius."

"I understand plenty, Mr. Sullivan. The medals, if you please."

Kelley stepped forward and handed him the box of Cadogan gold.

Darius took the box and dropped it unceremoniously into the fire. "By the power vested in me as the head of the Greenwich Presidium, I hereby break the bond between us. Your House is Decertified. Your vampires are unaffiliated, UnHoused, and lacking the rights and privileges that would otherwise be afforded to them. The papers," he added, then held out his hand. One of the other GP members, a tall and lithe woman who looked to be of Indian descent, handed him a folder. Darius held it over the flames, just low enough for bright orange tongues of fire to graze the paper.

Darius lifted his steely gaze to Ethan. "There is no going back."

"We move forward," Ethan said. "Always forward. To affirm our affiliation with you would not be a step forward."

"That's not the most positive statement on which to end your lengthy relationship with the GP."

"I come to bury Caesar," Ethan gritted out. "Not to praise him."

"Then let it be heard—this was their choice." Darius opened his fingers, and the portfolio fell into the fire and burst into flames. Along with hundreds of years of history.

For a moment, the vampires were silent. I'd expected to feel changed somehow. Lighter, or even more afraid when the deed was done. But I didn't feel any different, which was precisely the point Ethan had been trying to make. Being a member of the GP didn't make us vampires; it just made us members. We were who we were with or without our GP association.

Darius, not surprisingly, was the first to break the silence.

"It is done," he said. The change in attitude was clear in his tone. We'd left his secret society, and we were nothing now. We were outcasts, and he intended to treat us as such. No Grateful Condescension for the vampires of Cadogan House, no allowances for the age and respect of our House. Those things were irrelevant now, just as we were irrelevant to him.

"It isn't done," Ethan said. "There's something we wish to say."

"You have nothing to say to us, Rogue," said the woman.

Ethan's eyes flashed silver. *And so it begins*, he silently said.

So it does, I silently agreed.

"I have more than enough to say," Ethan said. "Words that have built over centuries. Words that you wouldn't hear then. Perhaps you won't hear them now, but I would be remiss not to try." He slid his hands into his pockets, the movement of a man calm and relaxed. But anyone who knew Ethan—and I'd bet Darius did—would have known his calm was only feigned.

"Peter Cadogan was a good man," Ethan said. "A good man and a good vampire. The GP, in the intervening years since its creation, has forgotten how to respect both attributes. It prizes that which is 'vampire' over that which is good or moral. You have lost your compass, and you perpetuate your own ignorance. Your own members cause strife for the Houses you are sworn to protect, and you ignore their actions and blame the Houses when they must defend themselves. You are an anachronism that has no place in this modern world.

"Our exit is not an aberration, Darius. It is a harbinger. Celina predicted war would come. If you ignore the rising tides, you do so at your own peril."

The speech was moving, Ethan's passion clear. But the only thought on my mind? That if he felt that way about the GP, maybe he wouldn't kill me after all.

"Hyperbole doesn't suit you," Darius said, little swayed by

Ethan's words. "And moreover, it's irrelevant, because there are two facts you've handily ignored. First, I believe you'll find it a challenge to move forward in light of the fact that any progress you've made since this House was founded is because of the GP's largesse."

"Malik," Ethan said, and Malik handed Ethan a slip of paper. Ethan immediately extended it to Darius.

"This is a check accounting for the increase in the value of the House's assets to which we assumed you would be claiming title. I believe you'll find the settlement to be very reasonable."

Ethan smiled smugly . . . but so did Darius. He handed the check back to the woman, whose eyes had grown wide with Ethan's revelation.

"That is only the first fact, Ethan. Much, much more important is the second."

One of the GP members whistled loudly. A shock of nervous energy blew through the Cadogan crowd at the sound, all of us looking around for whatever threat the GP had called or signaled.

Ethan's safety in mind, I put a hand on the pommel of my sword and moved forward through the crowd, closer to him. I didn't know what Darius had in mind, but there seemed little doubt it would be treacherous.

We didn't have to wait long. Only a second later, there was a thunder of sound and movement as a brigade of mercenary fairies burst into the backyard, swords bared. Each of them wore military black and fearsome grins . . . and their katanas were unsheathed and pointing at us. Other than Claudia, fairies looked nearly identical, so there was no way to tell whether these were the fairies at the gate or a new crew who'd been called in for the meeting. But it hardly seemed to matter—one way or the other, fairies had breached the peace between us.

Cadogan swords were drawn, and we moved closer together for

protection even as they attempted to surround us, the hypocritical bastards. So much for the progress we'd made, for the help we'd offered and the friendship I'd thought we were beginning to forge.

In front of us, smiling calmly and cruelly, stood the members of the Greenwich Presidium.

Gloating.

Anger drifted forward in waves from the betrayed Cadogan Novitiates and their Master, and I imagined more than a few eyes had silvered with anger.

But business first. *I'm here*, I silently told Ethan, checking the crowd for Luc and Malik. They stood nearby, and we formed a protective arc around our Master.

Hold your position, Sentinel, Ethan said, his voice tight.

"What is this?" Lacey asked. Her voice was calm, but there was a thread of irritation in it. She might be a GP-affiliated Master, but she was still one of Ethan's vampires. And for once, that might actually do us some good.

"This," Darius said, "is our second point. The Greenwich Presidium hereby reclaims ownership of Cadogan House."

Ethan laughed with such gusto that Darius's eyes narrowed with anger.

"This House and its remaining assets belong to the vampires within it," Ethan said. "I think you well know that."

"I know your disrespect for the GP has gone on long enough. You presume because we are located an ocean away, you can act with impunity. You are incorrect. The House's contract includes a proprietary clause allowing us certain damages in the event you breach your obligations to the GP. We have concluded you've breached those obligations throughout your history, and, as such, we claim the House by right. And obviously we have the muscle to back that up." He gestured vaguely at the fairies.

Ethan made a sound of disdain. "Because your pride has been hurt, you threaten the very vampires you just invited back into your fold? You kick us out of our home and incite a *war* between fairies and vampires for the sake of your egos? Peter Cadogan would be ashamed, Darius, but of your behavior. Of the entire Presidium."

"You're only making my point, Ethan. You bring drama, consternation, and media attention to the vampires of this state and nation, and you blame us for taking measures to protect our institutions? How very shortsighted. How very . . . human."

"I take that as a compliment."

"You would," Darius said. "Regardless your opinion of it, you should accept the state of the world you have created. In consideration of the rising sun and the number of vampires you'll need to displace, we'll afford you some time to gather your personal belongings and vacate. You have forty-eight hours. By then, you should be resigned to your fate and out of this House. Should you fail to do so, you'll find a contingent of armed fairies ready to escort you out. And think on this, Ethan: In consideration of the bridges you've burned, who will help you now?"

The GP and fairies disappeared. For a moment, we simply stood there in shock.

"The fairies," Ethan said. "The goddamn fairies."

The fairies weren't known to be lovers of vampires, but that didn't diminish the insult of their actions. They were our guards, for God's sake. They kept watch over us while we slept. Or at least they had.

"What could possibly motivate them to do this?" I asked. "What could they possibly want badly enough to do this?"

I looked at Ethan . . . and understanding dawned. It wasn't what the fairies wanted . . . it was what we had.

"Upstairs," Ethan said. "Check our apartments."

Already knowing what he was thinking, I ran back into the House and up the stairs, taking them two at a time. I reached the third floor and was nearly home when I stopped short.

The doors to our apartments were open. Alarm quickened my heart.

Malik appeared in the hallway behind me, his breathing quickened by the run. "I expect you know what you're looking for."

"I think I do." I waited outside for a moment to let my vampiric senses scan the room, and when I was sure it was empty of trespassers, I walked inside and looked around.

Nothing seemed immediately askew: no cushions ripped or bleeding their stuffing, no drawers or lamps overturned. In fact, nothing was disturbed at all . . . except the glass case in the corner of the room.

One side was completely shattered, and the dragon's egg was gone.

"Malik," I called out, as I moved closer to the case.

"A GP affiliate must have taken it," he said, disgust in his voice. "Undoubtedly during the ceremony. Even as they insulted us, they sent someone in here to retrieve an object to which they have no right. As if there wasn't enough drama in the world, Darius had to create more of it."

Malik moved closer, head tilted as he looked over the remains of the case.

"Should I clean up the glass?" I asked, but he shook his head.

"Leave it. Ethan will want to take a look anyway. We'll ask Helen to take care of it."

"We could file a police report," I suggested.

"For what purpose?" Ethan asked, stepping into the room behind us, Luc and Lacey with him.

Luc gave me a nod, and Lacey ignored me completely. Her eyes, and quite likely her mind, were on Ethan. Was it stupid to hope she'd see reason, forget about what she'd imagined she'd seen, and let us get through this crisis before creating another one?

Ethan deposited his suit jacket on a table by the door and walked toward the case. "I seriously doubt they'd care much for the missing trinket of a vampire."

It was an unfortunate point, but no less accurate for that.

"It was trinket enough for the GP to steal and hold before the fairies like a carrot on a stick," Luc said.

"The fairies want it back?" I asked.

"They must," Ethan said, "to be willing to raise arms against us."

"Why now?" Luc asked. "We've had the egg for more than a century, and they've been guarding the House for years. Why didn't they simply ask for it back?"

"Perhaps they didn't know where it was," I said. "Claudia mentioned it in her tower. Her guards were there; maybe that's when they learned it was here."

"And when Darius sought their help," Malik said, "they knew exactly what they wanted."

"Possibly," Ethan said. "Or it's possible they waited because they didn't want to risk the income they receive from the House. Once they believe our stability is questionable, they decide the income is no longer a given, and they're willing to take a chance to get the egg."

Malik nodded. "And perhaps they hoped Cadogan House's new 'tenants' would continue to pay them a fair wage for guarding it. They get both things they want."

Looking suddenly exhausted, Ethan sat down in an armchair and dropped his head back, loosening the tie around his neck. He closed his eyes for a moment, taking a haggard breath while Luc, Malik, and I waited for direction.

I took the opportunity to message my grandfather and Jonah about events, and the possibility that I'd be heading to my grandfather's house for an extended stay in the guest room.

"There were days," Ethan said, "when I considered a minor dip in the House's investments a tragedy. Oh, how times have changed."

"Same issues," Lacey said. "Only the scale is different."

"Hoss, you want some blood?" Luc asked Ethan. "Or maybe a drink?"

"Two fingers of whiskey, please. No, fuck it. Just bring me the bottle."

I was closest to the apartment's small bar area, so I made the drink. I wasn't sure even a fifth of fine Scottish whiskey would soothe the sting of Darius's betrayal. I poured the amber liquid into a short glass, the potent smell tickling my nose. When the bottle was recapped, I offered it to Ethan, and sat down in the armchair near his.

"The fairies are gone," Luc said, looking at his phone again, "and we've got the backup firm on the line. They'll have a full contingent of guards here within the hour, and Michael Donovan's agreed to rendezvous with them."

"Who'll guard us now?" I asked.

Luc leaned against a console table nearby. "Humans. We've had a security firm on retainer for years as a backup, but we don't reveal the firm's name even to guards. Or Sentinels," he apologetically added.

"It's a sabotage prevention mechanism," Lacey said, eyes narrowed at me.

Okay, so she clearly wasn't going to let us focus on one crisis at a time.

"Ya," Luc agreed, oblivious to the undercurrent. "We'd preferred fairies, since they're stronger and generally less fickle." His eyes narrowed. *"Generally."*

Ethan sipped his whiskey, then put the glass heavily on the cocktail table beside him. "Who, in God's name, could have predicted this? That the GP would force us to fight? That they'd prefer to leave us homeless instead of simply accepting our graceful departure? Goddamned bastards."

"They can't really take the House, can they?" I asked, looking from vampire to vampire, but no one offered a response.

My heart sank low in my chest.

I felt for the apartment key in my jacket pocket and looked around the space I'd only so recently moved into. This House had become my home; I didn't want to give it up, especially not to Darius West and his ilk. Talk about adding insult to injury.

"Darius has made his gambit," Lacey said. "For better or worse, he'll follow it through if he believes it's in his vampires' best long-term interest."

"The key phrase being 'his vampires,'" Luc said. "And we've just defined ourselves as falling outside that group."

"We knew he'd label us as the enemy," Ethan said. "I'd merely hoped for more of a 'live and let live' approach. And the irony? Michael broached the possibility the fairies were dangerous last night."

He'd mentioned it to me, too. Not that we hadn't known of the risks before. But we'd weighed the benefits against the costs, and we'd kept them around because the math didn't seem so bad.

"And so it begins," Ethan said. "More strife between vampire and fae. And I'd thought we'd made significant inroads."

"We did," I assured him. I hated to see him so defeated. "We were actually communicating with Claudia. We can't just let them get away with this."

I looked around the room, but no one met my eyes.

"There has to be some way to deal with it, some way to fix it. And we'll figure it out. All of us, together. Right?" I smiled at Ethan, feeling suddenly—weirdly—like a Cadogan House cheerleader, sans pleated skirt and bloomers. "I mean, you did ask your transition team to come all this way. At least now you'll get your money's worth."

Ethan looked back at me, and I saw that familiar spark light in his eyes. He sat up, and looked at each of us in turn. "She's right. We work this problem like any other, and we find a solution. Is that understood?"

We all nodded.

Ethan looked at Malik. "Start a timer. I want it in my office within the hour, counting down the hours we purportedly have to fix this situation. Thank God it's winter, and we'll actually be awake for a good portion of that time."

"Liege," Malik said, a little smile at the corner of his mouth at Ethan's sudden sense of action.

Ethan stood up and ran his fingers through his hair, then put his hands on his hips.

"I say this one time, and you may spread the word to the House as you like. We are *not* leaving this House. Peter bade me captain his ship, and as long as I am alive on this earth and Master of this domain, I will captain it. They will take this House over my dead body. Call Paige, the librarian, and Michael Donovan. I want them in my office within the hour."

Ethan could be frustrating at times. Infuriating at others. But there was no doubt he was a Master among men.

The troops inspired, I waited while Luc, Lacey, and Malik left the apartments to begin the process of beginning the process, then looked at Ethan. "You're all right?"

He walked toward me and pressed a soft kiss to my lips. "I've survived world wars, Sentinel. This is a drop in the bucket."

We both knew he was exaggerating, but I forgave him the boast.

I turned toward the door and held out a hand. "Then let's go downstairs and take care of this real quick."

He smiled a little, which was the point. "Real quick?"

I shrugged. "You know, since it's a drop in the bucket."

He put his hand in mine and we walked toward the door, pretending we had a solution. Pretending we had a fix.

And hoping to God we could find one.

We found Lacey in the doorway of his office, her eyes narrowing at the sight of Ethan and me together. I knew I had to tell him the truth about the RG—if nothing else to beat her to the punch—but this was not the time to add to his burdens. Hopefully she was mature enough to see that, too.

We walked inside to find Michael Donovan, Paige, the librarian, Luc, and Malik already in the room. On the wall was the timer Ethan had requested. It was large, with a black screen and squarish white numbers that ticked the seconds, minutes, and hours that we had left until the fairies tried to forcibly remove us from our home. Unless we figured out a way to stop them.

Luc had scrounged up another whiteboard and set it up near the conference table.

"This looks like a party."

We glanced back at the door. Gabriel Keene, head of the North American Central Pack, stood there with a black motorcycle helmet in hand. Memphis was his home base, but Chicago was, for all intents and purposes, his city. With sun-burnished hair and amber eyes, he looked like a force to be reckoned with. And was.

He took a step inside. "I hear you've got a problem. Thought perhaps you could use some assistance."

Word traveled fast among supernaturals—or in this case from my message to my grandfather, probably to Jeff, and then to Gabriel. The look on Ethan's face was priceless: Hope and joy blossomed, and perhaps for the first time, he believed there might actually be a way out of this.

He skipped the greeting, walked toward Gabriel, and offered a bear-sized hug. Gabriel slapped him on the back.

"All right, old man. Let's not make Kitten jealous." He glanced around Ethan and smiled at me. "Hello, Kitten."

Gabriel had taken to calling me that, mostly as a comic insult, kittens being among the least powerful of the animals shifters could change into. "Gabe. Welcome to the party."

"It means a lot to the House that you're here," Ethan said, as they moved toward the conference table.

"Yeah, well, don't take it too personally." He glanced around the room, his gaze falling on Michael Donovan. "I'm not sure I know everyone?"

Ethan made the appropriate introductions, and we began to gather around the conference table.

"Oh, one more thing," Gabriel said before sitting, swinging a black backpack off his shoulder. He unzipped it and produced a bundle wrapped in aluminum foil. The scent of barbecue filled the air.

"Mallory sends her regards," he said, handing the packet to me.

By having Gabriel bring me a bundle of meat? She most certainly did.

"Now that Merit's fed, which is clearly our most important consideration," Ethan snarked with a smile, "let's get down to business."

I put the meat on the table and sat down, but didn't open it. Now was not the time.

Ethan stood at the head of the table. "We have what's left of this evening and tomorrow night to figure out how to keep this House in our hands, and prevent the GP from destroying what we've built in this city. Failure," he said, looking at each member of the transition team in turn, "is not an option. I don't care what form the remedy takes—whether contractual, legal, or a good old-fashioned brawl. But we will have a plan in place that assures the continuation of this House in our hands.

"Now," he said, taking a seat, "let's get to work." He looked first at Paige and then the librarian, who sat beside me. "The contracts?"

The librarian nodded. "The contract has what amounts to a good-behavior clause," he said, handing Ethan a document with a flagged page. "It basically says the House is obliged to act in a manner consistent with GP values. If the House fails to do so, the GP is entitled to damages."

Ethan flipped the pages, glancing back and forth between them. "It doesn't say, specifically, the damages are comprised of the House?"

"It doesn't. But the language is vague, so there's no way to tell exactly how a court might interpret it." He shrugged. "But that's just my opinion, and I'm not a lawyer."

Ethan glanced at Malik. "And what do the lawyers say?"

"They're reviewing and researching now. They indicated they might not have a final answer until the sun rises again, but they do have some concerns about judicial interpretation."

"They always do," Ethan said. "The primary problem being we'd have to fight the GP in court, even assuming the courts have jurisdiction over vampiric problems. That 'solution' creates years of litigation, which does not accomplish my goal of resolving this issue before Darius leaves for London again."

He looked at Luc. "A show of force?"

"We could fight the fairies, but you know how they fight: to the death, or they deem it hardly worth the trouble. They prefer seppuku over losing, so any battle would result, at a minimum, in the deaths of multiple vampires or the deaths of all fairies."

Gabriel whistled. "The city of Chicago will not like that."

"No," Ethan agreed. "Nor is it something I can countenance. And I still find it hard to believe that Darius would condone such a thing."

"He doesn't think you'll follow through with it," Lacey said. She sat at the foot of the table, facing Ethan across the piles of materials. "He knows you wouldn't allow your vampires to be injured for the sake of a building, and assumes you'll bow out before then."

"Why the House?" I wondered. "Is it the symbolism or the structure?"

"Both," Lacey quickly answered, playing the authority on the GP's motivations, which maybe she was. "Symbolically, it demonstrates the GP's power—that the Houses are utterly within its control, and failure to fall in line will leave a House, quite literally, without resources."

"And structurally," Ethan put in, looking at me, "it defines who we are. We are unified by Peter's name, but it is the House that brings us together. If we will not follow the rules, Darius will strip away the tie that binds."

Gabriel leaned back in his chair, which squeaked beneath him. "That's a class act you have there."

"We're very proud," Ethan dryly said.

Gabriel sat up again and looked at Ethan. "We are friends," he said. "But I cannot offer soldiers now. Not when there's another way."

He meant not when we could leave the House and avoid the fight altogether. Ethan didn't look thrilled at the news the Pack wouldn't assist us in a fight—they were, by far, the largest group of nonvampire allies we had—but he took the news graciously.

"I understand your position," Ethan said. "It doesn't thrill me, but were I in the same place, I'd likely make the same decision." He looked around the table. "What else?"

"Extortion?" Paige suggested. "I don't know much about these vampires, but do we have anything on any of them we could use to change their minds?"

Ethan and I exchanged a glance. We knew Harold Monmonth had murdered at Celina's behest, but there was no way Darius or any of the other GP members would care. The GP generally thought human lives were beneath their concern. A centuries-old death wouldn't inspire much interest.

"Not that I'm aware of," Ethan said.

"We can't buy them off," Malik said. "We're out of money."

"What about the egg?" Gabriel asked.

Everyone looked at Gabriel. "What about it?" Ethan asked.

"It's the key to the entire thing. The fairies want it; Darius has it. I assume he hasn't given it to them yet and won't—not until they follow through on their promise to attack. If you can get it back . . ."

"Then we hold the trophy," Ethan said, "and the fairies won't care what the GP wants them to do." He sat back, then looked at Michael. "Thoughts?"

"It's an idea," Michael said, nodding at me. "Satiating the fairies would solve the immediate problem of keeping the House, but not the long-term issue. Darius isn't just making a one-time play here. If he wants the House, he'll try again to get it."

"A fair point," Ethan said. "But perhaps, for now, we play the hand we've been dealt. Where might the egg be?"

"Darius and the rest of the GP members are staying at the Dandridge," Malik said. "He might take it there."

"Eh, I'm not sure about that," Luc said. "They're gambling here, and he has to know we're having this conversation. That spot seems too obvious."

"Too obvious, and too hard to breach in any event," I said. "Celebrities and senators stay at the Dandridge. I'm not even sure we could get through security to check the rooms."

"I think it's safe to assume it's in the metro area," Michael said. "They can't take it too far away; there wouldn't be time to get it back into the fairies' hands again."

I bet he was right. Unfortunately, Chicago was a big city.

"We have to look," Ethan said. "The search begins now." He looked at Malik. "Start with the other Houses' Seconds. Find out what they know, if they have any information about where it might be."

"They may not want to help," Luc said. "This is precisely the kind of anti-GP behavior Darius wants to punish."

"Perhaps," Ethan said. "Convince them anyway. Someone knows how to fix this, and I want an answer tonight."

Unfortunately, he didn't get it. Two hours later, even after sharing the snack Gabriel had brought, we were no closer to a solution. Other than guessing it might be at the Dandridge, no one from the other Houses had any idea where the egg might be; nor were they forthcoming with even that unhelpful suggestion. Not that their mum's-the-word attitudes were surprising; neither Navarre nor Grey wanted to involve their Houses any more than necessary. That was how they'd stayed off the GP's radar before, and Darius's nuclear threat only reinforced the lesson.

Ethan rubbed a hand over his face. "Dawn is coming. We will reconvene at dusk." He looked at Gabriel. "I appreciate your time."

Gabriel smiled wolfishly. "Devil you know versus the devil you don't. I'd much rather have you in this House than a bunch of GP assholes."

We couldn't argue with that.

With minutes to spare before dawn, Ethan came to me with exhaustion, and sought solace in my arms. Fear hung over me: Lacey's knowledge of my meeting with Jonah. The unknown killer outside our gate. The threats against our House and home.

We lay together in the dark, bodies intertwined, as the sun rose outside. As the minutes and hours of our remaining sanctuary in Cadogan House slipped away, one by one.

"I cannot lose this House," he drowsily murmured, as the sun wandered into the sky again. "I cannot . . . disappoint them."

I ached for him, and swore to help him keep the House, but not even love could stop the rising of the sun.

CHAPTER TWELVE

THE FIRST RULE OF FRIGHT CLUB

I woke slowly after dreaming that I'd had to reapply for my position as Sentinel, and Ethan had found me utterly lacking for the job. It wasn't difficult to imagine the origin of that fear—namely, that I was being blackmailed by a woman in love with my boyfriend, even while my House was on the brink of destruction.

Ethan was already up, so the bedroom was utterly quiet. Indulgently, I pulled the sheet over my head and let myself pretend the world outside was empty and blackmail-free.

I didn't want to tell him. I wasn't *supposed* to tell him. After all, what was the first rule of the RG? *Don't talk about the RG.*

The entire point of the organization was to monitor the behavior of Masters and the GP so they couldn't act dictatorially and hurt vampires along the way. It was hard to do that when they'd identified you as a spy. How could I give up the Red Guard to a Master's scrutiny? How could I punish Jonah for my lack of discretion and Lacey's obsession with Ethan? If I confessed where I'd been, wouldn't I be negating the GP's careful effort to be anonymous, their decades of work, and all the members who'd given their twenty years of service?

Wouldn't I be betraying Jonah?

But I also couldn't let Lacey be the one to spill to Ethan what she'd seen. He wasn't supposed to know at all, but he certainly shouldn't find out from *her*. Especially not when she'd use it as an excuse to drive a wedge between us.

Maybe I'd wanted too much, hoped for too much—that I could be an RG member and have a relationship with a Master vampire, of all people. Maybe this would be the end of us: our friendship, our camaraderie, our relationship.

That conversation was going to suck. I knew he'd be angry and feel betrayed, just like Lacey had said. In true Sentinel form, I analyzed the risk, walking through every possible result of my confession:

1. Ethan, drunk on love, would tell me he was proud I'd agreed to serve vampires by joining the RG.
2. Ethan would dump me in a special ceremony in front of Cadogan House.
3. Ethan would kick me out of the House in a special ceremony in front of Cadogan House. Commemorative T-shirts would be prepared bearing the words I SURVIVED MERIT'S EXCOMMUNICATION.
4. Ethan would do both two and three, then kill Jonah.
5. Ethan would turn inward, then let loose a silent but deadly rage that would destroy Cadogan House and most of Hyde Park. Mayor Kowalcyzk would blame it on our genetics; Catcher would blame it on love.

The scenarios were the least comforting, because one way or the other, Ethan was going to find out, and Jonah was going to be exposed.

I had an unwinnable choice, which was hardly a choice at all.

I hated regret, and that was what I was feeling right now. Not so much regret that I'd said yes to Jonah, but that I hadn't been more careful the night before and that I'd baited Lacey enough to prick her into blackmailing me.

Unfortunately, sitting around and whining about it wasn't going to change anything. A killer was still roaming the city and my House was facing a ticking time bomb. Oliver, Eve, and Cadogan needed someone to fight for them, so I flipped off the sheet and climbed out of bed. The night would bring what the night would bring. Better to face it like a soldier—head-on, and without fear—than cower beneath a sheet.

I checked my phone and found a message from Jonah: CHECKING WITH RG CONTACT ABOUT CADOGAN; WILL ADVISE.

I wasn't sure how plugged in his contacts were. But he'd clearly been right about the contract clause. Maybe he could offer help. It would be an absolute godsend.

Since Ethan and the others were downstairs handling the House, I took a long, hot shower, trying to think through the murders I still hadn't managed to solve. We knew Oliver and Eve had been killed after visiting the registration office. Their bodies had been placed in a warehouse in Little Italy, and there were slivers of aspen near the body, possibly from a weapon created by McKetrick.

We also knew a black SUV was involved in their deaths and our House drive-by, and that McKetrick had used black SUVs in the past to terrorize us.

Of course, this was Chicago, and black SUVs were a dime a dozen. And McKetrick denied any knowledge of the murders, and particularly the idea that someone had used his weapon. Frankly, if he was so certain he had scads of political power, why lie? Why not admit to me what he'd done, and trust that no one would believe if I pointed to him as the culprit?

I wasn't ready to give up on McKetrick as a suspect, but I was beginning to think there was more to the puzzle than met the eye.

When I was clean and dressed, my hair in a ballerina-esque topknot, I downed as much blood as I could—the kitchen blissfully empty of Lacey Sheridan—and headed downstairs.

Ethan was behind his desk, the only one in his office. He wore a white button-down, the sleeves rolled up and the collar unbuttoned. He was ready for a long night of work, but he looked exhausted. He probably hadn't slept well.

"Good morning," he said.

There was no hint of anger in his voice, which suggested Lacey still hadn't spilled the secret she thought she knew. That made me breathe a little easier.

"Good morning." I sat down in a chair in front of his desk. "Any news?"

"Nothing of note. The humans are on guard outside, and we made it through the night without incident. I'm pleasantly surprised Darius didn't buy them off, too," he sardonically added.

"Bribery is clearly in his playbook. No news on the murder front, either. Or at least, no messages from the Ombud's office."

"The killer covered his tracks well," Ethan said. "But that doesn't mean there isn't a clue out there ready to be found."

Exactly why I wasn't ready to give up. Not yet.

"I'm going to ask everyone to pack a bag," Ethan said.

I stared at him, my heart deflating. He didn't think we could do it. He didn't think we could find a way to stop this, and thought we'd lose the House. That I'd be camping out on my grandfather's couch by nightfall.

The defeat in his eyes brought tears to mine. "We have tonight and most of tomorrow night. We can find a way."

"Can we?" he asked. "Without bloodshed?"

I opened my mouth, then closed it again, lacking a good retort.

There was a knock at the doorway. Lacey stood there in a trim black suit with white piping. She smiled at Ethan, but scowled at me.

"Lacey," Ethan said. "Coffee?"

"That would be lovely," she said, stepping inside.

He glanced at me. "For you?"

"No," I said, watching Lacey. "I'm fine."

Ethan put in a call to Margot, requesting espressos for both of them. As he offered the instructions, Lacey moved closer to me, her gaze growing colder with each step.

"Did you tell him?"

We were only a few feet from Ethan's desk, and my heart began to race. No doubt, in some primal part of her brain, she thought she'd ferreted out a traitor—and that bringing me to justice would bring her and Ethan closer together.

But I wasn't going to let her destroy my relationship, regardless her motive. I narrowed my gaze at her. "There is *nothing* to tell, and I have more important things to do than worry about what you think you saw."

"I saw enough," she quietly said, watching Ethan as he chatted with Margot on the phone.

"Can you please just focus on the drama we've got instead of creating drama that isn't really there?"

"Creating drama?" Her eyes flashed silver, which raised goose bumps on my arms. "I am here," she fiercely whispered, "in this city, because you are a child with no sense of how grave this situation is. Because you can't give him what he needs."

"I give him exactly what he needs."

"No," she said, "you're just easily accessible."

I nearly growled at her. "If he wanted you, he'd be with you. But he's not. At the end of the night, he comes home to me."

My mouth had gotten me in trouble before, and that had been exactly the wrong thing to say to a woman already threatening to tell Ethan what she'd seen after she'd followed me halfway across town.

"Ladies?" Ethan asked, staring at us from across his desk, the phone back in its cradle. There was no mistaking the tension and magic in the air. "What's going on?"

"It's about Merit."

My chest heaved as I tried to suck in air, waiting for my enemy to strike, to place her pawn before I made my own strategy.

I loved Ethan. But Jonah was my partner. I had to protect both of them. I just hoped I was clever enough to do it.

His gaze switched to me. "Merit?"

But before I could speak, she made her move. "She's having an affair with Jonah."

My eyes went dinner-plate wide. *That's* what she thought I'd been doing? "I most certainly am *not* having an affair with Jonah."

Ethan looked confused . . . and dubious. "Jonah? The Grey guard captain?"

"The same," Lacey said. "Last night she left the House. I thought her behavior, her disappearance, was suspicious. So I followed her."

Ethan looked equally suspicious. "You followed her."

Lacey slid me a glance over her shoulder, equal parts daring and accusing. "She drove to the harbor, where security let her in. She met Jonah on the harbor wall. They were alone. They embraced." She looked back at Ethan, ready to deliver the final blow. "There was blood in the air."

Ethan's gaze silvered.

"She isn't faithful to you, Ethan. You had to know that. I had to tell you."

"Lacey, leave us, please."

But she wouldn't listen. Her eyes were frantic, her voice panicked. She'd made her final play—her only play—and she wasn't sure whether it had worked. "Don't you see what she's doing to you? What she's done to you—to the House?"

"Lacey, get out!" Ethan bellowed.

"Ethan—"

He turned to glare at her, his expression no less polite than it had been with me. Sure, she'd accused me of cheating on him, but she'd also come tattling to Ethan. That wasn't exactly laudable behavior.

She did as she was told, slamming the door shut behind her.

Ethan stood up and walked toward me, a thousand questions in his eyes. "Tell me," he said. "Tell me now. Do not make me wonder, Merit. Do not make me put our relationship in her hands."

I swallowed down a bolt of panic. I hadn't prepared for this—for the assumption she'd actually made. What was I supposed to do now?

I certainly couldn't tell Ethan I was having an affair. I *wasn't* having an affair; I wouldn't do that to him, or anyone else.

There was no honorable exit strategy here, only a least offensive option. I could be honest, pray that he'd forgive me, and hope to God that Jonah did, too.

I called up every ounce of bravery I possessed, and it was only barely enough to force the words past my lips.

"I joined the Red Guard."

Ethan's face went white, and his eyes went huge. He stared at me, and my heart fell to my knees.

"You—you . . ." He tried to speak, but he was furious enough that he couldn't get the words out. "You did *what?*"

I cleared my throat, trying to find my voice and remember why I'd made the decision that I had. *Because I'd been given the choice to serve, and I knew my choice had been right.* "I joined the Red Guard. I'm a member now."

He just stared at me, as seconds or minutes or hours passed. I waited on tenterhooks while he assessed my dishonesty, and probably the validity of our relationship. Finally I broke, and filled the silence I could no longer stand.

"You were gone," I said. "And the GP was destroying us from the inside out. They came to me, and I said yes for the House—for what was left of us without you."

He put a palm against his chest. "For my House? To join an organization whose sole purpose is to spy on us?"

"We aren't spies," I insisted, holding my ground. "It was the right thing to do. *Is* the right thing to do. We were falling apart, and things certainly haven't gotten any better. I'm so sorry. I hated keeping it from you, Ethan. *Hated* it. But I couldn't tell you."

He glared at me. "Don't talk to me about your motivations." He wet his lips and looked away. "You've been inducted?"

Fear strangled me, and it took me a moment to answer. For both of us, there was no turning back. "Yes. Lacey saw it. She followed me to the meet."

His jaw clenched. "And he's your partner?"

I shrank back into myself, fearing this answer would seal my fate. If Ethan hadn't been at stake, I wouldn't have answered. But it would be disrespectful to lie to him.

"Yes," I finally admitted.

"Are you fucking kidding me?" His eyes flashed silver, and a pulse of bright, hot, furious magic filled the air.

I swallowed, and nodded. Ethan's chest rose and fell, shock and fury battling in his face. He looked like he couldn't decide whether to scream or cry, whether to bellow out his agony or curse the gods.

"You were gone," I repeated.

He barked out a laugh. "And that's the rub, isn't it, Merit? I'm back now."

I nodded.

"I've been back . . . for a month . . . and you hadn't bothered to tell me?" He took a menacing step closer. "I had to find out like this, from another Master, Merit? From a vampire I made and trained? A vampire who has, apparently, more honesty than my own girlfriend."

"I couldn't tell you. You may not agree with what I did, but you know why they exist. You know what they stand for." *Right and justice*, I thought.

That didn't seem to matter to him. "Did you share blood with him?"

"It was just a drop. Just a drop on a blade. There was no drinking. I swear it."

There was a sudden sadness in his eyes, a sadness that hurt me more than anything else and seared me to the bone. He wasn't just angry; he was hurt.

"I am so sorry. I didn't want this to come between us."

"*This*, Merit, is an organization that presumes I'm shitty at my job, that I require guarding, that I am like *them*, the members of the goddamn Greenwich Presidium, which is currently trying to take my House away."

I stood a little straighter; he was making my point for me. "That's exactly why I had to do it, Ethan—because that's what the GP is. They're *tyrants*. And we're trying to keep that from happening. I'm sorry I couldn't tell you. But for better or worse, the secret wasn't mine to tell."

Fury unabated, Ethan shook his head. "You told me Jonah helped you while I was gone. It appears that wasn't an accident."

"He helped me with the raves while you were busy taking care of the House. And after you were gone, we worked together to figure out what Mallory was doing."

"And have you lied to me about anything else?"

That question stung just like a slap. "I didn't lie about this."

"You significantly omitted. Regardless, you'll resign."

"What?"

"You'll resign." He took out his phone and held it out, fire in his eyes. "You'll call him right now, you'll tell him it was a mistake, and you'll resign."

I stared back at him. "I won't resign. I made a promise, and it was the right promise to make."

His eyes blazed again. "You took an oath to me. To this House."

"That's why I'm doing it! Ethan, now more than ever, we need the Red Guard. We need eyes on the GP. We need vampires who are willing to look beyond what the GP tells them to do and think critically. We need help."

"We need a Sentinel with undivided loyalties."

I stepped closer to him. My own temper was rising, but damn, did anger feel better than guilt and fear.

I put a finger in my chest. "I'm Sentinel of this House, and I'm loyal to it. My job is to do the right thing, and in my judgment, this is the right thing."

"You joined a secret organization whose goal is to undermine my leadership!" He sounded flabbergasted.

"No, I joined a secret organization to watch the bad guys who were undermining—and who continue to undermine—your vampires."

"And now you'll resign."

"I absolutely will not resign." Whatever doubt remained about my RG membership was quickly dissipating, despite Ethan's efforts to the contrary.

His nostrils flared. He wasn't used to being challenged. "I am Master of this House."

Finally, familiar territory. "And I am Sentinel of this House. Ethan, if the RG came to you tomorrow, you'd do the exact same thing. Yes, I made a difficult decision. I made a decision that clearly is making you ask questions about my loyalties, and that truly sucks. But this is the right thing for the House, and I stand by it. And if you'll stop acting on your prejudices and think—*truly think*—about the advantages this gives us, you'll know it, too."

"I know I trusted you with my House, Merit, and with my honesty, and with my heart. Was that the right thing?"

As if in answer for me, my phone rang. I didn't so much as reach down to turn it off, but his eyes narrowed anyway.

"Who is it?"

"Ethan—"

"Check the goddamn phone, Merit."

My hand shaking with adrenaline, I pulled it out of my jacket pocket and checked the screen. I closed my eyes.

"Who is it?" The words were half question, half accusation.

I opened my eyes, staring back at him, countering his distrust with irritation of my own.

And meanwhile, the phone still rang, the new sound track to our battle. "It's Jonah."

As Ethan's eyes narrowed, my heart raced faster. "Answer it," he gritted out.

"We're in the middle of a—"

"Oh, no," he said. "We are quite done here. Answer the phone, Merit. Let's see what brings the intrepid captain to your door."

His tone was insinuating and insulting, but I wasn't going to argue with him. Not about the RG. I'd made my decision, and he'd live with it.

Or he wouldn't. I replayed his words in my mind. *Done here?* I mentally repeated. What had he meant by "done here"? Done with me? Done with us?

I raised the phone to my ear, and had to work to keep my hand from shaking.

"I know my timing's bad," Jonah said, and my first thought was that he'd somehow psychically ferreted out our argument. "And you have House issues to deal with. But we have a problem."

"What happened?"

There was silence for a moment as Ethan stared me down. But even he could see the concern in my face, and his expression softened just a bit.

"Two of Morgan's vampires are dead. Decapitated, just like Oliver and Eve. They found them at dusk. Their guard captain just called me. But, Merit, it's worse. The murder was in the House."

I felt the blood drain from my face, even as I wondered—and then answered—why Morgan hadn't called us first. Because it was me, and it was Morgan, and the not-very-interesting history between us still made him weird that way.

"Okay," I said. "Let me see what I can do."

"I'm at Navarre now. Get here as soon as you can."

I hung up the phone and put it back in my pocket. I could see the debate in Ethan's face: *Should I show her how angry and hurt I am by asking something snarky, or lose the attitude, given the expression on her face?*

"What happened?" he finally asked, his voice carefully neutral.

"Two of Morgan's vampires are dead. They found them in Navarre House at dusk."

Ethan's eyes widened. "The killer was inside the House?"

I nodded.

Ethan ran a hand absently through his hair. "You should tell your grandfather. They can assist with arrangements or the investigation . . . whatever's necessary."

I nodded again. "I'm sorry this is happening right now," I said. "I know the timing is atrocious. I didn't mean for you to find out— about the RG."

For the second time tonight, that was exactly the wrong thing to say. I'd reminded him of what I'd done, and why he should be angry.

He snatched his suit jacket from the back of a chair.

"Where are you going?"

He slipped on the jacket, and slipped his phone into a pocket. "I think you'd know that, Sentinel. I'm going with you."

"But the House?"

"We have hours yet, and the lawyers are on it. Perhaps, should the opportunity present itself, I will have words with your new partner."

The expression on his face left little doubt about what those words would be.

Ethan gave Malik a heads-up that we were leaving. Malik was obviously surprised, but after scanning our faces for a moment, he wisely decided not to argue.

Ethan told him about the deaths at Navarre House and asked him to apprise Luc. I also stood by while he had a closed-door chat with Lacey, no doubt warning her to keep quiet about what she'd seen and dismissing her claim that I was having an affair.

I couldn't imagine he'd tell her about the Red Guard, but I wisely decided not to ask.

Navarre House was in the Gold Coast, north of Hyde Park and near the lake, and I was still the default transportation mechanism.

We drove in total silence. Ethan didn't mutter a word, too angry at me to speak. And I wasn't especially interested in talking to him. I'd opted to put my ass on the line to keep Cadogan safe from the GP. In my position, he'd have done the same thing.

And you know what? If I was the type of girl who quit an obligation because my boyfriend told me to, Ethan wouldn't have been interested in me in the first place.

So I concentrated on driving and not becoming any more furious than I already was.

When we reached Navarre House, an imposing white mansion with a turret at one corner, I parked in the first open spot I could find.

Ethan looked over at me, and his gaze was flat. "I presume, since Jonah called you, Scott knows about the murders."

Scott Grey was the Master of Grey House, the third of Chicago's three vampire Houses. "I would think so. I'm sure word has traveled from Noah."

"Does he know about the RG?"

"No. Just Jonah. And me. And now you."

"Is that why Jonah called you?"

"I doubt it. He knows we've been investigating the Rogues' deaths. Ethan—"

I said his name, unsure how to begin but knowing we needed to talk. But he held up a hand. He'd hear nothing more from me, not right now.

"Let's just get through this meeting," he said.

CHAPTER THIRTEEN

MADNESS

Ethan and I walked side by side down the sidewalk. His body language was clear—we were working together. Nothing more, nothing less, at least until we had a good talk.

But now was not the time for that talk.

We walked inside Navarre House and found the front desk empty. The three lovely brunettes who usually greeted visitors to the House were gone.

We walked into the House proper, and the mood was dark—grief stricken and silent. Every vampire House had a style. Grey House was an urban loft. Cadogan House had a European flair. Navarre House was sleek and modern. Although the exterior of the building looked more like a princess's castle than a vampire enclave, the interior looked like an art gallery. The walls and floor were gleaming marble, with occasional pops of art and furniture.

The first floor was full of vampires, but they'd clustered behind an invisible line, leaving a gap between themselves and the Masters, Morgan Greer and Scott Grey. Both were dark haired. Scott looked like a former college athlete—broad shoulders, small waist, and a dark soul patch below his lips. Morgan looked like a male model. His dark, wavy hair now reached his shoulders, but across his handsome face—strong cheekbones, cleft chin, dark blue eyes—was a mask of grief.

We hadn't exactly had the best working relationship, but this wasn't the time to dwell on our petty disagreements. He was suffering, and we'd do what we could to help. Besides, the last time I'd talked to Morgan, he'd saved my life. Being here was really the least we could do.

Jonah stood slightly apart from them. He and Scott both wore blue-and-yellow Grey House jerseys, which Scott had selected, in lieu of medals, to identify his House's vampires. A blond man I didn't know, but assumed was the Navarre House guard captain, stood with the group.

Ethan nodded, barely sparing Jonah a glance. "Our condolences for your loss."

Jonah looked at me curiously, and I found I couldn't make eye contact. My stomach felt suddenly raw. I was fighting with my boyfriend about my new partner—and my new partner was standing in front of us.

"What happened?" Ethan asked.

Morgan moved to the side, revealing the covered bodies of their fallen colleagues beside the stairs, a pool of blood beside them. They'd placed a blanket atop the bodies, giving them decency the killer hadn't bothered to show.

"Two of my vampires have been murdered," Morgan said. "The first is Katya. She's the sister of my Second."

My lips parted. Morgan's Second was a woman named Nadia, who was beautiful in an effortless, European way. I didn't know Katya, but I'd met Nadia briefly before.

"I'm so sorry," I said.

Morgan nodded. "The second is Zoey, a member of our administrative staff. They were friends."

"What happened?" Ethan asked.

"We found them at dusk. Will, our guard captain, found them." Morgan gestured toward the curly-haired blond beside him.

"May we?" Ethan asked, motioning toward the bodies.

Will nodded grimly, then took a knee and drew back the blanket. I didn't recognize the vampires, but then, I hadn't had much interaction with Navarre House other than Morgan and, once upon a time, Celina.

Katya was curvier than Nadia, with long, dark hair and angelic features. She wore what looked like sleepwear—a short satin nightgown of pale pink, and fuzzy white slippers. Zoey also wore pajamas—a tank and cotton pants. Her skin was dark and her hair was darker, cropped close to her head in tight curls.

Like he'd done with Oliver and Eve, the killer had separated the girls' heads from their bodies with the same long cut, and they were holding hands, their fingers stained with blood.

"Thank you," Ethan said, and Will covered them again. But covering the women didn't prevent the visage of their deaths from searing into my mind. Perhaps I was becoming desensitized, as it was less the blood and violence that affected me than the slippers on Katya's feet. They were soft and young and somehow pitiable, and made their deaths that much more offensive.

"Had they behaved unusually last night? Or perhaps disappeared for any time?" Ethan asked Will.

"They were hanging out together," Will said. "They spent the evening with friends at Red"—that was the official Navarre House bar—"and then returned here. They shared a room. No one noticed anything amiss until they were found this morning."

"What about the room?" I quietly asked, and eyes turned to

me. "I mean, they're in pajamas. Either they were taken from the room, or they left it to come out here for some reason."

Will nodded just a bit, as if appreciating the logic. "Their beds had been slept in, and the door was slightly ajar. The House kitchen is on this floor. We think they might have come downstairs for something to eat or drink."

"And the killer was waiting," Ethan finished.

Will nodded.

"Do you know how long they'd been dead when you found them?" Ethan asked.

Will cleared his throat, obviously uncomfortable. "The bodies were still warm. So not long."

"What about security cameras?" I asked.

"We have closed circuit, but it's not recorded," Morgan said, voice flat with grief. "And we don't have full-time external security staff. We don't need it," he added. But he didn't have to justify his decisions to me. Besides, it wasn't like our external security was working out so well right now.

"So it seems likely this happened just after dusk," Ethan said. "What type of security do you have on the doors? Who could get in?"

"Our security is biometric," Will said. "The system was on, and we've confirmed that it's functioning properly and has been. No breaches were registered."

"Can you track individual vampires?" Ethan asked.

"No. Our system doesn't record information; it operates like a door lock. If you match the data stored in the receiver, the door unlocks."

"That was Celina's preference," Morgan said. "She didn't want the vampires to feel they were living in a police state."

Or, I silently thought, *she didn't want anyone tracking the comings and goings of her lovers and secret allies.*

"What does the security system actually scan?" I asked. "Fingerprints? Retinal scan?"

"It's keyed for Navarre vampires," Morgan said.

His tone was matter-of-fact, but his implication was significant. Huge, actually. Because we'd found aspen slivers on the ground at the apartment building, we assumed McKetrick had been the killer. But McKetrick was human, as his daylight press conference with the mayor amply demonstrated. He wasn't a vampire, and certainly not a Navarre vampire.

Four vampires were dead, and the killer was a vampire . . . which meant we were looking at a vampire serial killer.

Ethan and I exchanged a worried glance. Thank God, even when he was angry, we could work together. That endeared him to me as much as anything else had.

"No one from Navarre House would do this," Morgan said, as if guessing our thoughts.

"Respectfully," Scott said, "if your security's working, only a Navarre vampire could have done this."

Morgan opened his mouth to respond, but he was interrupted by a commotion near the door.

Nadia, Morgan's Second and Katya's sister, ran into the room. Her cheeks were pink from cold, and she wore jeans, boots, and a long baggy sweater beneath the coat she hadn't taken time to button.

"Katya!" she screamed, her voice choked with tears, running toward her sister's body. But Morgan reached out and grabbed her before she reached Katya, wrapping his arms tightly around her and whispering softly in what I thought was Russian.

Since when did Morgan speak Russian?

Nadia screamed to be loosed. "She is my sister! Let me go!"

Morgan maintained his hold, and as her rage transmuted into

grief, she turned her body into Morgan as he kissed her temple, trying to comfort her through her gut-wrenching sobs.

It seemed Morgan and his Second were closer than I would have guessed.

"I'm going to take her upstairs," Morgan said, and we nodded as he escorted Nadia toward the staircase.

Will watched them leave, then looked back at us, desperation in his face. "Do you know who did this? Are you close to catching whoever murdered those two Rogues?"

I looked at Ethan, who nodded. "This is similar to Oliver's and Eve's deaths. The same method of death, and the same positioning of the bodies. Oliver and Eve were holding hands, too."

"But it's not in a hidden location this time," Jonah said, and I nodded.

"We'd thought McKetrick, the new Ombudsman, might be involved. But he's human, not a vampire. And if only Navarre vampires can get into the House . . ."

"Then you're out of luck," Scott said.

I didn't appreciate his tone or his conclusion, especially since he hadn't exactly participated in the investigation or offered any assistance. Thank God his guard captain was more willing to help.

"We have the information we have," Ethan said. "Nothing more."

Scott looked at him. "You'll look into this?"

Ethan looked at him silently for a moment. "Will, would you excuse us, please?"

Will nodded and walked away, leaving me, Ethan, Scott, and Jonah. Ethan took a step closer into the group, ensuring his words would stay private.

"Why not encourage Morgan to call the CPD?" Ethan asked.

Scott looked surprised. "Because they're part of the same city administration that hired McKetrick. Do you actually think we'd get a fair shake? Or that they wouldn't simply call this inter-House nonsense and attempt to oppress us even more? Or publicize the fact that it was probably a vampire who did this?"

I knew for a fact that there were perfectly honorable members of the CPD, my grandfather among them, but Scott had a point. If Morgan was right, and only Navarre vampires could enter and leave the House, that meant a Navarre vampire was the killer. Which was almost unfortunate, because we had no other evidence suggesting a Navarre vampire was involved.

"We will do what we can to bring the killer to justice," Ethan said. "But we are not here to dirty our hands so that yours and Morgan's can stay clean. We have reaped the punishment of that particular course of action for long enough. You owe favors to our House, and we will collect."

There was no denying the anger in Scott's expression; I doubted he was challenged by other vampires very often. But Ethan wasn't a Novitiate of Scott's House. He'd been a vampire—and a Master—longer than Scott had been alive.

I'd long thought that Ethan's premature death had changed him. Given him new bravado, perhaps. This was pretty good evidence that I was right. And since Ethan was one hundred percent correct, it was an attitude I liked. Cadogan didn't exist to serve Grey or Navarre, and while there was no question we wanted to find the perpetrator, I was glad they were on notice that their free rides were over.

There was something else in Scott's expression—a begrudging respect. Scott had seemed to me to be a forthright, balls-to-the-wall type of guy. Even though he didn't like hearing harsh truths, maybe part of him appreciated Ethan's frankness.

"Agreed," Scott said.

"In that case," Ethan said, "we'll leave the House to make its arrangements. We'll advise Morgan, and you, if we have any information."

Scott nodded, and the deal was done.

Ethan didn't spare him or Jonah another look, but headed back to the door. At least he'd managed to restrain himself from confronting Jonah about my RG membership here and now. Thank God for small miracles.

We left Navarre House through the cloud of grief and anger.

Unfortunately, those emotions followed us back to the House. Ethan wasn't talking, and I was becoming more upset. My RG membership was entirely justifiable, and it was supposed to be secret. Telling Ethan would have defeated the point of my being a member of a clandestine organization.

Not that I couldn't sympathize. I'd agonized about joining the RG for exactly the reasons he was angry now: because it would be perceived as slap against Ethan and the House. It wasn't; I knew that now better than ever. But that didn't ease the stone of guilt that settled heavily in my stomach.

When we got out of the car, Ethan waited for me before reentering through the Cadogan gate, but still didn't offer a single word.

"You'll tell Luc?" he asked, when we stepped into the House foyer.

I nodded. "Sure."

With a nod, he disappeared directly into his office without another word.

So much for our détente. I suppose it applied only to murder investigations, and not to the destruction of our House by contractual shenanigans.

My stomach clenched at the thought, but first problems first. I hadn't had a chance at Grey House to tell Jonah what had happened, and he needed to know, so I stepped outside onto the portico, dialed him up, and got right to the heart of it.

"Hello?"

"Ethan knows about the RG."

There was silence on the other end, and I could feel the disappointment radiating through the phone.

"I had to tell him," I said. "Lacey Sheridan followed me to our meet."

"She followed you? Why would she follow you?"

"Because she's in love with Ethan and is looking for an excuse to knock me out of the picture."

"Did she find one?"

"I don't know," I quietly said. "He's angry. The RG is kind of an insult to Masters, and he's taking it personally."

"That explains why he kept giving me nasty looks at Navarre House."

"Yeah," I said.

"Fuck, Merit. I do not want to add to an already shitty night."

"I know. I didn't plan on it, either. I'm not quitting," I added. "I made a commitment to you and the RG, and I know the RG is on the right side of things."

"What about Ethan?" he asked. It was hardly a question, but I knew exactly what he was asking: *Will Ethan rat us out?*

"He won't tell anyone," I said. "There's no one for him to tell anyway; it's not like he's going to call Darius up. I've told him I'm not quitting. I think he'll calm down—you know how strategic he is—but I have to wait him out."

My stomach clenched as I considered the worst-case scenario—that Ethan wouldn't get over my commitment, and that would be the end of us.

But I rejected that idea. Ethan loved me, and he wasn't going to leave because he disagreed with something I'd done, especially when that something was principled and intended to help the House.

Unfortunately, Ethan wasn't the only person involved in this drama. Lacey had inserted herself into it, too. God willing, he wasn't angry enough to fall into something with her that he'd regret later.

"What about Lacey?"

"She thinks we're having an affair. She and Ethan had a little chat this morning. I expect he explained away whatever she thinks she saw."

"I'll have to talk to Noah," Jonah said. "Theoretically, your cover's been blown. Since Ethan's no longer in the GP, it may not matter much to him. But we'll have to assess the risk."

My stomach fell. It hadn't occurred to me that they'd consider kicking me out of the RG because of what Lacey had seen, or what I'd confessed to Ethan.

This night was just getting better and better.

"Merit, hold on a minute, okay?"

Before I could answer, the phone clicked and he was gone. He must have been taking another call. Fifteen or twenty seconds passed before he came back again.

"I might have a solution to your House's problem."

Hope blossomed. "What's that?"

"The RG connection who told us about the contract bit? She says there's quite a bit of unhappiness with the way Darius is handling things. The situation is delicate—very delicate—but she's working it."

"She's working it? How?"

"We have someone inside the GP."

My eyes must have been as wide as saucers. "You . . . what?"

"A sympathetic member," he said, "but that's all I can give you right now. Let me talk it out and I'll see what else I can get you. I'll get back in touch as soon as I can."

"Okay," I said. "And I'm sorry. For everything."

"Things happen," he said. "They happen, and we pick ourselves up, and we get back out there."

He was definitely right about that.

The call done, I walked back into the House. Part of me wanted to run into Ethan's office and beg for forgiveness. But he hadn't invited me to his office, and I didn't expect I'd be welcome. I imagine he had enough on his mind without his girlfriend's presumptive betrayal staring him in the face.

I decided to visit the Ops Room, but stopped at the stairs when someone called my name.

"Merit."

I glanced over. Michael Donovan stood in the hallway near Ethan's office. He frowned when he saw me. "Are you all right? You look pale. Well, paler than usual."

"It's been a long night. I suppose you're brainstorming?"

He held up a bottle of Blood4You. "Yeah. We're looking at the contracts, trying to figure out a way to turn them around on Darius."

I nodded. "I need to get downstairs. Good luck with that."

"Good luck with your business," he said, offering a wave before he disappeared into Ethan's office again.

When I made it to the basement, I didn't find the mood in the Ops Room to be much better than mine was.

Juliet and Luc sat at the conference table together, both reviewing the House's evacuation procedures. Unfortunately, that they were reviewing evac procedures didn't say much for our chances when Darius showed up again with his hired thugs.

Lindsey sat at one of the computer monitors, and she looked

around in concern when I walked through the door. It wasn't hard to imagine that my mood was throwing off unpleasant magic.

"How bad was it?" Luc asked.

"As bad as you can imagine the deaths of two vampires being." I walked over to the whiteboard and added Katya's and Zoey's names, whispering a silent apology that I hadn't been able to do more to stop the killer before his spree encompassed them.

"We've got double the number of murders, and neither Navarre nor Grey is in much of a position to help."

"Not that they would," Luc muttered, and I smiled a little.

"You will, however, be pleased to learn that Ethan gave Scott the business for letting us do the dirty work."

Luc sat back in his chair, a smug expression on his face. "Good. He had it coming. Tell me what you know about the rest of it."

I nodded. "I'll call Jeff, and we can go through the entire thing together," I said, dialing his number on the conference phone.

"Milady," he answered.

"It's Merit and the Ops Room gang."

"You never have good news when you call me from the Ops Room."

"Sad, but true," I agreed, sitting cross-legged in the chair. If I was going to be miserable, I might as well be comfortable.

"Two Navarre vampires have been killed," I said. "Nadia's sister, Katya, and her friend Zoey. They were found this evening on the first floor of Navarre House. Both were decapitated, and they were found holding hands."

The room and phone were silent for a moment. Luc crossed himself, as if honoring the vampires' memory.

"That sounds like our man," Jeff said.

"It does," I agreed. "Same method, down to the placement of their bodies."

"And he only kills in pairs?" Luc wondered.

"So far as we know," I said.

"Different affiliations, though," Lindsey said, turning around from her computer station. "Two Rogues first, then two Navarre vampires."

"But random picks of vampires from each group," I said. "I mean, nothing we know suggests he targeted these particular vampires."

"Instead, he was targeting the groups," Juliet said.

I shrugged. "Maybe. I don't know if it matters, but there aren't any vampire registration issues with the Navarre House murder. Katya and Zoey were home in pajamas when they were killed. That doesn't fit the profile of a vampire who's pissed at Oliver and Eve because they were registering. Oh, and Navarre vamps are the only ones who can get into the House after hours. They've got biometric security."

"Biometric?" Jeff asked. "That's fancy. For a House anyway."

"I take it you don't know much about how they do it?" Luc asked.

"I don't. Normally biometric means a fingerprint or retina scan, but in this case I'm not sure. Theoretically, though, Merit's got it right: Biometric scanning would be a pretty solid method of security. I mean, it's easier to steal or swap a pass card or metal key than an eyeball, you know?"

"So, only a Navarre vampire could have murdered these two," Luc said.

"That's how it's supposed to work," Jeff said. "But I'll talk to Navarre."

Luc nodded. "Thanks. However they manage it, if it had to be a Navarre vamp, that takes McKetrick out of the equation."

"For the killing," I said. "But we still found aspen at the first murder scene."

Luc frowned. "Any aspen at the Navarre scene?"

"Not that I saw. And it probably would have been obvious on the marble floors. The aspen had to be at that first scene for a reason. Maybe our killer isn't McKetrick, but has ties to him or something. Like they're buddies?"

"That seems unlikely if the killer's a Navarre vampire," Luc said. "McKetrick doesn't like vampires."

"And nobody likes Navarre vampires," Lindsey muttered. Giving up the facade of working at her computer station, she pulled out a chair and joined us at the table. "Maybe the killer, the vampire, doesn't like McKetrick. Maybe he got his hands on a weapon, and he enjoys implicating McKetrick as much as McKetrick enjoys implicating us."

I nodded. That sounded entirely logical. Unfortunately, we had no evidence to support it.

"While we're talking," Jeff said, "I'm doing some poking around. I've got more evidence it's not McKetrick—at least, not him personally."

"That was fast," Luc said.

"Ya. I popped onto his official city Web site for 'S's and 'G's, and he's got an alibi. According to the numerous photos they've thrown onto the Web with no apparent artistic sensibility, he's been on a fund-raising junket with Mayor Kowalcyzk."

"Any chance the pics aren't legit?" Luc asked.

"Let me check," Jeff said. "I can run them through a program that flags image manipulation. *Beep beep boop boop.*"

Luc, Juliet, Lindsey, and I looked around at one another.

I squinted at the phone. "I'm sorry, Jeff, did you just say 'beep beep boop boop'?"

"Computer sound effects," he said, as if I'd asked him to explain the most obvious conclusion in the world.

"All right. Here we go. So, I've only checked one, but let's say it's obvious Diane's had a bit of digital work done. Unfortunately, the image of McKetrick is legit. It wasn't copied or pasted into the shot, which means he was really there with her. Sorry about that."

"Wait," Lindsey said, "what kind of digital work done?" She loved celebrity gossip, and had once graced the cover of a Chicago tabloid because of her fierce vampire style. Luc had not been amused.

"Focus," Luc said. "And never apologize for facts. We had questions about McKetrick's involvement, but you've helped us tie off that loose end. He's alibied for those murders, so we won't waste time on that angle. It is a bummer, though. I would have enjoyed pinning some good old-fashioned felonious behavior on him."

If Luc hadn't been a centuries-old vampire, I'd have called his expression a pout.

"It does leave us without a suspect," Juliet said.

"That it does," I agreed ruefully.

"What do we know?" Luc asked, scanning the whiteboard.

"Do we have any Navarre vamps even on the radar?" Lindsey asked, scanning the whiteboard.

"Not at the moment," I said. "But we're looking for one. Someone who kills in pairs, uses the same method of murder, and poses the bodies the same way. He's willing to cross the House/Rogue divide, as he's moved from killing Rogue vampires to killing Housed vampires."

"Or he's escalated from Rogues to the House," Jeff suggested, "depending on his attitude."

Luc nodded, pleased at the conclusion. "Good thought. Profile?"

I frowned, thinking it through. If I were this guy, and I'd done these things, who would I be?

"He's smart," I said. "Clever, and he likes to show off. He went from killing in an abandoned building to killing in Navarre House, with the bodies left in clear view of the House. He's methodical. He likes to set a scene."

Luc tapped his fingertips on the table rhythmically. "It's a good profile, except we have no concrete evidence to go with it."

He slapped a hand on the table. "And that's our job, people. Find me some evidence, before he decides to put Cadogan House back on his radar. I'll talk to Will at Navarre House. I don't think we'll be able to finagle interviews with the Navarre vampires, not given the mood over there, but it's worth a call. And maybe he's got some thoughts about any off-balance Novitiates who fit our profile. Mr. Christopher, I think we're done with you for now. Thanks for your help."

"Anytime," Jeff said, and the line went dead.

I turned back to the board, then walked over and erased McKetrick's name from our list of suspects. Where that left us I had no idea, but I had a very bad feeling more bodies were going to pile up before we got any closer.

When I'd stared at the board for an hour more, drawing and erasing straight and dotted lines between the facts that seemed to connect together, Luc suggested I take a break and say hello to Ethan. He was confident we needed to talk something out, and thought the middle of a crisis was a good time to do it.

"And, speaking of which," Luc said, "do you want to tell us what the hell went on with you and our beloved Master this evening?"

The entire Ops Room turned around to look at me. My chest burned hot. "I don't know what you're talking about."

Luc watched me for a moment, then shook his head. "Sentinel, that dog won't hunt."

"I don't know what that means. Is that cowboy wisdom, or a movie quote?"

Luc was a movie lover, and a constant movie quoter. But his eyes narrowed in disdain. "It's *movie* wisdom. And the next movie night, you're going to sit your butt down and watch *Roadhouse* like a good little vampire, or I'm giving you a nice little demerit for your file." He waved a hand in the air, dismissing the conversation. "But the sentiment stands. Go talk to him."

"We're in the middle of a fight."

Lindsey humphed. "All due respect, Mer, the cloud of emotional doom that is hovering over this House made that pretty obvious."

I winced. "Cloud of emotional doom?"

"You and Ethan have major chemistry, but you also have major magical spillover. When you're happy—when you're doing it regular, and don't give me that look—there's a nice, happy vibe in the House. When you're pissed off, the thundercloud of doom lurks above us and rains its funk down upon us all."

"I think you're overstating this a smidge."

She shook her head, convinced. "You say that because you can't feel it; you're already knee-deep in angst. Problem is, you're kicking it our way, too." She faux shuddered. "It's like a teenager's emo birthday party in here."

"And you don't think the GP ceremony and the chance we'll lose the House have anything to do with that?"

"Only thirty-five or forty percent," Luc said. "The rest of it's all you."

It wasn't exactly a vote of confidence that they thought I was sixty percent responsible for the House's bad mojo. But . . . "Be that as it may, they've created a war room up there, and they're focused on not losing the House. I'd prefer not to bother him until that problem's been solved."

Luc sighed. "Fine. Let him cool off, if you think that's best. We'll deal with the murder and let the upstairs staff deal with the House. Upstairs staff," he said with a chuckle, then looked at me curiously. "Your parents have money, don't they, Sentinel? Did y'all have upstairs and downstairs staff growing up?"

My father owned Merit Properties, one of Chicago's largest real estate development companies. We had a miserable relationship, mostly because he always wished that I was a different kind of daughter.

And also because he'd bribed Ethan to make me a vampire.

Ethan had declined, but the tactic—typical of my father's dictatorial style—hadn't done our relationship any favors.

I wasn't generally thrilled when people brought up my parents, but something happened when Luc spoke those words. A thought flashed, and I stared at Luc for a moment.

Luc grimaced. "Oh, sorry, Sentinel. I know they aren't an easy subject."

I shook my head. "I'm not mad," I said, then looked at the whiteboard. "I'm just thinking about property."

We'd identified the spots where Oliver and Eve were last spotted—the registration office—and where they'd been found—the warehouse. But we hadn't dug much deeper.

"The property where Oliver and Eve were found," I said, circling it on the whiteboard. "The warehouse. Jeff wasn't able to figure out who owned it."

"So?"

I recapped the marker and tapped it against the board. "Oliver and Eve were found in a secret room. James, one of Noah's friends, only suspected the room existed because he scented the blood. But how would the killer know about the room? Maybe the killer has some connection to the property."

"It seems unlikely the owner would use his own property to dump a body when it could be traced back to him."

"True," I said. "But the killer doesn't have to be an investor. He could be a former warehouse employee turned vampire."

"Turned Navarre vampire," Luc said.

"Even better. The list of people associated with that warehouse who are also Navarre vamps can't be long."

"Okay," Luc said. "But Jeff said the property records were a dead end."

"He did, but the records have to exist somewhere, even if they're somewhere Jeff can't get to them. On the other hand, I would bet my father can get anything he wants. I could talk to him."

The room went quiet for a moment as the group considered the gravity of that offer.

Lindsey grimaced. "Are you sure you want to do that?"

"I am absolutely certain I don't want to do it, but I've got to do something. I don't want to just sit around wondering if we're going to lose the House tomorrow . . . or waiting for another murder."

"You know, Sentinel," Luc said, "you've turned out better than I thought you would."

Proving she was my friend, Lindsey gave him a punch in the arm that had him roaring in complaint.

CHAPTER FOURTEEN

PARENTAL PATRONAGE

My parents lived in Oak Park, a suburb of Chicago known for its Frank Lloyd Wright architecture and beautiful homes. My parents' home wasn't one of those, at least in my opinion. It was a squat box of concrete slapped in the middle of prairie-style brick and honed wood. I completely understood why the neighborhood association had thrown a fit when my parents had shown them the plans.

Tonight, interrupting the usual peace and quiet of the neighborhood after dusk, men in J & Sons Moving T-shirts carried pieces of my parents' carefully curated furniture out of the house and into a waiting truck.

"You're moving?"

My mother's laugh tinkled. "Of course not. Just redecorating a bit."

Of course she was. My father had copious amounts of money, and my mother enjoyed spending it. "After dark?"

"They were two hours late, and I told their supervisor I wasn't releasing them until they were done."

And that, I thought, *is life in the one percent.* It was also a testament to how much furniture they'd amassed in their blocky concrete house.

"Why isn't Pennebaker out here?" Pennebaker was my father's skinny, fusty butler. He was probably my least favorite person in the house, which rather said a lot.

"Actually, he's at the opera this evening. It's his birthday." She glanced at me. "I presume you did not remember him with a card?"

"I did not."

Mom's upturned nose told me precisely what she thought of that breach of etiquette. She turned and walked into the house again, and I followed behind obediently.

"Why are you redecorating?"

"It's time. It's been fifteen years, and I wanted to breathe life into this house." She stopped and turned to look at me. "Did you hear that Robert is expecting again?"

Robert was my brother and the oldest of the Merit brood. "I didn't. Congratulations to them. When's the baby due?"

"June. It's very exciting. And this house isn't exactly grandchild-friendly, is it?" She put her hands on her hips and glanced around; she wasn't wrong—the house wasn't very grandchild-friendly. It was all concrete, monochromatic, and sharply angled. But it had been that way through the birth of my parents' other grandchildren, and they hadn't turned out any worse for it.

"If you say so," I said, not arguing the point. "Is Dad around? I need to talk to him."

"He is, and he'll be glad to hear from you. We won't be around forever, you know. You should consider giving him a chance."

I'd given him plenty of chances, although they were generally before he'd tried to bribe Ethan. But that was neither here nor there.

"I just need to talk to him," I said, willing to commit to nothing else.

We walked down the concrete-walled hallway and to my father's office. My mother's redesign had already found its way there.

The house had been a strict and sterile bastion of modernism; it had become the centerfold in an Italian design magazine. Pale carpet covered the concrete floor, and the office was lit by a chandelier of colored glass. Modern art canvases covered the walls. They were probably pieces my father had owned before my mother took charge of the room, but they looked completely different in this brighter, cheerier office.

My father, on the other hand, seemed unusually out of place.

Even at the late hour, he wore a black suit. He stood in the middle of the room, back bent over the undoubtedly expensive and custom putter in his hands. A few yards away, a crystal tumbler lay on the floor, poised to receive the ball.

He reviewed the lie and then, with a smooth motion, swung his outstretched arms in a perfect arc, sending the ball along the carpet to the hole at the end of his imaginary green. With a clink of glass, he sank the put.

It wasn't until he'd bent over to pick the ball up and cupped it in his hand that he finally looked up at me.

"Look who's here, Joshua." My mother squeezed my shoulders, then plucked an errant coffee cup from my father's desk and headed back for the door. "I'll just let you two talk."

"Merit," my father said.

"Dad."

He slipped the ball into his pocket. "What can I do for you?"

I was pleasantly surprised. He usually started off conversations with me with accusations or insults.

"I need a favor, actually."

"Oh?" He placed his putter into a tall ceramic vase that stood in a corner of the room.

"There's a warehouse in Little Italy. I'm wondering if you can tell me anything about it."

His toys put away, my father sat down behind a giant desk that looked like it had been made of recycled bits of discarded wood.

"Why do you want to know?"

Cards on the table, I thought. "The owner or someone involved in the property might have something to do with the murder of vampires."

"And you can't find this information online?"

I shook my head. "Nothing at all."

He regarded me skeptically. "I consider the assessor a friend, but I don't especially wish to burn that bridge completely by using the information she gives me to accuse someone of murder."

I pushed harder. "The clerk doesn't need to know what we're using the information for."

"We," he said. "You and Ethan?"

I nodded. My father and I hadn't discussed Ethan—or anything else—since Ethan had come back.

"He's alive and well, I understand."

"He is."

"That's good. I'm glad to hear it." He seemed honestly relieved. Since he'd put in motion the animosity between Ethan and Celina that had led to Ethan's death, he'd probably felt responsible for it, at least in some deep place in his heart.

It wasn't that I thought my father uncaring; he definitely cared, but he was so utterly absorbed in his own needs that he manipulated people like chess pieces to get what he wanted . . . even if he believed he was doing it for the good of others.

He looked up at me. "You and I haven't talked. About what happened, I mean."

"We've talked enough." My stomach clenched nervously, as it often did when my father suggested we should "talk" about things. Such conversations rarely ended happily for me.

"Have we talked enough for you to get some of the facts? Possibly. But the entire truth? Possibly not." He glanced at the array of photographs on his desk, and picked up a small silver frame. I knew what picture he held in his hand: a photograph of the child who would have been my older sister, the first Caroline Evelyn Merit.

"She was only four years old, Merit. It was a miracle your mother and brother walked away from the wreck, but that miracle wasn't large enough to save her."

His voice was wistful. "She was such a bright child. So happy. So full of life. And when she died, I think a bit of us did, too."

I sympathized. I couldn't imagine how hard it would be to lose a child, to bear witness to her passing, especially at such a young age.

But Robert and Charlotte had also lived through it, and they'd needed my parents, too.

"You were born, and we were so happy. We tried to give you the life we couldn't give her."

My father had an indefatigable belief that he could control and shape the world around him. He had grown up, he believed, without enough, because my grandfather brought home only a cop's salary. Solution? Create one of the largest businesses in Chicago.

I was the solution to Caroline's death. I was to be her replacement, down to the name, which is why even today I went by Merit instead of Caroline. But that burden was unfair, and it was much too heavy for a child.

"I can't replace her. I never could. And you decided to make me immortal . . . but you didn't ask me what I wanted."

He put the picture back on the desk and looked up at me, and his gaze was chillier now. "You are stubborn, just like your grandfather."

I didn't challenge that, as I didn't consider it an insult.

My father adjusted the items on his desk so they lined up just so. "I may be able obtain the information you're asking for," he said.

Relief flooded me. "Thank you," I solemnly said, hoping that he understood I meant it. I grabbed a pen and notepad from his desk and wrote down the warehouse's address, then put both back on his desk.

My father looked at the notepad silently for a moment, head canted as if he were debating something. "But keep in mind, I'm nearing retirement, Merit, and your brother will be taking over soon. I don't plan to set him up for immediate failure by arranging the city's chess pieces against him. So I'd like you to do something for me, as well."

I almost found it a relief that he'd asked. The request was a reminder—but a familiar one—that nothing was free when it came to my father. We were back on common ground, working in expected patterns.

"What?" I asked.

"You previously agreed to meet with Robert. I'd like you to follow through on that promise."

That was also a common refrain. My father believed being connected to a House would boost Robert's chances of making a further success of the company.

"Okay."

My father's eyebrows lifted. "That's it? No argument?"

"He's my brother," I said simply. "And you're right—I agreed to do it. But if this is for political benefit, meeting with vampires won't exactly endear him to humans. We aren't very popular right now."

"Perhaps not," he said. "But you are popular with your kind."

"What is 'my kind,' exactly?"

He gestured dismissively. "Supernaturals and the like."

I bit my tongue at the obvious stereotyping. He was, after all, doing us a favor. "Is there a market for you among the supernatural populations?"

"I'm not certain. But as there appears to be a substantial population of supernaturals in the city, we believe it's worth cultivating them."

I didn't tell him all the vampires living in Cadogan House might be seeking new living arrangements pretty soon. And speaking of which, I needed to get back to it.

"I'll get out of your hair," I said. "Please tell Robert to call me."

I walked out of his office, and I didn't look back to see whether he'd smiled in victory. But I'd have put good money on it.

I considered my visit to the Merit campus a success, but it wasn't going to be an immediate one. Even if my father made good on his promise to check the property, it was a long shot the information would be worth much. Plus, it was getting late, and the clerk's office would have long since closed for the night.

After saying good-bye to my mother, I sat in my car for a moment outside their house, the orange clunker no doubt depressing the property values by the minute, debating my next steps. I could return to the Ops Room and its sense of hopelessness, or to Ethan's office, which also wasn't exactly brimming with hope at the moment.

I checked my phone and found no messages, which made my

heart ache a bit. I wasn't expecting Ethan to suddenly blow through his anger and be thrilled that I'd joined a secret society, but a note would have been nice. Not that he didn't have other things on his mind. Like the House.

And perhaps the House was the key.

The RG was valuable. I knew it; I'd seen them in action. They'd helped me out of jams, and they'd given us a crucial bit of information about what the GP might try to do to the House, even if they hadn't correctly guessed how far the GP would go to screw us.

If I could use my RG connections to help save the House, wouldn't that solve all the problems? If I could help us keep the House that way, Ethan would see the RG was necessary and honorable—not a group that wanted to undermine him. If he saw that, he'd no longer think my joining was a betrayal of our relationship.

I closed my eyes and dropped my head back. Maybe, as Mallory once said, leprechauns would also poop rainbows on my pillow. We were talking about vampires here, and all of them stubborn . . . also like my grandfather.

But I had to try. I was useless to the RG, to the House, and to Ethan if I wasn't willing to try.

I started with Jonah.

He was immediately sarcastic. "Are you calling to tell me you've invited Ethan to our next RG meeting?"

"You're hilarious. Unfortunately, I have more bad news. McKetrick is alibied for the Navarre murder, so even if the biometrics weren't working, he wasn't there."

"At least we can tie off that thread," he said.

"That was our thought exactly. Any progress on getting help for Cadogan House?"

"Not yet. Our contact in the GP is skittish. And for good reason—if they find out she's been funneling information to the RG, she'll be the one facing down the aspen stake."

"That's not good enough, Jonah. This is my House on the line. Tell her . . . tell her I just want a meeting. Ask her if she'll do that."

"Merit, I can't."

But I wasn't taking no for an answer, and I'd been reading my *Canon* like a good little vampire.

"You said 'she.' There are only two female members of the GP, Jonah. The one from Norway—Danica—and the one from the UK—Lakshmi something. That means I have a fifty-fifty shot of guessing which member is the right one."

He muttered a curse; he hadn't meant for me to pick up on that. "It's not that simple."

"She's not helping us enough, Jonah. This is balls-to-the-wall time. Darius will either take Cadogan House away from us, or he'll start a war between fairies and vampires because his pride was hurt. Which one of those do you prefer as a precedent? The next time Scott does something Darius doesn't like, which way would you prefer Darius handle it? We cannot—as RG members or Rogues or whatever—let this stand. Darius cannot be allowed to break down what we've built just because we're doing it without him."

Jonah paused. "Her name is Lakshmi Rao. Let me talk to her."

"Thank you, Jonah. I'd do the same for you, you know."

"I know you would. And that's what scares me."

He hung up the phone.

I turned on the car and turned up the heat, still sitting outside my parents' house. It probably wouldn't be long before the neighbors were calling about the girl in the junky car "watching" the house, but I didn't want to go back inside while I waited for a response. Maybe my father and I had had a breakthrough; maybe he was simply feeling nostalgic. Either way, I knew when to quit.

The phone rang not even a minute later.

"Hello?"

"She's agreed to a meeting, but that's it."

"That's enough. Thank you."

"There's a Dirigible Donuts on State and Van Buren under the El. It's near the library."

"I know it," I assured him. It was near Harold Washington Library; it was also near the Dandridge Hotel, where the GP members were staying during their time in Chicago.

"Meet us there in one hour. And tell no one, Ethan or otherwise, about this. Consider this your first RG assignment—preventing the destruction of Cadogan House."

Instead of increasing the weight on my shoulders, which it should have done, it just made me feel more determined.

"I'll see you there," I assured him, and put on my seat belt. My baserunning might not have been pretty, but all that mattered was the final score.

It was late, and the Loop was relatively quiet. I parked on Van Buren, farther away than I'd have liked, then followed the El tracks back to State Street and the Dirigible Donuts location our reticent GP member had selected.

The chain's silver logo shone through the darkness: a gleaming blimp with "Donuts" in script across its side, the letters blinking in neon pink.

I opened the door and was hit by the scents of sugar and yeast. The restaurant was small and empty except for the tired-looking teen behind the counter and Jonah, who sat at a pink table in the corner, looking at his phone.

He looked up and nodded, then rose to meet me.

"She should be here any minute."

I nodded, my palms suddenly sweaty with nerves. This woman could make or break Cadogan House with a snap of her fingers— or perhaps the right words to Darius West.

Actually, by the look of her, she could make or break a lot of dreams.

Lakshmi Rao walked statuesquely through the front door. Like most other vampires (thanks to their selection process), she was gorgeous. Tall and lithe, with long, straight dark hair and caramel-colored skin. Her eyes were wide and hazel green, and she wore a printed designer wrap dress and stiletto heels beneath a long cashmere coat.

I'd seen her at the House, in formation with the rest of the GP members, but there she'd been one of many. Here she was a standout. She was obviously a vampire, and obviously a strong one. Even with no obvious vampiric features—fangs and silvered eyes hidden—she radiated magic in undulating waves. I had a natural immunity to glamour, but I felt it slip across the room and just touch the boy at the counter, who dreamily looked away and began counting aloud the donut holes in the bins behind him.

But most interesting? When Lakshmi caught sight of Jonah, she stared at him as if he were the first glass of water she'd seen after months in the desert.

His expression, on the other hand, was utterly businesslike.

So Ms. Rao, a member of the GP from Darius's home country, had feelings for Jonah, the guard captain slash member of the secret organization assigned to keep an eye on her. And he, by all appearances, wasn't feeling it.

How very Lifetime.

She looked at me, giving me a brief appraisal. "You must be Merit."

I had no idea of the etiquette. What was I supposed to call a member of the GP now? Without a better answer, I opted for a simple "I am."

She smiled gently. "It's nice to meet you. I'm sorry it's under such unfortunate circumstances."

"Were you followed?" Jonah asked.

"I seriously doubt it. And if I was, I'll lose them on the way back to the hotel. Unfortunately, I don't have much time. I'm afraid there's nothing I can do to help."

In a moment, my hopes were shattered. "Nothing? What do you mean, nothing? They're going to take away our House."

"Inside voice," Jonah murmured, casting a glance at the cashier, but he was still counting away.

"I am only one member of the organization, Merit, and I am by no means in the majority. Darius's punishment is much too dire, but I do not have the power to challenge him. I'm sorry."

"He's going to incite a war," I said.

"Only if Cadogan fights back, and we all know Ethan won't allow that. Not if it would bring harm to his vampires . . . or to you."

I suppose word about my relationship with Ethan had traveled among the GP members. "We cannot lose the House. It would be an insult to Peter Cadogan, to Ethan, to every other House that's tried to do its best since Celina forced us out of the closet."

Lakshmi looked at Jonah, who nodded at her. "Merit," she said, "please believe me . . . I have asked questions—surreptitiously, of course—but there's simply no way to steer Darius from his present course."

There was obvious regret in her eyes, which made me feel only minimally better.

"I'm sorry. But it's impossible. I don't have the power to over-ride him."

"What about the dragon's egg?"

Lakshmi paused. "What about it?"

"I assume Darius hasn't given it to the fairies yet and won't until he's sure they'll do what they've agreed to. Do you know where it is?"

She watched me carefully for a moment. "I do not know ex-actly."

"I will give you a boon," I said. "A promise, a favor, whatever you want. I will beg you, if that's what you want. Please, please don't let him take my House, Lakshmi. It is my home. For the first time in my life, it's really my home."

That thought—and the realization—brought tears to my eyes.

"I'm sorry," she said again. "I know only that it was hidden in a location of high regard."

I looked away, wiping back an errant tear that had slipped down my cheek. I didn't want to cry in front of my partner and the GP member. Maybe, like Darius said of Ethan, I was also too human.

"I should go," Lakshmi said. "And I wish you luck." She cast a lingering look at Jonah. "It was nice to see you again. I'm sorry it was under these circumstances."

Then she disappeared out the door and into the darkness.

I wanted to cry. I wanted to sit down and weep or, better yet, bury my sorrows in three or four dozen of the donut holes the cashier was so meticulously cataloguing.

"Let's go outside," Jonah said, gently steering me out the door. The cold air was refreshing, as was the numbing rumble of the El train above us.

We walked to the corner of the street, not far from where I'd parked, and stood in the darkness for a moment.

"She's in love with you," I said.

He cleared his throat nervously. "I know."

"That's why she agreed to the meeting, isn't it?" I looked at him. "That's how you got her to show up?"

He nodded, just once.

"This is just a clusterfuck. I suppose it would be wrong of me to suggest you offer to play Seven Minutes in Heaven with her so that she might give us the egg?"

He looked at me askance. "You want me to offer to make out with her so she'll save your House?"

I smiled a little. "Yeah, could you?"

"No. And you should get back. They'll be wondering where you are."

I wasn't so sure about that.

Feeling utterly defeated, I drove home again. Ethan's office door was open, so I took a chance and peeked inside, assuming Michael Donovan was in the room and heavy brainstorming and contract reading were under way.

But Michael was nowhere to be found; nor were Paige or the librarian.

Ethan and Lacey were alone, with a piano concerto on the radio and a bottle of wine on the table. They sat beside each other on the couch in the sitting area. Ethan, one leg crossed genteelly over the other, reviewed long documents on legal-sized paper. Lacey sat next to him, her boots on the floor, her feet tucked beneath her, scanning something on a tablet computer.

They looked utterly comfortable. Cozy, even, in a way that made my stomach drop and brought every teenage insecurity in my possession right to the surface.

But those weren't the only feelings in the chamber. I'd just begged a GP member to save this House—*cried* in front of that GP member—and I returned to *this*? Ethan may have been angry, but so was I.

Perhaps sensing the magical tsunami that accompanied me into the room, Ethan looked up.

"Yes?" he asked. His tone was flat; he was still angry.

That made two of us, since I'd walked in on a forthcoming chapter in Lacey's diary entitled, "The Cozy Night I Spent with Ethan Sullivan and a Bottle of Merlot."

I truly, *truly* did not like her.

"Could I speak to you, please, *Liege?*"

Ethan watched me for a moment before putting down his paper. "Lacey, would you excuse us?"

She glanced up and gave me a snotty smile he didn't see, then unfolded her legs and rose gracefully from the couch. "Of course. I could use a bit of fresh air." She walked toward the door, leaving her boots beside the couch, a clear indication she meant to return.

Of course she did.

"Time is ticking down, Sentinel. What did you want to talk about?"

I actually didn't have anything specific to tell him; I'd just wanted her out of the room, and perhaps a chance to clear the air.

But his tone was tight, and it took me a moment to gather words that weren't snarky, that didn't challenge her very presence in his office and her obvious intent to get her mitts on Ethan and not let go.

"Have you made any progress?" I asked.

"Not especially. The lawyers have prepared an emergency motion to halt the GP's actions, but, as we suspected, we're having a difficult time convincing a judge they have jurisdiction over this particular debate. None of the acquaintances from my very long life have any material worth GP blackmail, and Michael has determined that Claudia's tower is particularly well fortified right now, so there'll be no begging the fairies." His jaw was tight. He was obviously concerned, not that I could blame him.

"And you?" he asked.

"We've confirmed McKetrick didn't kill Katya or Zoey. He's alibied at a fund-raiser with Mayor Kowalcyzk."

"That doesn't leave us with much."

"It doesn't leave us with a suspect at all, except that we know the girls were killed by a Navarre vampire. Jeff's checking into the House's biometric system, and Luc is going to check in with Will and see if he's noticed any disturbed Navarre vampires recently."

"Hmm." He picked at an invisible thread on the knee of his trousers, then looked up at me. "Have you told Jonah about these latest developments?"

"Yes."

"Of course you have. Because you two are close." There was a dangerous edge of anger in his voice; it might have been motivated by fear or jealousy, but the only thing that mattered was that it was directed at me.

I had little doubt this change of attitude could be laid at the feet of the blond vampire I'd sent scurrying from the room. She was planting seeds of doubt about our relationship, and I'd bet money the more they spent time together, the bigger those doubts were going to become.

"We aren't close, not in the way you're suggesting. Not in the way Lacey has been suggesting to you. And that has nothing to do with this investigation."

"And you're willing to draw that line?"

"Are you willing to draw a line between you and Lacey? She looked quite comfy on the couch."

"That's completely different."

"Because Jonah knows that I'm committed to you, but she isn't entirely sure?"

His jaw clenched. "Are you suggesting I've been unfaithful?"

"Are you suggesting *I've* been unfaithful?"

"Have you?"

I flinched at the comment. "How dare you ask me that."

"There are rumors, Merit, about RG partners. That they work . . . closely . . . together."

His tone had gone condescending, and I suddenly felt like a very small child standing in front of my father, who was furious over something I'd done. Ethan was angry, and I wished he didn't feel my RG and Cadogan oaths—or my obligations to him—were in opposition. But I knew Jonah, and I knew they weren't. I still believed in the cause, and I was going to apologize for only so much.

My eyes silvered, and my heart beat faster, blood humming in my veins as my anger grew. "This is business. It is only business, and nothing else."

He arched an arrogant eyebrow at me, which irritated me further. It might have been his signature move, but it was a ludicrous response. A ridiculous response . . . to a truly ridiculous argument. Were we really arguing about infidelity? God knew I loved the man, but he was a stubborn, tight-assed control freak who really knew how to push my buttons.

"Ethan, we are better than this," I said. "I don't know what she's telling you, but you know I wouldn't be unfaithful. She is manipulating you, building a wall between us, and not for the better of this House, but because she has feelings for you."

"I'm not being manipulated," he said. He didn't sound entirely confident, but there seemed little point in continuing to argue.

"Okay," I said.

We stood there in horrible, awkward silence for a moment.

"I feel betrayed."

I bit my lip against the sudden onslaught of tears. "I know. And I'm sorry."

Ethan nodded, but said nothing.

"Okay, then," I said. "I should get back to work." Feeling dejected and angry, I walked toward the door.

"Where are you going?"

"I'm not entirely sure. But I think we need some space before we say something we're going to regret."

Assuming we hadn't already.

CHAPTER FIFTEEN

——— ⟡ ———

BOYS, BOOZE, BEEF, AND BETS

Fifteen minutes later I was still in traffic on Lake Shore Drive, with the lake to my right and Chicago's "big shoulders" to my left. Unfortunately, the drive hadn't done much to calm me down. The world was quiet, but my mind and heart were racing.

Probably Lacey and Ethan had been working. Probably they were taking a break after a long, miserable night. But probably that was time he could have spent with me, had he not been so angry.

He'd wanted a friend, someone who'd validate his feelings.

He couldn't have picked a better accomplice out of a catalogue. She was everything I believed I wasn't—graceful, stylish, cool under pressure. More like him than I was. Lindsey had once told me that was exactly why Ethan needed me, because I was fire to his ice. Lacey might never anger him, but she certainly wouldn't ignite him.

But none of that made me feel any better. Not tonight.

I slapped the steering wheel with both hands until my palms ached and the steering column felt loose. The poor Volvo. Fine

Swedish engineering or not, it wasn't designed for vampire aggression.

There seemed only one option.

I drove to Ukrainian Village and the dive the North American Central Pack called home, at least in Chicago—a squat biker bar called Little Red. (Now also home to some of the city's best smoked meats. And I would know.)

Even in frigid temperatures, shifters lounged outside along the row of Harley-Davidson and Indian motorcycles that lined the pavement in front of the door. I smiled politely as I passed them, but they were big and gruff and, frankly, didn't give a crap about a skinny vampire, no matter how well fitted and buttery her leather.

I walked inside and was immediately pummeled by the Clash and the smell of sour cabbage. It must have been sauerkraut-canning night at the bar.

Berna stood in her preferred position—behind the bar in a T-shirt one size too small for her heft. But this time, she had a buddy.

Mallory, her ombré hair in high side buns—couture à la dairy maid—stood beside Berna and practiced pouring liquor into a row of shot glasses.

As I walked closer, Berna's instructions became clearer. "No," she insisted. "You pour quickly, no spills. I show; I show." She nudged Mallory out of the way and took the unmarked bottle of liquor from her hand, then proceeded to fill six glasses in a smooth, fast line without spilling a drop.

Mallory gave her a begrudging nod. "I'm not sure if I like you," she said frankly. "But you know your meat and booze."

"Those are two of the four food groups," I said, sitting down at the bar. "Mallocakes and pizza being the other two."

God knew Mallory was far from perfect, and our relationship was still delicate. But it took only a glance at my face for her to realize the source of my troubles . . . and roll her eyes.

"What did you do now?"

"Why do you assume I did something?"

"Because you're across town at this bar when you have bigger problems on your plate."

"You've talked to Catcher?" I liked that news. It suggested—even if only a little—that things were getting back to normal.

"We've talked. We're talking. Lots and lots of talking and then more talking and conversing and communicating and talking." She snapped her thumb and fingers together, mimicking a mouth. "But you're not here to talk about us." Mallory narrowed her gaze at me, and I felt a faint prickle of magical interest—at least before Berna pinched her on the arm.

"Ow!" Mallory said, rubbing the spot, which was already turning red. "Damn it, Berna. He said I could use it a little bit."

"You use sparingly," she said, slapping one hand against the other, then gesturing at me. "Look at girl. She skinny vampire. She is in love, but is far away from lover. You don't need magic to know this." She tapped her temple. "You need eyeball."

They both looked at me. I nodded sheepishly.

"When you're right, you're right," Mallory said. "And since he took a stake for her, which pretty much proves he's in it for the long haul, I'm betting she's the current source of her own drama?"

I hated that conclusion. Not because it was wrong, but because it was humiliating. I was twenty-eight years old and headed for immortality. Was I destined to be forever awkward, at least where love was concerned?

And how often had I screwed things up when she wasn't around, and didn't even know it?

Mallory turned to Berna. "I'm taking fifteen, and we're moving this discussion upstairs."

"You can have here! I will not listen."

"You will listen," Mallory said, "and you'll tell your book club exactly what you heard."

"But is like *Twilight* in real life!" Berna protested. "Sparkles!"

But Mallory had already grabbed my hand and was pulling me toward the door.

"Ignore the half-naked shifters," she said, and before I had time to ask what she was talking about, we were rushing through the back room of the bar, where three or four—I didn't have time to count—shifters, most with their shirts off, sat at the old vinyl table playing cards. I'm pretty sure Gabriel was one of them.

And then we were in the kitchen, my retinas seared by the glow of gleaming pecs and abs, and she was dragging me up the stairs to the tiny bedroom where she'd been staying since she'd started her black magic recovery with hard work, shifter oversight, and lots of KP duty.

Mallory slammed the door shut and fell onto the small twin bed that was tucked against the wall. "Oh, my God, Merit, I'm going to kill her."

"Please don't," I said. "That would not improve shifter-sorcerer relations in Chicago."

"She's so nosy! And she's always telling me what do to!"

"She's like the parents you never had?"

She looked up at me. "Is that what it's like?"

"I'm afraid so," I said, sitting cross-legged on the floor.

"All right. I won't kill her. *For now.* And now that we have some privacy, why don't you spill what you did?"

This was the hard part, given the oath of secrecy I'd already inadvertently breached.

"I can't give you all the details," I said. "Suffice it to say he found out something I should have told him. And he kind of found out from Lacey Sheridan."

Mallory's eyes narrowed, just like they were supposed to. She remembered Lacey from her last trip to Chicago. "Why is she here?"

"To help with the transition from the GP. She's got a good relationship with Darius, and there was hope she might be able to smooth things over a bit. But since they're currently trying to take the House, that didn't work."

"Yeah, Catcher told me. What's that got to do with you?"

I struggled to find a way to give her the high points without revealing the secret. "Confidentially, while Ethan was gone, I agreed to help a friend in a way that helps the House, too. And I've continued to help since Ethan's been back. But I didn't tell Ethan about it, and then Lacey found out and told Ethan for me. Ethan was not thrilled."

The look on her face didn't exactly comfort me. "You betrayed him."

"I did not betray him. I understand that he's feeling betrayed, but I did what I thought was right. What I believed—and *still* believe—was right."

"Does this have something to do with that Jonah guy?"

Eyes wide, I turned to stare at her. "How do you even know about him?"

"Catcher," she dryly said. "He's in full-on relationship-autopsy mode. It's some kind of bizarre defense mechanism, probably prompted by the fact that he spends half his time watching those goddamn movies." She paused and turned to me. "Did I tell you about the time he auditioned for one of them? Before Nebraska, I mean."

Funny how well that simple phrase compartmentalized our relationship. "Before Nebraska" and "After Nebraska." "Before *Maleficium*" and "After *Maleficium*" would have been more accurate, but I wasn't eager to refer to an era in our relationship as "BM."

"Catcher auditioned for a Lifetime movie?"

"Yep. They were filming part of a rom-com in the Loop, and he auditioned to be an extra. Didn't get the part, although that clearly didn't sour him on the channel or the 'art form,'" she said, using air quotes. "Anyway, he said you were hanging out with this Jonah when Ethan was gone. Who is he?"

"Captain of the Grey House guards. He's just a friend. He helped me deal with stuff—deal with you—when Ethan was gone. He was at the Midway that night. . . ." I trailed off, not wanting to remind her in detail that she'd nearly burned down the neighborhood. She probably hadn't been paying much attention to my sidekick at the time, anyway.

"Ah," she said, obviously embarrassed.

"Yeah. Ah." I adjusted my ponytail. Not that it had needed it; I just wasn't sure what to do with my hands. The awkwardness with Mallory hadn't completely disappeared. "Lacey will grab him if she gets the chance, Mal."

"And you think he's amenable to grabbing?"

It was a good question; I knew he loved me, but he was angry and hurt, and he was probably questioning my trustworthiness.

"If you felt betrayed, and someone pretty came along and swore that she was the only one with your best interests at heart—that she was the only one who understood exactly what you and your House needed—would you feel amenable?"

She didn't answer, and when I looked over at her, I saw sadness in her face. My stomach fell, and I realized my error. "Oh, God, Catcher didn't, you know, find someone else?"

"No. I mean, not that I deserve his even talking to me—or your doing so for that matter—after what I did. I just . . . I could understand it if he had, you know, done that." Tears sprang to her lashes and she quickly wiped them away. "I left him in the middle of a crisis that I'd caused. Of course he needed comfort. Of course he needed a shoulder. I certainly hadn't played that part for him."

I blew out a breath. "Seriously, are we just incapable of not screwing up our relationships with people? Are we destined to do this for the rest of our lives?"

"Be screwed up?"

"Be screwed up and living with our shifter guardians or some crap like that, going to speed dating together because we can't maintain healthy relationships."

"If you get old and gray, I'll be honest about your roots."

"Vampires don't get old or gray. I'm stuck with this hair forever."

Mallory flopped back on the bed. "Woe is Merit, the immortal vampire with the never-gray hair and long legs and hot blond boyfriend."

"Whose boyfriend has a hot, blond hanger-on?"

She chuckled and sat up again. "We've gone full circle with this."

"What do I do, Mal? Seriously."

"You apologized?"

I nodded.

"Then you do the only thing you can do, and the reason you're here in the first place. You wait him out."

"That is truly just the absolute worst."

"It really, truly is."

We sat in silence for a moment while the laughter evaporated and the weight of the world settled heavily on our shoulders again.

"So this Cadogan House thing—do you think Gabriel has any dirt on Darius we could use to blackmail him?"

Mallory smiled sneakily. "Why, Merit, you sly girl. I am so proud that you've just asked that. It's so . . . vampiric. But honestly, I have no idea. He's downstairs, and you're welcome to ask him. But I will warn you—it's poker night."

"Meaning?"

"Meaning, if you want to talk to a shifter on poker night, you must play cards with the boys."

I arched an eyebrow at her.

She made an awful sound. "God, you're *already* Mrs. Sullivan. Let's go downstairs."

I checked my phone; still no messages. I didn't feel like there was any purpose to going back to the House without a solution, so I figured I might as well stay.

"Do I have to actually play poker?"

"You do. Fortunately, they will remain half-naked during the poker playing. If you like that kind of thing. Which obviously I don't."

I didn't need magic to know she'd been lying about enjoying the half-naked poker playing. I, too, could use my eyeballs.

There were four of them at the table. All shifters, only three of them half-naked, but the well-sculpted view was worth it.

Gabriel, the only one wearing a shirt, was shuffling a thick, well-used deck of cards. "Kitten," he said, sparing me a glance. "My brother Derek. I believe you've already met Ben and Christopher."

Mrs. Keene had named her children alphabetically in reverse order, starting with Gabriel, the eldest. Adam, the youngest Keene sibling, had been handed over to the CPD after his failed attempt to wrest control of the Pack from Gabriel. Ben, Christopher, and Derek were the next-youngest three.

Ben and Christopher were as broad shouldered and tawny haired as their brother; they sat at Gabe's left. Derek sat on his right. He had the same amber eyes as Gabriel, but darker hair and finer features. He must have taken after the other side of the family.

"Vampire?" Christopher wondered, eyes on the cards. "You running a way station for supernaturals in here, brother?"

"I have no need of a way station," I assured him.

"The kitten has claws," Derek said with masculine approval.

"*Rawr*," I said.

"You fight the fairies yet, Kitten?" Gabriel asked.

"No. And that's why I'm interrupting your game."

Gabriel's gaze flicked up to me, considered, then settled on the cards again. "Take a seat, ladies." Gabriel's magic was strong, and there seemed little doubt even that flick was meaningful.

"Can I ask about the shirts?" I asked, taking a seat beside Mallory. "Or the lack of shirts?"

"You may not," Christopher said.

"Yes," Gabriel mocked, "she may. Once again, the whelps have lost their shirts, Kitten. Literally and figuratively."

Derek grumbled something unflattering.

Gabriel gave him a quick and withering glance. "Pipe down, or I'll challenge you again, and we both know how that will work out." He began flipping cards across the table, creating a seven-card pile for each of us. "The name of the game is Nantucket."

"What's Nantucket?" I asked.

"It's a way to cheat," Derek said with a smile, sipping the glass of clear alcohol in front of him. "Don't let him fool you."

"I would never cheat," Gabe said. "I am as honorable as they come."

"Or else a really good liar," Ben said.

"I am not a liar," Gabe said, presenting the rest of the deck to Christopher. He cut it in half, put the bottom half on top, and slid it back to Gabe, who divided the cards into three stacks in the middle of the table. After dealing out the entire deck, he turned over the cards in the two outer stacks, revealing a spade in each.

"Spades are the cards to beat," he said. There was nary a spade in my hand, but I had no idea whether that was good. If spades were the cards to beat, what beat spades?

"High card, first trick," Gabe said, placing the queen of diamonds atop one of the spades. I wasn't sure why, or what I should play. I picked a queen of hearts and played it atop the remaining spade.

"Well played," he said, and began looking through his cards, frowning in concentration.

Each time I played a card, I tried to steer the conversation toward the House. But Gabriel wouldn't let me get a word in—not about politics, anyway. And so it went on for nearly an hour, at the end of which I still wasn't sure of the rules of Nantucket. I occasionally threw down a card I thought was appropriately strategic, while the shifters placed cards with apparent nonchalance. They'd have been sure winners at a poker table, assuming any casino let them play long enough to win.

Eventually, Derek threw his two remaining cards on the table. "Nantucket turtleneck," he said, and the other shifters threw in their cards, as well.

"Is it done?" I asked, looking at Gabriel.

But before he could answer, the door to the bar opened and Berna's head popped in. "Customers!" she said, pointing at Mallory with an arthritic finger. "You pour!"

Mallory sat quietly at the table for a moment, massaging her temples. It seemed her patience with Berna was definitely wearing thin.

"It's a good reminder," Gabriel said.

"Of what?" she asked.

"Of what happens when you eventually leave us, and you don't make a successful go of it. She's going easy on you this time."

"This is going *easy* on me?"

"Have you cleaned out the grease trap yet?" Christopher asked.

"No?" Mallory said cautiously, lip curled.

Christopher huffed. "Then she's going easy on you. Aunt Berna's a hard-ass."

I looked at Gabriel. "Aunt Berna?"

He smiled, then waved a hand at the vinyl-topped table, the framed B-movie posters, and the peeling linoleum floor. "Kitten, would we have allowed Berna into this bastion of class if she wasn't family?"

"Is that a compliment or an insult?" I wondered.

"Yes," he said. "It is definitely one of those."

Christopher, Ben, and Derek excused themselves and disappeared into the kitchen, presumably for one of the drinks Mallory was going to pour. Gabriel gathered the cards and began shuffling them again. Dawn, according to the beer-advertisement clock on the wall, was inching closer, and I still didn't have any answers.

"About the House," I said.

"What about it?"

"I'm out of ideas, the lawyers aren't helping, we can't find the egg, and Claudia's inaccessible. I don't suppose you've got any information on the GP members we could use to our advantage?"

He chuckled a bit. "You mean blackmail?"

"I do."

"I'm sorry, Kitten, but I don't. I don't know much about the GP other than their reputation, and from that I don't believe I care to know more."

I put my elbows on the table and rested my head in my hands. "Gabriel, we're going to lose the House. Time is ticking down. And we've got some crazy Navarre Novitiate out there taking out vampires for no apparent reason, and I don't have a clue who it is. What am I going to do?"

"You're asking me for advice?"

I tucked the edges of my bangs behind my ears and looked up at him. "Yeah. I think I am."

"And you aren't asking Sullivan because . . . ?"

"He's mad at me."

"Ahhh," Gabriel slowly said. "That explains the funk."

I tried not to sniff at myself. "There's a funk?"

"Psychic funk. A bad vibe. You're sad."

"I am sad. And you know what would help me? Advice. Do you have any thoughts at all?"

"Well, let's think it through: Darius wants the House, or to punish the vampires, or both. In order to get it, he's convinced the fairies to forcibly remove you, what, tomorrow night?"

"Yeah."

"And he's bribing the fairies with the dragon's egg, which is some trinket they made but gave to vampires, and are now claiming again, or some shit?"

"That's the meat of it, yeah."

"And where is the dragon's egg?"

"We don't know. The GP took it, but we haven't been able to find it, and the other Houses aren't cooperating."

"Well, at the risk of being blunt, if the fairies are the only leverage the GP has over you, and the fairies want the dragon's egg, then you need to find it."

"That's easier said than done."

"Is it? You're dealing with vampires, and a theft that occurred in a pretty short amount of time. Consider this." The card deck in hand, he began flipping cards onto the table one at a time.

For all his shuffling, and although I'd seen no trickery, he flipped over the jack of spades, then the queen of spades, then the king and ace. All in a row, all somehow organized without my being the wiser, and even as I'd watched him shuffle.

"The vampires of the Greenwich Presidium, who don't impress me much, managed to steal an object from Cadogan House right under your noses. I find that suspect."

"What do you mean, you find that suspect? You don't think they stole it?"

Gabe placed the deck on the table. "I don't know if they did or not. In my opinion the GP consists of the sneakiest vampires. Sneaky because they're double-dealers, not because they're skilled operatives who could pull off a heist beneath the noses of Cadogan House, its Master, and its Sentinel."

He had a point, although it didn't give me any better idea where the egg actually was hidden.

Gabe glanced at the clock. "The sun will be rising soon. You should get home."

I nodded and rose. "Thanks for your help."

He nodded. "It all comes down to this, Kitten: Don't let your fear of the GP guide you, especially not to give them more credit than they deserve."

Only half an hour before dawn, with my failure on my mind, I returned to the House.

The sight that greeted me in the foyer was enough to make me weep again. The holiday decorations were gone; in their place were dozens and dozens of black suitcases.

Granted, dawn would be here soon enough, but had we really given up? Were we simply going to hand Cadogan House to the GP without a fight?

I walked downstairs, found the Ops Room empty. Luc and the rest were probably tucking in for the evening. Because I wasn't up for another Lacey confrontation, I skipped a visit to Ethan's office and headed directly to the apartment to await him there.

As the minutes passed, I put on pajamas, then perused the House's evacuation procedures in our online security manual. Luc had been incredibly thorough, including creating a security "textbook" broken into chapters and thousands of footnotes. There were 142 footnotes in the third chapter alone, including lessons learned ("Garden rakes are less effective against wereracoons than you'd think"), anecdotes ("I remember when 'message' meant something carried on the back of a horse"), and tricks of the trade ("Honey is a good balm for a cobra lily scratch").

Luc, who'd penned the protocols, had also written tests to check our knowledge, like the following gem:

Q: What's the most effective way to corral a raging centaur?
A: Ha! There's no such thing as centaurs, newbie. Get your ass in a chair and read your Canon.

I did not, however, pack a suitcase. I refused to do it, to give in. There were only a few objects I cared enough to take with me— my family's pearls, my hidden Cadogan medal, the baseball Ethan had once given me. But they'd stay exactly where they were, because packing them away now would be a sign of defeat. And Ethan had taught me better than that.

I brushed my hair for the second time, then organized the drawer of my nightstand—tissues, lip balm, socks for cold winter days.

Just minutes until dawn, and he was still gone.

Surely he'd come back before the sun rose. Where else would he sleep?

I curled into his winged chair in the sitting room, listening to the clock tick away the seconds of his absence. The shutters over the windows descended, and the sun began to rise. My eyelids grew heavier, but still the door stayed closed.

The apartments creaked—the sounds of the ancient House settling and adjusting as the wind fought it outside.

I stayed upright until sleep threatened to knock me to the floor, then clumsily shuffled to the bed and climbed beneath the covers. The sheets were crisp and chilly, and I curled into myself to preserve warmth, an island of heat in the tundra of pressed cotton that our bed had become.

It was to be a war of attrition, of cold sheets . . . and I was losing.

CHAPTER SIXTEEN

CARD TRICKS

I woke up alone, the bed cold beside me.

I sat up, my mind whirling with possibilities—namely that he'd decided to let Lacey console him. But before I'd even put my feet over the edge of the bed, the door opened. Ethan walked in. He was in shirtsleeves, his jacket in his hand.

I said a prayer of thanks that he was okay, that the apparent vampire assassin hadn't snuck into Cadogan House and taken him out. But then the anger started to build again.

"Late night?" I asked, as calmly as possible.

"Continued strategy session," he said. "We nudged dawn, and I fell asleep on the couch in my office."

"And Lacey?"

"She was there," he simply said. He walked to the bed and laid his jacket across it, then took off his cuff links and watch.

"All this because you're angry at me?"

He didn't look back at me. "We were working, Merit."

"Until dawn? Without enough time to return to your bed? To me?"

"What do you want me to say?"

"I want you to admit that you're angry at me. That you want her to want you, and that you're giving her license because you're angry with me."

"You're just jealous." His tone was dismissive, as if I'd come to him with a childish complaint.

"Of course I'm jealous. You two were cut from the same cloth. And I think, in your heart of hearts, she's the type of woman you imagined you'd end up with."

"As opposed to the stubborn brunette I actually ended up with?"

"*Yes*," I pointedly agreed, then bucked up my courage. "Are you spending time with her to punish me about the RG?"

"I don't have time to play games."

"You're avoiding me."

"I'm busy."

"You're angry."

The dam burst. He glared at me. "Of course I'm angry, Merit. I am goddamn pissed off that you undertook a dangerous course without talking to me about it, and that you've been working with him all along without telling me about it."

He moved a step closer. "If I were to tell you Lacey and I weren't just working together because of our similar outlooks, our similar training, but because we shared a bond that you couldn't touch, how would you feel?"

He was right; I'd feel miserable. The hypothetical alone made me sick to my stomach. On the other hand . . .

"I don't spend time with Jonah to hurt you."

"If that's what you think I'm doing, then you must have forgotten the challenges facing the House right now."

The words notwithstanding, he wouldn't look at me when he answered. Yes, I'd hurt him, and there was little doubt his mind was on other things. But he knew damn well what he was doing and how it was affecting me. He was lashing out, even if he didn't want to admit it. Even if he wanted to imagine himself above such human concerns.

He put an elbow on the chest of drawers, then rested his forehead in his hand. "This won't help us. Fighting each other."

He was right. We were at a stalemate, and we would be until one of us stepped back, until one of us was satisfied about the fidelity of the other.

So he changed the subject. "The transition team is meeting in half an hour to consider our response. We have, we believe, some thoughts about the contract and the necessity of making the payment to the GP considering their bad behavior. We've called the bank, as well. But if we don't come up with a solution respecting the House proper, we'll have to give in."

"They mean to break us," I said, tears blossoming at the thought of leaving the House.

"They anticipate we'll bend."

But we wouldn't. We couldn't. The colonies didn't bend to the British, and I didn't imagine that we would, either.

"Your murder investigation?" he asked.

"We're no closer to finding out than we were yesterday. I have nothing, Ethan. Nothing at all."

And we're so far apart, I silently thought. *So far apart it's killing me. God, I need you. I need help. I need someone to steer me in the right direction. I need an answer.*

But I'd already asked him for more than he was able to give. He offered up a good-bye, then headed downstairs for another meeting with his team.

Which I was apparently no longer a part of.

————

I showered and donned leathers in case the transition was messier than we'd expected, and made the usual beauty arrangements—bangs brushed, hair ponytailed, lips glossed.

I walked downstairs, a couple hundred suitcases for the ninety-ish vampires who lived in Cadogan House still staring back at me like a reminder of my failure: *If you'd found a way out of this, convinced Lakshmi to help, we wouldn't have to leave.*

I glanced into Ethan's office, saw that it was full of vampires. Ethan, Malik, Lacey, the librarian, Michael Donovan, but empty of mementos. Despite the crisis—or because of it—someone had packed away Ethan's knickknacks: trophies, photographs, physical reminders of his time in the House.

That was utterly depressing.

I'd be in and among vampires for the rest of the night, most likely. But for now, I wanted a moment with the House, with my home, to say good-bye, so I bypassed the office and headed through the hallway to the back door, and then outside.

The cold was jarring, but refreshing, as if the cold had cleansing power of its own. I walked down the path to the garden in which Ethan and I had shared moments, and where the fountain had finally been turned off for the winter.

I glanced back, the House glowing gold in the darkness of Hyde Park, three stories of stone and blood and memories.

A GP issue we hadn't been able to fix.

Four murders we hadn't been able to solve.

A relationship I'd broken.

What if I'd been wrong? What if joining the RG had been a violation of my obligations to the House and his trust in me? What if I'd managed to take everything that was good in my life—my place in the House, my vampire family, and Ethan—and tossed it in the trash on a whim? Out of some misguided belief that joining the RG had been the right thing to do? What if I'd played my hand incorrectly, made the wrong decision, and because of that I'd lost everything?

Why was everything so complicated? The politics. My friendships. My family.

My love.

But as good as a pity party sounded, this wasn't the time for regrets. It was the time to savor memories I'd soon be giving away. I took a seat on a nearby bench and recalled the things I wanted to remember about Cadogan House. Dinner with Mallory and Catcher in Ethan's office. The first time I'd walked into the library. The night I'd been Commended into the House, when Ethan had named me Sentinel.

The flap of wings overhead drew my attention upward. A dark bird—a crow or a raven, maybe—flew across the lawn and over the fence again. Wouldn't that be nice? To be able to disappear from our drama and bad decisions so easily?

I dropped my gaze to the garden around me. It was winter, so most of the beds were brown and bare of flowers. Someone, probably Helen, had installed a gazing globe on the other side of the bench. It was a perfect sphere of blue glass. Surrounded by inground lights, its convex surface warped the image of the garden.

I scooted across the bench and stared into it, wishing for enlightenment and wisdom. My face was warped in the glass, my nose hawkish, my cheeks pink. It was a different perspective on who I was . . . and what I'd become. A soldier, perhaps, if not always a successful one.

I stood up and straightened my jacket. If I was going to be a soldier, and if we were all going down with this particular ship, I'd much rather do it with the rest of my team in the House in which

I'd built so many memories, rather than here, in the dark and cold, alone.

My phone signaled a new message just as I walked back into the House.

It was from Jonah. MESSAGE FROM LAKSHMI, it said.

My heart began to pound. AND? I asked him.

SHE SAYS, "MERIT OWES ME A BOON."

I stopped still, staring at that message. I'd offered her a favor last night in exchange for the location of the egg. She thought I owed her a boon . . . because she'd already told me the location?

SHE ISN'T RESPONDING TO MESSAGES, Jonah added, which I presumed meant we'd gotten out of her what we were going to get.

My hands began to shake with adrenaline. I squeezed my eyes shut, blocking out distractions, and tried to remember what she'd said about the egg, about where it had been hidden. It was hidden in a high place? A place of high esteem?

"No, a place of high *regard*," I whispered, opening my eyes again.

But where could that possibly be? A "place of high regard" could be virtually anywhere, if she had literally meant "high." Chicago wasn't without its tall buildings, after all. Could the GP have gotten it to the Willis Tower? Or the Hancock building?

What had Gabriel said? That I should be careful not to give them too much credit for a heist.

The GP had clearly accomplished a heist—the egg was no longer in its case. I'd seen that for myself. But what if, like Gabriel's skillful card dealing, the theft was somehow an illusion?

Maybe it was time to take a look at exactly what had happened during the GP ceremony.

I put the phone away and ran back down to Ethan's office,

where Malik and the transition team were settled in around Ethan's conference table.

Ethan stood a few feet away, not yet sitting, but clearly taking in the lay of the land—the vampires and stacks of materials at his table. Tools unable to help him solve the problem that confronted him.

But perhaps I could help.

I walked toward him, put a hand on his arm. "I need to speak to you outside."

He glanced back, dubious of the suggestion. "Time is a bit crucial, Merit. We have less than an hour before they arrive."

"I promise it will be worth your time."

He watched me for a moment, his trust in me clearly not back to usual levels, but nodded and followed me into the hallway.

"I think we should check the security tapes from the GP ceremony. There should be video of the back half of the House. I'd like to see exactly what went on when the egg was stolen."

His expression didn't change; I could tell he was trying not to get his hopes up. "Why?"

I wet my lips nervously. "I'm not entirely sure yet. But I've spoken with the particular source you don't approve of, and let's just say I think it's worth checking out."

He looked at me in silence for a moment. "Merit—" he began, and I knew he was going to tell me I was wrong.

But I wasn't wrong. I was right, and I knew it. I just wasn't sure *how* I was right.

"I'm asking you to trust me. I know I'm not good at being a girlfriend, but I've tried my best since I joined this House—without my consent, I might add—to protect it. To keep it safe."

"Without your consent?"

I smiled a little. "I just threw that in for tension relief. But that's not the point. Just give me a few minutes, Ethan. Humor me."

Ethan tapped his fingers against his hip, undoubtedly debating the value of spending precious minutes on an untested plan, instead of working on the plans he already had in place.

Without a word, he started down the hallway. I followed him, hope deflating, afraid he'd refused to believe me because he was still angry, or because the idea was really just that bad.

But he passed his office and headed for the stairs, and then walked down to the basement.

The Ops Room was abuzz. The overhead screen showed a group of photos, pictures of the Navarre House vampires, some of them crossed out, presumably because Luc had eliminated them as murder suspects.

I would have been surprised that the electronics were still here and operational. But there was an emergency plan for the Ops Room, too—an electromagnetic switch that, when pushed, would wipe clean the electronics where they stood. Luc didn't have to worry about packing; nor did he have to worry about any new residents of Cadogan House taking our sensitive information.

"Liege?" Luc asked, glancing between us when we entered. "Is everything all right?"

"We need to see video of the GP ceremony," Ethan said. "Can you arrange that?"

"Um, sure. Do I get to know the punch line?"

"We're curious about the egg theft."

"I'm listening," Luc said, tapping a tablet to pull up video from the security cameras.

The screen went dark, and then the video popped up. It was black-and-white and grainy, but the figures posturing on the lawn were clear enough. The GP appeared in its typical V formation.

"Goose on the lawn," Luc said.

"Goose?" I asked.

"That V formation. I like to use derogatory terms to describe the GP whenever possible."

I couldn't disagree with that.

"They're all there," Ethan said, his gaze tracking the screen as he counted the GP members. "No one's missing."

"Patience," I said, hoping that I was right and wasn't wasting his time.

In the video, Ethan and Darius faced off, and the fairies arrived for their show of strength.

That was when I saw it.

"There," I said, pointing to the video. In the back corner of the "goose," Harold Monmonth, Celina's GP buddy, disappeared from view.

"That little shit," Ethan said. "Move the video forward."

Luc fast-forwarded the video, and it skipped ahead. Four minutes later, Harold Monmonth popped back into the V like he'd never been gone.

"Check his hands," I said, and Luc zoomed in closer.

His hands were empty.

"Can we be sure he went into the House?" Ethan asked.

"We can," Luc said. "Camera on the back door, too."

Luc switched the view and rewound a bit, and sure enough, Harold walked inside . . . and four minutes later walked back out again, empty-handed.

"He went into the House; he came out again," I said. "The egg was taken, but it's not in his hands when he leaves."

I glanced at Ethan. "The GP knew they'd have to come right back to Cadogan House with the egg to pay the fairies, kick us out, and take control. In fact, they were *counting* on the possibility we'd give up and walk away rather than risk bloodshed. They also had to think we'd comb the city looking for it . . . and the last place we'd look would be right here, under our feet in Cadogan House."

"The dragon's egg is in the House," he said, astonishment in his voice, looking at me with awe, then wrapping me into a giant hug that soothed my heart . . . and every other part of me. "He left it in the goddamn House!"

"Damn, Sentinel," Luc said, standing up and clapping me on the back. "You have been listening to me."

Him, and a renegade GP member, and a shifter. But sure, him, too.

"One problem," Luc said, checking the clock on the wall. "We don't have much time until they arrive, and it's a big House."

Ethan looked at me. "Did your, er, source provide you with any clue about where it might be?"

"High regard," I said, and luckily thought to disguise my pronoun: "They said it was in a 'place of high regard.'"

Ethan and Luc exchanged a glance. "My apartments," Ethan said. "Perhaps the library?"

Luc shook his head. "The librarian didn't leave for the ceremony. He'd have known if someone came in. The ballroom?"

Ethan nodded. "You stay here. I'll check the ballroom. Merit, check the apartments."

I nodded and dashed back to the stairway and up three flights of stairs. I tore open the doors to our apartments and began combing the room. I pulled open cabinet drawers, pushed back curtains, pushed clothes aside in closets. I unzipped pillows, checked beneath ottomans, and crawled under the bed.

I tossed the rooms, but I found nothing.

Defeated, I walked back into the hallway just as Ethan bounded up the stairs, chest heaving.

"Anything?"

I shook my head, just as his beeper sounded.

Blowing out a breath, he looked at it. "They're here," he said. "The fairies are outside."

I shook my head. "This isn't the end. It's here, Ethan. I know it."

"I cannot allow them to bloody this House," he said, his posture and expression beaten. He turned back to the stairs . . . but I refused to give up.

"High regard," I muttered, taking only a single step farther toward the stairs. "High regard. High, like prestigious? High, like on drugs? High, the opposite of low?"

I stopped. "High, like the opposite of low."

Ethan glanced back. "Merit?"

"It's high, as in height," I said, realization and memory coalescing together. "I know where it is. Go, go downstairs. I'll come to you. *I promise.*"

He looked dubious, but I didn't wait for an argument. I ran back to the door at the end of the hallway that led not just to a room, but to an attic . . . and onto the Cadogan roof.

The room was empty but for the set of fold-down stairs, already unfolded. Air from the attic, cold and stale, rushed through the opening, and I climbed through it and emerged into rafters and insulation. I glanced around, but saw nothing.

But the window outside, which led to the House's widow's walk, was open.

"Hot damn," I said, rushing to the window and climbing outside into the night and onto the tiny balcony ringed by a railing of wrought iron.

I dropped to my knees and searched the shingles, one by one, in the dark, waiting to feel the lump of gold and enamel I knew I'd find . . . but still I found nothing. I stood up again, glancing down at the vampires and fairies assembling on the lawn just as Ethan walked outside.

The vertigo made me momentarily dizzy, and I put a hand out to balance myself—and felt the lump beneath the sandpaper shingle. I lifted it up and squeezed my hand into the opening I'd created . . . and pulled out a silk-wrapped package.

"I believe you have something that belongs to me."

I glanced back. Harold Monmonth stood in the window, scowling at me with dark eyes and a darker expression. The fairies were here, and it was time to produce his trophy.

But I had different plans.

"I believe you're wrong," I said, not waiting for his argument.

As he reached out to grab me, I hopped up to the railing of the widow's walk, then took a step into nothingness.

Vampires had a special relationship with gravity, and it was one I'd learned to exploit.

A second later, the dragon's egg safely in hand, I dropped down to the grass below, landing in a crouch with a thud that drew all attention to me.

With all the bravado I could manage, I rose and walked toward Ethan, trophy in hand. I smiled slyly. "Liege, I believe you were looking for this."

The crowds erupted into sound and noise—cheers from the Cadogan vampires, jeers from the GP members and the fairies. Not that they cared who carried the token. They just wanted it in hand.

Swollen with pride, and as Harold, Darius, Lakshmi, and the rest of the GP members watched, Ethan gazed across the lines of fairies in the yard.

"I presume you're here to retrieve the dragon's egg?"

"It is ours," said one fairy, stepping forward. "Made by our hands."

"Perhaps," Ethan said, "but it was created for one of our own, given to us by royalty among you. It is rightfully ours. Although by your deeds, you have proven how little you care for what is right."

There were scowls aplenty among the fairies.

"But tonight I offer this: Take our dragon's egg. And in return, swear to us that fae will do no more business with the Greenwich Presidium or threaten harm to Cadogan House, and we will consider our business here concluded."

Concluded, I presumed, because we could no longer trust them to guard the gate.

The fairies communed together for a moment, and then the fairy who'd stepped forward nodded at Ethan. "Accepted," he said, and took the dragon's egg from Ethan's hands.

Like a defeated army of the supernatural, they marched out the gate again.

Slowly, Ethan glanced at Darius, eyebrow imperially raised.

I had to bite back a smile, and I'm sure I wasn't the only one in the crowd.

"It appears your plan has been . . . thwarted," Ethan said.

"They are only our tool," Darius said. "You have wronged us, and we have a right to your House, irrespective of the arms we bring to bear in the conversation."

"Well, that position is as unfortunate as it is wrong. What you failed to anticipate, Darius, is that your little power play—your raising arms against our House and its vampires—is a fairly significant breach of your contract with Peter Cadogan."

Darius's smile faded.

Ethan put his hands in his pockets. "And do you know what happens when you breach the contract? By its terms, Cadogan's obligations to the GP are dissolved." Ethan snapped his fingers. "*Gone.* Not only don't you get the House, you also don't get the check. We called the bank, and they are more than happy to keep our rather substantial assets safe and sound within their vault."

Ethan crossed his arms and arched an eyebrow at Darius. "As you've lost your army and your battle, I suggest you get the hell off my lawn."

"This isn't over, Ethan," Darius gritted out.

"I'm sure it isn't," Ethan said. "All's fair in love and war, after all."

Their current state of defeat obvious, Darius and the GP members began to slink toward the front of the House, and Ethan was swamped by Cadogan vampires celebrating our very close call.

But he met my gaze over the crowd, a promise in his eyes—and his words. *All the chocolate in the world*, he silently said.

I presumed that was my reward, but this hadn't been my doing. I was only the vessel for the clue someone else had given me. I glanced across the sea of vampires, and locked eyes with Lakshmi Rao. She stood her ground, shoulders straight, expression just haughty enough to qualify for GP membership.

She looked back at me, and there was a very clear reminder in her eyes: *You owe me.*

As she disappeared from the Cadogan grounds with the rest of them, I shuddered.

The cold drove us inside, and we gathered in the foyer while Helen, Margot, and her staff unboxed crystal flutes and poured champagne.

"Novitiates," Ethan called out, "it would be naive of me to say that we are now in a world free of challenges. We are Rogue vampires, and if they weren't already, we have undoubtedly made an enemy of the GP tonight. Our guards still search for a killer who haunts our city. But most of all, we are Cadogan vampires. Drink up," he said, lifting his glass, "and then back to work."

Like a boss, I thought with a smile.

For a few minutes of bliss, I let Luc ply me with beef jerky and I pretended I was as competent as he made me out to the vampires sitting around us. But the fact that we'd found the egg was a lesson in human (and vampire) nature: Be nice to people (and shifters), because you never knew when you were going to need to pick their brains.

After a few minutes, I stood up to find Ethan. I needed to get back to work, but we needed to clear the air. I'd shown him, I hoped, that the RG was a benefit to the House, not a burden. A bond that worked both ways—and worked for the overall good of vampires.

I walked down to his office and found his door slightly ajar. I peeked inside. He and Lacey stood in the middle of the room.

Ethan's expression was polite. "I appreciate that you came. You're a good Master; you're an even better ex-Novitiate."

He teased Lacey, but her expression was serious, and there seemed little doubt of what was on her mind.

"Ethan, I have to say this: I think it's time you gave serious thought to your relationship with Merit."

"Lacey—" he began, but she interrupted.

"You need someone strong. Someone honorable. Someone who isn't going to run into the arms of another vampire in the middle of a crisis. You need someone worthy of this House. Someone worthy of you."

However much she wanted him, she had no right to diminish the gravity of what he'd done—the stake he'd taken for me—by suggesting he hadn't done it on purpose.

It was time to clear the air with her, too, so I pushed open the door and stepped inside.

Lacey caught a glimpse of me, and before I could speak, she reached out, grabbed Ethan by the lapels . . . and kissed him fiercely.

"Jesus!" Ethan said, pushing her back and wiping his mouth with a hand. "Lacey, get ahold of yourself."

"She let you *die*," Lacey insisted. "She failed to protect you. Do you know what that did to us? To all of us?"

Thinking it best to keep the witnesses to this drama to a minimum, I closed the door behind me with a resonant thud.

Ethan looked back, his eyes widening, probably wondering what I'd seen.

"If you're going to insult me, at least respect me enough to insult me to my face." I kept my tone calm, but my voice was loud enough to carry across the room.

For a split second, I saw fear in Lacey's eyes. But then in an instant it was gone, replaced by haughty arrogance.

"This is how you train your Sentinel? To be disruptive? To be dishonorable? She's cuckolding you, Ethan. And lying to you about it." She reached into her pocket and pulled out the Saint George coin Jonah had given me. "I found this on the floor of your apartment, and it stinks of Grey House."

My eyes widened, and I only just managed not to reach into my pocket and confirm the coin was gone. It was clearly gone; it must have fallen from my jacket.

Ethan's expression was a sad mix of fury, disappointment, and bewilderment. "You were in the apartment?"

"Yes, because I'm right, Ethan. I've always been right about her. I don't care who her father is. She's dishonest, and she's hurting you."

I wondered if Ethan appreciated the irony that two of his vampiric students had acted without his permission because they were sure they were right. I'd acted for the House. Lacey had acted . . . for Ethan? Or for herself? Did she truly believe I was as dangerous as she said, or was that the best excuse she could imagine to in-sinuate herself between us?

And then there was the shot about my father, which certainly didn't endear her to me. It was a sensitive spot, which she must have known.

Ethan sensed my rising anger; he held up a hand to stop me from speaking. "It is unacceptable for you to go into our home without permission."

Our home, he'd said. Tears nearly popped to my eyes from the rush of relief prompted by those two little words, but I held them back. I did not want to cry in front of her.

She blanched, just as I had. "I did it to help, Ethan. You have to know that." She thrust out the coin again. "Look! Look at this. It proves what I've been saying."

"Merit has no reason to be ashamed about that coin. And you have no reason to concern yourself with it."

Wait, did Ethan just *defend* me . . . and the RG?

"You knew about it?" she asked.

Ethan didn't answer. He just extended his hand, kept it there until Lacey dropped the coin into it. And then he turned and held it out to me.

"I suppose you dropped this, Sentinel?" His eyes were unfath-omable.

"Yeah, yes," I said, then tucked it into my pocket again.

Ethan looked back at Lacey. "I think it's time you return to San Diego," he said. This time his tone wasn't that of a Master speak-ing to a colleague, but a Master speaking to a Novitiate who'd dis-appointed him.

"Ethan—"

"Lacey, I don't care to be manipulated. While our relationship is long-standing, and I appreciate your service to this House, for the sake of that relationship, this is a chapter you must close. If you cannot close it on your own, I will close it for you."

She nodded curtly, tears beginning to swim in her eyes. "Liege," she said, then turned on her heel and walked toward the door, opened it, and disappeared into the hallway, leaving it ajar. I wondered if that was symbolic of her hope that perhaps Ethan might change his mind and call her back.

Ethan looked back at me. For the first time in days, I saw the hint of a smile. "Saint George?"

"It was a gift from the RG. For my membership. Thank you for covering for me."

"The last thing we need is Lacey believing she's discovered a conspiracy between you and Jonah to take down the House."

I nodded. "I'm sorry for all of this. I'm sorry Lacey and the RG had to come between us. It wasn't the way I wanted this to work."

"I understand why you'd be attracted to the RG," he said. "It's because of who you are. Your recent humanity, your rebellious nature, your disdain for authority. And as we saw tonight, your RG connection is quite clearly a very effective defense against the GP."

"I told you it would be," I said.

"You'd have a heart attack if I forced you to quit, wouldn't you?"

"Yes, because you wouldn't force me, and I couldn't do it. That's not who you are, Ethan, and that's certainly not who I am. I'm Sentinel of this House for a reason—because you knew I wouldn't blindly follow your dictates or the GP's dictates."

Ethan made a sarcastic sound. "There seems little chance of that."

I took his hands. "If I thought for one second that I needed to join the RG to keep an eye on you and make you a better Master, we wouldn't be together. You taught me to be a vampire, to be a soldier, to stick up for those whose voices aren't heard by the politicians in our world. Even if it doesn't feel like it, the RG is an homage to you, not a rebellion."

He looked back at me, and must have been satisfied by what he saw in my eyes. "Follow your instincts, Merit. If you believe the RG is part of your path as a vampire, see it through. But remember that *we* are your priority."

He smiled a little, so I leaned up and pressed a kiss to his lips. "Always," I said. "I love you."

"I love you, too. I can accept your RG membership because I know who you are. Because I know you will wear it to better the lives of vampires of this city. But times are what they are. That I find it acceptable doesn't mean that others would. Who else knows?"

"No one else. Well, the House knows we were fighting, but not what we were fighting about. Ditto Mallory."

Ethan narrowed his gaze.

"What? I needed to talk to a girlfriend."

"And what did she have to say?"

"She was irritated on your behalf."

He looked smug. "Do try not to tell anyone else about your top secret affiliation, if you can manage it."

"I'll do my best. And consider this—if I forget and put an ad in the *Sun-Times*, at least we have each other."

"So we do. I will accept your membership in the RG. But should you ever share blood with him again, you will answer to me."

His eyes had silvered, and he stared at me intensely.

The heady mix of fear and lust in the air made my head spin. "You said you weren't jealous," I countered, stepping backward. "You said you and I were inevitable."

"That was before I knew that you'd blood-bonded yourself to a man of another House, Sentinel."

Without warning, and before I could correct him, he reached out, gripped the edges of my jacket, and kissed me fiercely. "You are mine and mine alone, and it appears you need reminding. I suggest you return to our apartment; otherwise you'll be ravished here and now where you stand, and the door is open."

I stared at him, all rationality leaving me, any objections I might have made to his attitude completely slipping from my mind. I was grateful to be alive, and this was Ethan in his prime—vampire, alpha, predator. And it was intoxicating. But that didn't mean I wasn't going to challenge the attitude. I knew my eyes had silvered—and that he'd seen it, too, but ignored it.

"You wouldn't."

He dropped his head, his lips at my ear. Instinctively, my blood singing, I dropped my head back, giving him access to my neck. "Try me, Sentinel."

"Ethan," I muttered, the sound pushing him over the edge.

"Too late," he said, moving to the office door, slamming it shut, and locking it behind him.

Before I could object, he'd reached me again, and his mouth was on mine, feasting, his hands claiming every inch of my body as he pulled away my jacket and dropped it to the floor.

"You're ravenous," I said lightly.

He stepped forward to keep our bodies aligned, and took my chin in his hand. "I will have you. Body, mind, and soul. And I won't share you with anyone else."

He was in full alpha mode, playing out some part about possession and ownership.

I was a smart woman. Well educated and plenty schooled. But

that didn't lessen the effect of his primal, predatory desire. If he'd asked me to drop to my knees and crawl toward him, I might have done it.

Fortunately, there was no need.

I gripped the hem of his shirt and pulled it upward and over his head, taking a long moment to enjoy the view: smooth, eternally golden skin over lean muscle. I slid my hands from his waist to his chest, reveled in the feel of him. He stepped back and raised both arms, then ran his hands through his golden hair. The motion pulled his obliques into view and tightened his flat stomach. "Show-off."

Ethan grinned and crooked a finger at me.

"I don't perform on command," I reminded him.

He unsnapped the top button on his jeans.

My eyes widened. "Sneaky bastard."

I gnawed my lip in pleasure, watching the past, present, and future Master of Cadogan House in a state of utter abandon: shirt on the floor, jeans unbuttoned, his arousal obvious.

Without bashfulness, he took my hand and guided it to his erection. With rhythmic motions, he moved my hand back and forth across denim-clad steel, eyes closed as he tilted his head back, teeth clenched, breath hitching. His hips canted against my hand.

I watched him for a moment, utterly entranced, his expression wrenched with the sensation, the sensuality. And then his eyes opened, his lips curled, and he watched my face as I moved him, rocked him, brought him close to the edge of his passion.

When he decided he'd had enough, he found my mouth again, then wrapped my legs around his waist and maneuvered me backward until my thighs hit the back of his desk, and I was perched on the edge, my legs wrapped around his hips.

"You want me," he said.

"I don't stop wanting you. Not since the moment I walked into this House all those months ago."

He momentarily stilled—maybe shocked by the admission—but his eyes flattened again.

"Take off your shirt," he said.

But I hadn't won Ethan Sullivan—and he hadn't won me—by my playing the wilting lily to his alpha predator. I lifted my head. "I am not your possession."

"Aren't you?"

At my refusal, he moved forward and gripped the hem of my shirt. With fingers trailing over my skin, he pushed it upward, farther and farther, until he'd revealed my bra. Then shirt and undergarment disappeared, and he trained his eyes on my bare breasts.

He used mouth and teeth and tongue to incite me, and when I was aflame, stripped me of the rest of my clothing. His hands aroused my body, a ship at his command. There wasn't a bit of me that wasn't on fire for him, and when I silently called his name—*Ethan, please*—he reacted.

He didn't waste time on preliminaries—not that I needed any. A thrust of his hips and he was inside me, pushing a bare whisper of sound from my lips and the very breath from my body.

"Look at me," he said. But when I buried my head in his shoulder, he took my chin in hand and turned it toward him. "Merit. Look at me, goddamn it."

His irises, already silver, spun with mercurial motion. He held my gaze as he moved faster, as our bodies and hearts collided, and I watched with awe and shock and utter arousal as his pupils contracted and his lips trembled . . . and he reached his pleasure.

I watched the delicious agony of release cross his face, and I thought I'd never seen anything so memorable, that burrowed so deeply into my soul, as the expression on his face.

But to every story, there is another chapter.

Two hours later, we'd found our way upstairs and were still lying languorous and naked across the bed we'd reclaimed together, with love.

I lay on my stomach; Ethan lay beside me, his fingers trailing up and down my back as dawn approached again.

"So, are we good?"

"I'm definitely good."

I swatted his shoulder. "You know what I mean."

"We're good," he confirmed. "And if he so much as lays a hand on you, he won't live to regret it."

"Egotistical much?"

He smiled that leonine smile, utterly masculine, utterly arrogant, utterly proud. "It's not egotistical if it's well earned. Shall we see, Sentinel, how well earned it is?"

Far be it from me to argue.

CHAPTER SEVENTEEN

NEVER GONNA GIVE

I woke drowsy to find Ethan on the other side of the bed, tying his hair back with a bit of leather cord. He was shirtless, but wore martial arts pants.

"Going somewhere?"

"Workout," he said. "The tension of the last few days has built up. I need to work through it."

I propped myself up on my side, grinning at him. "And last night wasn't workout enough?"

"Less so for me than for you, although I bless the day you decided to train as a ballerina and work on your flexibility."

I could feel the blush to my feet.

Ethan headed toward the window. I pulled the sheet around my body, then padded to the window, a train of Egyptian cotton behind me.

Outside, the night was overcast and still, like the precursor to a winter storm.

"Snow later tonight," Ethan said.

"It feels like it." I looked back at him. "What are you doing after your workout?"

"Working with Michael regarding our security protocols. Since an RG member was able to enter and exit the premises in fairly quick order, we've obviously got holes to fill."

"Good call," I said, although I wasn't sure anything other than alarms on the bedroom doors and interior cameras would have solved that particular problem.

"I presume you're heading to the Ops Room when you're up and around?"

"That's my plan. Luc was looking at the Navarre vamps, so I'm hoping something popped up there. I also want to call Jeff to see if he's found anything new. And I visited my father," I added.

Ethan looked at me, obviously startled. "When?"

"During our escalation of tensions."

"What did he have to say?"

"He apologized for the vampire thing, in his way. I asked him to get information about the owner of the building where Oliver and Eve were killed. Jeff didn't find anything, and maybe it's a throwaway fact, but I thought it was worth asking."

"It's a good thought, Sentinel. Perhaps you'll get your clue. I'll see you later."

He kissed my cheek and headed for the door, feet padding across the hardwood floors. With one crisis down, but one substantial crisis yet to go, I dropped the sheet and dived into the shower, where I dunked myself under steaming hot water, thanking God I was still in Cadogan House and not at a hotel across town, living from a suitcase as I contemplated my vampiric future.

When I reached the Ops Room, everyone was engaged in a task of some kind, but Luc was nowhere to be seen. In fact, the Ops Room was virtually empty except for Lindsey and a few of the temps.

"Where is everyone?" I wondered.

"I believe you'll want to go next door," Lindsey said. "Ethan and Jonah are sparring."

"Oh, you cannot be serious," I said, positive she was joking.

But she definitely, definitely was not.

They stood in the middle of the mats, both shirtless, Jonah also wearing martial arts pants. The air was thick with magic and the smells of sweat and blood.

In the time I'd gotten dressed and come downstairs, they'd been beating the crap out of each other, and they clearly hadn't pulled any punches. Jonah's eye was bruised, and his lip was cut and swollen. Ethan limped, his left foot obviously tender, and his knuckles were bloody and torn.

I walked into the room as Jonah wiped a smear of blood from his jaw. He nudged Ethan, who looked back at me.

I crossed my arms and stared back at him.

"Jonah volunteered for a little sparring practice," Ethan said.

The liar.

But Jonah, who'd worked out the cover story with him, nodded. "The old man picked a fight. I thought it was a good idea, so I went along with it."

I glanced up at the balcony, which was full of well-entertained vampires. "Could you excuse us for a moment?" I asked.

Seeing as I had no authority over them, they all looked at Ethan, who nodded; then they filed out of the room. When it was empty, I looked back at Ethan and unloaded the cannons.

"There's a vampire assassin on the loose in Chicago," I said, "and I could use a little cooperation. What the hell is going on?"

"We needed to clear the air," Ethan said, silver eyes blazing as he stared at Jonah.

Jonah, his expression surprisingly serene, nodded in agreement.

"About what?"

"You," they simultaneously said.

I was completely flabbergasted that two grown men—more than grown, chronologically—would waste their time throwing punches at each other.

"And this was the best way you could do it?"

"Yes," they simultaneously answered.

I put my hands on my hips and closed my eyes. "This is completely ridiculous, and completely insulting."

"It was necessary," Ethan gritted out. "Boundaries needed to be set."

"As if there was any risk of boundaries being breached," Jonah countered, magic rising again, and it was clear they hadn't really settled anything.

"You've deemed yourself her 'partner,'" Ethan said.

"In the RG. You're her romantic partner."

"So I am. Can you remember that?"

Jonah's eyes flattened, not, I thought, because he was jealous, but because Ethan had taken a stab at his honor.

"She is my partner," Jonah said, "because she agreed to fight with me to protect the vampires in this city. If you don't understand that, or can't respect it, you're the one with the problem, not me."

"*Hey*," I interrupted, "I am not a toy to be fought over." I pointed at Jonah. "I'm his colleague"—I pointed at Ethan—"and his girl-friend. Those are the boundaries, and that's where they'll stay."

"We needed to be sure of it," Ethan said.

"You needed to whip them out and compare notes," I countered. I looked at Jonah. "I'm still learning who you are. And you're my partner, so I appreciate that you're willing to take a punch for me."

I walked to Ethan and glared up at him. "But you know better than this, Ethan Sullivan."

I strode toward the door, then peeked back to watch Ethan reach out his hand. After a moment, Jonah shook it.

God save me from boys.

While Ethan and Jonah finished their testosterone fest, I went back to the Ops Room to stare at our whiteboard. Unfortunately, no clues had miraculously appeared overnight.

"It looks like you've gotten a lot done," I said to Luc, but the Navarre vampire photos on the projector screen answered the question. Every photograph had been covered with an "X."

"Yeah, but not the kind I prefer. I talked to Will; there's not a single option in the group," Luc said, swiveling around in his chair in a full circle before landing at the head of the table again. "They're either alibied or completely motiveless."

I frowned. "But how is that possible? We know it was a Navarre vampire, right? So it has to be one of them."

Luc ran his hands through his curls. "You'd certainly think so, wouldn't you? But unless Will is lying, which I highly doubt, they're all off the hook."

I grimaced. "Is there any chance Will's the killer?"

"There's a chance of everything you can imagine, Sentinel," Luc said, going philosophical on me. "But that doesn't mean the chance is large."

"What about the biometrics?" Lindsey asked. "Have we heard from Jeff about that?"

"We have not," I said, picking up the phone. "Let's do that now."

Jeff answered the call almost immediately, but there was such a cacophony of music and screeching in the background that I could hardly hear him.

"*Turn the music down!*" I yelled, holding the speaker away from my ear until the volume was only slightly above bar brawl. "What's going on over there?"

"Nymph birthday party!" he yelled over the remaining musical din.

I rolled my eyes. "Could you maybe go outside?"

"Oh, yeah! Sure!"

A moment later, I heard the slamming of the screen door and the din quieted considerably.

"Sorry. It's a nymph obligation thing. I was going to call you as soon as we were done."

"Got anything on the biometrics?"

"Actually, yeah. Turns out this is pretty state-of-the-art stuff. It's not a scanner for fingerprints or retinas—it scans your blood."

"Your blood? How? And for what?"

"Tiny pinprick," he said. "A little lance pops up and scans the blood. But it's not looking for type or anything—it's looking for vampiric heredity. It only lets in vampires who were made by Celina."

And we had a winner.

"So to get in, you don't have to be a current Navarre vampire— you just have to be one of *Celina's* vampires."

"Correctamundo."

"Thank you, Jeff. That's great. Have fun at your party."

"Later, Mer."

He hung up the phone, and I did so gratefully, rubbing my ear a bit for good measure. I was pretty sure I'd just heard Rick Astley at eardrum-popping decibels, which wasn't anything I needed to ever experience again. Ever.

"News?"

"One of the nymphs is celebrating, and the biometric scanner at Navarre determines whether you were sired by Celina."

Luc whistled. "That's nice technology. And it gives us suspects." He walked to the whiteboard, scratched out NAVARRE VAMPIRE under the suspect list, and added SIRED BY CELINA.

"Would there be a lot of Celina-sired vampires not in Navarre House right now?"

"I have no clue. Typically, you wouldn't think many, but Celina was an odd duck. There's no telling exactly how she ran her House."

Since we had to identify the killer she'd made, not terribly well, in my opinion.

A little while later, I was nominated to make a snack run to the kitchen. Although I wouldn't wish murder on anyone, it was nice to be back in the Ops Room and operating on a relatively normal schedule.

After taking the roll of any other Ops Room food requests, I walked upstairs and down the hallway to the kitchen. Ethan's office was still closed, and I expected he and Michael were working on our revised security plans.

I peeked into the kitchen, making sure I wasn't about to barrel over anyone headed out of the swinging door with breakables, and found the room abuzz with activity. It looked like they were preparing for a cold-fusion experiment.

The stainless-steel countertops were covered in vials and beakers, and two-foot-tall assemblages of glass pipettes and other assorted equipment.

"What's going on in here?" I wondered aloud.

Margot, who'd paired her white chef jacket with the loudest pants I'd ever seen—an insanely bright neon chartreuse that looked nearly radioactive—glanced back and smiled.

"We're making condensations," she explained. "We're reducing food to its chemical essentials to get to the heart of the flavor."

"Cool," I said, although I still preferred a hamburger over any whip, mousse, or elixir I'd tasted at my father's house.

"Yeah. This seemed like the kind of night to try something new." Her voice had gotten quieter and more solemn. "Like we're on the verge of something, you know?"

"Believe me," I said. "I get it."

Margot helped me fill a tray with beverages and snacks—including bottles of the sarsaparilla that Luc favored.

I was halfway down the hall when Ethan—now in jeans and a three-quarter-sleeved T-shirt—stepped out of his office. "Would you like to go have dinner?"

I looked down at the tray in my hands. "I have dinner."

"I was thinking about an actual meal, with tables and waitresses. I'm starving, and I don't want to eat at my desk. I'd like to grab a quick bite, just a few minutes away from the House. I don't suppose you'd happen to know a place?"

Of course I knew a place; I knew plenty of places. If only the questions he usually asked were so easy to answer.

"What are you in the mood for?" I asked.

He ran a hand through his hair. "A burger, maybe? But nothing trendy, and nothing kitschy. No shade-grown beef or organic spring mix or beet consommé," he said, mirroring the thoughts I'd just been having.

"Shade-grown beef. That's funny." I bobbed my head back and forth, debating a couple of options. Chicago was a food-friendly town. Shade-grown beef was an option if you wanted it; so were modernist foams, authentic *pho*, and diners where the waitress offered you just-fried donuts when you walked through the door. I didn't mean to put Chicago on a pedestal. Undeniably, it had issues: poverty, crime, and strife between folks—including vampires—

who thought they were all "different" from each other. But you truly couldn't fault the food.

When I settled on a restaurant, I looked at Ethan. "I'll drive."

"You have to. I don't have a car anymore," he reminded me. "But, out of curiosity, why do you need to drive?"

"Because we're going to a place for locals. Low-key. Good food. Good atmosphere. Whatever car you might borrow would be . . . too much."

"Despite the fact that I've lived in this city longer than most anyone alive, you're afraid they'll think I'm a tourist."

"Your cars are always so flashy."

"Your car is so . . . orange." The distaste in his voice was obvious. Not that he was wrong.

"My car is also very mine, and very paid off. I'm driving." I lifted the tray in my hands. "I'll take this downstairs. You grab your coat."

He grumbled a few choice words, but only because he knew I'd won. Heaven forbid Ethan Sullivan should let me get in the last word.

Giant neon capitals above the sidewalk read CHRIS'S BROILER. When we opened the door, a giant brass bell on the handle chimed our arrival. The decor was simple and homey, the restaurant populated by small tables, plastic chairs, and a line of orange vinyl booths along one wall.

"Take a seat," said a waitress in a black uniform dress and white apron who breezed past us with a tray of what could only have been manna from the gods. I didn't see what it was, but it smelled like heaven on a plate.

"Shall we?" Ethan asked, putting a hand at my back and guiding me toward a booth.

We weren't seated for more than fifteen seconds before a blond waitress with a ponytail put water glasses and laminated menus in front of us. "Get you something to drink?"

Ethan's gaze didn't waver from the menu he'd already snatched up.

"Water's fine," I said, and she smiled and moved along, giving us time to consider our orders.

We sat quietly in the booth, the few other diners around us enjoying their late-night meals.

The bell on the door rang, and two uniformed officers walked inside and headed to the counter, where they took seats and began chatting with the waitress.

"What do you recommend?" Ethan finally asked, oblivious to my mental wranglings.

"Patty melt," I said, pointing to its spot on the menu. "With fries. It's their specialty."

"And it appears I can add any number of toppings. Peanut butter. Eggs. Pickles." He looked up at me. "What's a jalapeño popper?"

"Nothing that's made it into the awareness of a four-hundred-year-old vampire, evidently. It's a cheese-filled jalapeño."

"Ah. Sounds . . . unhealthy."

"I wasn't finished," I said. "It's also breaded and deep-fried."

His eyes widened comically. I needed to get him to a state fair and a booth where everything was fried and served on a stick. He'd probably have a heart attack just looking at it.

"Pick the patty melt," I repeated, looking at my menu and scanning the options. What was the best thing to eat when you were trying not to think about the murder you couldn't solve? Salad? It was the classic food of self-denial. The meatloaf platter was a protein- and carb-laden behemoth—more an indulgence than a punishment.

In the end, I settled on something simple. Foods that would sit easy in my gut, even if my conscience wasn't sitting easy.

"Morning special," I said when the waitress returned, handing the menu back to her.

"I suppose I'll have the patty melt special," Ethan said, giving the waitress a smile and returning his menu, as well.

"Anything you want, sugar," she said with a wink, tapping the edges of our menus on the tabletop to straighten them, then disappearing into the back. I wondered whether they had a Mallory in the back of Chris's Broiler—a disgraced witch doing her best to atone for her sins with dishwashing and onion chopping.

I sprinkled salt on the table, then put my water glass over the salt.

"What's that for?"

I smiled a little. "It's supposed to keep the glass from sticking to the table if you don't have a coaster. I don't know the science of it or if it even works. I've just seen it done."

"Hmm," he said, then mimicked my movement and sprinkled salt on the table in front of him. "We'll test the theory and see if it works." He glanced up at me. "Are you okay?"

"I'm good. Tired."

I could see a hint of sadness in his eyes, too. He'd reached the end of an era, and certainly the end of Ethan's particular brand of international strategy.

"You're mourning, aren't you?"

He looked up at me. "Mourning?"

"You're grieving about leaving the GP, not being involved in international machinations. Your world—the House's world—is contracting. You aren't thrilled about that."

"I am a very strong Strat," he said. Vampire strengths were divided into categories—psychic, physical, strategic—and levels—

very weak, weak, strong, and very strong. Ethan was as strategic as they came, quite literally.

"It will be a different kind of politicking from here on out," he admitted, pausing while the waitress placed plates in front of each of us.

We checked out our meals. It was clear after a moment that Ethan was coveting my stack of hash browns, biscuits, and gravy; frankly, his patty melt looked pretty delicious, too.

"Switch?" I asked.

"I knew I loved you for a reason," he said, switching our plates' positions and diving into the biscuits and gravy with the abandon of a starved man. Not that there was anything wrong with a patty melt. It was hot and greasy and just the right balance of salty and cheesy.

I flipped the bread from my sandwich and doused the meat with ketchup—an abomination to some, but delicious to me. I also poured a separate puddle for my fries. When the ketchup bottle was in place again and I'd settled my sandwich in hand, I took a bite, and then another, and another. We ate quietly and companionably, two emotionally exhausted vampires struggling for energy.

When I'd finished off half my sandwich, I took the paper wrapper from my napkin and folded it lengthwise into a thin strip, and then around into a ring, tucking the ends together. I handed it to him. "Now you have a memento of this wonderful date at Chris's Broiler."

"Sentinel, are you giving me a ring?"

"Only the temporary kind."

After glancing at the check, Ethan pulled his long, thin wallet from his interior coat pocket, slid out bills, and placed them on the table. Minutes later, we were in the car, driving home again.

———

We'd only just parked my car when Lindsey ran out to meet us on the sidewalk.

"You need to get inside," she said. "Margot's hurt."

A bolt of adrenaline sent me running down the sidewalk, Ethan's footsteps behind me.

When I stepped into the House, I stopped short. Malik stood in the middle of the foyer, Margot in his arms. Her eyes were closed, and there was a smear of blood around her neck.

Holding in a scream, I covered my mouth with a hand.

Malik carried Margot into the sitting room and laid her carefully on the couch, brushing the hair back from her eyes. Her chef's jacket was red with blood from a gash on her neck.

"Is Delia here?" Ethan asked.

"Delia?" I asked.

"She's a doctor," Malik said. "And a friend of Aaliyah's." Aaliyah was Malik's wife. "She usually works a split shift. I'm not sure if she's in the House."

"Someone get her," Ethan snapped.

"I'll do it," said one of the vampires behind us, rushing out of the room.

"What happened?" I asked, falling to my knees beside the couch. Someone handed me a scarf, and I pressed it to Margot's neck to stanch the bleeding.

My heart pounded, my fear and anguish matched only by the fury I felt on Margot's behalf. Someone hurt Margot. My friend. My culinary ally.

But not just hurt—someone had tried to *kill* Margot. And given the wound at her neck—an unsuccessful decapitation?—our serial killer was the number one suspect.

"I was talking to her a minute ago in my office," Malik said. "She was asking me about kale. She said there were winter vegetables outside in the garden and she was going to pick some things. I don't know what happened after that. Next thing I know, she's stumbling into my doorway."

Ethan's eyes went silver. "Someone attacked here? In my home?"

Now our attacker wasn't just a Navarre vampire, but a Cadogan vampire, too?

"I'm here," said Delia, stepping into the room with the vampire who'd fetched her. Delia was tall, with dark skin and straight dark hair that reached her shoulders. She wore pale blue scrubs and flip-flops.

"I was about to hop into the shower. What happened?"

"She was attacked outside the House," Ethan said. "Her throat was cut."

I moved out of the way so she could get closer to the sofa. "Someone applied pressure," she said. "Good."

Carefully, she peeked beneath the scarf I'd put on the wound. She grimaced a bit. "It's a very clean cut—sharp weapon. Those often don't heal as well as more jagged cuts. It's deep enough that it will take a bit yet to stitch together, but if I can get some blood into her, we can keep her stable until she heals completely." She glanced back and found Helen in a corner of the room. "Can you get me the House emergency medical kit, some water, clean towels, and a knife? I want to get her cleaned up so it heals well. Less risk of a scar that way."

Helen nodded and disappeared.

"A knife?" Ethan asked.

"We'll need a blood donor," Delia said. "Not everyone prefers to break skin with teeth."

"She came to me," Malik said. "When she was injured, she came to me. I'll give her blood. And I don't need the knife."

Without waiting for approval, Malik bit into his own wrist, and the smell of sweet and powerful blood and magic filled the air. I closed my eyes, enjoying the scent before Delia cleared her throat and gestured toward us.

"This isn't exactly a sterile environment, and you're not making it any cleaner. Disperse, please. I'll keep you updated."

Her authoritative tone didn't leave any room for argument, so we climbed to our feet and walked into the hallway just as Malik placed his open wrist to Margot's lips.

"A knife wound at the neck," Luc said. "Similar MO, if we assume he ran out of time."

"We so assume," Ethan said. "Check the security video. I want to know exactly what happened out there. We work from the presumption this was another act of violence by our killer. And until he's caught, no one leaves this House. Not without the express permission of a senior staff member. I don't care if they're going to work, to dinner, to the bar, or to do a good deed."

Luc grimaced. "Liege—" he began, but Ethan stopped him.

"No excuses. I don't want to hear how it can't happen. I want to hear how it will happen. Figure out a way. Make it clear to them that they don't have a choice. That asshole has targeted my vampire, which means he's under my authority now."

"On it," Luc said, trotting toward the basement stairs.

Ethan looked at me, helplessness in his eyes. He didn't have to speak for me to know what he was feeling: fear that he'd somehow allowed Margot to be hurt.

"What could we have done differently?"

"I don't know," I told him. "But we'll find out."

The front door opened and shut behind us, and we glanced around.

My father stood in the foyer in a crisp tuxedo, a large set of rolled papers in his hands. The security guards had let him through the gate, probably given our family ties. I sincerely hoped he had evidence in hands.

"Merit, Ethan," my father said.

"Joshua," Ethan said. "What brings you by?"

"Meredith and I are on our way home. We were downtown, and we picked these up while we were there."

"It's nice to see you," Ethan said, "but if you'll excuse me, I need to get back to this."

Ethan disappeared. Given the drama in the front parlor, I opted to guide my father toward the front door. "Why don't we just chat outside?"

Brows knitted, my father glanced back as we stepped outside. "Is everything all right?"

"Unfortunately not. One of our vampires was attacked. We think the murderer might have done it. What have you got there?"

My father unfurled the roll, revealing several large sheets of white paper. There was a building plan, several contract documents, and a map of land plots, dozens of square and rectangular puzzle pieces fitted together to form some part of Cook County.

My first thought was that he'd discovered something about the property in Little Italy, but I didn't recognize anything on the map. The boundaries were strangely drawn, and there were no buildings to be seen.

"What am I looking at?"

He tapped a spot on the map. "That is the address you asked about. These parcels are owned by a limited liability company. That company is, in turn, owned by another limited liability company, and so on up the chain. Ultimately, you get to a single owner: Carlos Anthony Martinez."

"Who is that?"

"I have no idea. I thought you might."

Unfortunately, I didn't. My heart sank. I'd been holding out hope the property was owned by Vampire H. Killer or some equivalent name that would ring obvious bells and send me in his direction.

My father looked at me for a moment, then nodded almost imperceptibly. "The land is valuable. If you have discovered untoward activities there . . ."

"You can jump in, buy the property for a song from the current owner, and turn it into something else."

He nodded. "It's a good location. An area that's troubled, but it's up-and-coming. It could be a positive arrangement if we can make it work."

And that was how my father operated, and probably the secret of his success. There was always a deal to be done, money to be made. And if the opportunity arose, you didn't let little things like murder—or your strained relationship with your daughter—impede your financial progress.

"Thank you for the information. If this leads to anything, I'll let you know."

My father looked appreciative, which seemed a fair trade for the information. Problem was, I was left standing on the front porch with a map and a reference to a man named Carlos. What was I supposed to do with that?

———✠———

CHAPTER EIGHTEEN

SEALED WITH A KISS

I rolled up the map and walked back toward Ethan's office; no point in delaying bad news any longer than necessary. The door was open, but Ethan was gone. Michael Donovan stood in front of the bar.

"Is Ethan around?" I asked.

He looked up. "He just popped into Helen's office; they're making arrangements for Margot. Would you like a drink?"

I blew out a breath. "Sure. Whatever you're having."

He smiled thoughtfully. "I knew I liked you." He opened one of Ethan's decanters and poured Scotch into two glasses, then handed one to me.

I wasn't much of a Scotch fan, but tonight I wasn't going to argue. I sipped it, letting the fire burn down my throat, savoring the warmth. There was too much violence in the air for even an old Scotch to touch, but that didn't make the sensation any less pleasurable.

"How goes the securing?"

"Slowly. We're working on cameras right now, making sure we

can fill the necessary gaps while still giving the vampires their privacy."

I smiled. "I can see how that would be tricky. We do like our privacy."

Michael sat down in one of the chairs in the sitting area and waved me over. He crossed one leg over the other. "What have you got there?"

"Property maps," I said. "From my father. I'd hoped they'd help us identify the vampire killer, but I'm not sure they'll actually lead anywhere."

Ethan walked in just as Michael's phone rang. Frowning, Michael excused himself from the room and began chatting with the caller.

"Have you heard anything about Margot?" I asked Ethan.

"I just checked in. She hasn't yet regained consciousness—which isn't unusual for a wound of this magnitude—but she's healing very well. Delia expects she'll make a full recovery."

"Good," I said, feeling a wash of relief. Margot was an awesome person and a good friend, not to mention a great chef. She was also a potential witness, and that would be handy in preventing any more attacks.

"What do you have there?" he asked.

I glanced down, just realizing that I still held the rolled-up map in my hand. "Info about the property in Little Italy."

Michael stepped back into the room. "Ethan, if you'll excuse me, I've got a personal matter I need to address. I should be back shortly."

Ethan nodded. "Of course."

Michael waved at me, then disappeared into the hallway.

Ethan's desk phone rang, so I took my maps over to the conference table, hoping he might have a clue about our secret property owner. As I waited for him to finish his call, I sat down, my gaze falling on a stack of papers marked with the same kind of crimson wax seal Ethan had used during his second Master ceremony.

I'd always liked wax seals. They were so old-fashioned, so evocative, so secretive. I ran my fingers across the wax, expecting to find the Cadogan House seal there. But instead, the seal was smooth except for three small indentations.

Curious, I rotated the paper—which looked like an elevation of Cadogan House—toward me. The seal consisted of three letters inside a circle.

The letters? C.A.M.

My heart began to thud, and I unrolled my father's map of the warehouse property and placed it on the table.

There, at the bottom of the page, was the property's owner. Carlos Anthony Martinez. C.A.M.

That was quite a coincidence.

Ethan finished his call and moved toward me, putting a hand on my shoulder. He must have sensed the magic. "What's wrong?"

"The seal," I said, looking up at Ethan. "Whose seal is this?"

Ethan moved closer and looked down at the papers. "Those are plots Michael prepared with potential camera placements. It's an antique seal he uses. He says he likes the mystery."

"What do the initials mean?"

Frowning, Ethan picked up the seal and stared at it. "I've no idea what they mean. It's a handy thing, though. The seal's in his signet ring. Why do you ask?"

I turned the map so he could see it. "The property in Little Italy where Oliver and Eve were murdered is owned by a guy named Carlos Anthony Martinez. Michael's using a seal with the initials 'C.A.M.'"

Ethan blanched. "Carlos Anthony Martinez? You're sure?"

"Yes, why?"

"Carlos was Celina's Second, the one who served before Morgan."

Of course. I'd heard of Carlos, but not frequently, and I hadn't heard his last name.

"Michael said he knew Celina. Do you know how?"

Ethan shook his head. "No. He wasn't a member of Navarre House."

"Yeah, that's what he told me, too. What do you know about Carlos's tenure as Second?"

Ethan put a hand on the chair beside him, the other on his hip, as he frowned in remembrance. "He was ousted as part of a scandal. Although I'm not sure what it was. Celina didn't say; she was tight-lipped in those days, didn't enjoy her notoriety the way she did in later years."

He dialed a number on the conference phone.

"Library," answered a male voice through the speaker.

"Carlos Anthony Martinez," Ethan said. "What do you know?"

"Navarre House Second before Morgan. Stripped of his title, reportedly staked, but I've never seen anything official on that."

"Why was he kicked out?" I asked.

"There's no official record," the librarian said. "But I was a friend of the Navarre House archivist a few years back, and she hinted he might have been siring vampires on the side."

"Siring vampires?" I said. "As in, he was making vampires without Celina's consent or knowledge?"

"The very same. Anything else?"

"No, thank you," Ethan said. He hung up the phone, then looked at me.

"We need to talk to Morgan," I said. "Although I hate to ask him questions at a time like this."

"Unfortunately, the feeling is mutual. But this concerns his House, so we can't avoid the discussion. But I will try to ease into it. I won't go in 'with guns a-blazing,' as Luc might say."

Ethan walked back to his desk and began perusing his computer for files. After a moment, he opened a portrait of Michael Donovan. It was a professional-looking photograph in front of a white backdrop, probably a marketing shot.

Having found what he wanted, Ethan dialed the phone on his desk. Morgan quickly answered.

"Yes?"

"I'm going to send you a photograph. Can you tell me if you recognize the vampire?"

"Why?" Morgan managed to imbue those three little letters with a lot of exhaustion.

"It's background," Ethan said. "It will assist us in the investigation of the murders." Without waiting for permission, Ethan e-mailed the photograph. There was a pause on the other end of the line.

"I got it," Morgan said. "His name is Stephen Caniglia. I haven't met him personally, but I've seen his face."

"He was a Navarre vampire?" Ethan asked.

"Not exactly. He wasn't Commended into the House. How much do you know about Carlos?"

Ethan met my gaze. "Fill me in," he said.

"Carlos was Celina's first Second. She made him a vampire; he was one of the earliest she'd made. I didn't know him very long—Carlos hadn't been in the House very long—when the scandal broke."

"The siring scandal?" Ethan asked.

"Yeah. Carlos had been recruiting vampires who weren't entirely convinced about becoming vampires. He pushed and changed them anyway without their consent. I replaced Carlos not long after that."

"And what happened to Carlos?"

"I don't know anything officially, but I heard she had him taken out. Frankly, it wouldn't surprise me. She didn't take kindly to his exercising her authority behind her back."

Ethan frowned. "And how does that relate to the vampire whose picture we just sent you?"

"He was one of the unfortunate few whom Carlos turned without consent. Celina offered him membership in the House, but he declined."

A burst of magic spilled across the room as Ethan's anger rose and expanded. I'd seen him angry before, but nothing compared to the fury before me.

"Did Carlos, perchance, have a signet ring with his initials carved into it?" Ethan asked.

Morgan's eyes widened. "Yeah, he did, actually. A big gold thing. He wore it on his pinkie like he was a mobster."

"Thank you," Ethan said, and without ceremony hung up the phone. For a moment he stood there, simply breathing, taking in what we now knew.

So Michael Donovan had been sired by Carlos, made a vampire against his will. Michael was now using Carlos's signet ring, and someone—Michael?—had dumped two bodies at a property Carlos, or maybe now, his estate, had owned. But why?

"Why would Michael Donovan care about the warehouse?"

Ethan shook his head. "I don't know. It must have been meaningful to him somehow. Otherwise, there are easier ways to hide a body."

"And how did he get into Navarre House? Jeff said the biometric security was linked to vampires Celina sired, not current members of Navarre House."

"Michael Donovan was sired by Carlos, and Carlos was sired by

Celina. The chemistry would be the same for both, as they'd both carry her particular mutation."

If that was true, Michael Donovan could be our killer.

Ethan cursed. "That son of a bitch. I let him into my House, Merit. I asked him for advice and shared our security protocols with him. How could I have been so stupid? How could I have been so naive?"

"Oh, God," I said, looking up at him. "I told him I had the map, and then you walked in, and that's when he left. Does he know? Does he know that we know?"

"Christ," Ethan said, vaulting from his seat and running to the front door, then out to the gate where humans now stood watch. I followed behind.

"The brown-haired vampire," Ethan said, then indicated a height. "Is he here?"

The humans exchanged a glance. "He left," said the one on the right. "About five minutes ago." She put a hand on her revolver. "Is there trouble?"

"We aren't sure. What was he driving?"

"Tonight, a black SUV."

Just like the vehicle that had lured Oliver and Eve into the alley and stopped me and Ethan on the street a few nights ago.

Ethan swore out another string of curses, this time including words I'd never heard before; in fairness, some of them may have been in Swedish.

"Assemble the team, if you would, Sentinel. I think it's time we explore a plan to handle Michael Donovan."

Luc, Malik, and the guards were easy to assemble. We gave them an overview of our theory, then called Catcher, Jeff, my grandfather, and Jonah, as Scott's proxy, and patched them in by phone.

I considered calling Morgan, but thought it best to wait until we'd finalized a hypothesis.

When the Cadogan vampires took seats around the Ops Room table, Ethan got the ball rolling.

"We believe the man I hired as a security consultant, Michael Donovan, is the killer of Oliver, Eve, Katya, and Zoey. He also injured a member of my House."

He paused to allow a moment for shocked noises and expressions.

"Morgan Greer has confirmed that Michael Donovan was made a vampire by Carlos Anthony Martinez, Second to Celina before Morgan was appointed. Unfortunately, Carlos made Michael a vampire without his consent and, in fact, over Michael's strong objection. We believe Carlos is deceased.

"We believe Michael killed Oliver and Eve and placed their bodies in a building owned by Carlos's estate. We have learned he stamps his documents with a signet ring that bears the initials 'C.A.M.,' and that once belonged to Carlos. Because Celina made Carlos, and Carlos made Michael, we believe that would have given him entry into Navarre House despite their biometric protocols."

"Jeff," I asked, "do you think that would work?"

"Without a doubt," he said grimly. "Vampirism is genetic, so Celina's genetic marker would be the trigger. If she sired them, or she made a vampire who sired them, they'd be there."

Ethan nodded at me. He'd been right about that.

"We also know Michael drives a black SUV of the same approximate size and color of the vehicle that lured Oliver and Eve into the alley and followed me and Merit."

"Our working theory," Luc said, "is that Michael Donovan was made a vampire mostly without his consent. He takes that personally, maybe has a secret vendetta against vampires who took away his humanity and so on and so forth. He'd have to be a self-hating son of a bitch, but we've heard weaker reasons for murder."

"All this because he's still angry at Carlos," Jeff marveled.

I understood Jeff's surprise, but also a touch of Michael's anger. Ethan had made me a vampire without my consent. He'd done it to save my life, but my initial nights as a supernatural had included frustrating realizations of all I'd be giving up.

"The fact that he makes use of the ring and the initials suggests he's harboring some anger," my grandfather said. "He is, in a sense, reliving his experience each time he kills, but he gets to be the attacker."

I nodded. "He kills Oliver and Eve, placing them in a secret room in a property owned by Carlos. We aren't yet sure why he picked that particular property or that particular room, but it stands to reason there was some connection between him and Carlos."

"Maybe that's the place Carlos turned him," Catcher said. "It's unlikely to be a place he'd soon forget."

"That's a good thought," Ethan said. "We'll check with Morgan."

I nodded. "After Oliver and Eve, he gets brave. He walks right into Navarre House, takes them out while everyone else is asleep."

"The connection there is easy," Luc said. "Revenge against the House that created the monster who attacked him."

"And earlier tonight, he attacks Margot outside the House."

"Unfortunately," Luc said, "the video doesn't help us on that one. Coincidentally, after the GP ceremony, Michael recommended we upgrade the cameras to get a better view, so we're in between hardware. There's no video in the back of the House." Not that Luc sounded bitter. At all.

I saw the flash of regret in Ethan's eyes. Michael had been his hire, and he'd been badly bitten.

"Why Cadogan?" Jonah asked. "What's the connection there to Carlos?"

"We aren't sure," Ethan said. "It could be part of his escalation. He killed Rogue vampires, then Navarre vampires, then attempted to kill a Cadogan vampire."

"And Grey House would be next?" Jonah wondered.

"Perhaps," Ethan said.

"I obviously can't let that stand," Jonah said. "What's our approach?"

"He might suspect we're onto him," I said. "My father dropped off a map of the warehouse plat, and I mentioned it to Michael. Michael left the House quickly after that."

"In that case," my grandfather said, "he might make himself known, especially given the theatrical way he's arranged the bodies. He'll want us to know who he is and what he's doing."

Ethan's phone rang. He checked the screen and seemed surprised.

"Who is it?"

"Diego Castillo. He's a member of the GP," he said, for the nonvampires on the call. "A representative of Mexico."

Something uncomfortable thrummed in my chest. Why was a member of the GP calling Ethan?

Ethan answered the phone. "Ethan Sullivan."

I could have used my vampiric senses to listen in, but since I was already in RG hot water, I thought it best to trust Ethan would tell us what we needed to know.

But when he sat straight up, my heart sped exponentially.

Ethan? I silently asked, but he didn't answer.

"Diego, I'm here with my team. I'm going to put you on speakerphone." Ethan put the phone on the table and pressed a button. "Go ahead," he said.

"Darius and Lakshmi have been taken." Diego's accent was melodically accented, but his voice was firm.

A shock wave of alarmed magic crossed the room.

"Taken?" Luc asked. "What do you mean, taken?"

"We were at the Dandridge waiting for our ride to the airport. Darius stepped outside to smoke a cigarette, and Lakshmi joined him."

Darius liked to smoke cloves, and I had a sudden vivid memory of their peppery smell.

"I saw through the window," Diego continued, "a vehicle pulled to the curb. The driver got out, began to chat with Lakshmi and Darius. I thought perhaps he was a vampire, although not one I knew."

"Brown hair?" Ethan asked. "Slender build?"

"*Sí.* You know this man?"

"I may," Ethan said. "What happened next?"

"Our limo pulls up and we walk outside, but the car is gone, and so are Darius and Lakshmi."

"What kind of car?" Ethan asked.

"I do not know. It was large. Black with dark windows."

Ethan's eyes narrowed, and it didn't take much to guess the direction—or violence—of his thoughts.

"Wait," Luc said, leaning toward the phone. "So someone forced Darius and Lakshmi into the car? How?"

Probably the same way Michael Donovan had done it before, I thought.

"He's got a weapon that shoots bullets made of aspen," I said. "A direct shot and they'd both be dead."

"There were no human witnesses?" Jonah asked.

"The bellmen were inside," Diego said, guilt in his voice. "They were helping us gather our luggage."

"How long ago did this occur?" Ethan asked.

"Seven or eight minutes?"

"We will find them," Ethan promised. "Stay at the hotel, inside, around humans, and do not leave until you hear from me."

He didn't wait for an argument, but hung up the phone, then glanced at us. He looked suddenly tired.

"He'll kill both of them," I quietly said. "If we don't get there and stop him, he'll kill both of them."

"There seems little doubt of that," Ethan said. "I have no love for the GP. We are enemies, but that hardly matters now. We cannot blithely turn them over to a murderer." He glanced up at Luc. "And more important, if we do not find them, there is little doubt the GP will blame their deaths on us."

Luc nodded.

"We have to find them," Jonah agreed. His interest was differently motivated from Ethan's. Lakshmi was a friend, an insider who'd helped save the House . . . and to whom I already owed a favor.

"Why Darius and Lakshmi?" Jeff asked. "What does he get out of it?"

"What did he get out of any of them?" my grandfather asked. "He's looking for emotional closure, or absolution, or something he likely won't find with violence. But that doesn't mean he'll stop looking."

I nodded.

"At this point, the reason hardly matters." Ethan stood up. "The rescue mission begins now. Where will Michael go?"

"The warehouse was his chosen location," Luc said. "But now that we know about his connection—and he knows that we know—he won't go there."

"True," I agreed. "But he might look for another place that's meaningful to him. I'll be right back."

I ran upstairs to Ethan's office and grabbed the papers my father had brought over. When I was downstairs again, I spread them out across the conference room table.

Fortunately, my father was very thorough.

"Someone fill us in," Catcher said.

"The materials Joshua provided," Ethan said, scanning the materials. "He's given us information about all the properties held by Carlos Anthony Martinez."

I picked up the contract and skimmed it. "There are three. The warehouse, then the Comstock building, which is a few blocks north of Streeterville."

"That's not far from Navarre House," Jonah added.

"Yep. And the third"—I ran a finger down the paper, which had minuscule type—"is some kind of strip mall in Roseland."

"Opposite directions," Ethan said. "Would he go north or south of the Dandridge?"

"Roseland is a longer drive," my grandfather said, "and for him to delay the thing he's looking forward to doing—the killing . . . I'm not sure he'd opt to make the trip that long."

"Agreed," Ethan said, decision made; he flipped through the documents, but didn't find what he was looking for. "There's no blueprint for the Comstock building."

"Jeff," I said, looking at the phone, "can you get us details on the Comstock?"

"Pulling it up now," Jeff said. "It's a twenty-story building. The floors are divided between commercial units on the bottom and residential on the top."

"How will we find them in a twenty-story building?" I asked.

"Thermal scanners," Jeff said. "We can use satellites to scan at a temp range for vamps, which will give us an idea where he is. Easy-peasy."

Ethan looked skeptically at the phone. "That doesn't sound especially 'easy-peasy.' Are you just saying that to make us feel better, or do you actually believe it?"

"I didn't say it could be legally done," Jeff said. "I just said it would be easy."

Somehow, that actually made me feel better.

"The problem is," Jonah said, "the scanners will also flag any other vamp in the building."

"Yeah, but what are the odds there's a cabal of vampires in the Comstock building?" Jeff said. "If we find a group of three vampires together, it's probably them."

"So we scan the building," I said. "We go in, take out Michael, take Darius and Lakshmi home."

"I want to see the inside of the building," Ethan said. "Can we do that?"

"I've logged into the property manager's site," Jeff said. "Pulling up schematics . . . now. I'm sending them to you."

Luc pressed some keys, and an elevation of a building appeared on-screen.

"Should we ask how you got into the client section of the Web site?" I wondered.

"Better if you don't. Suffice it to say '123kitty' does not a strong password make."

"Duly noted."

"Merit and I will go," Ethan said, standing.

"You need more bodies than that, especially if there are two wounded vamps," Jonah said. "I'll get permission from Scott to go, too."

Ethan was quiet for a moment, debating the offer. "I'm in charge," he finally said. "What I say goes. No heroics."

"I hadn't planned on it."

"Excellent."

"Glad to hear it."

Jeff whistled, and they shut up. "Vampires, please. It's going to take time to get the scanners in place. I can do it, but I've got to finagle a satellite, and that's going to take a phone call and some security clearance."

"You can find it while we drive," Ethan said.

"Working on it. Hit the road and I'll update you as soon as I can."

"Luc, technology?"

"On it." Luc jogged to a nearby cabinet, then brought out some of his prized possessions—incredibly small earpiece-and-microphone combos that would allow us to talk to one another inside the building.

"One for each of you," Luc said, handing them to me and Ethan. "There's an extra there for Jonah. We'll coordinate the comm here, and keep Jeff and Catcher patched in."

Ethan nodded, slipping the earpiece into his ear, and I did the same.

"We find him, we get Darius and Lakshmi out, and we take out Michael," Ethan said. "Any objections to that plan?"

My instinct, in times of stress, was to be sarcastic, but I managed not to ask if we'd get mission T-shirts after we were finished, or maybe a group photo op as at so many other Chicago attractions.

"No objections," Jonah gravely said.

Swords at the ready, earpieces in place, we headed upstairs and walked outside. Great white flakes of snow were falling across the city, and they'd already collected into a white blanket that covered the lawn.

"Snow is coming," I said.

"Indeed," Ethan agreed, as we walked through the gate. Ethan was driving the two of us, and Jonah would meet us there.

As Ethan and I buckled up, Luc's voice rang through our ears. "Audio working?"

"It's working," Ethan said. "We're leaving now. We'll get this done."

I certainly hoped he was right.

CHAPTER NINETEEN

GIVING CHASE

Ten minutes later, we were zooming down Lakeshore as fast as the Volvo could go. Luc had patched Jeff and Jonah—who didn't yet have his earbud—into our connection system so we could make final arrangements on the way.

"Guys, I've got good news and bad news. And since we don't have time for debate, you're getting the bad news first: The Comstock building's scheduled for demolition tomorrow morning. The Web site I'd found was an old one; the building changed hands, and the new property manager decided to go in a different direction with the property."

My heart throbbed in my chest as fear overwhelmed me. Murderous vampires were one thing. Exploding buildings? Something altogether different.

"The building will be guarded," Jonah said, "but there's a good chance some of the explosives and wiring have already been placed."

"If there are guards," I said, "Michael's probably already taken them out. He won't think twice about taking out humans."

"Agreed," Ethan said. "You said you had good news, Jeff?"

"Two parts: Catcher and I are on our way. I had to let him drive, you know, since I'm working my keyboard magic, but we thought you could use some help. And also, helpfully, the building's now a husk. Drywall, interiors, everything's been cleaned out in preparation for the demo."

"Which makes the thermals operate a lot more effectively," Jonah said.

"Precisely. The satellites are queued in—you can thank Big Brother and some lovely white-hat hackers for that—and I've got thermal. But there aren't any vampires in the building yet."

"Shit," Ethan muttered. "Does that mean he isn't there yet, or he's on his way?"

"I don't know. I'm still working on it. I'm logging into the security feeds I can find between the Dandridge and the Comstock."

"Shit," Ethan muttered again, cracking a fist on the dashboard.

"Hey," I said. "She's the only transportation we've got at the moment."

Ethan looked around, eyeing an exit, doubt in his eyes. "We could go south back to Roseland. He could be there."

"He wouldn't be there yet," I said. "You thought Comstock first, and I agree. It's closer to the Dandridge, and it's the murder he wants. He can do it faster if he goes to the Comstock."

He didn't look convinced, so I pushed on, just as he had for me. "Remember what you told me? Trust your instincts."

Ethan's gaze intensified, and he pushed the Volvo's engine even more . . . zooming past the exit that would have given him a chance to get to the other building.

And thank God for that.

"I've got it!" Jeff suddenly exclaimed.

Ethan blew out a breath in relief.

"I'm matching security footage and imaging," he said. "We've got a black SUV across the street from the building, three vampires inside . . . and they're moving."

"You got it," I said, squeezing Ethan's hand. "Now get us there."

Ten minutes and multiple moving violations later, we pulled up across the street from the Comstock building, or what remained of it. It was only a concrete skeleton, its plastic walls flapping in the breeze. The block had already been fenced off, the neighborhood prepared for the destruction to come.

On the upside, parking was abundant.

We met Jonah outside the building; Catcher and Jeff hadn't yet arrived. I gave Jonah his earbud, and we belted on our swords as snow fell around us. We saw no guards to speak of, but the smell of blood was in the air. It seemed likely the guards had been sacrifices to Michael's evil intent.

"Jeff?" Ethan said, touching his earpiece. "What can you see?"

"Two vampires on the roof. One on the sixteenth floor."

"He wouldn't separate them," I said. "That can't be right."

"Oh, crap," Jeff said. "The color of the one on sixteen is changing."

"Changing?" Jonah asked.

"Cooling," Jeff said. "Dying."

My stomach fell, tears blossoming at my lashes. We were so close.

"We go in now," Jonah said. "Ethan, take the vampire on sixteen. Merit and I will take the roof."

"No way," Ethan said, but I shot him a glance.

"I'm not letting you within five feet of an aspen gun," I said. "No arguments. Find whoever that is. They aren't dead yet. *Save* them."

"We climb the fence," Jonah said. "Then we go inside. Swords drawn and at the ready."

We nodded, and then we did our things.

The fence was chain link and made for an easy climb. We hopped down on the other side and found the building creepily quiet. Snow already covered the concrete outside, which made the steel exoskeleton look as if it had risen straight from ashes. Not exactly a comforting metaphor.

"The roof?" I asked, casting a glance upward. "Can we even get up there?"

"They keep ladders and stairwells open for the demolition crew," Jonah said. "Getting up there won't be a problem."

We crossed the dirty and dusty hull of a lobby and went into the stairwell. We began the climb, and said good-bye to Ethan on the sixteenth floor.

You'll be careful, Ethan silently said.

I promise, I assured him, and he disappeared into the hallway.

"Focus," Jonah said, and I pushed Ethan's safety from my mind and we made the slow climb to the top of the building.

We emerged into a kind of waiting area, with a door marked ROOF in front of us. I swallowed down a dose of fear.

"You ready?"

"On three," I said.

One . . . two . . . three, he mouthed, then pushed open the door.

A freezing wind met us on the other side. It whipped around us at this height, biting through my jacket and quickly numbing the hands around my sword.

The roof was still covered in gritty tar paper, and it looked like every rooftop I'd seen on cop shows—a flat surface marked with vertical pipes, antennas, and skylights. Around the roof was an edge of concrete that kept folks from tumbling over the sides.

I sincerely hoped we weren't going to need that.

Ethan's voice burst into my earpiece. "I've got Lakshmi," he said. "Bleeding, but I'm stanching the wound. I'm going to get her out. Luc, get Delia ready for an incoming."

"On it," Luc said.

"Michael and the other vampire are on the north side of the building," Jeff said.

We took cautious steps forward. The snow was still falling, but it had melted to slush on the roof's dark fabric.

"Behind me," Jonah said.

The roof was dotted with small outcroppings—utility sheds and HVAC units that hadn't yet been removed. We hustled across the surface from obstacle to obstacle, trying to get as close to Michael as possible without blowing our cover . . . or risking his taking out a vampire before we could reach him.

"Twenty feet," Jeff said, and we stopped behind a bank of air conditioners.

I dropped my guard and reached out for the magic in the air—and there was plenty of it: a cloud around us, and a swell emanating from the other side of the utilities. That was Michael's location, and I signaled it to Jonah.

"I'll step in front and distract him," Jonah whispered. "Go around; cover his other side. I'll wait ten seconds before I move."

I nodded. "Be careful."

I crept along the air-conditioning unit until I'd passed Michael's position, crouched behind a gigantic vent pipe, and glanced around the corner.

Michael Donovan stood beside a bit of plumbing that pushed through the roof's surface, his long black coat swirling in the wind.

Darius kneeled on the ground in front of him, cowed by the katana that Michael held in his right hand and the gun in his left.

The latter was the same weapon I'd seen McKetrick raise against me, and likely the same one that Michael had used to threaten Oliver and Eve.

With bullets of aspen, it was decidedly deadly.

"You had to run," Michael said to Darius. "I tried to arrange you just so, and you had to run. And now she's down there alone."

Michael lifted the sword.

Jonah stepped into Michael's line of sight. "Michael, you're surrounded. Drop the weapon and step away from Darius."

Shocked, Michael jerked, glancing around the roof. I crawled around the vent and began to creep along the edge of the roof toward him.

But he wasn't going to simply give up. "I can't allow you to interrupt," he said. "I'm obviously in the middle of something here."

"You're going to have to hit 'pause,'" Jonah said. "I've got guards on the roof and around the building."

"Great," Michael said. "Then you won't mind when I do this."

Jonah jumped, but not before Michael slashed out, the tip of his sword catching Darius across the throat. Blood spilled, filling the air with the scent of heady vampire magic.

As my eyes silvered, Jonah leaped for Darius.

It was a perfect distraction. I extended my katana, and before Michael could react I sliced forward, hitting the underside of his left hand. The wound wasn't deep, but it was enough to startle him. He instinctively dropped the gun, and I used the tip of the sword to change its trajectory, batting it away like a crappy pitch. Instead of falling at Michael's feet—within easy reach—it flew fifteen feet away, then skittered beneath one of the utility units.

Michael's smile drooped, and he took a step backward, katana still in hand.

Darius whimpered as Jonah worked to stop the bleeding at his throat. I moved closer to Michael, forcing him backward and away from the pair.

Now that we had equal weapons, it was up to me to bring him down. But first and foremost, he was going to answer some questions.

I kept my katana at heart height. "You've murdered four vampires. You killed Oliver and Eve."

Michael looked confused. "Who?"

"The vampires you slaughtered at Carlos's warehouse."

"I didn't even know their names until you told me. They were the first vampires who stumbled along."

He'd just admitted to murder—serial murder—as if it were nothing more than admitting he'd run out of milk or forgotten to vote on Election Day.

Michael slid a glance to Darius behind him. Michael's expression was cold, as if he were irritated that Jonah was interrupting his plans—and Darius's death.

"Why kill them at the warehouse?"

"It seemed as good a place as any."

His nonchalance had to be feigned. No one went to all that trouble—killed multiple vampires with linked locations and meticulous placement—and didn't care. That is, he might not have cared for Oliver, Eve, Katya, or Zoey, but he cared about the killing.

Time to poke the bear, I thought.

"So Carlos made you a vampire?"

Michael glanced back at me. Concern flashed in his eyes, but disappeared. But that flash was enough for me.

I pulled up every memory of the night I'd been made a vampire, digging into the feelings of fear, horror, and brutality, and used them against him.

"You didn't want it, did you? You didn't want to be a vampire.

You didn't want to be a part of that lifestyle. But Carlos found you. Selected you. And then he subdued you. Restrained you, maybe? And bit you."

Michael's gaze snapped back to me, his eyes swirling silver. "You don't know what the fuck you're talking about."

This wasn't Michael the security auditor. This was Michael's darkness, the anger he'd been holding inside . . . and had finally decided to unleash.

But I didn't need him angry. I needed him to break.

I provoked him further. "Are you sure you didn't want it? That you didn't secretly want the immortality? The strength? Are you sure Carlos didn't give you exactly what you wanted?"

Michael bared his fangs with a hiss, and slashed forward. I jumped away from the tip of his katana, then sliced out with mine, catching the edge of his duster and ripping the fabric.

"You don't fucking know what it was like. The blood. The darkness. He was sick. He had a sickness."

Darkness, I thought. That was an important word, wasn't it?

"The room at the warehouse. No windows, no light. Utter darkness. That's where he made you a vampire?"

Michael turned in a circle and kicked out. He was fast, but his moves were sloppier tonight than they had been when he'd fought Ethan. He was angry and afraid, and he wasn't focused.

I dodged the kick easily.

"He forced me into the room," he said.

"I'm sure of it. And you took your revenge, didn't you? You killed Oliver and Eve in that same room."

"I eliminated vampires."

"And the vampires at Navarre?"

"She made him," Michael said. "She made him, and she ig-nored what he did."

She, I assumed, was Celina. He couldn't take her out, because I'd already done that.

"Why Cadogan House? Why Darius and Lakshmi? What do they have to do with Carlos?"

"They don't," he said. "They were just bonuses. Their price was much, much higher."

I froze, sword in front of me, hands shaking with tension and fear and cold. "What price?"

"The price McKetrick paid me to kill vampires."

"Holy fucking shit," said Luc's voice in my ear. He must have heard that confession. "Sentinel, you were right."

Right or not, I kept my gaze on Michael Donovan. "McKetrick paid you? Why?"

The surprise in my eyes must have helped Michael regain some control. He stood a little straighter, adjusted his grip on his katana.

"He wanted to create havoc," Michael said. "He hates vampires. And, frankly, I don't disagree with him."

"What about the aspen gun?"

"Test shot. McKetrick suggested I use it. I found it sloppy."

"You prefer steel."

His gaze narrowed. "Guns make good threats, but vampires should die by their own weapons."

That he was also a vampire didn't seem to matter. But maybe he wasn't really a vampire, not emotionally. My own transition had been difficult; his couldn't have been a walk in the park. Ethan had saved me from death, but Carlos had stolen life from Michael Donovan.

"Oliver and Eve were holding hands. So were Katya and Zoey. Why?"

Michael's lip quivered with anger. "I wasn't the only one. He took many of us to the warehouse. We knew he was coming for us. The monster in the dark."

Humans, I thought he meant.

"They didn't want to change. Didn't want immortality. Didn't want the blasphemy of being a vampire. So that night, while they waited for him to come, they killed themselves. Took something, some poison. I don't know." He waved away the thought. "I was already a vampire, and I wasn't strong enough to fight back when he used glamour against me."

Michael looked up at me. "I found them lying together, hand in hand. He made me get rid of them." He shook his head, as if reminding himself of his own motivations. "And now I get rid of the Carloses of the world."

"And your security consulting?"

"You gave me plenty of information about your defenses that I will happily share with McKetrick." He smiled just a bit. "And what better prize to my employer than the king of the world?"

Darius, I realized.

"And now what?" I asked.

Michael pulled something from his pocket. There in his palm was a small black remote control with a very large red button.

I'd seen plenty of action movies. Nothing good happened when a red button was pressed.

"Detonator," he said. "The building was already wired, and the guard had the button. This was Carlos's building. He kept an office here, you know. An office Celina didn't know about." He shrugged. "I didn't want them to destroy it, not without me. And now I can do it myself. I can take down what he built. I can ruin him, the way he ruined me."

Michael moved toward the ledge, hands out apologetically. "I'm so sorry, Merit. It was nice working with you."

He punched the button, and sirens immediately began to wail, followed by the cry of a female voice on a loudspeaker that echoed through the silence.

"Five minutes until detonation."

The demolition contractors must have installed a warning system for the building's destruction.

"Goddamn it, Michael," I said, raising my sword again. "You'll kill more innocent people."

"No," he said, his eyes flat and emotionless. "The neighborhood's already been cleared out. All that remains are vampires and their legacies. You have a choice now, Merit. You can follow me down and try to apprehend me, or you can help your friends with their burdens. Frankly, if I'm analyzing this from a strictly strategic standpoint, I find your chance of success either way to be pretty damn unlikely."

"Fuck you, Michael."

He clucked his tongue, tossed away the remote, and resheathed his sword. Then he ran to the edge of the roof. He stepped onto the edging, outstretched his arms, and dived.

I gripped the rail and peered over. The distance gave me momentary vertigo—I really hated heights—but it passed quickly enough for me to see him strike the ground with force enough to buckle the sidewalk in a six-foot radius. The ground shook with it, but he straightened up as if he'd barely felt the shock.

"Catcher? Jeff?" I called into the receiver. "Are you here? Michael Donovan just jumped down to the street. He's working for McKetrick and he's been hoarding information about the House's security. We cannot let him get that back to McKetrick. Can you get someone to him?

"Hello? Jeff?" I said again after a couple of seconds, but there was no answer.

Michael Donovan looked up, pausing to straighten his jacket and spare a glance—and a disturbing smile—for me.

I could jump, but I'd never jumped that far before. Not even close. Unlike Michael, I wasn't sure I could survive the fall. Vampires were certainly strong, but we weren't guaranteed to stick the landing.

On the other hand, didn't I have to do it? I couldn't just let him walk away.

My hands shaking violently, my stomach a mess, I gripped the edge of the concrete and began to hoist myself up. What was the point of being here, of promising to face my fears and help my vampires, if I wasn't willing to put my money where my mouth was . . . or my feet in the air?

But before I could move, a blur of white blew through the darkness toward Michael. Long, pale, and furry.

I had to blink to be sure I wasn't hallucinating: a massive tiger, ten feet long from nose to tail, white with dark stripes, pounding the pavement in the middle of Chicago.

"What the hell?" I murmured, staring down as the scene unfolded.

Michael ran, but his speed was no match for the tiger's. Front feet, back feet, front feet, back feet, and then it pounced.

It knocked Michael to the ground with a single blow, but Michael was a vampire, and he wasn't going down without a fight. He kicked the tiger backward, and it rolled before standing again.

The tiger unbalanced, Michael rose to his feet. Before he could grab his sword, the tiger attacked again, rearing up and hitting Michael Donovan across the nose. I was too high up to scent blood, but there seemed little doubt the tiger would have drawn it.

Michael didn't delay. He pulled the sword from its scabbard and struck out at the tiger, slicing the animal across the back of its shoulders. The tiger roared but didn't cease its attack.

They parried back and forth—the tiger slapping out with a paw, Michael slicing back when he could, but his opponent was enormous, and Michael was tiring. He raised his sword again, and the tiger knocked it out of his hand. Panicked, without a weapon, Michael stumbled, and the tiger took its turn. It pounced—all four feet in the air—and made for him.

Michael took the tiger's full weight, falling backward onto a pile of lumber—sharp planks and sticks that had probably been pulled from the building. There must have been aspen in the mix of wood; Michael screamed, and then he was gone, only a cone of ash in his place.

The tiger stepped back, panting. Ears flat against its head, its teeth bared, it roared into the night, the sound deep and loud enough to shake the foundations of the building and rattle my bones.

Goose bumps lifted on my arms.

And then, in only a moment, the tiger shape-shifted. I'd seen it happen before, but that didn't make the visual any less amazing. A flash lit the night as magic swirled around him, changing the massive predator . . . into Jeff Christopher.

He shook out his arms and legs, then popped his head back and forth as if stretching his neck. He looked up and met my gaze, and in the eyes of this young man—often silly, sometimes costumed, always flirty—I saw a world of understanding and experience and maturity.

Not that I'd had any doubts, but Jeff Christopher was a marvel.

"Three minutes until detonation."

Not that there was time to be impressed.

"Merit? Are you there?" A voice sounded over the constant beeping of the alarm. "Get the hell out of here."

I pressed a finger to the earpiece, trying to improve the reception. "Ethan? Is that you?"

"It's me. I'm on sixteen. Get your ass out of the building."

I'd be damned if I was leaving without my crew. I ran back across the roof and found Jonah walking toward the door, Darius in his arms. Darius looked limp and pale, but he was still breathing.

"Little help?" Jonah asked.

"Working on it." I ran to the door and propped it open just as Jonah hustled through.

Awkwardly, he trotted down the stairs, arms bulging under Darius's weight. Vampires were strong, but he'd given Darius blood, and weakened himself in the process.

"Two minutes and thirty seconds until detonation," said the warning voice.

"This is going to be close," I muttered, gripping the interior railing as we moved as quickly as possible down the stairs to the sixteenth floor. When we reached it, I burst through the door and came face-to-face with the pointy end of Ethan's sword.

"It's me," I said, tipping it out of the way. "Where is she?"

Lakshmi lay prone in one corner, unconscious, her arms chained to a length of plumbing that rose through the floor.

He looked at me. "I'll get her. You get the hell out of here."

Jonah appeared in the stairwell behind me, face pale, Darius in his arms. His eyes widened in surprise as he caught sight of Lakshmi in the corner.

"Michael chained her because they were trying to get away," I said. "That's how Darius made it to the roof."

"And you hired that asshole?" Jonah asked Ethan, placing Darius on the floor and jogging toward Lakshmi.

"I didn't know he was an asshole at the time," Ethan murmured. Together they pulled at opposite ends of her chain, sweating with the sudden exertion of trying to break it apart.

"Katana," I said. "I'll aim for a link in the chain; you both pull her away."

"Your katana isn't strong enough," Jonah said.

"It's been tempered by my blood," I said. "It's strong enough."

I had no idea whether my bluff was right, but what choice did I have? We had to try something.

"Two minutes until detonation," said the announcer.

I didn't give them time to argue, but raised my katana in the air. Realizing I was serious, they each grabbed one of Lakshmi's arms and braced themselves.

"One, two, *three*!" I yelled, and, silently apologizing to the blade, I brought the katana down with all the force I could muster.

Sparks and metal flew, and I heard a pop that I bet was Lakshmi's left shoulder, but the chain broke, and she tumbled into Ethan.

"One minute and forty-five seconds until detonation."

"I really hate that lady," Jonah said, helping Ethan lift Lakshmi into the air. "Let's get out of here," he said, and cast a glance from Ethan to the edge of the sixteenth floor, which disappeared into darkness.

"Let's do it," Ethan said.

We ran to the edge and looked down. We were sixteen stories up, and it was a long way to the ground.

"One minute and thirty seconds until detonation."

"We'll jump it," Jonah said.

I shook my head, panic suddenly setting in. "It's too far. I've never jumped that far before."

"It's not too far," Ethan said. "Jonah taught you to jump, and I saw you do it in Nebraska. You can do this, too, Merit. Trust me."

He looked over at me, and our eyes met. Promises and hopes and dreams swirled there, adrift in an ocean of fear. But we had to keep trying.

"One minute and fifteen seconds until detonation."

"I love you," he said.

Tears swam in my eyes, blurring my vision. I wiped them away with the edge of my sleeve. "I love you, too."

"Anytime now, kids!" Jonah yelled out.

"Jump!" Ethan said, and I didn't bother to hesitate. I hit the ledge at a full run and bounded over it toward the ground. Jonah did the same, with Darius in his arms, then Ethan, with Lakshmi in his.

We jumped.

For a split second, the entire city swam before us, the edges bent by the curvature of the earth. And then, as if gravity bowed to us instead of the other way around, the world slowed, and that single, gigantic leap became one small step.

But one small step with a hell of a lot of acceleration.

We hit the ground, buckling the asphalt before us. My knees ached with the force of the fall, but we were all still standing.

The percussions began to sound behind us. "Time's up," Ethan yelled out. "Run!"

Pain and fear disappeared. We were driven only by survival, by the need to escape the heat of the blasts that had already begun behind us.

We ran with speed that would have blurred our movements to any onlookers, then vaulted the fence just as the heat of the explosions began to grow. We made it a few more feet before the shock wave pushed us forward. Jonah and Ethan put me, Darius, and Lakshmi on the ground, then covered us with their bodies as the explosions shook the earth.

I'd felt earthly and magical earthquakes, but the building's detonation was a force of an altogether different magnitude. My chest rumbled from the vibrations, and my eardrums ached from the noise. They went on for an eternity; even when the detonations stopped, the building crumbled into a pile behind us with earth-shattering force.

A minute later the percussion was over, and the air was filled by a thick cloud of dust and the sounds of sprinkling dirt, steel, glass, and gravel.

"Everybody okay?" Jonah asked above me.

"I'm good," I said. "Ethan?"

He grunted, which I took as a good sign.

"How's Lakshmi?" I asked.

Another grunt. "She just elbowed me in the ribs, so I think she's good."

I didn't bother asking if Darius was okay.

————— ✦ —————

CHAPTER TWENTY

LET THEM FLY

When we returned, dusty and victorious, to the House, Ethan thanked me with steak and chocolate. The healthy members of the Greenwich Presidium thanked us with effusive praise and their promise they'd note the House's courageous actions toward the GP.

I guess only near-death experiences were sufficient to prove to the GP that we weren't common criminals.

Regardless, a bit of postcrisis praise wasn't enough to make me feel better about the GP. Although we'd made a pretty large bang, rescuing Darius and Lakshmi wasn't the first good deed we'd done as a House, and the GP had ignored the others.

Besides, Darius was still recuperating from his injuries; it remained to be seen whether his opinion of us had truly changed.

But those were worries for another night. Tonight, when we were clean once again, we raided the kitchen before returning to the bedroom—and the bed.

"You're all right?" I asked him.

"I am angry at myself for what I missed. That I didn't see

who Michael Donovan was. But there's little to be done about that now."

"Would you feel better if I slugged you in the arm?"

He gave me an arched eyebrow. Classic Sullivan. "How would that make me feel better?"

I shrugged. "It would make me feel better, which would make you feel better."

My only warning was the narrowing of his eyes . . . and then he pounced. I squealed as he pushed me back onto the mattress, but not because I was in pain.

"You know," I said, "we're still going to have to deal with McKetrick."

"And his mayoral dispensation? Yes, I know. It's unfortunate our primary witness to McKetrick's wrongdoings made a very bad decision in the vicinity of an angry shifter."

Not that Michael would have come out any better in the hands of the Rogue or Navarre House vampires who would have liked to get a piece of him.

I frowned up at Ethan. "Will there be a time when things are normal? When vampires are loved or hated just like everyone else? When we live simpler lives?"

Ethan settled himself on an elbow, and pushed a lock of hair from my eyes with his free hand. "I'm not sure you were cut out for a simple life, Merit. You don't seem a suburban type of girl."

I understood his point, but the comment made me suddenly melancholic. "I would have liked children someday," I confessed. But it wasn't in the cards for me; no vampire had ever successfully borne children.

His expression fell. "I didn't know. You hadn't mentioned—"

I tried to smile a little. "I know it can't happen. And it's nothing I'm actively thinking about. But I do wonder what it would be like to be a parent. To experience the world again alongside a little person who's only just beginning to understand it. To learn with them all the things that make life worthwhile."

Ethan's eyes, green and fathomless, seemed to grow larger.

I thought, just for a moment, of a prophecy Gabriel had once made. Of the pair of green eyes he'd seen in my future—eyes that looked "everything and nothing" like Ethan's. Children were impossible, but that begged the question: Whom had he seen?

Ethan caressed my cheek. "You are a remarkable woman, Caroline Evelyn Merit."

"I try. But it's exhausting."

"I am your Master and your servant. Just tell me how to please you."

"Just hold me," I said, moving closer to him.

He stilled. "That's not entirely what I had in mind."

"Long night, tired Sentinel."

Ethan wrapped his arms around me and nestled his chin atop my head. "In that case," he said, "try to stop me."

Those were the last words I heard before dawn closed my eyes.

The next evening, Ethan asked us to assemble on the lawn at the fire pit. He'd refreshed the stack of wood the GP had used for its ceremony, and the flame there now glowed with a wonderful warmth.

Ethan turned toward us, his face lit by the fire. "We have made a decision no vampires before us have made. We have chosen liberty and self-respect. Darius and the GP have undertaken the rituals they believe in. It is, in my estimation, important that we have our own rituals, as well. Rituals that remind us who we are, and why we make difficult decisions instead of letting others justify their ignorance and decide for us.

"Helen," Ethan called out, and she stepped forward, a square of white gossamer paper in her hands. She extended it to Ethan.

"Centuries ago," Ethan said, "we were visited by a samurai, Miura, who taught us the way of the sword. The way of honor. He also told us of the tradition of the sky balloon."

Helen and Ethan gently pulled the opposite sides of the paper, and it opened into a squarish shape like a paper party lantern.

While Ethan held the lantern by a small loop on the top, Helen dipped a long matchstick into the fire and pulled it back, its end now alight.

"The lantern is symbolic," Ethan said.

Helen carefully touched the flame to a wick in the center of the lantern. The flame filled the air inside the lantern and gently expanded the walls. It glowed with a pale white luminescence, and bobbed in the breeze, clearly eager to be free, even as Ethan held it firm.

"We place our worries and our concerns inside this lantern," Ethan said. "We give it the weight of our fears . . . and we set it adrift."

He released his grip, and the lantern floated into the air, rising slowly above the House like a star taking flight from earth.

It was such a simple thing, such a simple act, but filled with hope and promise and beauty. I brushed away a tear, and heard sniffles in the crowd behind me. I hadn't been the only one moved, which had undoubtedly been Ethan's intent.

We watched the lantern drift higher and higher into the sky, the star rising as the winter breeze drew it farther from Ethan's still-outstretched fingers. And then it disappeared, the wick extinguished by a sudden burst of chilling wind.

"Our fears fly," Ethan said into the quiet that had fallen. "We face them and then we set them aloft until they are extinguished."

He looked back at us again. "Tonight, my Novitiates, we embark on a new journey. We decide the manner of vampires—the manner of House—we are to be. And we make that decision for ourselves, without the political interference of the GP. We do this with honest intention and without fear, for we have already set our fears adrift, and the world owns them now. Good night, my brothers and sisters, and may the falling of the sun again bring us peace and prosperity."

It wasn't a prayer, not exactly.

It was a promise.

Photo by Jeremy Dixon

Chloe Neill was born and raised in the South but now makes her home in the Midwest—just close enough to Cadogan House and St. Sophia's to keep an eye on things. When not transcribing Merit's and Lily's adventures, she bakes, works, and scours the Internet for good recipes and great graphic design. Chloe also maintains her sanity by spending time with her boys—her favorite landscape photographer (her husband) and their dogs, Baxter and Scout. (Both she and the photographer understand the dogs are in charge.)

CONNECT ONLINE

www.chloeneill.com
facebook.com/authorchloeneill
twitter.com/chloeneill